MY DARK ROMEO

Parker S. Huntington is a stay-at-home dog mom from SoCal, where she discovered her allergy to rain.

In spite of her shoddy attendance record and strong aversion to homework, she earned a B.A. in Creative Writing from the University of California, Riverside and an A.L.M. in Literature from Harvard.

When she's not writing or exchanging food pics with her friends, she's binge-watching an unhealthy amount of Netflix while curled up with her dogs.

Parker hates talking about herself and is (also) allergic to social media, but you can catch up with her in her newsletter or through the occasional TikTok video.

L.J. Shen is a *Wall Street Journal, USA Today, Washington Post*, and #1 Amazon bestselling author of contemporary, new adult, and young adult romance. Her books have been translated in over twenty different countries, and she hopes to visit all of them.

She lives in Florida with her husband, three rowdy sons, and even rowdier pets. She enjoys good wine, bad reality TV shows, and reading to her heart's content.

MY DARK
ROMEO

WALL STREET JOURNAL BESTSELLING AUTHORS
Parker S. Huntington
L.J. Shen

ORION

First published in Great Britain in 2023 by Orion Fiction,
an imprint of The Orion Publishing Group Ltd.,
Carmelite House, 50 Victoria Embankment
London EC4Y ODZ

An Hachette UK Company

13 15 17 19 20 18 16 14

A CIP catalogue record for this book is
available from the British Library.

ISBN (Paperback) 978 1 3987 2199 9
ISBN (eBook) 978 1 3987 2200 2

Typeset by Born Group
Printed and bound in Great Britain by Clays Ltd, Elcograf S.p.A.

www.orionbooks.co.uk

To all the girls eager to marry a grumpy, tortured billionaire . . . This one's not for you.

"Thus with a kiss I die."

William Shakespeare, *Romeo and Juliet*

Soundtrack

Starphucker — **Beauty School Dropout**
heartbreak honeymoon — **Mad Tsai**
I'm Not Sorry — **Dean & Eric Bellinger**
Lover Like Me — **CL**
Take What You What — **ONE OK ROCK ft. 5 Seconds of Summer**
favorite crime — **Olivia Rodrigo**
WE MADE PLANS & GOD LAUGHED — **Beauty School Dropout**
Wedding Dress — **TAEYANG**
Strawberries and Wine — **Jaylon Ashaun**
Easier — **5 Seconds of Summer**
End Game — **Taylor Swift, Ed Sheeran, & Future**
HABIBI (MY LOVE) — **Faouzia**
Control — **Halsey**
Born Without a Heart — **Faouzia**
The Happiest Girl — **BLACKPINK**
Crush — **Yuna & Usher**
Oceans & Engines — **NIKI**
Si Fueras Mia — **D.O.**
Lay Your Head on Me — **Crush**
Time — **The Rose**
Die for You — **Beauty School Dropout**
Bonnie & Clyde — **YUQI**

Prologue

Dallas

I always assumed my life was a romance novel. That between my pages nestled a happily ever after. It never occurred to me that I miscategorized my genre. That it could be a horror story. A blood-chilling thriller.

Then Romeo Costa typhooned into my world, ripping off my rose-colored glasses.

He taught me darkness.

He taught me strength.

Most importantly, he delivered the cruelest lesson of all—there's beauty in every beast. Thorns in every rose. And a love story can blossom—even from the carcass of hate.

Chapter One

Dallas

"Oh, Lord, they weren't bluffing, were they? He really is in town." Emilie latched on to my wrist, coffin nails sinking into the tan flesh.

"So is Oliver von Bismarck." Savannah extended her arm. "Someone pinch me."

I did so with pleasure.

"Ow, Dal. Stop being so literal."

I shrugged, fixing my attention on the catering beside us. The real reason I'd appeared at the debutante ball tonight. I plucked a chocolate-covered pomelo peel from a crystal tray and crushed it between my teeth, savoring the bitter-sour nectar. God wasn't a man. God wasn't a woman, either. God was probably a piece of Godiva-covered fruit.

"What are they doing here? They're not even from the South." Emilie stole Sav's debutante program and fanned her face. "And they're definitely not here to meet women. Both are die-hard bachelors. Didn't Costa dump a whole-ass Swedish princess last summer?"

"As opposed to a partial-ass Swedish princess?" I wondered aloud.

"*Dal.*"

Where were the Portuguese custard tarts? I was promised Portuguese custard tarts.

"You said there'd be pastéis de nata." I snatched a consolation prize—melopita—and waved it at Emilie. "Serves me right for trusting you again."

Her hawk eyes caught me slipping two Polish donuts into my bag. "Dal, you can't hide that in your Chanel. You'll ruin the calfskin."

Sav shoved a frantic fist into her clutch, retrieving a tube of lipstick. "I heard von Bismarck is in town to buy Le Fleur."

Jenna's daddy owned Le Fleur. They manufactured percale sheets for five-diamond hotels. In eighth grade, Emilie and I ran away from home and slept in their showroom for a week before our daddies found us.

"What does he need Le Fleur for?" I picked a kanafeh next, my back still to the mythical creatures my best friends had collectively lost their minds over. Judging by the urgent whispers around us, they were not the only ones.

Emilie snatched the Bond No. 9 from Savannah, applying a generous coat to her lips. "He's in hotels and hospitality. Owns a little chain called The Grand Regent. You might've heard of it."

The Grand Regent began as an exclusive, invite-only resort before metastasizing into more branches than the Hilton. So, I gathered Pompous von Fancypants wasn't strapped for cash. In fact, obscene generational wealth was the unspoken entry ticket to tonight's event.

The 303rd Chapel Falls Royal Debutante Ball was a glorified dog show that attracted every billionaire and mega millionaire in the state. Fathers paraded their cotillion-bred daughters around the Astor Opera House in hopes they'd perform well enough to be courted by men in the same tax bracket.

I hadn't come here to find a husband. Before my birth, Daddy had already promised me to someone, which the diamond ring on my engagement finger reminded me. This always seemed like a problem for the future—up until I discovered the official announcement on the society pages two days ago.

"I hear Romeo is dead-set on becoming the CEO of his daddy's company." Lord, Sav was still droning on about him. Were they planning on penning the man's Wikipedia? "Already, he's a billionaire."

"Not just a billionaire. A mega billionaire." Emilie fingered a marquise diamond on her Broderie bracelet, her poker tell. "And he's not the type to blow it all on yachts and gold toilet seats or funding self-indulged pet projects."

Sav snuck a desperate glance at them through her compact mirror. "Do you think we can be introduced?"

Emilie's eyebrows pinched together. "Nobody here knows them. Dal? Dallas? Are you even listening to the conversation? This is important."

The only grave situation I'd witnessed was the lack of shortbread, too. Reluctantly, I fixed my eyes on the two men that parted the thick crowd of silk chiffon and frozen updos.

They both stood at least six-three. A towering height that made them look like giants trying to squeeze into doll houses. Then again, nothing about them was conventional. Their similarities ended with their height. Everything else was arctic opposites. One was silk and the other leather.

If I had to guess, the live-action Ken clone was von Bismarck. Dirty-blond, square-jawed, and adorned with shabby whiskers of stubble, he looked like something only a Walt Disney illustrator could sketch. The perfect European prince, down to the scandalous blue eyes and Roman-like structure. *Silk*.

The other man was a polished savage. Menace decanted into a Kiton suit. He wore his inky hair in a gentleman's cut, trimmed into submission. Everything about him seemed carefully crafted. Intentionally designed to deliver lethal doses straight into a woman's bloodstream. Sharp cheekbones, thick brows, lashes I'd risk jail time for, and the frostiest gray eyes I'd seen to date. In fact, his eyes were so light and frosty, I decided they had no business coupling with his otherwise tan Italian features. *Leather*.

"Romeo Costa." Savannah's voice curled with longing as he breezed right past us, heading toward the table reserved for VIPs. "I would let him ruin me as thoroughly and impressively as Elon Musk destroyed Twitter."

"Oh, I would let him do heinous things to me." Emilie toyed with the blue diamond on her neck. "Like, I'm not even sure what they might be, but I'd still be down for them, you know?"

It was a problem. Being church-going, Bible-thumping, virginal Southern girls in the twenty-first century. Chapel Falls was known for two things: 1) Its filthy-rich residents, most of them conglomerate owners of high-profile Georgian businesses. And 2) being extremely, outdatedly, lock-your-daughters-up conservative.

Things worked different down here. Virtually all of us never went further than sneaking a few sloppy kisses before marriage, even though we all scraped the age of twenty-one.

While my well-mannered friends kept their glances discreet, I had no trouble glaring. As a nervous host led them to their table, they surveyed their surroundings. Romeo Costa with the dissatisfied detachment of a man who had to feast on back-alley garbage for dinner; and von Bismarck with amused, cynical playfulness.

"What are you doing, Dal? They can see that you're staring!" Savannah nearly fainted.

They weren't even looking our way.

"So?" I yawned, swiping a flute of champagne from a tray hovering in my periphery.

While Sav and Emilie gushed some more, I set off, passing banquet tables lined with imported sweets, champagne, and goodie bags.

I did the rounds, greeting peers and distant family members if only to access the catering trays on the opposite end of the room. I also kept an eye out for my sister, Franklin. Frankie was here somewhere, probably setting a small fire to someone's toupee or losing the family fortune in a game of cards.

If I was branded the lazy one, with the lack of ambition and abundance of free time, she was the designated banshee in the Townsend household. I had no idea why Daddy brought her here. She was barely nineteen and interested in meeting men a little less than I was interested in chewing unsterilized needles for a living.

Strutting in my limited-edition Louboutins—five inches, black velvet, and needle-thin heels made of stacked pearls and Swarovski crystals—I offered smiles and blown kisses to everyone in my path until I bumped into another body.

"Dal!" Frankie wrapped her arms around me like she hadn't seen me just forty minutes ago when she'd sworn me to secrecy after I caught her shoving nips of Clase Azul into her padded bra. The plastic edges of the miniature bottles dug into my boobs as we hugged.

"Are you having fun?" I righted her in place before she toppled over like a goat. "Do you want me to get you some water? Advil? Divine intervention?"

Frankie smelled of sweat. And cheap cologne. *And* weed. *Lord, help Daddy.*

"I'm fine." She waved a hand, peering around. "Did you see there's some duke from Maryland here?"

"I don't think monarchy exists in the U.S. of A, Sis." Just because von Bismarck's last name sounded made up didn't mean he was royalty.

"And his super-rich friend?" She ignored me. "He's an arms dealer, so that's fun." Only in her universe would an arms dealer be something enjoyable.

"Yeah, Sav and Emilie were so pumped, they were ready to wrestle a mountain lion. Did you meet them?"

"Not exactly." Frankie scrunched her nose, still surveying the ballroom, probably for whoever made her smell like an oopsie-baby in the back of a drug dealer's car. "Guess whoever invited them wanted to make an impression, 'cause their table has shortbread specially prepared by the late queen's beloved baker. Flown here straight from Surrey." She flashed me a crooked grin. "I stole one when no one was looking."

My heart squeezed. I loved my sister so much. I also wanted to *kill* her right now.

"And you didn't steal one for me?" I nearly shrieked. "You know I've never tasted authentic British shortbread. What's the matter with you?"

"Oh, there's still plenty more there." Frankie dug her fingers into her tight updo, massaging her scalp. "And people are lining up to talk to these jerks like they're the Windsors or something. Just go there, introduce yourself, and casually take one. There's a mountain of them."

"Shortbread or people?"

"Both."

I craned my neck above her head. She was right. A line of guests waited to kiss the rings of these two men. Since I wasn't above lowering myself for something tasty, I marched to the cluster of people haloing Costa and von Bismarck's table.

". . . disastrous tax plan that would create economic mayhem . . ."

". . . surely, Mr. Costa, there must be an off-ramp for all this spending? We can't keep funding these wars . . ."

". . . true about their lack of technological weapons? I've been meaning to ask . . ."

While the men of Chapel Falls blabbered their way into giving these two a coma and the women leaned down to show off their cleavage, I weaved into the thick crowd, my eyes on the prize—a three-tier tray full of mouthwatering shortbread. First, I casually planted my hand on the table. *Nothing to see here.* Then I inched deeper toward the British treats—the centerpiece. My fingers skimmed a square when a biting voice turned my way.

"And you are?"

It came from Leather. Or rather, Romeo Costa. He sat lounged back on his chair, staring at me with all the friendliness of a Nile crocodile. Fun fact: they considered humans a regular part of their diet.

I bent my knees with flourish. "Oh, I'm sorry. Where are my manners?"

"Not in the shortbread tray, that's for sure." His voice was dry and disinterested.

Okay. Tough audience. But I *did* try to steal his biscuits. "I'm Dallas Townsend of the Townsend family." I flashed him a warm smile, offering him my hand to kiss. He appraised it with repugnance, ignoring the gesture. Totally disproportionate to my alleged crime.

"You're Dallas Townsend?" A tinge of disappointment marred his godly face. Like he'd expected something entirely different. That he would expect anything at all was a stretch. We didn't move in the same circles. In fact, I was ninety-nine percent sure this man only moved in squares. He was a sharp-edged kind of guy.

"For the past twenty-one years." I eyed the shortbread. So close, and yet so far.

"My eyes are up here," Costa bit out.

Von Bismarck chuckled, snatching the largest square, possibly to spite me. "She's darling, Rom. Quite the pet."

Darling? Pet? What did he mean? With much reluctance, I dragged my gaze up the length of the table, from the shortbread to Romeo's face. He was so handsome. Also—dead in the eyes.

He leaned forward. "Are you sure you're Dallas Townsend?"

I tapped my chin. "Hmm, now that I think about it, I'd like to change my answer to Hailey Bieber."

"Is this supposed to be funny?"

"Is this supposed to be serious?"

"You're being obtuse."

"You started it."

Gasps pinged from every corner of the table. Romeo Costa, however, appeared more indifferent than offended. He sat back, forearms meeting each seat handle. The posture—and his perfectly tailored Kiton suit—granted him the aura of a terse king with a flavor for war.

"Dallas Maryanne Townsend." Barbara Alwyn-Joy rushed forward to intervene. Emilie's mother was a chaperone for the event. She, like the rest of them, took the job way too seriously. "I should get your father to escort you out of this ballroom right this minute for speaking to Mr. Costa like that. This is not the Chapel Falls way."

The Chapel Falls way would have every redhead in this town burn at the stake.

I made a show of lowering my head, tracing the shape of a round shortbread on the marble with my toe. "Sorry, ma'am."

I wasn't sorry. Romeo Costa was a prick. He was lucky we had an audience, or he would have gotten the unfiltered version of me. I turned, about to extract myself from the premises before I caused even more commotion and Daddy canceled my black card. But then, Costa just had to speak again.

"Miss Townsend?"

Bieber, for you.

"Yes?"

"An apology is in order."

Swiveling on my heel, I glowered at him with every ounce of wrath I could muster. "You're high if you think I'll apo—"

"I meant *I* should apologize." He stood, buttoning his blazer with one hand.

Oh. *Oh.* Dozens of eyes ping-ponged between us. I wasn't sure what was happening, but I did think my chances of getting my hands on that shortbread just increased tenfold. Also, I really needed to get in on his talent for being controlled and confident to the nines, even when delivering an apology. Apologizing always made me feel so helpless. Costa, on the other hand, treated an apology as a tool to catapult himself further up the hierarchy of humans. Already, he seemed an entirely different species from his peers.

I knotted my arms over my chest, ignoring everything etiquette classes taught me, per usual. "Yeah. I'd be open to that."

He didn't crack a smile. Didn't even look at me. Rather, he looked straight through me. "I apologize for doubting your identity. For uninformed reasons, I thought you'd be . . . different."

Normally, I'd ask who told him what, but I needed to cut my losses and run before my mouth got me into more trouble. There was a reason I kept it munching on something eighty percent of the time. Plus, I couldn't stare directly at that man without feeling like my legs were constructed of instant pudding. I didn't like how woozy he made me. Or how my skin flushed wherever his eyes rested.

"Hmm, sure. That's okay. Happens to the best of us. Enjoy your evening." With that, I beelined back to my table.

Luckily, Daddy sailed through dinner in a great mood, talking business with his friends. Barbara must not have acted on her threat to narc, because shortly after the fourth entrée, he granted me permission to dance.

And dance I did. First, with David from church. Then, James from high school. And finally, Harold from one street over. They spun me, dipped me inches from the marble floor, and even let me lead in a few waltzes. All in all, I almost restored my confidence that the evening was a success. Until Harold bowed his head when our song ended and I started for my seat. Because when I turned, Romeo Costa was there again. Like a summoned demon. About two inches from my face.

Sweet Mother Mary, why must sin always be so tempting?

"Mr. Costa." I placed my hand over my bare collarbone. "Sorry, I'm rather dizzy and exhausted. I don't think I can da—"

"I'll take the lead." He swept me up, my feet hovering over the floor, and began waltzing with me without my participation.

Hello, red flag the size of Texas.

"Kindly put me down," I requested through pursed lips.

His hold on my waist tightened, the contour of his muscles engulfing me. "Kindly drop the lady façade. I've seen Olivia Wilde performances more convincing."

Ouch. I distinctly remembered wanting to bleach my eyeballs after watching *The Lazarus Effect.*

"Thanks." I loosened my muscles, forcing him to hold all my weight or render me limp on the marble. "Being a respectable member of society is honestly exhausting."

"You came to my table for the shortbread, didn't you?"

Perhaps any other girl would deny it through her teeth. As it happened, I liked the idea of him knowing he wasn't the main attraction for me.

"Yes."

"They were spectacular."

I peeked at his table over his shoulder. "There's still some there."

"Very perceptive, Miss Townsend." He twirled me with the frightening expertise of a competitive ballroom dancer. I wasn't sure whether I was nauseous because he moved too fast or because I was in his arms. "I don't suppose you'd also be interested in champagne to go with it? Oliver and I just attained a bottle of Cristal Brut Millénium Cuvée."

That thing was thirteen thousand dollars a pop. *Of course*, I was down. I tried to match his lackluster tone. "Actually, I think a glass would be a perfect companion to the shortbread."

His face remained impassive and still. Lord, what did it take to muster a smile out of the man?

I was faintly aware of people staring at us. It occurred to me that Mr. Costa hadn't danced with anyone other than me. It made me uneasy. Savannah and Emilie had mentioned he wasn't here for a match, but they'd also told me brown cows made chocolate milk when we were in preschool. They were clearly an unreliable source of information.

I cleared my throat. "There is something you should know." He peered at me through his English winter-grays, his expression telling me there couldn't possibly be something I knew that he didn't. "I'm engaged to be married, so if you're looking to get to know me—"

"Knowing you is the least of my intentions." As he spoke, I noticed, for the first time, the tiny ball of gum crushed between his incisors. Spearmint, by the scent of it.

"Thank God." I relaxed into the waltz. "I don't like turning people down. It's a pet peeve, you know?"

I didn't love the idea of marrying Madison Licht, but I didn't hate it, either. I'd known him all my life. As the only child of Daddy's college roommate, he showed up during holidays and the occasional dinner party. Everything about him was adequate. Adequately attractive. Adequately rich. Adequately mannered. He did, however, tolerate my brand of quirkiness. Plus, his eight extra years gave him the shine of a worldly, experienced man. We'd gone on two dates, where he made it clear he'd let me live my life as I pleased. A rarity among arranged couples in Chapel Falls.

Romeo Costa stared at me like I was flaming poop at his doorstep he needed to stomp on. "When's the wedding?" His voice was mockery tightly wrapped in velvet.

"No idea. Probably when I graduate."

"What are you studying?"

"English Lit at Emory."

"When are you graduating?"

"Whenever I stop failing my semesters?"

A bitter smile touched his lips, as if he recognized it was supposed to entertain him. "How do you like it?"

"I don't."

"What *do* you like, other than shortbread?" He seemed to humor me just so I wouldn't leave.

I had no idea why. It didn't look like he enjoyed my company all that much. Still, I gave it some genuine thought, since I didn't have to concentrate on getting my steps right. He did all the work for us.

"Books. Rain. Libraries. Driving alone at night with my favorite playlist in the background. Traveling—mainly for the food. But the historic stuff is decent, too."

Chapel Falls knew me as the girl who spent her days upcycling Daddy's money into luxury bags, frequenting fancy restaurants, and hunting down every decent novel in the Bible Belt. It was a well-known fact that I possessed no worthy aspirations. But the gossip hadn't gotten it all right. I had one secret desire. A clandestine wish that, unfortunately, demanded a man to fulfill. More than anything, I wanted to be a mother. It seemed so simple. So attainable. And yet, there were important steps required for such a goal, none of which I'd ever come close to achieving in stuffy Chapel Falls.

"You're very candid." He didn't say it like it was a good thing.

"You're very curious." I let him dip me, even when it brought us closer. "What do you like?" I asked after a beat, because it was the polite thing to do.

"Few things." He spun us in swift circles, right past a slack-jawed Savannah. "Money. Power. War."

"War?" I choked out.

"War," he confirmed. "It's a lucrative business. A steady one, too. There's always a war going on in the world or countries gearing up for it. It's extraordinary."

"For the politicians, maybe. Not for the people suffering. The children soiling their beds from fear. The casualties, the families, the pain-stricken—"

"Are you always this taxing, or did you save this beauty-pageant speech especially for me?"

After being rendered speechless by his assholery, I answered, "All for you. Hope that makes you feel special."

He snapped his gum. So gentlemanly. *Not.* "Meet me in the rose garden in ten minutes."

Everyone knew what happened in the rose garden.

I pursed my lips. Was he not here for the last five minutes? "I just told you I'm engaged to be married."

"You aren't married just yet." He dipped me again while correcting the sequence of the sentence. Show off. "This is your last hurrah before you tie the knot. Your moment of weakness before it's too late to try something new."

"But . . . I don't like you."

"You don't need to like me to let me make you feel good."

Rearing my head back, I glared at him, my pupils running wild in their sockets. "What are you offering, exactly?"

"A reprieve from this mind-numbing event." Another spin. More whiplash. Or maybe it was from this conversation. He kept his voice low and even. "Full discretion guaranteed. Ten minutes. I'll bring the shortbread and champagne. All you need to bring is yourself. Actually . . ." He paused, giving me a onceover. "I wouldn't mind if you left your personality at the table." With that, he broke off from me mid-dance, setting me down on the floor.

My mind reeled as I watched his back while he sauntered away. I didn't understand what had just happened. Had he offered me a hookup? He seemed appalled by our conversation. But maybe that was just his default setting. Glacial, reserved, and offhanded.

Part of me reasoned I should take what he'd offered. Not go all the way, of course. I was saving my virginity. But a few fumbles in the dark wouldn't hurt. Not like Madison sat at home, working on our couple's scrapbook. I knew for a fact he went out all over D.C., enjoying brief affairs with models and socialites. My friend Hayleigh lived across the hall from him and told me about the women coming in and out of his condo. I mean, we weren't even together-together. We spoke on the phone once a month to "get to know each other," per our parents' request, but that was it.

A man like Romeo Costa was a once-in-a-lifetime event. I *should* take advantage of it. Of him. And maybe he could teach me a few tricks. Something to impress Madison with. Besides . . . shortbread.

As soon as Daddy turned to speak with Mr. Goldberg, I dashed toward the restroom. I white-knuckled the edge of the gold-specked limestone sink, blinking into the mirror.

It's just a few kisses. You've done this before with plenty of boys.

He was so new, so mature, so sophisticated, I didn't even care that he was downright mean. Let's get real here—Mr.

Darcy wasn't exactly swoon-worthy until the last twenty percent of the book.

"Nothing bad will happen," I assured my reflection. "Nothing."

Behind me, a toilet flushed. Emilie escaped a booth, frowning as she settled beside me to wash her hands. "Did you smoke the same thing that waiter gave your sister?" The back of her soapy hand rose to my forehead. "You're talking to yourself."

I dodged her touch. "Hey, Em, did you meet Romeo Costa?"

She shook her head, pouting. "He and von Bismarck are the main attractions. Always surrounded by herds of people. I couldn't even get a picture of the guy. I saw you dancing with him. So lucky. I'd kill for the opportunity."

A breathless, reckless laugh escaped me. I shook my head.

"Where are you going?" she called after me.

To do something wild.

Chapter Two

Dallas

That this could be a mistake didn't once occur to me as I waited, perched on the stone bench behind the rose bushes. Summer's warm breath clung to the crisp night, humid residue weighing down roses in full bloom. Romeo Costa was three minutes and thirty-four seconds late. Yet, somehow, I knew he'd come. I bit my lip to stem my giggles. Adrenaline coursed through my veins.

When crunched leaves penetrated cricket chirps and hums from faraway cars, I straightened my spine. Romeo's flawless features came into view, illuminated by the moon's sleek blue shadow. He was even more beautiful in pure darkness. Like he was in his natural habitat, playing on his home field.

True to his word, he held an open champagne bottle by its neck in one hand and a handful of shortbread squares tucked inside a napkin in the other.

"My precious!" I growled in a Gollum voice, extending my fingers. He gave me the bored glare of a man used to fending off fangirls, before realizing I'd reached for the shortbread, not him. I shoved an entire square into my mouth, tipped my head back, and groaned. "So good. I can practically taste London."

"Surrey," he corrected, staring at me as if I were a wild

18

boar he needed to wrestle. "Do you enjoy the taste of ancient ruins and manure?"

"Buzzkill."

For a reason beyond my grasp, he seemed really unhappy about spending time with me, even though he'd initiated this meeting.

"Let's go somewhere discreet." It was more of a demand than a suggestion.

"No one will find us here." I waved a hand. "I've been attending this ball since I was sixteen. I know every nook and cranny in this place."

He shook his head. "Some waiters come here for a smoke."

Romeo must've not wanted to be seen with me just as much as I didn't want to be seen with him. I was a provincial, silly girl to his billionaire-tycoon reputation.

I sighed, dusting shortbread crumbs onto the cobblestone. "Fine. But if you think I'm going to go all the way with you, you're gravely mistaken."

"I wouldn't dare assume." He punctuated the dark mutter with his back, starting for the other side of the courtyard. It seemed like he was running away from me, not leading the way. I followed him nonetheless, munching on my third shortbread. "What made you come to the rose garden? The snacks or the proposition?"

"A bit of both." I licked my fingers. "And the fact that I bet Madison doesn't stay fai—" I stopped myself. I shouldn't talk badly about my fiancé, even if he did do me dirty. We weren't officially together. We hadn't even kissed. It wasn't like I was jealous. I couldn't give the first dang about whom he hung out with before we truly became a couple. "Curiosity killed the cat," I amended.

"Your cat will survive. Though I'm tempted to leave it in less-than-pristine condition."

My cat? Did he mean my pu . . .

Oh. My. Lord.

My body, which didn't get the memo that we were both supposed to dislike conceited jerks, got tingly in places I normally forgot existed. "You're terrible," I informed him cheerfully. "You're going to be my favorite mistake."

He stopped on a rolling green hill at the back of the opera house. It seemed secluded enough, with a dark wall to our right. Romeo passed me the champagne bottle. "Drink."

Pressing it to my lips, I drained a fifth. "You're not a master of seduction, are you?"

He leaned against the wall, hands tucked inside his front pockets. "Seduction is an art I rarely have to perform."

The fizzy liquid ran down my throat, cold and fresh. I coughed a little, forking over the bottle. "So humble."

He took a generous swig, the gum still in his mouth. "Are you a virgin?"

"Yes." I glanced around, suddenly wondering if it was worth it. He was hot. But also, kind of a pig. "Are you?"

"Close enough."

The question had been a joke, so it took me a while to register his answer. Tipping my head back, I laughed. "What do you know? There *is* a sense of humor under all this ice."

"Have you considered how far you want to take this?" He passed the bottle back to me, two-thirds empty.

"Can I just tell you when to stop?"

"From my brief history with you, my guess is you won't stop until you've not only lost your virginity, but have lost the virginity of every other well-bred girl in this zip code, too. Let's agree to keep your hymen intact." Someone needed to work on their dirty talk.

"Sounds good. Are you from New York?"

"No."

"Then wher—"

"Let's not talk."

Oh. Kay. The man wasn't going down in my history book for the nicest hookup, but he *was* the hottest one by a thousand miles, so I let it slide. We shuttled the champagne back and forth until it emptied. My body felt like a live wire, humming with anticipation. Finally—*finally*—he set the bottle on the ground, pushed off the wall, and pinched my chin between his thumb and index finger, tilting my head up. My heart somersaulted, diving to the pit of my stomach, where it liquidized into sludge.

For the first time, his eyes glittered with warm approval. "I've met IRS agents more likable than you. I'll give you one thing, though. You're quite delicious, Miss Townsend."

My mouth fell open. "How would you kno—" But I never finished the sentence because he spat his gum on the grass and shut me up with a searing kiss.

His mouth was warm and smelled of bonfire, expensive perfume, and spearmint. It sucked all logic out of me, rendering me dizzy. His body felt strong, hard, and foreign. I molded into him, wrapping around him like an octopus.

He darted the tip of his tongue out, parting my lips. When I opened them eagerly, his satisfaction reverberated in my stomach. He cupped the back of my neck to deepen the kiss. His tongue was fully in my mouth now, exploring the grounds like it was conquering every inch. The bite of freshness from his gum filled me. He tasted delicious, applying just the right amount of pressure. Just like that, his harsh words and stony exterior melted into passion, fire, and a depraved promise for things I didn't know if I could handle.

The place between my legs throbbed. I tried to remember if anything I'd ever done before felt like this. The answer, depressingly, was *no*. This was completely new territory. Unchartered waters I wanted to dive right into. I whimpered into his mouth, yanking the lapels of his jacket, my tongue chasing his. I didn't care what he thought of me. I'd never see him again.

My hands roamed his sleeves, clutching the expensive material and sinewy muscles beneath it. He was athletic and built without looking bulky. Lord, he was beautiful. Cold, smooth, and imperial as marble. As if somebody had breathed just enough soul into a Roman statue to make it move—but not enough to make it feel.

As we devoured each other, I wondered if I could feel each individual ridge of his six-pack. I patted down his abs. I could. Wait until Frankie heard about this. She was going to cry horny tears.

Romeo pushed me against the wall, wrapping my dark tresses around his fist two times over like reins of a horse. He tugged, slanting my head up and deepening our kiss. His massive erection dug into my thigh, pulsating with heat and need. A thrill shot up my spine.

"My, my." His grip tightened. I felt him unfurling, the walls around him cracking just a tad. "You were made for corruption, weren't you, Shortbread?"

Did he just call me . . . Shortbread?

"More." I clawed at his suit. I didn't know what I was asking for. All I knew was it tasted and felt better than any dessert. And that it would be over in a few minutes. I couldn't afford to be gone too long.

"More what?" His hand had already snaked into the slit of my dress.

"More . . . I don't know. You're the expert here."

He gripped my ass. An index finger slipped under the elastic of my cotton panties, plowing into my butt cheek.

"Yes. Yes. That." I broke our kiss, biting his chin, my inexperience bleeding into the encounter when I couldn't help myself. "But . . . the other way. Up front."

"Sure you want to lose your virginity to the fingers of a stranger who gave you shortbread?"

"Don't push inside, then." I jerked my head away, frowning at him. "Just work around . . . you know, the frame."

He shoved his hand between my legs, covering my heated center with his palm, squeezing hard. "I really ought to fuck the sass out of you right here and now for that smart mouth of yours." It marked the first time this artful Mid-Atlantic man had used profanity, and somehow, I knew it was a rare occasion for him.

Arching my back, I plastered myself into his hand, searching for more contact. "Mmm. Yes."

He stroked my slit through my panties, drawing an oval around it with his finger without actually touching it. Maybe it was because his touch was unhurried, fleeting, and designed to drive me wild, but my panties dampened. Sweet torture, it was amazing.

"Does your mouth always get you into trouble?" He finished kissing me and graduated to driving me nuts by stroking my pussy, staring down at me with open irritation. Weird man. Very weird man. But not weird enough for me to walk away from whatever was currently happening between us.

"Always. Momma tells me if I ran my legs as much as I ran my mouth, I'd be an Olympic—*ohhh*, this feels good."

His finger dipped into my slit, curling over my clit, then retreated as quick as it came. To my horror, I heard my wetness as he parted my lips.

"Do that again." I nuzzled into his neck, high on his scent. "But all the way."

He groaned, followed by what I was pretty sure was a harsh whisper of *what a mess*. Hey, no one was holding a gun to his head.

"Are you even having fun?" I was beginning to think he regretted the whole thing. Even through my lusty haze, I could tell he appeared more irritated than turned on. I mean, his leg-length cock definitely told me he wasn't suffering, but he seemed very upset about finding me attractive.

"Ecstatic." His voice dripped sarcasm.

"You can suck on my nipples if you want. I heard it's hot." I reached for my corseted breast, tugging at the fabric.

His hand rushed to grasp mine and cupped my breast, keeping it clothed. "Generous of you, but I'll pass."

"They're pretty nice, I swear." I tried tugging harder to show him.

His hold tightened around my hand. "I like my things mine. Concealed from view. For my own private entertainment."

His?

I sobered up. "Yours?"

Just then, the wall we'd leaned against collapsed. The hostess of the ball stood on a podium, holding a remote to fireworks. *We* were standing on the podium, too. *Oh,*

Lord. This wasn't a wall. It was a curtain. And in front of us sat the entire three-hundred-strong guest list of the ball. All slack-jawed, wide-eyed, and judgmental as heck.

I spotted Daddy immediately. Within nanoseconds, his olive skin turned eggshell, yet his ears grew redder and redder. A couple thoughts finally filtered into my lust-fogged brain. First, Daddy was definitely, two-hundred percent going to cancel all my cards, from the Amex to the library one. And finally, I realized what everyone was seeing. Me, in the arms of a man who sure wasn't my fiancé. His hand shoved between my legs through my dress. My lipstick ruined. My hair a mess . . . and I knew I'd given him a few visible love bites.

"Dude." That was Frankie from the deep jaws of the crowd. "Momma's gonna ground you till you're forty."

The throng erupted in excited chatter. Phone flashlights attacked my face as I stumbled backward, pushing Romeo Costa away. He wasn't having any of it, though. The psychopath pretended to protect me, shifting me behind him. His touch was careless and cold. An act. What on earth was happening here?

". . . ruined for every other man in this zip code . . ."

". . . poor Madison Licht. Such a good fella . . ."

". . . always been problematic . . ."

". . . a scandal magnet . . ."

". . . horrible fashion sense . . ."

Okay, that last one was a flat-out lie.

"D-d-daddy. It's not what it looks like." I tried to smooth out my Oscar de la Renta and stomped Romeo on the foot with my spiky heel, finally breaking free from his hold.

"Unfortunately, it's exactly what it looks like," he countered, stepping deeper into the stage and scooping me by the elbow to join him. What in tarnation was he doing? "The secret is out, my love." His *love? Me?* He made a show of wiping the hand that was between my legs just seconds ago on my designer dress. "Please, don't call my Dallas a ruined woman. She merely yielded to temptation. As Oscar Wilde pointed out, it is naught but human." His eyes remained hard. Dead on Daddy's.

Naught but? Why was he talking like a *Downton Abbey* extra? And why did he say I'm ruined?

"I should kill you." My father, the great Shepherd Townsend, shouldered through bodies to reach the stage. "Correction—I *will* kill you."

Cold white panic coursed through me. I really wasn't sure if he was talking to me, to Romeo, or to both of us. My fingertips were so frozen, I couldn't even feel them. I shook like a leaf blowing in the autumn wind.

I'd really done it this time. This was no longer about failing random courses, sassing off to someone whose opinion my parents sought, or not-so-accidentally eating Frankie's birthday cake. I downright and single-handedly ruined my family's good reputation. Tarnished the Townsend name to rubbles of gossip and condemnation.

"Shep, is it?" Romeo un-pocketed the hand not wrapped around me and checked the Patek Philippe on his wrist.

"It's Mr. Townsend to you," Daddy ground out, now onstage with us. "What do you have to say for yourself?"

"I see we've reached the bargaining portion of the night." Costa gave me a once-over, as if trying to decide how much he wanted to bid on me. "I know Chapel Falls has a you-break-it-you-buy-it policy in place when it comes to your maiden debutante daughters." His words thrashed against my skin, leaving angry red marks everywhere they touched. Now that no one could hear us, he no longer pretended we were an item and spoke to Daddy like a businessman. "I'm willing to buy what I've broken."

Why was he talking like I was a vase? And what on earth was he proposing, exactly?

"I'm not broken." I shoved him, halfway toward feral. His hold on me only tensed in response. "And I'm not a product to be bought."

"Zip it, Dallas." Daddy's breaths came out labored and heavy. Sweat like I'd never seen on him before raced down his temples. He inserted himself between us as if he couldn't trust either of us not to launch into a fresh session of lovemaking. And finally, Romeo released me. "Now, I'm not sure what you're proposing, Mr. Costa, but this was nothing but a few kisses on a drunken night—"

Romeo lifted his hand to stop him. "I know what your daughter's pussy feels like, sir. Tastes like, too." He licked the pad of his thumb, never breaking eye contact with Daddy. "You can try to talk your way out of this until you're blue in the face. The world will buy my version. We both know it. Your daughter is mine. All you can do now is negotiate a decent deal out of it."

"What's going on over there?" Barbara stood in the crowd. "Is there a proposal?"

"There better be a proposal," someone else warned.

"I didn't even know they knew each other," Emilie cried. "All she talked about was the dessert."

Shame colored my face pink. The only thing keeping me up on my feet was the deep-set knowledge that I'd never let this awful man win. My anger was so poignant, so tangible, I tasted its sourness in my mouth. It coated every corner, dripping into my system like black poison.

Daddy lowered his voice, leveling Romeo with all the hatred he possessed. "I promised my daughter to Madison Licht."

"Licht won't touch her with a twenty-foot pole now."

"He'll understand."

"Will he?" Romeo arched a brow. "Put aside the fact that his fiancée was caught with my fingers up her dress in front of her entire hometown, I'm sure you're aware we're bitter business rivals."

Ladies and gentlemen, the man who apparently wants to marry me. Safe to assume Edgar Allan Poe wasn't churning in his grave, worrying about being knocked down from the Great Poet pedestal.

"Hey, now. This is my daughter, and I—"

"Gave her away to a well-off prick, who I'm sure is going to treat her like a piece of baroque furniture." There was no mirth in Romeo's voice. No victory, either. He delivered the news like a sulky Grecian god deciding on a mere mortal's fate. "There is no difference between what I offer her and what Madison Licht brings to the table, other than the fact that I am soon to be worth twenty billion dollars, and his company isn't even public yet."

The entire weight of the world came crashing down on me when I understood two things: 1) Romeo Costa had known exactly who I was when he'd arrived at this ball. He sought me out. Lured me in. Made sure he had my attention. I was always his objective. After all, he'd said it himself—Madison Licht was his enemy, and he wanted to ruin things for him. And 2) Romeo Costa was such a bastard, he would marry me despite making every single person involved in this union miserable, just to spite my fiancé. Former fiancé, more likely.

I raged forward, palms connecting with his chest. "I don't want to marry you."

"Feeling's mutual." He stepped into my fiery touch, picked up my left hand, and glided Madison's engagement ring off my finger. "Alas, a tradition is a tradition. I touched; I ruined. Say hello to your new fiancé." Romeo examined the ring pinched between his fingers, unimpressed. "This thing barely costs sixteen grand." He tossed it into the crowd, and a few less-than-honorable girls tried to catch it.

The air drained from my lungs. Romeo examined my father with a perfect poker face, confident that, despite my recklessness, I wouldn't dare defy the patriarch's order if he decided we should marry.

No. *No, no, no, no, no.*

"Daddy, please." I rushed to him, lacing my arm with his. He jerked away from my touch, scowling at his loafers, struggling to regulate his breaths. My cheeks pricked with rejection, as if he'd struck me. My father had never been so cruel to me before. I wanted to cry. I *never* cried.

Evil had a face. It was breathtakingly beautiful . . . and belonged to the man who had just become my future husband.

"Why don't we discuss this away from prying eyes?" Daddy peered around, worn out and pain stricken. I'd probably tarnished that tux for him, too, just as I'd tarnished my future. "Mr. Costa, report to my house immediately."

Romeo Costa brushed his arm over my shoulder as he passed, not sparing me the faintest look. "Ruined by shortbread." He popped a cube of gum into his mouth as his imposing figure descended the stage. "How the mighty have fallen."

Chapter Three

Ollie vB: @RomeoCosta, how's it feel to pop your scandal cherry? Welcome to the club, son. We've got snacks. And the Kennedy family.

Romeo Costa: www.dmvpost.org/ Von-Bismarck-Heir-Caught-Cozying-Up-To-Georgia-Governors-Wife

Ollie vB: Call me daddy, and I might just pass along my skills.

Zach Sun: Homewrecking is not a skill.

Ollie vB: Tell that to Rom. He just broke an engagement, reputation, and future in the span of ten minutes. The student has surpassed the master.

Ollie vB: [Shia LaBeouf standing ovation GIF]

Zach Sun: Where is Rom now?

Ollie vB: Her house, probably torching her childhood memorabilia and drowning her pets.

Zach Sun: If I had a heart, it would break for her.

Ollie vB: Judging by the fight she gave him, if anything is going to break here, it'll be your boy's spirit by the end of the month.

Chapter Four

Romeo

A million Dallas Townsends waltzed on my brain, their pointy heels stabbing each fold. I peeled my eyes open. The room rocked back and forth as if I'd stowed away on a sinking ship.

"Shouldn't have finished that Pappy Van Winkle by yourself, buddy." Oliver's spirited voice echoed from the depths of a toilet. "Sharing is caring."

Zach *tsked* from a distance. "For the last time, von Bismarck, that Agent Provocateur model didn't want a threesome."

I hissed into a silky pillow at the Grand La Perouse Hotel, regretting every decision I had made that landed me in this hellhole. Spurred on by a last-minute discovery, the three of us had arrived in Chapel Falls half an hour before the ball.

Presently, we occupied the four-bedroomed presidential suite. Not so much because we enjoyed each other's company, but because we knew some schmuck had booked it ahead of the ball. Taking joy in other people's misery was one of the smallest pleasures in life. One I often indulged in.

Oliver ambled into the room, his mouth enveloping an unlit cigar. "You needed to numb the pain away. Erase the memory of fingering a prepubescent girl in front of

Fortune 500's finest." He shouldered into a polo. "The tab was forty grand on alcohol and cigars alone, by the way. We should get into the business of throwing debutante balls. The world would never be short of privileged young women in need of billionaire husbands."

The idea of ever wasting my time like this again revolted me. "You'd turn the place into a gambling joint and father a few bastards before the first waltz."

He plopped onto the edge of my bed, hiking up his riding boots. "Yes, to gambling. No, to bastards. I always pack my meat. No glove, no love." Considering he viewed women as a conveyor belt of warm holes to park himself inside for the night, I doubted Oliver was familiar with the notion of love. He paused, his lips bowing around the cigar. "Not everyone is scrupulous enough to practice your method of ensuring no illegitimate children are in line for the throne."

Zachary Sun—tall, lithe, obnoxiously genius, and as emotionally available as a pet rock—breezed into my room with his laptop tucked under his bicep. "What's Rom's method?"

He'd opted to stay in the hotel yesterday. His presence at the ball would have been redundant. Just the thought of her son marrying a Southern girl would send Mrs. Sun into heart failure. No common woman could suit their old-money lineage, which traced back to the Zhou Dynasty

"There's one hole he never fucks, and it's the one where babies come from." Oliver delivered the piece of information with unnecessary jollity.

Zach frowned, probably recalling my past. "Recently or ever?"

We shared the same worldview—that the oxygen provided by Earth's dwindling forests was a privilege wasted on humans. Against my better judgment, I'd made one exception in my thirty-one years of life. Which I'd come to regret. In spectacular fashion, too.

"He's been abstinent long enough to be considered a born-again virgin." Oliver shrugged into an equestrian blazer. "Not to mention—a loser."

If the words were supposed to offend me, they missed their mark by about two thousand miles. Women didn't interest me. Neither did people in general.

Zach observed me with equal wonder and confusion. "How come I never knew that about you?"

"You must've missed my three-month ad on the front page of the *New York Times*." I emptied a water bottle in one gulp, placing a piece of mint gum on the tip of my tongue. "What's the time?"

"Glad you asked." Oliver lit his cigar and sucked hard. A plume of smoke crawled up from the amber tip. "It's high time I remind you what happened last night. The incident that preceded you polishing off an entire bottle of brandy in hopes you'd die of alcohol poisoning after you returned from the Townsends' premises."

I slam-dunked the bottle into the trash. "Have your moment in the sun. Tell me how bad it looked from the outside."

"It didn't look bad." Zach parked his laptop on the table in front of my bed. "Bizarre? Yes. Scandalous? As intended. But you came off as a good guy trying to win over a girl. At least in the videos plastered all over TikTok and YouTube, many of them viral. They call it the proposal of the century."

Oliver whistled. "You have your own hashtag."

I'd never created a scandal in my entire life, and I certainly did not relish being a part of one now. However, the ends justified the means. I'd done it. Stolen Madison Licht's fiancée and made her mine. The little cretin always ended events with an underaged gold digger, who thought she could keep him for more than one night. Imagine my surprise when, two days ago, Oliver overheard him waxing poetic about his fiancée's delectable body, perfect face, and luscious hair. For once in his miserable life, it appeared he hadn't lied.

I rubbed my chin. "Was she at least as beautiful as I remember?"

"Exquisite. Chef's kiss." Oliver brought his fingers to his lips. "Also: hardly pubescent. Is she even legal, Rom?"

"Legal." A teeth-shaped valley at the tip of my chin rippled across my fingertips. The manic little vixen had bitten me and left a mark. "Been in college for at least two years."

Three or more, if she hadn't exaggerated about failing her semesters. How one could fail in English Lit evaded me, but leave it to this hell-dragged phantom to manage it.

"Zach, when I tell you that woman was livid . . ." Oliver shook his head. Smoke poured from his nostrils like a demonic dragon. "She nearly stabbed him to death. I think the only thing that stopped her was the likelihood of embarrassing her family further."

Thankfully, Dallas Townsend harbored a red line. Based on our fleeting introduction, it was her only one. I'd be hard-pressed to conjure a woman as colorful as her. She remained in constant sixth gear, ping-ponging from stealing food to running her mouth like it was a Boston Marathon contestant. Her mere face made me want to pop four Tylenols and wash them down with brandy. If I'd known her personality prior to acquiring her as my newest investment, I would've chosen to hear that pasty brute wax on about her for the rest of his pathetic life over marrying her myself.

Oliver slapped his knee, laughing. "She gave him hell."

"I'm sure he'll retaliate in kind once they tie the knot." Zach typed away on his laptop, only half-invested in the conversation. "What happened after you got to her house?"

I propped against the headboard, massaging the foot my future wife had pierced a straight hole through with her heel. "Her father sent her to her room. Then we closed a nice sweetheart deal. I'm going to hemorrhage donation money into his non-profits for the next five years and introduce him to some people he wants to pitch businesses to."

And for what? I could count on one hand the number of times I would see Dallas Townsend after the wedding ceremony—and have fingers left over.

"Well." Oliver tugged his brown leather gloves up his fingers, tossing the butt of his cigar through the window. "As much as I enjoy reciting the night Romeo ruined his life, I have horses to see and women to corrupt."

Zach popped a dark eyebrow. "Any woman who is dumb enough to end up under you has already been thoroughly tarnished."

Oliver sighed. "It's true."

Zach's nose scrunched. "Aren't you bored?"

Whereas Oliver loved all women, Zach couldn't find a single one that lived up to his unreasonable ideals. In fact, Mrs. Sun arranged weekly dates with ABC heiresses to shipping, copper mining, and software companies. His favorite pastime was shutting them down on absurd bases, such as too pretty, too smart, too rich, too charitable, and my personal favorite, too much like him.

"I'll stop chasing tail when I die." Oliver rose to his feet, slipping his wallet and phone into a sleek leather courier bag. He frowned. "Actually, even then, the worms aren't safe from my libido. Now, if you'll excuse me, I'm going to make the most out of this shithole before we depart, and there's no better way I can think of spending my time than not with you."

With Oliver off to make the world a worse place, Zach and I stared each other down. On paper, we shared much in common. A single entity motivated us. Money. Zach had two multi-billion-dollar exits under his belt on self-developed apps. Meanwhile, I reigned over my father's company as CFO, dabbling in hedge funds and high-risk investments for fun. Since graduating from MIT, I'd tripled Costa Industries' revenue. We were reserved, calculated, pragmatic, and unmoved by societal expectations. Both our parents pressured us to marry. And they would go to extreme lengths to walk us down the aisle with the future mother of their grandchildren. But our similarities ended here.

Unlike Zach, I didn't possess a single nerve in my whole body. Not to mention integrity, a concept I found as mythical as mermaids. I did atrocious things and still slept like a baby at night. Zach, on the other hand, was genuinely decent. It didn't matter much, since he found ninety-nine percent of the population hard to stomach due to lack of sufficient intelligence.

"So." Zach didn't lift his eyes from the screen. "Think you'll develop a conscience and let the poor girl loose?"

I swung my feet to the floor and planted my elbows on my knees, digging my palms into my eye sockets. "No."

"Why not?"

A million reasons existed, but only one mattered. "Because she was Madison's, and he deserves nothing good in his life."

"So, she *is* good."

"Did I say good? I meant insufferable."

"High praise."

"Insufferable *is* praise, as far as she's concerned. The woman could drive a monk to murder."

"Interesting." He did not find that interesting. He did not find anything that wasn't money, technology, and art even remotely stimulating. "I've yet to hear you so passionate about a woman, one way or the other, since Mo—"

"Do not speak her name. At any rate, Dublin and I will be married on paper only."

Was I telling this to Zach or myself?

"Dublin, huh?" He ripped his gaze from the screen only to deliver a pitiful look. "Don't underestimate the power of paper. Money's made of that shit."

"Twenty-five percent linen. Seventy-five percent cotton," I corrected. Not that he didn't know.

"Checks, then. What do you know about her?"

Not much. After yesterday, my curiosity wasn't piqued, to say the least. Seducing her had been easier than taking candy from a baby. Ironically, taking candy from *her* was something I didn't think was possible without losing an arm.

"She's beautiful, unhinged, and would rather eat her own eyeballs than marry me."

Zach saluted me with his electrolyte water. "I'll make popcorn."

"Don't be so smug. You're next in line."

"But the line is long." He clicked away on his mouse, already drifting from the conversation to his work. "And I'm very good at stalling."

Chapter Five

Romeo

The day progressed like a night terror. At an excruciating pace. Zach fielded back-to-back conference calls for his impending hostile takeover. Oliver busied himself riding racehorses and getting oral—possibly at the same time.

Meanwhile, I wolfed down chicken breasts and Brussel sprouts, washed the bitter aftertaste with Chicory coffee, and stocked up on gum, demanding Mastika brand from the concierge. When I could no longer delay the inevitable, I left the hotel to purchase a ring for the bane of my existence.

It was of great importance that Dallas wore an engagement ring at least three times the size of the one her ex-fiancé had gifted her. This had nothing to do with her and everything to do with ensuring that Madison wanted to stab his own pupils whenever she flashed it in public. And if it proved too heavy for her delicate fingers, she would have to manage. It wasn't as if she ever put them to use and actually worked. I'd heard the whispers. My future wife was exceedingly, notoriously, incomparably lazy.

As the store manager rang up the two-million-dollar statement ring on my limitless card, along with the hefty insurance that accompanied it, my phone buzzed with an incoming call. *Mother.* I pressed accept, but did not grace her with actual words.

"Well?" Romeo Costa Sr. demanded, instead. "How is it going?"

Leave it to my father to not know what half the Internet had already made memes about. It was unfortunate, if not downright gauche, that I had become a social media sensation for ruining a young woman's honor at a debutante ball. In fact, much to the appreciation of the DOD, I'd made it thirty-one years without a single blemish. I'd given Dallas Townsend my first scandal; she'd given me her future. It did not seem like an equitable exchange and marked the first time in my adult life that I'd ended up on the losing side of, well, anything. All over a girl who would sprint into a stranger's white van if it meant she could get her hands on a piece of candy.

"Chapel Falls is lovely." I snatched the turquoise bag from the sales associate's fingers, strolling out to the sidewalk. "How're y'all doing?"

"Romeo, my goodness." A distinct horrified tone vaulted forward, seizing the call. No doubt my mother clutched her signature pearls as she spoke. "I didn't send you to Sidwell Friends, MIT, and Harvard, so you'd pick up horrid Southern lingo."

"You also didn't send me to Sidwell Friends, MIT, and Harvard for me to be a mere CFO at your husband's company, yet here we are." We all knew I deserved the COO position, which the other bane of my existence, Bruce Edwards, currently occupied.

My father ignored my dig. "Did you find a bride? Remember, Romeo—no bride, no company."

Ah. The crux of my existential problem. The whole reason I was in this humid hellhole in the first place. Ideally, I'd have simply tarnished the Townsend girl and sent Madison my Egyptian sheets as a souvenir. As it happened, my parents had delivered an ultimatum earlier this week—find a bride and settle down, or the CEO position would go directly to Bruce Edwards.

Bruce was the byproduct of top-tier Massachusetts inbreeding. Nine years at Milton Academy, four at Phillips Andover, and two Harvard degrees. He and Senior shared the same dorm room in Winthrop House, eighteen years apart. Both initiated into The Porcellian Club, where good ole Senior served as his alumni mentor.

Though not a drop of Costa blood ran through Bruce's useless veins, an affront to centuries of Costa nepotistic tradition, Romeo Costa Sr. considered himself too honor- able to forget his Harvard juniors. So, Bruce was, to my great displeasure, a fixture in our lives. He possessed the infuriating habit of referring to me as Junior at every public opportunity. Eight years ago, he'd even taken to addressing my father as Romeo instead of Mr. Costa for the sheer justification of assigning me the nickname.

He was also, apparently, in the same room as my parents. His deep, nerve-grating voice soothed Senior. "Romeo, Mon." Mon, not Monica, as if they were golf buddies. "Children mature slower these days. Perhaps Junior isn't ready. Not for marriage and not for the job."

This. This was why I preferred numbers and spread- sheets to humans. I knew Senior half-expected—maybe even wished—I'd flake on his dare and stay single. The only thing Bruce had that I didn't was a wife. A mousy thing called Shelley. There was nothing overtly wrong about Shelley, other than her taste in men. There was nothing overtly right about her, either. She was the white bread of humans. As bland as unseasoned chicken breast and just about as alluring.

"I'm not going to hand over one of the most profitable corporations in the United States to a soulless bachelor half the company is too scared to approach." My father was wrong. It was precisely my soullessness that made me the perfect candidate for the job of delivering heavy-duty weapons into the hands of dubious governments and banana republics. Not that he cared about my marital status. He only cared about one thing—continuing the Costa bloodline.

"Come on, Romeo." Bruce wedged himself back into the conversation. "This can't be good for your blood pressure."

Bruce's brother ran a goliath pharmaceutical corporation that made Pfizer look like David, so he often pretended to care about Senior's health. The truth was, we both wanted the man dead. And we both played nice to succeed his position as CEO before he kicked the bucket. Well, I played nice. Bruce had his tongue so far up my father's rear, I was surprised it didn't tickle his tonsils.

Senior ignored Bruce, continuing his rant. "Especially with Licht Holdings breathing down our necks."

Licht Holdings—you guessed it—belonged to Madison Licht's father. A rival defense firm gaining popularity with the bigwigs in D.C. To be sure, by calling it defense, what I truly meant was weapons. My family made an extraordinary volume of weapons and sold most of them to the U.S. of A. Underwater guns, precision-guided firearms, armed robotic systems, taser shockwaves, hypersonic missiles. If it could kill thousands in one blow, we probably manufactured it. War was a profitable industry. Much more than peace.

Sorry, Tolstoy. Commendable idea, though.

"Actually, I found the one." I sighed with displeasure when I remembered that my so-called one was probably currently changing her name, forging a fake passport, and running off to a country without extradition laws.

"You did?" Monica gasped with excitement.

"You did?" Senior asked skeptically.

"You did?" Bruce sounded like I'd just shoved a ballistic missile up his rear.

"Indeed." I called an Uber to take me to my future bride's residence, since this hellhole didn't even have a car service. "I cannot wait for you to meet her."

"What's she like?" The pearls in Monica's fingers probably twisted with her eagerness.

"The proud owner of a pulse and a womb, your only two requirements."

Not that she'll be using that womb of hers.

Monica barked out a delighted laugh. "Oh, Rom. You really can be crass sometimes."

An Uber Lux pulled to the curb. Last year's Range Rover. I needed out of Chapel Falls yesterday. I slid into the cab of the vehicle, ignoring the eye contact the driver tried to impose on me. The only thing that would make today even more inconvenient was small talk with a stranger.

"When are we going to meet the girl?" If it were up to Monica, Dallas would be delivered to her doorsteps via Two-Hour Prime shipping.

"As soon as humanly possible." I needed to destroy any chances of Bruce becoming a viable alternative to me as CEO. That, unfortunately, meant a few more hours in a confined space with Dallas Townsend.

Monica hovered on the cusp of exploding with joy. "*Aww.* Are you really that excited to show her off?"

I stared out the window. "Bursting at the seams."

"Junior . . . Christ, kid." And that was when I knew Bruce had found one of the viral videos from last night. "Mon, Romeo, I think you should see something. Remember Clinton Brunswick from the Pentagon? His wife forwarded a video to my Shelley. I regret to bring it to your attention, but I wouldn't feel comfortable not addressing it since Junior did a terri—"

That was my cue to hang up. As I killed the call and watched Chapel Falls zip past me in all of its small-town glory, I thought marrying the Townsend girl wasn't such a bad idea after all. I would leave her to tend to her own business—shopping? Luncheons? Botox parties?—only reentering her life periodically to drag her to black-tie events or important summits that required me to appear like a respectable family man. She'd probably slink back to Chapel Falls within a year or two and age ungracefully, spending her time drowning in materialistic extravagance and meaningless gossip to numb the taste of her own pointlessness.

I would return to my normal life in Potomac. My work. My friends. *My plans.* After a few years, ten or twelve, when the burn of becoming a mother really seared through her, I would consider granting Dallas a divorce. Depending on how useful to me she'd be by then.

She'd sign a prenup, though. That woman was not worth half the Costa fortune.

Yes, I decided. *Marrying the Townsend girl will be an anecdotal incident in my life, not a pivotal moment.*

It didn't matter how loud she was.

My silence would always be louder.

44

Chapter Six

Romeo

It seemed fitting that a cookie-cutter mansion housed my cookie-obsessed bride. With its fresh coat of white paint, black shutters, imperial columns, and bright-red door, the pre-War Colonial could grace the pages of *Southern Living*.

On the second-floor balcony, two rocking chairs swung from the force of whoever had occupied them seconds ago. That confirmed my suspicion. Shortbread had waited for my impending arrival to claim my newest acquisition. *Her.*

I'd toyed with the idea of giving her the entire weekend to say goodbye to her family and friends, mainly to relieve myself of her burdensome existence. But it was best to get it over with as soon as possible.

Shep Townsend opened the door in his Sunday's best. Of course, they'd just returned from church. Nothing screamed devout Christian like getting caught with a stranger's hand between your thighs.

"Is the ring acceptable?" He snatched the jewelry bag from my hands, ripping it open. "Because I won't let you humiliate my daughter any further."

I might have been a deplorable human for dragging his daughter kicking and screaming into marriage, but he was a first-class prick for allowing it. And for originally fixing her up with Madison Licht, who was a bag of STDs draped in a Prom suit.

He popped the ring box open. His eyebrows shot to his hairline, throat bobbing with a swallow. "This'll do."

Shouldering past him without acknowledging his words, I surveyed his foyer. My future wife was nowhere to be seen. A smaller, scowling version of her—her little sister, I assumed—stood at the foot of the stairway, holding tight to the banisters, watching me like a woodland creature about to pounce on its prey.

I glanced at my Rolex. "Where's Dallas?"

"Upstairs, resting." Former Miss U.S.A. Natasha Townsend traipsed out of the kitchen in a respectable Gingham dress, appraising me with open hatred. Thankfully, Dallas had inherited her mother's face rather than her father's.

"From what?"

The girl sure didn't have a busy schedule. She didn't have *any* schedule.

"Stop goading her. You catch more bees with honey." Shep placed a hand on my arm, ushering me to the drawing room. "Just yesterday, you disgraced her, killed her engagement, and strong-armed her into marriage. She needs time to process."

It had never once occurred to me that Dallas Townsend was a three-dimensional character with needs, wants, and motivations. From where I stood, she seemed like a gorgeous, spoiled, petulant child accustomed to getting her way. One who nursed a somewhat unhealthy obsession with food.

I invited myself to sit at the head of the room in front of Dallas's shocked family. "Tell her to come down right this second. We need to discuss schedules."

Little Townsend surged forward. "Why don't you go scre—"

"Go get your sister, Franklin." Shep's lips twisted downward. "And wash your mouth with a bar of soap right after."

With a shake of her head, Franklin fled my periphery. Shep remained standing. So did his wife. They both glowered at me.

I produced my leather business case and began spreading the paperwork my bride needed to sign on the table. "A cup of coffee would be nice. No sugar, no milk, no spit."

Mrs. Townsend's eyes flared. In the end, Southern hospitality beat her resentment. She scurried into the kitchen. Probably speed-dialing Jesus with a request to give me an early and deadly heart attack.

Shep braced the back of a chair. "Did you do this to get back at Madison or because your father is making you wed?"

I wiped invisible lint from my suit, marking everywhere Dallas needed to sign with an x. "It was a two-birds-one-stone situation."

He sat and laced his fingers on the table, tight-lipped. "My daughter is very special."

Fighting an eye-roll, I muttered, "They all are."

"No," he insisted. "Dallas is nothing like what you've seen and known. I assure you." If I had a penny for every time a proud father tried to sell me his daughter based on her merits . . . well, I'd still be a billionaire. "When you fall in love with her, make sure you don't resent her for it." So. Delusion was something that ran in this family. As luck would have it, I didn't need Dallas's DNA.

I glanced around me, bored. "I'll try my best."

"I mean it." His jaw set. "I know you don't feel this way right now, but my daughter is utterly irresistible.

There wasn't one man in this town and the next who didn't offer for her. I hope that, when she captures your heart, she'll have the right mind to break it. Just like you're breaking hers."

That really did it.

"She isn't in love with Madison Licht."

"How do you know?"

"While I'm no expert in relationships, I'm pretty sure it would've taken me more than thirty seconds of waltzing to convince her that shoving my fingers inside her was a good idea if she were madly in love."

The man never failed to wince when I mentioned my sexual encounter with his daughter.

"She is definitely fond of him, though."

"She'll be fond of me, too," I snapped. I didn't even want her to be fond of me. I simply hated the idea of losing to Licht.

Shep sat back. "That remains to be seen."

My bride interrupted the bizarre conversation, stomping into the drawing room in a dark-green satin dressing gown. Her chestnut hair spilled down her shoulders all the way to her waist. A rush of relief eroded my lungs. Dallas Townsend really was a beauty. Even more striking than I'd remembered. With long, curly lashes, lofty hazel eyes, and pillowy lips.

Oh, well. I supposed it was only fair that, for the price I'd agreed to pay, I should truly and genuinely ruin her. Intercourse was out of the question, but a few ideas sprung to mind. No doubt it would take me two minutes and a bag of Skittles to make them happen.

Shortbread regarded me with open disdain, still standing.

"My sweet," I drawled. "How you must've missed me."

"What do you want?"

Bruce and Madison dead. And for you to undergo an entire personality transplant.

"We're boarding a plane to Potomac in three hours."

"Good riddance. Send von FancyPants my regards." She stole my cupcake from the plate Natasha had dropped off for me, finishing it in two bites.

Dallas Townsend, ladies and gents. She possessed half the manners and twice the beauty of any woman I'd ever met. Such a shame a personality that insufferable was attached to a face that stunning.

"You're coming with me."

"Oh." She pursed her lips but didn't argue.

"Go pack."

She swiveled to her father, biting down on her lip. "Do I have to?"

He nodded. She huffed. Great. I was marrying a woman who was mentally twelve.

"Trust me, Dal, your mother and sister won't forgive me, either."

"But it's improper for me to move in with him before marriage."

I stacked our prenuptial papers, already bored with this. "Everyone knows I sampled the goods."

"You sampled nothing." She whipped her head to glare at me. "You barely touched me, and you and I both know it."

Knowing it and admitting it were two different things. Expecting honesty from me was as ridiculous as expecting loyalty from a prostitute.

"You have two hours to gather your things." I forced direct eye contact, raising the stack of paper. "After which, you'll sign this prenup. I'll wait here."

She shrugged. I narrowed my eyes. From my limited knowledge about her, she didn't take instructions well, especially from me. It was on the tip of my tongue to warn her grave consequences would follow if she didn't fulfill my orders.

Then I realized I no longer needed to seduce her. To coax her into my sphere. She was already securely caught in my spiderweb. Thrashing and resisting, yet glued in place.

Next time she did something stupid, she'd pay.

There was no better lesson than experience.

Chapter Seven

Romeo

The residents of the Townsend home weren't among my rabid fans, to say the least. They considered it impolite to kick me out, but definitely didn't offer any entertainment. With my fiancée locked in her room, I invited myself to a tour of her childhood home.

It was impressive, yet boring. Or so I thought until I reached the end of the hallway. The library. Sensing Shortbread's sanctuary, I stepped inside. I was right. It smelled of her. A scent I recognized from the debutante ball. Of baby powder, roses in bloom, and a deranged woman.

I ran my finger along the spines as I strolled past books, crushing gum between my teeth to relieve some annoyance. They were cracked, the leather abused. Shortbread clearly wasn't gentle with the things she cherished. She had a fitful nature, a goliath temper, and a tongue that could slice through metal. I couldn't imagine her with someone like Licht, who was the human answer to a radish.

Dallas was a versatile reader. The genres varied. From romances to thrillers. Fantasies to detective mysteries. The only thing to stand out was the fact that she was the proud owner of all thirteen books in the Henry Plotkin world. A blockbuster series even I knew about. It revolved around a young wizard learning to use magic to transport late loved ones back into the land of the living. *Henry Plotkin and the Mystic Potion. Henry Plotkin and the Girl who Dared. Henry Plotkin and the Magic Wand.* I bet that last one sounded better in the author's head.

"Don't touch that." The bite in her voice lashed across the room.

I grabbed the book on principle and turned to find Franklin in front of me. She marched forward, snatching it from my hand. Her puffy eyes told me she'd spent the past hour crying.

"Dal is a huge fan of this series. She pulls all-nighters outside of bookstores on Christmas Eve to buy the new books when they release. No one's allowed to touch those. No one. Not even me." She guided the book back to where it belonged, then pivoted to me. "I have a proposition for you."

"Not interested."

"Take me, not her. I'll be your girlfriend . . . your wife . . . your *whatever*." She rolled her eyes. "I'm strong. I can take it. And you'll never be bored with me."

Franklin was a less refined version of her sister. Not as beautiful. Not as tempting. And—probably—not as reckless. She was also very distinctly a girl. Though I possessed no morals to speak of, putting my dick in a high schooler's mouth was where I drew a limit.

"Your offer holds no allure for me." I slid a hand into my front pocket. "I've already got more Townsend on my hands than I desire."

"Please." It came out as a demand instead of a plea. She stood tall, staring me dead in the eyes. I wondered where the Townsend sisters got their spine from, because it sure wasn't from Daddy dearest. "We fit better, you and me. I'm more pragmatic, she's more . . ."

"Unhinged?"

She bared her teeth. "Impractical."

I leaned a shoulder against the shelf. "There's only one problem."

"Yeah?"

"I'm not a pedophile."

"First, I'm nineteen, you jackass. Second, you don't want to marry her. Trust me."

I had to give her one thing—she was smart enough not to appeal to my heart, probably sensing I didn't have one.

"And why's that?"

"Because she's in love with Madison."

That caught my attention. Unlike her father, I assumed Franklin discussed such things with Dallas. I also remembered Shortbread complaining about Madison's infidelity.

I studied her, almost interested for once. "That so?"

"Yes." Ire singed her eyes. "Take me. I'm unattached."

"Also: unfit."

"She'll never love you."

"I'll try to carry on."

Her demand metamorphosed into a desperate plea. "*Romeo.*" She sauntered into my space, running her hand down my tie. Her fingers stopped just above my navel—and only because I snatched her hand before she cupped my junk. I'd sooner be seduced by a rotten egg sandwich than this child. Franklin leaned closer, still, pinning her flat chest against my upper stomach. "Let me prove myself to—" Stepping back, I let her fall and tumble onto the carpet, face-first. She groaned, her mouth inches from my loafers. "You sick bastard."

I used the tip of my loafer to kick her phone away. The device turned on its back. On her screen, the recording app flashed. A setup. Very *One Tree Hill.*

Franklin scrambled to her feet. A deep frown stamped on her face. "Know what? I'm actually happy you're marrying her. She won't stop until your life is ruined."

"That, I can believe."

Her lips parted, preparing to launch into more verbal diarrhea, but my phone's ringtone informed me that Shortbread's two hours were up.

"Go call your sister."

"I'm not your secretary, ass-face. You go get her."

It'd be my displeasure.

I saw my way out of the library and up the winding staircase to the second floor. Shortbread's room stood at the end of the hall.

I knocked. "Time's up."

No response.

Rather than repeat the entire process again—I knew she wouldn't budge—I pushed the door open. If she was indecent, fine. Nothing she hadn't offered to show me before. But Shortbread wasn't naked. Nor was she crying hysterically in a heap of emotions, perched on a windowsill like a damsel in distress. She was, in fact, sleeping peacefully on her queen-size bed, still in her dressing gown, *Cheaters* dancing on her television. A single snore rattled her shoulders.

Words failed me. For the first time in my life, it occurred to me that my vocabulary might be insufficient. Needless to say, Dallas had not packed a single item. There wasn't even a suitcase in sight.

As if sensing the impending storm, Shep and his wife materialized at her door.

Shep clutched the frame. "Remember, Costa, honey attracts more bees."

I waltzed to Dallas's bed, perching on its edge. Her hair—thick and wavy and impossibly soft—framed her face. I skated my knuckles over her spine. She fussed, her exposed skin pebbling with goose bumps. A soft moan fled her lips.

"Wakey, wakey, Shortbread." My voice glided over her skin like velvet. "It's time to say goodbye."

She was so disoriented, she actually followed instructions for once, opening her eyes. Then the small serene smile on her face twisted into a frown. I didn't break character, though.

I picked up her hand from under the covers and slipped the 20.03-carat emerald-cut engagement ring onto her finger. "Sleep well?"

Behind my back, Shep released a relieved exhale.

Dallas eyed me skeptically, ignoring the ring. "I guess. Sucks that I woke up, though."

Trust me, sweetheart, I am disappointed, too.

"Our plane departs in forty minutes. We should leave right away."

"Fine." She rose, duvet pooling around her waist. "Let me just pack—"

"Sorry, Shortbread. As I said before, you had two hours."

"Stop calling me Shortbread. I have a name."

"One that is arguably more ridiculous."

"Dude, your name is Ro—"

"Do not call me dude."

"Lord. Okay, go away. I'm packing."

"You're coming with me right now, or I withdraw my engagement offer."

Her eyes flared. "You think that's a *threat*?"

"Certainly." I stood, fishing my phone from my pocket to call an Uber. "If I retract now, you'll be a ruined, sullied girl with no prospects of marriage to a respectable Southerner. One infamous for getting fingered by a stranger at a ball, only to be dumped by two men in twenty-four hours. How do you think that'll work for your family? Your reputation? Your life goals?"

She didn't answer. She understood the gravity of her situation. I snatched her by the elbow and escorted her downstairs. Gentle but firm.

She stumbled into the hallway, now fully awake. "At least let me get dressed."

"You're perfect just the way you are, *darling*."

I valued punctuality. My wife didn't even know the definition. Yet another reason our marriage would be a miserable one. There would be no time to sign the prenup. We could do it when we arrived in Potomac, I supposed.

"I need clothes. I need underwear. I need—"

"Better time management. As for all the rest, you'll have a credit card and access to shopping centers and the Internet. You'll survive." *Much to my dismay.*

We descended the stairs. The Uber would be here any minute now. Shortbread swung in the opposite direction, trying to beeline for the shoe closet.

I tugged her back to me. "The rumors were wrong. You aren't lazy at all. When incentivized, you're a ball of energy."

She faced me, fuming. "I'm not leaving here without shoes."

"Care to bet on it?"

"Let my sister put shoes on." Franklin galloped toward us, fists waving in the air. She rained those little balled hands down on my chest. I didn't feel a thing.

"She had two hours to put on shoes. She chose to watch *Cheaters*."

Mr. and Mrs. Townsend hovered before the landing, arguing.

Natasha covered her face with her hands and sobbed. "Oh, Shep, who cares about our reputation? Stop this nonsense right away."

He patted her back. "You know as much as I do that Costa is her best bet right now."

"I really hate you right now."

Shortbread threw herself into her mother's arms. "Don't worry about me, Momma. I'll be okay."

"Oh, honey."

More wailing, arm-clutching, and general theatrics. I looked away. Not because I was uncomfortable by the *Jerry Springer* production, but because I wanted to see through the window if the Uber had arrived. It had. Oliver and Zach were probably already on the plane.

"Time to go."

Shortbread swiveled to me. "Can I at least take a book to keep me company on the flight?"

I couldn't help but notice her face was dry and stoic. Her entire family cried behind her, but she had not shed one tear. A strange pang of respect zinged through me.

I opened my mouth to say no, then realized she'd try to make conversation if she was bored. "Pick a classic. Your head is already full to the brim with nonsense."

She rushed to the library and returned a minute after with *Anna Karenina* tucked beneath her bicep. Shortbread made one last attempt to retrieve her shoes, but I scooped her up and hurried out the door, depositing her into the Uber before she could get away with more bad behavior.

The driver put the car into gear and pulled from the curb when the vehicle slammed against something. Or rather, someone. It sounded serious. What did they feed the stray cats in Georgia?

"Frankie!" Shortbread rolled her window down, heaving half her body out of the car. "Are you okay?"

Franklin banged her palms onto the hood, stopping the car. "Here!" She shoved a small suitcase through the window. "No way was I going to let you leave without them."

So Dallas managed to escape this hellhole with clothes and undergarments, after all.

Shortbread hugged the case to her chest. "Are they all inside?"

Franklin nodded. "All of them. Arranged by date of publication."

"Oh, thank goodness."

What?

"Henry Plotkin will keep you safe." Franklin squeezed her sister's hand. "House Dovetalon for the win."

My bride spent our journey to the airport hugging her suitcase to her chest, eyes everywhere but on me. The woman was a certified agent of chaos. And now Oliver and Zach would see what I had to deal with.

I would never live it down.

Chapter Eight

Dallas

It seemed my future husband used his mouth exclusively to chew gum and piss me off. When he wasn't doing the latter, he engaged in the former, content to spending the entire ride to the small airport in silence. Fine by me. Judging by the way he sneered at my suitcase full of Henry Plotkin hardbacks, he broke my cardinal rule: Never trust someone with poor taste in books.

Once we arrived, Romeo's shiny Gulfstream G550 waited on the runway. We shuffled into a passenger cart, which drove us the short journey from the hangar to the tarmac. At the plane's stairs, he collected my small suitcase and climbed the steps, ignoring the fact that I was barefoot.

I'd get back at him. But first, I needed to find my footing in Potomac.

I already had a plan. I knew someone there. *Madison.* We'd never really broken off the engagement. Not officially. This morning, my daddy had called his daddy and informed him of the chain of events (obviously omitting rather unflattering bits). The Lichts insisted they understood, promising they were still fond of me. Madison was Romeo's enemy. We could get back at him together.

When I entered the plane, I was met by an array of men. We passed the cockpit, where two attractive men in

59

their 30s discussed a Ravens draft pick just outside. The captain and the co-pilot. In the cabin, Oliver von Bismarck lounged on a crème sofa, drinking imported beer and watching something on his phone. His face was seraph, nearly cherubic. With a red pout and light curls twining around his ears and forehead just so. How fitting it was that the devil was masquerading as a perfect angel. While Romeo's proposal was the biggest news to come out of the debutante ball, the rumor mill spun stories of Oliver getting into the skirts of at least three local divorcées. *At the same time.*

Yet another tall, handsome man in the casual rich-boy uniform of ironed khakis, a dress shirt, and a fleece jacket sat behind a compact table, holding a business conversation on his phone. He had a top-dog appeal. Of a man whose attention everyone craved when he entered a room.

"Oliver, Zach, this is my fiancée, Dallas." Romeo made dismissive introductions, not even bothering to approach each of his friends individually. "Dallas—Oliver and Zach."

Oliver raised his hand in a hello motion. Zach sent me a smile so impatient and impersonal you could mistake me for a maid giving him room service.

Romeo parked himself in a recliner. "Make yourself comfortable. Takeoff is in ten minutes."

I did just that, refusing to look intimidated. It helped that there was a charcuterie board. Rows of shortbread adorned a crystal plate beside it. I pushed the tray away. For obvious reasons, I found the treat rather off-putting these days.

"Did the shortbread offend you, Dover?" Oliver gestured to an imported snack basket in front of him. "It's all yours."

First Shortbread. Now Dover. Lovely.

I wanted to politely offer him the finger. Then I spotted shrimp chips and abandoned my dignity quicker than the chick who'd turned Jesus Christ into a monkey in the *Ecce Homo*.

I'd emptied half the bag when Romeo's sharp voice sliced through the silence. "Miss Townsend, are you feeding yourself or your clothes? There is a time and place for scarfing down a village's worth of sustenance with your mouth open. I suggest you refrain from indulging your poor manners during your stay in Potomac."

"Or what?" I punctuated my question with a chip, tossing it past my lips and grinding it between my molars as loud as humanly possible.

"Or you'll find yourself in a miserable position under the scrutiny of the viperous DMV media."

"I've already found myself in a miserable position. With you. The first time we met. In front of all of Chapel Falls."

"As I recall, you enjoyed every second." He slanted his head, producing a matte-black rectangular tin from his pocket.

"You must have drugged the shortbread."

"I stand corrected. You do have a talent. Deliberate misinterpretations."

I frowned. "When did you accuse me of not having a talent?"

Oliver threw his head back and laughed. "This is fantastic. Turns out Bruce won't have to kill you to land your job, after all. Your wife will do the job for him."

Bruce? Swapping notes with the man who wanted to kill my future husband seemed like a swell idea, but before I could request a last name, they moved on to discussing stocks.

With that, I pressed the chip bag to my lips and tilted my head back, finishing it down to the last crumb. Romeo unwrapped a new pack of gum and transferred each cube into his tin container with deft fingers, forming a perfect, straight row. Then he offered a piece to each of his friends, forgetting me.

And *I* was the one with poor manners?

I glared out the window, trying to find some silver lining to my situation. Anything.

First, we'd make beautiful babies. No way anything that came from his sperm and my eggs could be anything less than aesthetic perfection. Second, from what I'd gathered, neither Romeo nor I cursed. Our child would exit the womb speaking like a fourteenth-century duke, hopefully sans the misogyny. And third . . . there was no third. Lord, even the second kind of sucked. I slumped in my seat, depressed.

After takeoff, Zach spoke to me first. Romeo appeared to be typing emails on his phone, and Oliver's snores drifted from the couch.

"You're not suicidal, are you?" He didn't seem like he genuinely cared, but the fact that he'd asked made me want to sag with relief. At least *someone* recognized the horridness of my situation.

I shrugged. "Murderous, more like. Why should I be punished for Romeo's bad behavior?"

"Potomac is nice."

I shot him a glare. "What's so nice about it?"

"Its proximity to New York, mostly."

That earned him a chuckle. Why couldn't Zach force me into marriage? And what was it about tall, dark, and handsome men with the emotional capacity of an ingrown toenail?

"Don't encourage her, Zach," Romeo warned. "Once she starts talking, it's impossible to stop her."

Since my future husband was dead set against having me around, I got up and slipped into the cockpit. I'd always wanted to visit one. Growing up, my parents thought it uncouth to peek inside just because we always flew first class.

I slid past the door. "Mind if I look around?"

"Not at all." The co-pilot waved. "I'm Scott."

"And I'm Al." The pilot saluted me with two fingers.

I explored the small space, the many buttons, the thick white clouds we pierced through, surrounded by an inky night.

"You can sit by my side if you'd like." Scott scooted to give me space. "A bit tight, but you can squeeze in."

I hesitated. Momma wouldn't approve. It was improper to sit so close to a man. Then I remembered I was engaged to be married to the reaper of hearts himself, and being inappropriate was my new lifelong goal.

"Okay." I slipped into his seat, cemented to his side. I leaned down, inventorying the array of buttons and screens. A map lit up his side. My fingers fluttered along a central console full of little switches. "It looks like a spaceship."

"Nice, huh?" I heard his smile. Al released an impatient sigh. I had a feeling Al wasn't a fan of his co-pilot cozying up with me. Scott jerked a thumb to his right. "Wait till you see the view from my window. Underneath, it's a solid white blanket of clouds."

"I want to see." I leaned across his body and glanced down the cool glass. He was right. Fluffy clouds curled over one another, thick and dense like snow. "Wow," I breathed out. "That's amazing."

Another thing that was amazing was how my boobs pressed against Scott's lap in this position. His face was in my hair. I realized I harbored pent-up sexual rage from yesterday's encounter with my dear fiancé. He never did finish the job.

I was about to straighten back into a sitting position when the cockpit door flung open.

Of course, it was Romeo.

And, of course, from his vantage, it looked like I was sucking Scott off. My head in his lap, my whole body concealing his lower half. Despite the eternal urge to piss him off, I didn't quite want him to think I went *that* far.

I rose to my feet, meeting Romeo's gaze. As always, his expression was resigned and dead.

Obstinate silence filled the small space. Scott broke it first.

"Mr. Costa, I can assure you it is not what it look—"

"Sweetheart." Romeo surprised me by lacing his hand around my lower back and drawing me to his chest. He grinned, but he didn't seem amused at all. It looked like someone had carved that smile with a Swiss knife. "Enjoying the cock . . . pit?"

My goodness, he really thought I'd given Scott sexual favors. Well, I sure as heck wouldn't fall all over myself, trying to explain my behavior.

Scott and Al were now on their feet, staring at him expectantly.

I smiled, ignoring Romeo's tight jaw. "Yes."

"Yes?" He narrowed his eyes at me, waiting for an apology, an explanation, anything.

"I enjoyed it very much. Thanks, boys." With a toss of my hair, I marched out of the cockpit, as dignified as one could be barefoot and in a house gown.

Romeo stayed back a few minutes while I loitered around the snack bar, munching on wasabi peas. Oliver and Zach shared a chess game in the corner, sparing me no attention. About fifty packs of luxury gum formed militant stacks across the table. What was up with my fiancé's oral fixation? Maybe he had bad breath. A side effect of being full of crap.

Suddenly, rough, warm fingers wrapped around the nape of my neck from behind. I sucked in a breath while my future husband angled my face upward to meet his frosty grays. He towered over me, his chest flush with my back.

I thought he would comment about what had happened in the cockpit, but he surprised me by saying, "Might I remind you, Miss Townsend, that your father confiscated all your cards after you got caught riding my fingers? Your ability to eat, shower, clothe yourself, and sleep under a roof rests solely upon my good will. Govern yourself accordingly."

"Are you done?" I yawned. "I'd like to sit down and read my book."

"And I have just the place to put you in."

He snatched the *Anna Karenina* copy I'd left on a table and guided me to his recliner. I followed, confused, as he sat, handing me my book.

I quirked an eyebrow. "You want me to stay standing?"

He shook his head no, grabbed my hand, and began lowering me between his legs. My eyes flared. Would he make me service him in front of his friends? Force me to give him oral sex as punishment for what he thought he'd seen with Scott?

From the corner of my eye, I spotted Zach's hand freezing, a rook in it, hovering over the chessboard. Oliver, too, gawked at Romeo like he'd completely lost it.

I didn't care if he tossed me out of the plane. I refused to do it.

"No." I tried to free myself from his grasp, but instead of pushing my head into his lap, he turned me until I faced the wall. My butt landed on the floor between his thighs.

"Here. Now I can keep an eye on you."

"I didn't do anything with Scott," I said, even though I promised myself that I wouldn't. Anger anchored my lungs, weighing them down until I couldn't breathe properly.

Romeo sank toward me, his lips brushing the shell of my ear from behind. "You think I'm under the impression you sucked the co-pilot's cock? If that were the case, he would've been flung from the plane through the emergency door. Now read your book and pretend to be a semi-respectable woman."

No point fighting with him right now. I needed to get to Potomac, recalculate, and strike back.

For the rest of the flight, I sat tucked between my future husband's legs like a loyal dog. My hair spilled over his thighs. I could feel his stare boring into the side of my face. Every now and then, his hand drifted to the crown of my head, patting my hair, reminding me I was nothing but a pet to him. I loathed him with every cell, every atom, every molecule in my body.

His friends remained so deathly silent, I could hear every time they swallowed. I bet Romeo loved seeing me degraded like this. On my knees, on the floor, reading *Anna Karenina* with my head bowed down.

He continued sending emails on his phone, but I somehow knew his entire attention was on me. Thirty minutes later, the plane lowered in preparation for landing.

"Shortbread."

66

That nickname again.

"Asshole?" Hey, it was only polite to reciprocate.

"It's been a while since I've read *Anna Karenina*, but I'm pretty sure I would remember if Anna and Count Alexei engaged in praise kink."

My back stiffened. I said nothing. I felt Romeo lean downward until his chin brushed the edge of my collarbone. He peered straight into the book, his stubbled cheek pressed against mine, and began reading.

"'. . . he thrust his cock into her dripping cunt, pushing only halfway, driving her mad with desire and pleasure. In and out. In and out. 'Please,' she begged. 'Please, I need you to fill me. Every hard inch of you.' 'Only good girls get rewarded,' the handsome stranger maintained, bringing his hand down to her plump rear. 'And you've been very, very bad.'"

First of all, the man could narrate romance books and make a fortune if the whole perpetuating-a-Third-World-War gig didn't work out. Second of all, I was incredibly dumb to even notice. He was a terrible human. Who cared that he had a sexy voice and a jawline I could cut cheese with?

Romeo plucked the hardcover from between my fingers. I turned to look at him. He stripped the dust jacket, revealing a completely different book beneath the *Anna Karenina* cover.

A frown touched his lips. "*Zaddy Knows Best*?"

I snatched it from his hands. "It's a work of art."

"It's smut."

"What do you think Anna did with Alexei? Same stuff. Just off-page."

"Yes. I'm sure Tolstoy chopped the anal-beads scene during the final edits."

"He might have." At this point, I was arguing with him for the sport of it. It was also the *only* sport I was eager to engage in.

Oliver barked out a half cough, half laugh behind my shoulder. Zach ran his hand down his face. I could've sworn I saw his lips twitch up behind it. Courage blossomed in my chest.

"Stop defying me," Romeo warned.

"Then stop being impossible. You don't let me breathe."

"Now there's an idea."

"It's not my fault you decided to marry a woman you can't stand just because you're engaged in a pissing contest with Madison. I never asked for any of this. Not for you, not for him, not for anything."

Incredibly, this penetrated his numbness. His usually tense jaw loosened a little. He sat back, finally giving me some space. "Continue reading your book and stop talking."

"My knees hurt on the floor," I lied. I was perfectly comfortable, but an idea sprouted in my head. "Can I sit in the recliner next to the cockpit?"

"Absolutely not."

"*Romeo.*" Zach's voice was sharp as a blade, chilling against his otherwise wholesome look. "Cut this shit out."

My soon-to-be husband's nostrils flared. "Sit in my lap."

I considered defying him, but produced a better idea. With an exaggerated sigh, I stood and parked my butt on his lap. His friends continued watching. Maybe I should have felt self-conscious, but I didn't. None of this was my fault.

"Better?" Not an ounce of concern coated Romeo's voice.

I huffed in response. He didn't deserve my words.

For the next thirty minutes, I shifted and stretched in his lap, pretending to search for a comfortable position, rubbing against his crotch. He became hard and engorged beneath me until it felt like I sat on a water pipe.

"Stop moving." He barely rasped out the guttural command.

"Just trying to find a comfortable spot." I raised my head and chanced a glimpse at Oliver, who grinned ear to ear. I felt like Bugs Bunny, driving Elmer mad but somehow getting away with it.

"How hard could it be?" Romeo bit out.

"Oh, trust me, *very* hard."

Oliver erupted into full-blown laughter. I tilted my head a smidge to observe Romeo's reaction. He looked ready to wrap his fingers around my throat and strangle me. I waited for him to tell me to leave his lap. But the words never came. He knew he'd lose our little game if he told me to go.

"I love her, Rom." Von Bismarck slow-clapped from his seat. "If you won't marry her, I will."

"You should marry Oliver." Everything that came out of Zach's mouth sounded like a business proposal. "He's better looking, generally more pleasant, and richer than God."

"Please." Oliver waved a hand. "God's entire net worth is not even what I pay the IRS annually. But do I get that kind of following and appreciation? No."

"I'll join your cult," I volunteered.

"Somehow, I don't doubt that."

Zach tipped his chin down, flashing Romeo a taunting smirk. "Well, what do you know? Da Nang turned out to be a success."

I waited for a reaction from my new fiancé. None came. He acted as though I didn't exist. Now, if only I could follow his wish and vanish.

Chapter Nine

Dallas

My relief when we landed could solve a humanitarian crisis. Possibly of my future husband's doing. For the last thirty minutes, I couldn't concentrate on a word in my book. Sometimes, when I read, I realized I was happiest in a world that wasn't mine. This time, however, the only happy thing here was Romeo's erection bobbing beneath my butt. There was no love lost between us. Lust, however, was lost, found, and begging to be converted into filthy sex.

When the plane came to a full stop, the stewardess opened the door. "We're just waiting for the car." She aimed her sunny smile at Romeo, the owner of the jet. "Shouldn't be more than a few minutes."

Al and Scott emerged from the cockpit, standing beside her. I tasted the danger before it happened. Tension crackled in the air like a whip. Romeo stood, toppling me into his warm recliner in the process. He sauntered toward Scott, tall and menacing and, frankly, terrifying.

Scott's face wilted. He fell back a step, bumping into the cockpit door. "Sir." He raised both palms. "I don't know what you think happened between me and your fiancée, but I can assure you—"

Without a word, Romeo scooped him by the collar and dragged him to the cavity the plane's door once occupied.

He threw Scott face-first to the floor, dangerously close to the open exit. His head lolled in the air while the rest of him flailed on the hardwood.

My future husband pressed his loafer between Scott's shoulder blades. A scream wedged in my throat. What was he doing?

"Touch my fiancée in any capacity whatsoever—even breathe in her direction, in fact—and I'll relieve you of your lousy excuse for a spine." The words were cold, calm, and callous.

"*Aow!*" Scott wormed beneath him. "My back."

For once, pure serenity settled into Romeo's features. "Tell me you understand, and you may return to your miserable existence."

Oliver frowned at what appeared to be a broken nail on his otherwise flawless hand. "Christ, Costa. Who pissed in your pea soup?"

Zach speed-dialed Romeo's assistant, unruffled as though this was just another Sunday. "Hey, Cara. Call Hayward or whomever Romeo has on retainer now." Pause. "Assault, of all things." Another pause. "No, I am not interested in a blind date with your niece, but thank you for the offer."

Finally, the haul in my throat loosened. I released the scream. Romeo didn't even spare me a glance.

"I promise," Scott spluttered. "I swear on my life I'll never look at her again."

"I believe you." Romeo removed his foot from Scott's back, rolling him face up with the tip of his shoe. "Because you're fired, effective immediately."

Everyone on the plane went silent. Even I couldn't find the right words. Guilt consumed me. This had happened to Scott because of me and my thoughtlessness. My juvenile need to stick it to my fiancé.

"But your father hired m—"

"My father's not here now and will expire soon enough. I make the calls."

I didn't know how much time passed, but eventually, Al dragged Scott out, the car arrived, and Zach and Oliver moved in my direction.

Oliver tapped my shoulder. "Come on, Davenport."

I didn't even have the energy to correct him.

When Zach strode past Romeo, he shook his head. "In the twenty-nine years I've known you, I haven't seen you lose your temper once. I've seen you lose it three times tonight alone."

Romeo flashed him a glare. "If you have something to say, say it, Sun."

Zach dusted his cashmere-clad shoulder. "A picture's worth a thousand words, but your face only says one—*pussy-whipped*."

Chapter Ten

Dallas

Utter silence suspended in the air. Sensing the dark mood, Jared shut off the classical radio and raised the divider of the S600 Maybach. Of course, Romeo had a chauffeur. And, of course, his chauffeur wore a three-piece uniform, ornamented with a black cap and leather gloves. Romeo seemed very fond of treating everyone around him like they had the depth of a Sims character. He considered people as placeholders that existed solely to advance his personal plot.

I glared out the window, watching cars zip past, knowing I'd lose control if we got into an argument. A D.C. license plate winked at me, *taxation without representation* inked across in bold script. It snapped the last thread holding my anger at bay.

Talk about kindred spirits. I paid a heavy price for one mistake and had no voice of my own.

If only I could angry-cry. Find some sort of relief. But Romeo Costa didn't deserve my tears. Heck, he didn't deserve *any* of my bodily fluids.

Eventually, we turned onto an endless street lined with trimmed privacy hedges and rows of looming double gates that hid dozens of mansions from view. It seemed only fitting that the tyrant beside me lived on the aptly named Dark Prince Road.

Several minutes later, a towering set of iron gates came into view. A quarter-mile driveway flanked by cherry blossoms guided the Maybach to Romeo's house. Perhaps house wasn't the right word to describe a 30,000-square-foot Italian villa, sprawled over ten acres of historic pre-Civil War property. Six bedrooms, twelve bathrooms, two pools, and a private vineyard. I'd Zillow'd it on my phone the moment my eyes landed on the mammoth structure.

When we passed the first dozen trees, Romeo finally remembered my presence. "Due to the risks involved in my line of work, there are security cameras installed everywhere, in case you're planning your grand escape."

I wasn't. Mainly because I had nowhere to go. My father would never accept me—I wouldn't do that to Frankie, anyway—and I refused to leave before I retaliated for all the things Romeo had done to me.

I chose not to answer him.

His jaw clenched. "He stepped over the line."

"You stepped on *him*." I tried my hardest to keep my voice from shaking. "Why must you humiliate everyone who crosses you so harshly? It is such an unbecoming trait."

"We don't choose our traits. We merely endure them."

It was obvious he had enough baggage to fill an airport carousel, but I refused to humor him. No excuse could pardon his behavior, no matter his backstory.

The nearer we got to his mansion, the more I could see of it. Lush greenery enfolded the statement manor in Potomac fashion. The property hosted separate grounds for staff. On the opposite end, an engineering shop nestled between the edge of a small forest and an entire security building. And here I thought my family was well-off.

"Wipe off that expression of yours," Romeo demanded. He really had an issue with everything I did. Or didn't do.

"What expression?"

"The one that plans to tarnish every single piece of furniture in my house in retaliation."

It hadn't even occurred to me. I preferred to deliver my revenge with finesse. But I certainly wouldn't reassure him.

"No promises."

"You're going to be a headache, aren't you?"

"A headache?" I cocked my head. "You kidnapped me, you psycho. I'm not gonna be a headache. I'm going to be, at the very least, a deadly brain tumor."

They say fate is nothing but the consequences of our decisions. Well, I planned on being the worst thing fate ever had in store for him.

"Fine," he bit out. "You get one."

"Theo James," I said without missing a beat. "On the off chance I ever meet him."

"I wasn't giving you a free pass with a celebrity." Romeo's face clouded. Clearly appalled by my answer. "I meant one wish." He scanned my face, like he already regretted extending an olive branch. "One thing you can request of me. I'll give it to you. No questions asked."

I side-eyed him. "What's the catch?"

"You need to promise you'll behave."

I would never behave. But my anger wouldn't allow me to keep my mouth shut, either. A bitter smile carved up my cheeks. "You want to know what I wish for?"

His scowl told me the answer was *no*. The Maybach stopped in front of the estate's double doors. I faced him, my gaze pinned on his, unblinking.

"My one and only wish is for you to die in my arms, Romeo Costa. I want to see you when you draw your last breath. To feel your skin turn cold and lifeless beneath my fingers. My wish is to witness your nostrils struggle to move as you consume oxygen for the last time." I paused, drawing my hand to my chest. "I want to watch you suffer for all the suffering you did to me. And there is nothing and no one I want more in this life."

Chapter Eleven

Dallas

Karma must be on a lunch break, because a full twenty-five minutes had elapsed since I wished my fiancé would drop dead, yet he remained very much alive.

So did my anger as I dragged my luggage to the door-steps myself, waited for Romeo to finish a sudden business call, and debated whether to smash down his door with the shovel I'd spotted resting against the greenhouse.

In the end, I eavesdropped on the man I would soon share a home with. I sat on the top step and observed Romeo, elbow on my knee, chin clasped in my palm. The sun cracked through a marshmallow-white cloud, pouring the first rays of sunshine as dawn crawled up the sky. The light haloed around my fiancé. For a moment, he appeared angelic. Then he opened his mouth.

"The shipment requires extra security. I don't have to tell you activity among armed rebels has spiked in recent months." Pause. "Or *do* I?"

Weapons. They were talking about weapons. The imported snacks I'd eaten on the plane churned in my gut.

"Mess this up and I assure you, your next job will require an apron and extensive knowledge of operating an industrial fryer."

Romeo killed the call and turned to me, again jarred and

annoyed by my existence. "Hettie is in the kitchen, should you require food. If anything needs fixing, Vernon can be reached on the intercom. I understand it'll be difficult for you, but refrain from wreaking havoc on my property. In the city, actually."

"Yeah, because I'm the destructive one between us." I rose, dusting off my sleeping gown. "Bro, you sell *death* for a living. Who are you trying to fool?"

"Next time you *bro* me, I will confiscate your phone, TV, and snacks. You will handle yourself in accordance with your pedigree."

"I'm a person, not a golden retriever." Then, before I forgot, I added, "*Bro.*"

A muscle in his jaw threatened to jump out of his skin. "Have you finished, Miss Townsend?"

"I haven't started." I clutched my suitcase handle. "You sell weapons to the highest bidder—"

"That is factually incorrect. It's not always the highest bidder." Already, he appeared bored with this conversation. "Unfortunately. Patriotism is the root of most geopolitical disputes and is too dichotomous for full-rounded individuals."

That wasn't even in English, so I refused to speak to his point.

"You provide armies with the means to kill people," I explained, as though he was a toddler. "And you do it for the sake of money."

"It's not for money."

"If not money, then what?"

He didn't answer, advancing to the front door and entering the code. "4-8-1-0-4-3-2-4-1-5. The code rotates once a week."

"You expect me to remember that?" At this point, I needed to build an ark to save myself from drowning in his bull-crap.

"There's a cot in the shed, should you forget."

I didn't budge, refusing to step through the doors without regaining at least some of my dignity. "Let's make a deal."

"A deal requires each party to possess leverage. I know what I have. I also know what you do *not*. What could you possibly exchange?" His utterly unmoved glare raked down my body, from my head to my bare feet.

I resisted the urge to cover myself, slamming the door shut to busy my hands. "Not *that*. My body is a temple."

"And you litter this temple with three tons of sugar-laced, artificial-flavored junk food every third hour."

Judging by his glowing review of me, I suspected that he wanted me to be more refined. I refused. If you had to change yourself to be accepted, you didn't need that person in your life in the first place. Because it wasn't you they wanted to be with. It was their version of you. There would be no universe in which I caved to Romeo Costa's expectations.

Harsh laughter fizzed up my chest. "You believe you hold the power in this relationship, don't you? Well, *hubs*, you're wrong. We're equals."

A feral grin hiked up his cheeks. "Equals? From a woman with no life goals. No dreams to speak of."

"I *do* have dreams."

A baby. Well, babie*s*. Plural. Somehow, I knew he'd find that unworthy. And he'd be wrong. Every dream is worthy. Even if it is tiny and insignificant to one person, it may be impossible to another.

Romeo waited for me to elaborate. I didn't.

He filled the silence with, predictably, more bull-crap. "It is unwise to anger the man who holds your fate in his palm, Miss Townsend. Consider this advice my second gift to you."

"Second?"

"The first was when I spared you a lifetime of mockery. Dallas Licht sounds like the name of an STD clinic."

Did he think this was about Madison? It wasn't. I didn't even like Madison. Not really. I just didn't want Romeo, either.

"Fine. Wanna know what my wish is?" I advanced on him, poking his chest dead in the center. "For you to quit your job."

"Give me one good reason."

"Because what you do disgusts me."

"What I do will finance your existence. At least until your trust fund kicks in." Romeo punched in the door code again. "And you can continue your life as you always have. Without responsibilities. Without a purpose."

The adrenaline in my body crashed, burning my energy with it. I pivoted, realizing I wouldn't win this argument. "Is Zach single?"

"Irrelevant. He wouldn't touch you with a gun aimed at his head."

"That's all right. Weapons have never been my kink." I licked my lips, grinning. "He's hot."

"He's incapable of any emotion that isn't boredom."

"At least he is cordial about it. He'd still be an upgrade from you."

He ignored my barb, pushing the door open. "Get inside and find a room to lodge in. Anything other than the master. That one is mine."

"Aww. So territorial. Why don't you piss on the carpet, just to mark your ground?"

"The only pissing happening is *you* pissing *me* off. I suggest you work on your likability skills during the time I'm gone."

"Wait. Where are you going?" It was hard to keep up with what was happening. I tried gathering my wits like they were scattered marbles on a sleek floor.

"It's called work." He turned, descending the steps back to the car, which he'd left running. "You wouldn't be familiar with the concept."

"It's five in the morning."

"War never stops. It rages all hours of the day."

My mouth hung open. "You can't be serious."

"I can be nothing *but* serious, Shortbread. I forgot to mention—I do not have a sense of humor."

In that moment, hungry, frozen, and confused, I truly wished to die.

"You're just leaving me here?" I didn't know why I'd asked. I already knew the answer.

Without a single backward glance, Romeo slammed the door to his Maybach.

His answer came in the form of exhaust smoke and a faint trail of dark laughter.

Chapter Twelve

Dallas

The urge to flee to Chapel Falls electrified my heels. Who cares if I caused a scandal? The word had long lost its meaning since Daddy used it to describe *everything*. From the flan incident to that thing with the family Aspen trip. Really, if he wanted me to take him seriously, he needed to be more selective in his application.

Then I remembered my sister and mother. *I* could suffer if it meant *they* didn't.

Nestled in a luxurious four-poster bed, I tossed and turned for hours until my once-fluffy duvet pancaked beneath me. Alone, in a room that smelled different and looked different and *felt* different, a breakdown should've been inevitable. But I *never* cried. According to Momma, I'd left her womb without a single tear, not even when the nurse pinched me.

I missed Frankie, and Momma, and—pathetically—even my poor excuse for a father. So much so that my lungs felt as if they'd warped into a pinball machine, each breath bouncing off them with a sharp pang. Left. Right. Left. Right. And *still*, I couldn't cry.

The clock on the nightstand read half past noon. I'd been in bed since Romeo left me on his doorstep and I stormed straight to the second floor, choosing the room furthest from the master. I couldn't even bear sharing a zip code with him, but this would have to do.

Eyes pinched shut, I counted sheep. When that didn't work, I counted the ways I'd make Romeo pay. Finally, I drifted into a peaceful slumber.

Bullets poured from the jaw of a machine gun, rattling the air. *Boom. Boom, boom.* Breath baited, I waited for one to reach its intended destination. The withered heart of the beast who had captured me. *Boom. Boom, boom.*

My eyes shot open, sweat slicking my temples. White stars cartwheeled across my vision. The clock on the nightstand read half past noon. Seconds passed before I realized I'd slept through an entire day.

I glowered at the door as if it would reveal the culprit that had awakened me before the best part of my dream. Another knock shook its frame. Hazy afternoon light trickled through the burgundy curtains of my new room, warming my skin.

"Come in." I pulled the blanket to my chin.

A weathered man in muddy clothes waddled inside. Dirt streaked his cheek, a shock of white hair sprouting from his scalp in every direction. He wore the easy, genuine smile of someone who harbored no ulterior motives.

"Hello, my dear. I'm Vernon." He stopped by the foot of my bed. "Don't be afraid. I have a grandchild about your age. I couldn't bear thinking she feared me."

I hiked the cover further up. "Why're you here?"

"I'm Mr. Costa's groundskeeper." He eyed me with unabashed interest. "Thought I'd introduce myself, since our paths will cross. There's dinner in the kitchen. Hettie prepares three meals a day. Snacks, too."

"Thank you."

Vernon still didn't move.

I still didn't show my face.

Surely, he'd realized something was amiss. That I wasn't here of my own free will.

"Romeo is misunderstood, but quite the phenomenal man." He bit his lip. "A beautiful, complicated soul. Once he opens up."

"I have no intention of opening him up." Unless he meant carving him with a steak knife.

Vernon hesitated. Finally, he produced a plain white rose from his back pocket, setting it on my nightstand. Dirt caked his fingernails, too. I found this small detail oddly reassuring.

"Do you know Venus et Fleur?"

I nodded. "It's a type of rose that lasts a year."

Momma loved them. Every holiday, she'd gift them to neighbors, family, and friends.

Vernon's face lit up. "A rose can live up to thirty-five years with the right care and weather condition. Do you ever think how sad it is that most don't last through the winter?"

I shook my head.

I'm more worried I won't last through fall.

Sensing he'd lost my attention, Vernon cleared his throat. "I dabble in cross-breeding flowers. I managed to combine two rose species to create something pretty remarkable."

I sat upright, plastering my back against the headboard. "Remarkable how?"

Poison? The appeal of delivering slow, cadaverous revenge should have terrified me. I wasn't normally this violent. For Romeo, I'd make an exception.

"There she is." A relieved smile spread across Vernon's face. I had a feeling he wouldn't be so happy if he had a direct line to my thoughts. "This rose can live for six months without an ounce of sunshine or warmth. Maybe even more. The perfect amount of time to fall in love."

My excitement blew out of me, slumping my shoulders and clouding my face. "No one is falling in love in this place."

"Just because you don't plan on it doesn't mean it won't happen." Vernon bowed his head. "Take my rose as an example. It can survive the roughest conditions and still flourish. Maybe you can, too."

I held my tongue back. No point in lashing out at the poor man.

Vernon stepped back without turning away. "Well, if Mr. Costa gives you trouble, you know where to find me. Take care of that rose for me, will you?"

When he left, I kicked the blanket off and snatched the rose, willing to snap it in half. *Fall in love, my butt.* I'd be lucky not to fall into depression. It was only when my fingers wrapped around its delicate spine that I realized I wasn't Romeo, who'd crushed a flower beneath his heel in the rose garden. I didn't want to kill something beautiful just because I could.

And the rose really was pretty. White as snow with sickle-shaped pricks adorning it.

"It's not your fault." I sighed, talking to the flower. "You're right."

With a frustrated groan, I tromped into the en suite bathroom, collected a Q-Tip container, and filled it with fresh water. I stuck the rose in it, placing it on my nightstand.

The rose could live.

Even if *my* life had ended.

Chapter Thirteen

Dallas

Cages aren't made of bars. They're made of thoughts, expectations, and fear. My favorite quote—now ruined by Romeo Costa, who made a liar out of Henry Plotkin. The cage *Romeo* trapped me in was a Corinthian palace made of cobblestone piazzas, antique pavements, and gold-plated everything. A home clean and tidy. With a floor so spotless, you could eat off it.

When I ran out of rooms to explore, I slipped into the garden and soaked the last sunrays in the sky, tucked between lush lilac bushes. Afterwards, I retreated inside to scour through every landing, hallway, nook, and corner.

The haunting quiet made the little hairs on my arms stand on end. Absolute, utter silence. To the point where I couldn't hear a thing. Not the birds chirping, the AC buzzing, nor the appliances humming. Each wall must've been padded from within. How fitting that my future husband—the one with thick, unbreakable layers of ice around his heart—guarded his house in the same exact way. No wonder he hated me. I had zero inhibitions, wore my heart on my sleeve, and as Daddy often said, could be heard from most states in North America.

Around six in the evening, my stomach rumbled, reminding me I hadn't eaten in almost forty hours. Not since Romeo forced me on that plane and I binged on cheese, crackers, and shrimp chips. It was time to explore the most important room in the house.

Squaring my shoulders, I paraded to the lavish chef's kitchen. The faint scent of cooked food drifted from pots and pans on the stovetop.

I placed a hand on a lid—*still warm*—and peered inside. My face fell. "Ugh."

Brussel sprouts and chicken breast? I knew the man didn't have a heart, but did he lack taste buds, too?

"Problem?" The voice was so loud compared to my recent noiseless existence, I jumped.

Swiveling, I came face to face with a woman. Hettie, I assumed. Petite, edgy, and no more than a few years older than me, she wasn't at all what I'd expected. Though I hated my future husband, I couldn't help but feel a little panicked by the idea that someone so lovely roamed his house all hours of the day.

He literally put you between his legs and patted your head. You should be rooting for these two to fall in love.

I pursed my lips, moving to the fridge. "No problem."

Why did the hot-pink tips of her blonde hair look so cool? And why did her lip ring make me want one of my own? Momma would have a heart attack.

Hettie wrinkled her nose. "Then why the *ugh* when you opened the lid? Is my food not good enough for your majesty?"

"I'm sure it's great." I threw the fridge open. "But I want something comforting. And this is . . ."

She snorted. "Terrible?"

I whipped my head to stare at her. Despite my dark mood, a smile tugged on my lips. "I was going to say healthy, but . . . Brussel sprouts? Dude, hardcore."

She giggled. "Blame Romeo. His diet is so strict. It's all oatmeal and lean protein and leafy greens twenty-four seven. That six-pack-flaunting peacock."

So, she knew he had a six-pack. A wick of interest ignited in me.

"Is that all you make for him?" Hiring a personal chef to make you chicken breast and Brussel sprouts every day was like going to a Chanel store to buy nail polish. Unless she was doing more than cooking.

"Yes!" Hettie flung her arms up, leaning back on the stool she'd claimed. Her cropped Joy Division shirt rose, exposing flat abs above her skinny jeans. "It's terrible. I took this job straight from Le Cordon Bleu. Figured it's rent free and pays a ton, so I could save up and pay back my student loans. But it is painfully boring to make healthy, fat-free food."

Had I found my kindred spirit? Maybe she'd be open to slowly poisoning him. I made a mental note to dive into some murder-mystery books for inspo.

I shut the fridge, giddy from the prospect of having someone who actually talked and behaved like she was living in the same era as me. She was just like a friend from home, only cooler. And worldlier. *And probably sleeping with my fiancé.*

"Think we can make something else?"

She quirked a brow. "What do you have in mind?"

"Truffle fries, bacon-wrapped pork roast, candied yam, and monkey bread." I licked my lips. "You know, just as an example."

Hettie stood, literally rising to the challenge. Instead of preparing the meal alone, she doled out tasks to me. As we cooked, she told me about herself. That she hailed from

Brooklyn, traveled the globe on a food tour, and would kill for another round.

She spoke of Romeo with respect and curiosity. Like he was an unsolved puzzle she still hoped to find all the pieces for.

Hettie slid the monkey bread into the steam oven. "So, can we address the elephant in the room?"

I stabbed a yam I was supposed to cube. "All right."

"Hmm . . . who the hell are you?" She laughed. "Like, what are you doing here?"

Romeo hadn't told her? Actually, now that I thought about it, he hadn't told Vernon, either. I added poor communication skills to my never-ending list of things I disliked about him.

"I'm . . . well, I guess I'm Romeo's fiancée."

Her brows shot up. "You *guess*?"

"Can you ever be sure when it comes to men like him?"

Hettie poured the truffle fries into a basket padded with paper towels, signaling for me to try one. I picked one up and popped it into my mouth. *Heaven.*

"You don't look too surprised." I studied her, stealing another fry. "Is this a normal occurrence? Romeo bringing a fiancée home?"

"No." Hettie sucked honey off her thumb. "But his dad was on his ass about getting married, so I figured it was bound to happen eventually. I just expected something . . . *different.*"

"Mail-order bride?"

She snorted. "Girl, that man has women lining up and down his gate twenty-four seven. It's a nuisance at this point. Can you water spray them away or something?"

Despite my good senses, I blurted out, "Who does he normally go for?"

Hettie frowned, setting the table with two plates. She was sharing the meal with me. Stupid butterflies fluttered across my rib cage.

"Actually, I've never seen him with a girlfriend before. But the women that usually hang on his arm during events are kind of stuck up, I guess. Pencil skirts and season tickets to the opera. They barely say a word, and they definitely don't indulge in truffle fries. Not that it should matter to you. He never brings them home." She gestured around. "Guess he's too freaked out about them dirtying up the place or something."

I filed this as crucial information. I intended on being especially loud, uncultured, and tacky just to spite my neat-freak fiancé.

We tucked into the food, which was totally delicious. I moaned, earning a grin from Hettie.

"So good, right?"

I nodded.

About the only decent thing about this place.

Chapter Fourteen

Dallas

It was to my great disappointment that Romeo wasn't here to admire my handiwork. I'd stained his two-hundred-year-old restored sofa with French dip while watching pay-per-view. I didn't even like boxing, but I *was* fond of wasting his precious money.

I hadn't planned on messing up his place. Truly. It was never my intention. Then I saw how awfully clean it was and couldn't help myself.

Where the heck was he, anyway? It wasn't like I had anyone to ask. I didn't even have his phone number. What I *did* have was his Centurion card, which I'd found on the kitchen island, along with a business card for a chauffeur. Since I was one hundred percent sure the bastard hadn't made a pit stop here, I gathered the elusive Cara was responsible for this sliver of humanity.

As a matter of principle, I didn't buy anything wearable. I continued prancing around in my sleeping gown, even as it began to smell.

Hettie scrunched her nose, abandoning her fruitless attempt to erase my French-dip stain. "There's a laundry room upstairs."

"I know." I spiraled my fork, reeling in pappardelle noodles. "Aren't you hungry?"

"I ate dinner with you two hours ago." Her eyes followed the arrabbiata sauce as it splashed onto my gown, followed by the wool upholstery. "Aren't you worried Romeo will flip out when he sees"—she twirled her finger—"all this?"

"Nope."

"Are you guys in a fight?"

If this is a fight, World War II was a neighbor dispute.

Sensing my mood, she stood, returning with an expensive bottle of champagne. "We can get drunk to forget about our woes."

I shoved pasta down my throat. "So, I can continue to remember them tomorrow, but with a hangover?"

"Point taken."

At midnight, Hettie left me to simmer in my thoughts. Violent fury eclipsed the relief of not having to deal with Romeo. How dare he lock me in his mansion and continue to live his best villainous life?

In lieu of a fiancé to take my anger out on, every single item in his bedroom and office was at my mercy. I left no stone unturned in my bid to discover more about the man who had waltzed into my life in an expensive tux and turned it upside down just because it suited him.

I spent the entire night sifting through paperwork in his study, going item by item, and putting it back in non-chronological order, just to mess with his psyche. By the time the sun crested the sky, I'd learned a few things about my future husband:

1) He was exceptionally, alarmingly, *obnoxiously* good at making money. His talent of turning a dime into a Benjamin was unmatched.

2) For the past few months, Senior had pressured him into marriage in exchange for the CEO position at Costa Industries, following Senior's impending retirement.

3) The unfriendly, terse email exchanges between Romeo and his father also included harsh words about the Licht family. The Costas were intimidated, and I was their way to up the ante in the battle.

Satisfied that I'd put a dent in my research, I stopped by the kitchen to inhale Hettie's blueberry and pecan waffles before retiring to my room for a nap.

The following evening, I sat shoulder-to-shoulder with Hettie, slurping Chai tea she'd brought from Darjeeling. "Does he usually sleep out of the house?"

In front of us, a news segment danced across the screen. Something about a ring of brazen daylight robbers, who crashed restaurants and luxury stores, robbing the DMV's wealthiest.

"Not usually." Hettie sank into the cushions. "Sometimes, when he pulls really late nights, he stays in his Woodley Park penthouse. But he doesn't like his schedule out of whack. He's kind of peculiar about his meals staying the same."

So . . . Romeo had an apartment in D.C. Another piece of information certain to come in handy. "Why?" Hettie grinned, bumping our shoulders. "Missing your dreamboat?"

If by dreamboat you mean the Titanic, then . . . still no.

I hadn't confided in Hettie about the nature of my relationship with Romeo. Though it didn't take a degree in neuroscience to put two and two together.

I smiled at her question. "I can't wait to see him again." This part wasn't even a lie.

Next time I met Romeo, I'd remind him of my existence. Loudly. Messily. And unapologetically.

Chapter Fifteen

Dallas

There was only one thing worse than awakening from peaceful slumber—and that was being *rudely* awakened from peaceful slumber by a harem of middle-aged, white-privileged men with enough chins between them to sculpt another full-sized person.

"Is this her?" I didn't recognize the voice.

"Regrettably." That terse reply could only belong to one person.

My eyes fluttered open. Sure enough, two men I didn't know hovered at the end of my bed beside another man I knew but wished I didn't—my fiancé. I sat up, leaned against my headboard, and rubbed my eyes, yawning.

If I'd hoped Romeo would be disheveled and unrested, having spent several nights away from his home, I was gravely mistaken. He appeared as fresh as the gum he now chewed, with a crisp light-gray suit, powder-blue dress shirt, and Panerai timepiece.

He glanced at his watch. "It's almost six in the evening."

I drew a hand to my collarbone. "Goodness gracious, you can read the time. What other distinctive qualities must be hidden in you, my darling?"

The look he launched at me could freeze the arctic back to its pre-global warming state. I glanced between his two companions. I already knew who they were. Daddy had texted me about them. A message that remained unanswered, despite frequent pleas to return his calls.

I sank back into my mattress, shutting my eyes. "Well, this has been fun. Don't forget to turn off the light on your way out."

"What do you think you're doing?"

"Sleeping."

"In the middle of our conversation?"

"Was that a conversation?" I shimmied the comforter up my shoulders. "As I'm sure you remember, you once accused me of having no dreams. Can't dream without sleeping." I yawned, shooing them with a wave. "Well, off to chase my dreams. Tootles."

Romeo jerked the duvet off me. "This is Jasper Hayward, my lawyer. And this is Travis Hogan, your lawyer. We're signing a prenuptial agreement this evening." He sauntered to the windows, drawing the curtains open in a sharp movement. Even the sunset singed my hooded eyes.

"You hired a lawyer for me." I slipped out of bed in my six-day-old nightgown, strutting to him. "Why, that's so sweet of you. I'm sure he'll have my best interests in mind."

Romeo sneered down at me. "Your father approved the contents of the agreement this morning. Rest assured, it is on par with standard prenuptial agreements." His words were so reserved and careful, I wanted to shake him. Grab him by the suit and rattle him until his inhibitions rolled down the floor like pennies.

"Relax, darling. I trust you." I advanced to the beverage cart, pouring myself a few fingers of whisky from the decanter, knowing he wouldn't approve. "So far, you haven't done me wrong." If sarcasm were poison, he'd be dead five times over by now.

"Day drinking." He pursed his lips. "Dare I ask if this is a habit of yours?"

I could count on one hand the number of times I'd drunk in my life, having grown up under such strict religious rules. But he didn't need to know that. I sighed, swirling the drink. "Lighten up. Could be worse. I could be a coke addict." I took a sip. "Unfortunately, coke smells like nothing. Can you believe it? That was five hundred bucks I'm never getting back. Hopefully, I'll have more luck with crack."

Jasper hacked out coughs. Travis patted him on the back, looking at anything but me.

Judging by Romeo's dispassionate glare, I knew he'd begun to truly regret his decision to marry me, just as I knew it was too late for us to back out of the arrangement now.

"Clothe yourself." His eyes catalogued every stain I'd acquired in Potomac. "You look like a dumpster diver."

"Clothes?" I frowned, playing dumb. "But, baby, I have no clothes. Remember we had to rush to the airport so we could be together? I didn't have time to pack."

"The credit card I gave you wasn't ornamental."

"It wasn't?" I shrieked, widening my eyes. "But it looks so pretty on the kitchen table. Anywho, I was too busy pining over you to use it."

The two lawyers glanced between us in confusion.

Jasper readjusted his briefcase. "Would you like a few moments?"

"Yes," Romeo barked out at the same time I raised the drink in the air, announcing, "Moments? I would love a whole *lifetime* alone with this dreamboat."

Jasper and Travis fled, tossing awkward looks at one another.

With just me and Romeo in the confined space, I felt smaller. Not as brave. Nonetheless, I stepped forward, coming toe to toe with him. The sooner he realized I'd make his life hell on Earth, the sooner he'd let me go.

"Where were you, baby?" I tacked on a thick, deep-fried Georgian accent I knew would drive him mad, lifting my hand to drag the damp glass across his cheek. "I wanted us to go over wedding brochures. I'm thinking peonies for flowers. Glitter-themed. You'd look real good in a sequin suit. Summer in Portofini. To honor your Italian heritage, you know."

"Portofi*no*." He grabbed the whisky from my hand, gliding it between my breasts. Delicious shivers broke over my skin. "The ceremony will take place at the end of the month in von Bismarck's backyard, and the guest list is already locked, curated by both our families." His cutting, harsh words made me dizzy. There was a date. And a place. "You can have your peonies—and your sequins. If you think a bad suit will veer me off track from my plan, you haven't been paying attention."

He tipped the glass down, letting a few drops of whisky run between my breasts, slide down my stomach, and disappear into my underwear through my gown. It was erotic, maddening, and infuriating all at once. I breathed harder just so the tips of my nipples brushed against his chest each time I exhaled.

"Can't wait," I choked out.

"Good. Here's another event to fawn over. You're coming to my parents' shortly after we sign the prenup, where you will be on your best behavior, which, for you, possibly means using utensils and refraining from sniffing people's behinds as a way of hello."

I stared at him with all the hatred in the world, shaking with rage. His complete indifference undid me. He was the coldest, meanest man I'd ever met. His eyes snapped from my face to my nightgown. My chest heaved. I wasn't wearing a bra, and my nipples pearled, erect from the adrenaline rush.

"You can't help yourself, can you?" A sadistic glimmer flickered through his pale eyes. "Such a basic creature." Through the satin fabric, he ran the frosty rim of the tumbler over the tight bud, raising his phone to his ear with his free hand.

I couldn't move. Couldn't even breathe. The sensation was so intense and incredible, my whole body turned to clay. With this simple touch, it felt like he owned every inch of me. Heat swirled below my belly button. My breasts felt heavy, full, and sensitive, begging to be cupped and played with.

"Cara?" Romeo drew a lazy circle around my nipple with the glass. I resisted the urge to plaster myself against him. To beg for more. For the millionth time, I cursed my father for my sheltered upbringing. If only I'd been less innocent about these things, Romeo wouldn't have such a strong grip on me. "Head over to Tyson's Galleria and get me every single item for women from Yves Salomon, Celine, Burberry, and Brunello Cucinelli's latest season. Size small."

He set down the whisky, reaching for me. His entire hot palm covered my right breast. "Bra size: 32B."

Spot on. Dang it.

Grabbing my hip bone, he spun me so my back faced him. I felt his eyes on my ass. His hand slipped beneath the material of my robe from behind, stroking my bare chest. "Pants size: four."

"Six, asshole." A weird tingling feeling between my legs made my skin hum with expectation. The thought to resist crossed my mind, but I knew if I did, I might never explore this pleasure again.

Cara said something I couldn't decipher through the phone. I burned with shame. He was talking to another woman while playing with my body like it was his personal toy, yet I loved the way he made me feel too much to stop it.

"Short boot for pants. She is the height of a garden gnome." Romeo pinched my nipple, causing my knees to buckle. I bit down on a moan. I had the distinct feeling he was taunting me sexually just to prove to me he could. Another one of his control games. He pressed his hard-on against my ass, squeezed my breast, and trailed his hand from my nipple to my neck, scooping it and tilting my head up to face him. "What's your shoe size, Shortbread?"

My shoe size? I couldn't even remember my middle name with his cock pulsating between my butt cheeks.

Think. You know that one.

"Six point five." My voice came out thick and raspy.

He released my throat at once, stepping back, completely unaffected by my body. By my readiness for him. "Six point five. Kindly deliver all items within two hours. Time is of the essence."

He killed the call. I spun to face him, disappointed in myself for letting him strum my body like an instrument. Again. Hadn't I learned anything from the debutante ball?

"Tonight, you will present yourself to my family as a proper, levelheaded lady." He snatched the Macallan M by its neck, confiscating it. "If you succeed in fooling them into thinking you are, in fact, marriage material, I'll reward you accordingly and relieve you of your pent-up sexual frustration."

"You mean what you did just now was to blackmail me into good behavior so we can have sex tonight?"

The whiplash his last sentence gave me singed my cheeks. He really thought I'd be his little sex doll just because the tricks he used on my body provoked my curiosity.

He made a disapproving face. *Lord, so stuck-up.* "We're not wedded quite yet, Miss Townsend. What I alluded to was oral favors."

"Oral favors?" I scrunched my nose, noticing he spoke as if he'd just strolled out of the worn pages of a historical romance. That just so happened to be my least favorite genre. "And why do you talk like you fled the cast of *Bridgerton*?"

There was no point in telling him there'd be no oral-giving lessons, no cordial dinner, and no suitable fiancée tonight.

"Our lawyers must be running out of patience." He sipped whisky straight from the bottle. "Frankly, so am I."

Don't worry, honey, I thought as I breezed past him, refusing to look distraught. *After I'm done with you, you'll be running, period.*

Chapter Sixteen

Ollie vB: How is Delaware settling in?

Romeo Costa: Dallas.

Ollie vB: What is a show my grandmother was fond of?

Romeo Costa: We're not playing Jeopardy, you mediocre man child. Her name is Dallas.

Zach Sun: That's quite unfortunate for her.

Zach Sun: But not as unfortunate as marrying your ass.

Ollie vB: @ZachSun, agreed. That girl must've been in the Judenrat in a previous life to deserve this kind of karma.

Zach Sun: Mussolini's right hand.

Ollie vB: *Mussolini's jerk-off hand.

Romeo Costa left the chat.

Ollie vB added Romeo Costa to the chat.

Zach Sun: Is she still feeding you enough shit to cover the Northern Hemisphere?

Ollie vB: I'm never going to unsee the picture of Romeo turning blue when she wiggled her little ass on his lap. Boss bitch move.

Zach Sun: Or when Rom threw a hissy fit after she hit on the co-pilot. His self-control evaporated quicker than a thought in Ollie's brain.

Romeo Costa: She did not hit on the co-pilot. She was just being difficult. Brat is her entire personality.

Ollie vB: Have you consummated your engagement yet?

Romeo Costa: Are you familiar with human customs? There is nothing to consummate until marriage.

Ollie vB: Yikes. That's a definite no.

Romeo Costa: A gentleman doesn't kiss and tell.

Ollie vB: Asshole, please.

Ollie vB: Drop the gentleman charade. I've met dildos more honorable than you.

Zach Sun: @OllievB, you've met dildos? Socially or intimately? Or both?

Romeo Costa: I cannot believe nearly two decades of education in America's finest establishments bred me you two as best friends.

Ollie vB: I'll have you know I'm a fucking
delight and a top-notch friend.

Ollie vB: And I'm happy to prove it. Shall I
break her in for you?

Romeo Costa: Joke about it one more time,
and I'll personally cut off your dick and feed
it to you, bite by bite, until you choke on it.

Zach Sun: Hissy fit #2 duly recorded and
entered into the meeting's minutes.

Zach Sun: The woman turned you into an ape.

Ollie vB: . . .

Ollie vB: Is that a no?

Chapter Seventeen

Romeo

The warning signs flashed bright and loud, daring me to heed them. As it happened, I was so content watching my bride's golden blush, tantalizing neck, full breasts, and macabre beauty, I lowered my guard. She looked delectable, even in her stained nightgown. So painfully young and innocent and alive. Fondling her breasts felt like pouring ink all over freshly fallen snow. Like the perfect sin. Corrupting the uncorrupted.

The prenuptial agreement passed without a hitch. Shortbread scoured through every word, jotted her name on the dotted lines a dozen times, and listened, nodding whenever appropriate. It marked the first time she'd exhibited signs of rationality. That should've been my first warning.

Her feistiness returned in full swing when our lawyers departed and Cara arrived to drop off a trillion new outfits. Shortbread soaked up an eyeful of fifty-seven-year-old, wedding-band-sporting Cara. Her shoulders sagged. My bride had the poker face of an eager puppy.

"These clothes are an insult to eyes all over the world. It's going to look like I'm playing dress up as a sixty-year-old." Dallas flung cashmere dresses and hand-knitted cardigans on the hardwood while picking an outfit for dinner. My body temperature spiked. I positively despised messes, and everything about her was untidy.

Cara hovered around Dallas, thrusting different garments at her. Hettie joined the party, cracking up each time Dallas tested Cara's patience. I suspected they'd become fast friends in the time I'd spent in my Woodley Park penthouse. I didn't mind. It was good that Shortbread had someone to talk to. Because that person wouldn't be me. Nonetheless, I wasn't thrilled to have a front-row seat to this tableau.

Cara picked up a plaid sweater. "What's wrong with this dress?"

Dallas blew a raspberry like a toddler, just to get on my nerves. "I'll look like I'm about to launch into a monologue about how I haven't seen my lover in eighty-four years."

Hettie, who'd gotten the *Titanic* reference, toppled to the floor, clutching her stomach with each laugh.

A flustered Cara planted a fist on each hip. "This is the sixteenth gown you've tried, young lady. It is a terrific gown. A classic. Costs a fortune. I didn't hear any complaints when Romeo bought it for his ex-girlf—" She didn't finish the sentence, but it was enough to paint disgust on Shortbread's face.

"Well, in *that* case, he is welcome to marry her."

No, thank you. I'd take Dallas over Morgan every day of my cursed week.

After forty minutes of this spectacle, I snatched a dress from Dallas's fingertips. "If you're not going to choose an outfit, I'll do it for you. Dare I suspect our tastes run different?"

A violent glare swaddled her cheeks. "I want to be left alone. Everybody out."

With pleasure.

I waited in the foyer, glued to my messages.

Ollie vB: That couch needed a makeover, anyway.

Zach Sun: Hate to break it to you, but you married the female, virginal version of Oliver.

Romeo: Zach, sweetheart, you sure you're doing lines of code and not lines of coke?

Beside me, Hettie whistled. "Holy. Crap."

I pocketed my phone, lifting my head. Shortbread descended the stairway, reminding me why I'd stolen her. For the first time in my life, I regretted my no-sex rule.

My future wife looked sensational. Ample cleavage shot past the corset bodice of her solid-gold dress. Her tiny waist swayed as she walked, guiding the floor-sweeping train. A loose bun rested on her head, tendrils of dark locks framing her face. She was so absurdly beautiful, I watched her every move like she was a Fata Morgana. Alas, even Miss Townsend, as alluring as she was, couldn't break the no-heirs rule.

Dallas reached the last stair, where she thrusted her Chanel purse in my chest. I caught it, indulging her. If holding her purse tonight meant she'd be a good girl when I introduced her to my parents, I was willing to play the gentleman for a short while.

"I'm going to get a snack to-go. I haven't eaten in two hours."

Where did she fit all this food?

"Hurry up and mind the dress."

She started to the kitchen, then stopped, frowning. "Is your family terrible? I need to know whether to compliment my snack with a shot of something strong."

"Get yourself two shots. Actually, bring the whole bottle. We'll share."

Chapter Eighteen

Romeo

On second thought, I had buyer's remorse. I spent the drive to my parents' house staring at my future wife, wondering if she'd been raised by coyotes. Dallas's long, shapely legs strewed beneath her like excess fabric of a newly worn dress.

She split open an Oreo and licked the cream with a moan, washing it down with the vintage champagne we shared. "You know in Japan they have Bourbon choco and coffee biscuits? Imagine what that must taste like."

The only thing I imagined was my cum in the Oreo cream's place, dripping from between her succulent lips. It infuriated me that I'd momentarily fallen for it when she claimed to be an alcoholic. The woman was straight as an arrow. Lazy, spoiled, and reckless, sure. But her only vice seemed to be food that would send her into the arms of type 2 diabetes and an early grave.

Unfortunately, Dallas interpreted my glaring as an open invitation for conversation. "So, why does your daddy want you to marry so bad?" She flicked a cream-less Oreo cookie into the trash and picked another one, cracking it open just for the filling.

I didn't bother asking how she knew this. The cameras in my study had caught her snooping on my desktop in 4K Ultra HD.

"Because he gets off on control as much as I do and knows I'd sooner obtain a pet bear than a wife if it were my choice."

"Yay me." Her tongue swept up the cream. *Christ.* "And why do you go along with it?"

"Because he's dangling the company I'm set to inherit as a carrot, and I won't lose it to that brown-nosing bag of STDs, Bruce."

"Tell me about this Bruce." She stopped licking the cream and scanned me, her interest piqued. It was the first time the woman hadn't actively tried to either kill me or drive me to madness, so I threw her another bone.

"He's the COO of Costa Industries, an unbearable prick, and worst of all, phenomenal at his job. You will notice when we get there that my father treats Bruce like a prized poodle. Senior met Bruce a year before Monica became pregnant with me. They'd tried for years with no luck, so he figured Bruce was his one and only chance at a legacy."

"What about Bruce's dad?"

"Irrelevant. Owns a pharmaceutical empire, which will go to Bruce's older brother, then pass down that lineage."

"So, Bruce wants into the Costa legacy."

"Precisely. Months before he discovered Monica's pregnancy, Senior took Bruce under his wing, signing him with Costa Industries. Bruce has done his bidding since, getting married to a horsey fashion-empire heiress just so her dad would invest in Senior's endeavors. Senior wants us to be his puppets. Whatever is ours must be his, too."

Shortbread tucked a tendril behind her ear. "Your daddy sounds even worse than mine."

"Doubtful."

"How come?"

"No one decent would ever hand over their precious daughter to someone like me."

"You admit that you're horrible, then." She celebrated with a single fist pump.

"I admit I lack compassion, sympathy, and empathy. Which is why I would have been better off staying single."

"And your mom?"

"She mainly lacks a backbone. Her compassion levels are adequate."

Dallas rolled her eyes. "I mean, are you close with her?"

"Not remotely." I sipped our champagne. "She's nothing to write home about."

"Shouldn't *she* be your home?"

God, Dallas sounded like a children's book again. "Enough chitchat, Shortbread. You're here to look pretty and alive. The free therapy is redundant."

Dallas sighed. "It's awful, isn't it? How, at the end of the day, all we are is a byproduct of our parents' ambitions, principles, and desires. A collection of memories, mistakes, and unexplainable yearning to please those who gave us life. Look at us." She gazed out the window, her perfect cupid's lips drawn downward. "Both stuck in an engagement we want nothing to do with because of our parents."

I stared at her, the ice block padding my chest somewhat thawing. It was the first profound thing she'd said, and I wondered if other interesting things filled that beautiful head of hers or if this was an accidental soundbite she'd memorized by chance.

Dallas scooted away from me, probably afraid I'd make her almost come again, my new unfortunate hobby. "Why are you looking at me like that?"

"Because," I said as the Maybach pulled to a stop in front of my parents' residence, "I think you just unintentionally made sense."

Chapter Nineteen

Romeo

My parents lived in a French Country-style manor wrapped in Boral bricks. Despite living on the same street, it took a solid ten minutes to reach their gates, followed by another two minutes to traverse their mile-long driveway. Their four-acre house was both grand and understated enough to scream old money. Inviting yellow lights glimmered through the vast windows, illuminating a long table filled with professionally prepared food. I knew that, to anyone who wasn't me, this looked like the picture of domestic bliss.

I shot Dallas a final warning before pushing the doorbell. "Remember—tonight, you are a well-bred woman."

"Did someone say bread?" Dallas gasped, playing dumb. "Please tell me there will be gravy, too. Or anything I can dunk it into."

Monica's pumps clunked on the other side of the door. As soon as it opened, I thrust Shortbread into her arms, my human sacrifice. "Mother, Dallas Townsend. Dallas, this is Monica, the woman who gave me life, possibly to spite me."

"My goodness, look at you." Monica neglected all decorum and etiquette by clutching Dallas's cheeks with her talons, examining my bride's delicate face with hysterical pupils. "I won't pretend I didn't make some calls to find out more about you. Everyone said you're gorgeous, but the word doesn't do you justice."

Shortbread gathered my usually reticent mother into an embrace with theatric flourish. Though I didn't particularly like either of them, I was satisfied they were a good match. "Well, Mrs. Costa, I can already see you and I will get along just fine."

"Please, call me Mom."

I didn't even call her Mom. Also, why did she use an exclamation point for every sentence that left her mouth?

"Oh, if you insist. Do you know any good shopping spots around here, *Mom*?"

"Know?" Monica almost suffered a cardiac arrest. "I have a personal shopper in each of them." Her eyes caught the pearl necklace Dallas must have stolen from my room. I knew she'd snooped—left her greasy fingerprints everywhere—but just now noticed it on her collar. Monica covered her lips with her fingertips, sparing Senior a glance. "Oh, honey, Rom gave Dallas your great grandmother's necklace. They really are getting married."

Behind her, Senior, Bruce, and Shelley peered at Dallas. I studied my father. The hard set of his shoulders. The way they rattled with each exhale. He planted a hand on the railing. For support, I gathered, though he'd never admit it. He hated weaknesses. The bad news was—Senior was still alive. The good news? He seemed a little less so than the last time I'd seen him.

Bruce and Shelley advanced after Dallas managed to unplaster herself from Monica's hold.

"Dear." Shelley squeezed Shortbread's shoulder, a grim expression eclipsing her face. "We heard what happened at the debutante ball. Are you okay?"

"Miss Townsend." Bruce slipped between them, grabbing Dallas's hands in an Oscar-worthy performance. "If you need to discuss anything privately for a moment, I'm at your disposal." The prick wanted Shortbread to fall at his feet and beg him to save her from the big, bad wolf.

I'd predicted this behavior from Bruce, as well as Dallas's response—she knew she had no way out of this. No home to return to. Chapel Falls would only accept her as my wife after our rose garden debacle.

Though I'd expected Dallas to shut Bruce down, I hadn't foreseen her upturning her nose, regarding him as if he were a lowly servant. "Bruce, is it?" Her eyes narrowed, foot sliding back.

"Yes." He inclined his head in faux modesty. "No need to put on a brave face, my dear. I've seen the social media videos—"

"You know what they say about social media." Shortbread examined her manicured fingernails with a patronizing pout. "It's nothing but a false reality."

Shelley stepped forward, trying to milk some kind of confession out of my fiancée. "But you looked so livid—"

"Oh, I was." Dallas laughed, twirling a lock of hair around her finger. I noticed she had a wing-shaped constellation of freckles on her nose. "But then I had time to cool down and consider how completely obsessed with me this man is. Look at the lengths he went to in order for us to wed. I swear, every time he stares at me, there are tears in his eyes. He can't contain himself. I hold his happiness in my fist. How romantic is that?"

I could kiss her in that moment. Of course, she'd probably bite my lips off as payback.

Disappointed, Bruce and Shelley scampered to the sidelines as Senior finally strode toward Shortbread. My blood cooled in my veins. My muscles tensed. I parked a possessive hand on her waist.

Dallas took in my father's general welfare. Or lack thereof. A million questions danced behind her honey-hued eyes. I hoped Senior saw each and every one. He hated the idea of people knowing what had happened to him. That his imperial body had failed him, and he'd soon wither into himself. Which was why he'd chosen to retire before the general public could witness what his disease did to him.

Senior captured Dallas's hand and brought it to his lips, making eye contact with her. "Romeo, she is ravishing."

"I have eyes," I informed him.

"You have hands, too, and they seem to be all over her. Relax." He chuckled. "She isn't going to run anywhere, is she?"

Dallas studied the human ring surrounding her, trying to read the atmosphere. It was obvious bad blood ran between the men present. Hedging her bets on a safe stock, she laced her arm in Monica's and smiled. "I'd love to help you in the kitchen, Mom."

"Oh, I haven't entered my kitchen since 1998." She waved a hand. "It's all servants."

Dallas flashed her dazzling smile, but I could tell she didn't like Monica's usage of the words servants. Did my young bride have morals? Unlikely. Best not to find out.

"Shall we sit down for dinner?" Senior suggested.

"Certainly, Romeo." Bruce all but rolled over and showed him his tummy for a rub.

When the four of them poured into the dining room, Shortbread held back and leaned toward me, her voice low. "Is your father okay? Is something wrong with him?"

There was a lot wrong with Senior. Friedreich's ataxia happened to be the only thing right about him. It would kill him, eventually. Too slow for my liking. But in the meantime, I enjoyed the progression of his symptoms. Each time he struggled to walk in sudden bouts. The fatigue. The slowed speech. The only time I ever listened to him speak, really.

"He has a rare inherited disease that causes progressive nervous system damage." I strode to the dining room, refusing to match her volume. I didn't care if Senior heard me. In fact, I would enjoy it.

Her forehead creased. "Inherited? Will you—"

"Get it? No. It requires two recessive genes." I leaned into her, my lips brushing the shell of her ear. "Careful, Shortbread. Wouldn't want to mistake you for caring."

Dinner consisted of Bruce and Shelley cross-examining Shortbread about the debutante ball, Monica trying to lure Dallas to European shopping sprees, and Senior prying her for obvious flaws. Of which there were many. My bride slumped in her seat like an overcooked shrimp, most certainly to grate on my already raw nerves. I could tell Shortbread didn't enjoy defending our relationship, for the simple fact that it did not exist. She was forced to lie through her teeth for a man who had plucked her from her charming life. By the time dessert was served, shockingly, she didn't even touch it.

Bruce and Shelley grilled her with their millionth question about her relationship with Madison Licht. She took frequent sips of water, her usual fire long doused.

". . . just find it odd that after Madison sang your praises to half the DMV, you two would break off an engagement following a short flirt with our little Junior—"

Bruce would've drilled the subject until oil poured out if Shortbread hadn't blurted, "May I be excused?"

My parents shared a puzzled look.

"Go ahead." I stood, pulling her chair for her.

She disappeared faster than a bikini top in a Cancun spring break party.

Bruce turned to me. "Junior, son, what you are doing to this child is deplorable."

"So is what you're doing to me," I pointed out.

"What am I doing to you?"

"Existing."

"Romeo," Senior faux-chided. He fucking loved our competition for his throne. "Stop mocking Bruce. You know better than to disrespect your elders."

I sipped my brandy. "He started it."

Bruce frowned. "How so?"

"By being born."

Nothing brought out my inner child like arguing with my nemesis in front of my father.

"Madison is going around telling people the DOD will make them an offer for an annual contract." Senior dug into his pie, changing the subject. The fork pinched between his fingers rattled, either from irritation or his disease. "The one we're currently grandfathered into. You know, their company holds the rights to the taser shockwave system prototype. My sources tell me it's a deal breaker. They have cutting-edge blueprints we don't."

A direct consequence of Senior relying on engineers and experts with dated knowledge and no field experience to speak of. Senior hadn't just dropped the ball. He'd let it roll all the way to our enemy's home field. During my undergrad at MIT, he'd admonished my engineering degree as wasteful since Costa Industries boasted an army of engineers, yet here we were. A decade behind, pants around our ankles.

"Madison is right. We're old blood. Weak in the teeth." I slammed the tumbler on the table, staring Senior in the eye. "Make me your CEO, and I'll give you a state-of-the-art weapon. I'm talking nuclear-level destruction."

"Romeo." Bruce gulped. He was in it for the money. We both knew Senior needed to make a decision soon— and that decision would either be our windfall or drought. "You should sleep on it. At the very leas—"

"Let's see you walking down that aisle first, Son." My father tried and failed, yet again, to slice his pie. Definitely his disease. His fork clattered to his plate as he reached for his drink. "And then I'll seriously consider it."

I'm not your son. Not where it matters.

I crushed my gum between my teeth. Other than wanting the Costa dynasty to continue, Senior also saw my reproduction as entertainment for his wife. He figured that if he blackmailed me into marriage, I'd have children, a family, something to keep Monica engaged and fulfilled. She wanted grandchildren and cheesy Christmas vacations and Hallmark-worthy holiday cards. The makeshift family she'd never had because my father was too busy dicking down anything on the East Coast with a skirt to pay us any real attention.

Monica lifted her glass. "Romeo?"

"Yes?"

"Where is Dallas?"

Good question. She'd escaped my mind. And possibly the premises.

Since there was a reasonable chance the answer to it was running off to live in the woods with a family of badgers,

I tossed my napkin over my plate and stood. "I'll check on her."

Monica touched her throat. "Look at him. I haven't seen Rom so involved with anyone since Morgan."

Morgan.

I didn't even bother checking if Shortbread was in the kitchen, the garden, or Senior's library. I knew exactly where I'd find her and took the stairs two at a time. I rounded the massive mahogany hallway, flinging the door open to my childhood room. Sure enough, Dallas was there, perched on the edge of my teenage bed, flipping through an old photo album. Morgan and me vacationing in Aspen. Morgan and me in New York. Morgan and me kissing. Hugging. Existing in our own little universe.

She didn't look up, even when I entered the room and shut the door behind me. "Why didn't you marry her?" Her voice sounded faraway. In another galaxy. "Morgan. You obviously still love her."

Why wouldn't Dallas assume so? My old room was a shrine to my ex-girlfriend. Photo albums. Framed pictures. Stubs from concerts we'd attended. Memorabilia from exotic places we'd visited. I refused to throw away the evidence that I was once a fully functioning human. Morgan's face stamped every inch of this room. Her slight ballerina frame. Her dimpled smile. She was as graceful as a perfect autumn day. Exceling everywhere my current fiancée fell short.

Approaching my future wife, I swiped the album out of her hands and tucked it back inside the nightstand drawer, its usual residence. For all I cared, I could burn every memory of Morgan to the ground, then piss on the remains to avoid a fire. I'd completely recovered from our five-year relationship and the broken engagement that had followed it. But I couldn't destroy the proof of our relationship, or the members of my so-called family would misinterpret the reason.

"Marrying her wasn't an option." Mainly since I'd kicked her out of our shared penthouse stark naked on the day our engagement had fallen apart, then filed a restraining order against her when she continuously found her way to my door, begging for forgiveness.

"You're still in love with her, aren't you?" Dallas slanted her lovely face upward, blinking with those dark, curly lashes that made her look like a Disney animal.

Denial settled on the tip of my tongue before I realized that, if I said yes, I'd spare Shortbread from heartbreak when I eventually got rid of her. Already, her body was too attuned to mine. Beneath the rebellious streak was a young woman capable of great love. Love I certainly wouldn't return. It was better to establish we'd be nothing but a business transaction.

"Yes," I heard myself say. It was the first time in years that actual laughter gathered in my throat. Me. In love with Morgan. I had more sympathy for the devil.

Dallas's throat bobbed. She nodded, gathering her dress and standing.

"What about you?" I asked. "Does Madison have your heart?"

This was what Frankie had claimed. I'd been meaning to sniff around the subject. Not because I cared, but because I needed to know if I should monitor her. Just because I didn't have feelings toward her didn't mean I was receptive to a scandal that would rock D.C. to its core.

She paused at the door, her back to me. "Your co-worker and his wife are getting on my last nerve." She ignored my question. "I would like to go home in the next ten minutes."

I would've pushed her about Madison, but I simply couldn't find it in me to muster the curiosity.

"I'll call Jared."

Chapter Twenty

Dallas

At the very least, I could rest easy knowing my husband's lack of civility extended to others, too. Jared pulled in front of the mansion near midnight. My future husband unfastened his seat belt, his face still buried in his phone screen, reading an article on *Forbes Money*.

"Jared," Romeo snarled, touching the door handle. "Stick around. I'll head to the penthouse in about an hour."

No please. No thank you. *And*, I realized, this poor excuse for a man, who had just confessed to being in love with his ex, expected me to perform oral sex on him before he retired to his bachelor pad. As a reward for my good behavior, no less. I could inform him he was wrong . . . or I could teach him I was more than an innocent little fawn and scare him off until the wedding. For the first time in my life, I chose education.

We made our way to the door. Silence hummed between us like a dramatic backing track. He opened it, letting me walk in first. "Your posture was weak, but otherwise, you performed well." His version of a compliment, I guessed. No wonder Morgan had dumped him. The man was as warm as Uranus.

I kept silent, focused on storming up to my room without stabbing him. A win in my book. He followed one step behind.

"Actually." I turned, placing a hand on his chest. His pecs flexed beneath his Eton dress shirt. He appeared mildly aware of my existence for a change. "Could you bring some whipped cream from downstairs?" I bit my bottom lip. "I've always had this fantasy . . ."

His expression clouded. "No."

"Romeo, O, Romeo." I knotted my arms over his shoulders, pressing my body against his. He was hard everywhere. And I meant *everywhere*. Poor Morgan might've had his heart, but his cock, it appeared, was community property. "That's my *dream*."

He peeled my arms off him. "Find a better one."

Plastering on my longing, purest gaze that always got Daddy to bend for my will, I whispered, "It's my first . . . *experience*." That seemed to do the trick.

"It might just be your last if you continue acting like a brat." He turned, trampling his way down to the kitchen. *Holy crap*. He was doing it. Momma was right. Men are more basic than a little black dress.

I hurried to my room, slipping into a soft-pink lingerie nightgown with crisscross satin bows wrapped around my chest. *Thank you, Cara, for pimping my ride*. Romeo appeared a few minutes later, a whipped cream can in his hand. It was beyond comical to see the most stuck-up, serious man I'd ever come across holding something so . . . random.

His eyes raked down my body. "Cara bought you this?"

"Yes." I forced out a smile. "Do you like it?"

"I'll like it more when it's in tatters on the floor." He pushed the whipped cream into my hands. "On your knees. Now, Miss Townsend."

"Can you . . . get undressed first?" I swallowed, feigning

shyness. "I've never been completely naked in front of a man before."

"Full nudity won't be necessary for what I have in mind for you."

A scream lodged in my throat. Selfish bastard. His ego needed its own zip code, a talk show, and a harem of agents.

"Just . . . just lie in my bed, all right?" I ground out.

"I'd rather do this standing up."

"If you don't indulge me at all, I'd rather not do it altogether," I snapped. Then, to conceal my plan, I gentled my approach. "Everything we've done so far has been on your terms. This is important to me. I need to feel like I have a say, too."

Romeo frowned, weighing my words, finally complying. "Take advantage of my goodwill, and I assure you—you'll be reminded I lack it altogether."

With wobbly knees, I waited until he flattened against my mattress before I mounted him, straddling his narrow waist. He stared up at me, indifference making room for a glint of desire in his fog-colored eyes.

"It's all so new and foreign to me." I licked my lips, feeling myself blush, because this wasn't actually a lie. I fumbled with the buttons of his shirt, undoing them with shaky fingers.

"I said I won't undress."

"I'll get undressed, too. I promise." I got stuck on his custom RF cufflinks. He took over, removing them with an impatient snarl. I hesitated. "I hope I won't disappoint you."

"While I'm not a fan of your personality, I'd pay good money to watch you sit and breathe," he admitted, his voice roughening. "All you have to do is be alive for me to get a hard-on, so don't worry your pretty head about underperforming."

Sadly, that was the sweetest thing he'd ever said to me.

His shirt feathered to the floor, exposing his sculpted upper body. My fingertips tingled, begging to run over his work-of-art abs. All smooth tan skin, bulging six-pack, perfect pecs, and lean muscles. The veins running down his biceps and forearms told the story of a man who kept himself in brilliant shape. I was also acutely aware of how easily he could crush me with his strength should he wish to.

I licked my lips, allowing my hands to roam his chest down to his belly button. "Lord," I breathed out. "You're beautiful."

He caught my wrist between his fingers when my hand was halfway down the path to his pants. His eyes bore into mine. "If you sit on my face and let me eat you out through your nightgown, I'll buy you the Astor Opera House."

The sentence didn't fully register for the first fifteen seconds. This didn't sound like him at all. The possessive tone. The carnal urgency in his usually shark-dead eyes.

"Uh . . . what?"

"I'll buy it for you." He didn't blink, my wrist still clasped in his hand. "You'll be able to do as you please with it. Cancel the annual debutante ball. Burn it down to the ground. Flatten it and build a tacky strip mall instead as payback for the way Chapel Falls judged you the night of the ball. The entire town will know your husband bought you the place just because you fancied it."

My eyes flared, heart wedged in my throat. The man was dead serious. He obviously wasn't playing with a full deck, as Daddy said. No point in reminding him *he* was the reason I was now a social pariah.

"The Astor Opera House isn't for sale," I said once I found my voice. "It belongs to my daddy's friend, Paul Dunn—"

"Everything is for sale if you offer over value. Test the theory yourself. Sit on my face, Dallas, and I'll give you anything you desire. I'll buy you that Japanese cookie factory if you let me feast on your juices."

I eyed him curiously, thrill coursing through my veins. My sexuality held potent power over him once he let his guard down. Which had only happened once so far.

"But you'd go back to your penthouse afterwards? After we . . ."

"Yes." Remembering himself, he released my hand as if it were fire. "Don't confuse lust with like. Lust is an urge. Like is a sentiment. I hold no sentiments toward you."

I planted my hand over the hem of his pants. "Then I'd rather do things my way."

This time, I didn't fumble. I rolled his zipper down all the way and sat on my knees as he pushed his cigar slacks down. His black briefs came into view. Givenchy waistband. The man was so rich, I suspected he wiped his butt with Egyptian silk sheets. The outline of his cock made my mouth water. For a second, I genuinely considered having a brief taste. It was long and thick, the shape of its perfect engorged crown obvious through the luxurious fabric. Funny how all my married friends told me penises were a sore sight for the eyes. I found my fiancé's penis pretty attractive. Its only downfall was that it was attached to a prick.

"Shortbread." His tone held a warning.

"Hmm?"

"Tit for tat. Lose your top before I do it for you."

Tearing my glare from his cock, I unfastened the pink satin ribbons, which kept my modesty intact. His eyes alight with desire as the two ribbons fell to his chest. He grabbed me by the waist, hoisted me in the air, and pulled me down so my entrance pushed against his clothed cock, dragging me along his length with a pained hiss.

My head spun with stupid yearning and adrenaline. Time to act before I drowned in sweet temptation and gave him what he wanted. The *only* thing he wanted from me. I picked up a bow and reached to plaster his wrist against my bed's poster behind his head.

"I want to explore you first. I've never touched a man before."

No longer tied together by the flimsy strings, my breasts hung out of my nightgown, full and round, dangling from side to side as I quickly tied his wrist to the headboard.

"I will not be tied down."

"Oh, please." I dipped one of my nipples into his mouth, knowing he'd catch and suck on it. "I'll probably butcher the job. Humor me."

Romeo was so laser-focused on watching my tits pendulum, trying to catch a rosy-peaked nipple between his teeth when I bent down, that he let me tie his left wrist to the pole.

"You do have the tendency to make a mess of things," he muttered around my tit, licking it. Tremors ran through me.

"Now the other hand."

I bent lower, my stomach flat against his hard chest as I tied his other wrist securely to my bed. He clasped his hot, wet lips around my nipple and sucked almost all of my breast into his mouth. I shuddered at his warmth, my palms dropping to his shoulders. The nightgown was damp between my legs. I felt empty. Mad with need. I ran my fingers through his thick, inky hair, dropping my head back with a moan. His teeth scraped my nipple at the same time his tongue swirled its tip. I rocked back and forth against his cock, knowing I left stains of my desire all over his briefs.

"The things I'm going to do to you, Shortbread . . ."

My nickname kicked me back into reality. I remembered his words from the debutante ball. *Ruined by shortbread.* Squaring my shoulders, I pulled away, swinging my legs and standing up beside the bed.

Romeo tried to pull himself up, his magnificent abs contracting, when he comprehended that I'd tied him to my bed with a triple-knot from each side. His head dropped to my pillows. He arched a dark brow, perfectly calm and collected. "Mind the whipped cream, Miss Townsend. I loathe dirt and messes, and judging by your clumsiness, your aiming skills leave a lot to be desired."

Dropping the façade, I rolled my eyes and tugged at the tied ribbon chaining him to my bed to ensure it stayed in place. "No wonder Morgan dumped you. As a partner, you stink worse than the inside of a teenager's ball cap."

He opened his mouth, about to say something, but I showed him I didn't really care by turning and picking up the whipped cream spray from the credenza. I swaggered to him, dangling my hips seductively. My breasts were still completely exposed, but somehow, I didn't feel self-conscious at all. The man treated my looks as if they were my flaw—taking me against my will. Well, now I'd turned my weakness into my strength.

I noticed a few scars on the sides of his rib cage. Old and pink against his tan skin and pretty major. Curiosity nipped at my throat, but knew if I ever asked, he'd bite my head off.

Romeo's expression darkened. "Don't try me, Shortbread."

"Why not? It's not like you ever held back on punishing me before." I shot him a sugary smile, reached for his waistband, and pulled it down in one go. His dick sprung out, heavy, pulsating, and engorged. That thing was huge. He wanted it in my mouth? I'd hardly be able to fit the thing into my suitcase. Maybe Morgan had broken things off because he'd sprained her jaw with it. Welcoming such a thing into your vagina seemed akin to giving birth to a full-size German shepherd.

"Oh, I forgot to mention." I shook the can in my hand, watching my future husband try to jerk his wrists free, writhing like a caged beast. "I was in the Scouts my entire childhood. Side effect of being raised a goody two-shoes. I know how to bond all seven knots by heart, blindfolded, with a hand tied behind my back. No pun intended, of course." I winked.

His eyes tapered. He lurched even harder, shaking the entire bed. The satin ribbons dug into his flesh, creating angry red bracelets on his skin.

"Why do you chew gum all the time?" I demanded, standing a safe length away from him.

His jaw locked.

"Answer me, and I might spare you," I lied.

"You won't. And even if you did, I don't negotiate with terrorists."

"It's an obsession."

"*A coping mechanism*," he corrected.

"Like the silence in your house. Your idea of heaven is most people's hell."

"Hell gets a bad rep. Sunny all year round, plenty of interesting neighbors, and no Sunday church."

He was picking a fight with a religion now? The man truly was headed to the nadir of the cosmos.

Without further discussion, I aimed the nozzle at his junk and pushed, spraying a thick, fluffy cloud of whipped cream on his cock and balls. The chill made his skin rise with goose bumps. He sucked in a hiss.

Romeo glared at me with murder in his eyes. "You've had your fun. Now untie me or face grave consequences."

I freed a laugh. "You blackmailed me into marriage, annihilated my reputation, and ruined my relationship with my father. What more can you do?" I aimed the nozzle at his chest, coating each of his nipples with the white fluff, then drawing a smiley face on his abs. "Aw. You look *adorable*. I cannot wait for Hettie or Vernon to find you like this."

His brows shot up to his forehead. "If you don't free me right now, Dallas—"

"Freedom isn't free, buddy. You're the one who taught me that lesson. That credit card you gave me is going to come in handy tonight." I swiveled, grabbed a dress he'd bought me from the floor, and slipped it on. "I'm going to spend tonight in a hotel. Order some room service. Maybe dessert. I didn't even have an appetite when we visited your parents." I approached him and set the can in his bound hand, leaning to whisper in his ear. "*Ruined by whipped cream.*" I tsked, just the way he had the night we'd met. "How the mighty have fallen."

There was a spring in my step when I strode to the door, knowing Romeo would stay right where I'd left him, naked and covered with sticky goo, until morning rose and his staff trickled into his mansion.

Before I left, I bent my knees in a mock bow, imitating his grandiose manner of speech, down to the high-brow Potomac accent. "Perhaps we shall reconvene in the next century, Lord Costa. Or the one after that."

He didn't answer.

Tough crowd.

I just knew this moment would come up on my Judgment Day.

Chapter Twenty-One

Romeo Costa: @OllievB, are you still interested in taking the banshee off my hands?

Ollie vB: Why?

Romeo Costa: I'm putting her on the market.

Zach Sun: Oh, no.

Zach Sun: What could possibly have gone wrong?

Zach Sun: [GIF of a person skydiving with an umbrella instead of a parachute]

Ollie vB: IDK if I'm willing to commit to marrying her, but I am happy to give her a bed to sleep in until you cool off.

Romeo Costa: Would you extend this offer to me? The penthouse is undergoing renovations, and there's no way I'm returning to the manor before the wedding.

Ollie vB: Sorry, but the offer is exclusive to people I'd like to give a cum facial.

Zach Sun: The mental image is exquisite. Thank you, @OllievB.

Ollie vB: What happened? Show us on the sex doll where she touched you.

Romeo Costa: @ZachSun? You have five spare bedrooms.

Zach Sun: Sorry, I'm expecting guests from Guangzhou.

Romeo Costa: Your family isn't visiting until New Year.

Zach Sun: Nice memory.

Zach Sun: In that case, you can't crash at mine simply because you're unbearable.

Ollie vB: I know a nice hotel chain if you're looking for recommendations.

Romeo Costa: How charitable of you.

Ollie vB: Are you going to tell us what happened?

Romeo Costa: If I do, I'll ruin whipped cream for you for eternity.

Zach Sun: I'm lactose intolerant.

Ollie vB: And I'm red-lines intolerant, so nothing can put me off.

Romeo Costa: All right. Here goes.

Chapter Twenty-Two

Romeo

I would never make eye contact with Hettie again. The silence that gripped Dallas's bedroom when Hettie had found me at eight in the morning and untied me from the bed—sticky, melted whipped cream scarcely covering my morning wood—was deafening.

She tried to loosen the knot manually at first. Then, after a three-minute struggle, she huffed. "Goddammit, out of all the women you could've gotten engaged to, you chose the one with James Bond's combat skills?"

"Trust me, no one is less excited than me about the pending nuptials. Now go get some scissors, and while you're at it, drape the blanket over my nether region."

File under: a sentence I never thought I'd tell someone I hired to steam my broccolini.

"Nether region?"

"My cock, Hettie. By God, does anyone under thirty have a vocabulary not borrowed directly from TikTok?"

She'd seen my scars. I was certain of it. So had my fiancée. Both had the good sense not to probe, though. Still, I didn't like that people knew. I didn't like that they could guess. I didn't like the reminder that once upon a time, I was weak, too.

My first stop was the shower, where I scrubbed off any remains of sugar and cream and punched the tiles until at least two of my knuckles bled. Afterwards, I wore my best suit, slipped three gums into my mouth, and grabbed my phone, informing the world I was, much to its disappointment, still alive. I'd never gone MIA for over four consecutive hours to sleep. Work thought I'd accidentally driven myself off a cliff. No doubt Costa Industries' employees were saddened to discover I was still among the living. My bedside manner didn't win me many fans and admirers.

While Jared drove me to work, he also informed me that my cunning fiancée was lodged in The Grand Millennium Regent. One of von Bismarck's high-end elite hotels. In a fifteen-thousand-dollars-a-night suite, of course. It took me less than five minutes to cancel all of her credit cards, relocate her Henry Plotkin books from her room to a locked safe in mine, and wipe the kitchen and pantry of anything savory. Needless to say, whipped cream was permanently banned from the premises.

I also cut Netflix and the Xfinity package, then the Internet, for good measure. My tantalizing bride didn't need entertainment. She needed to think about what she'd done.

Next time I saw her, she was going to promise me her forever.

And I was going to take it.

Just to fucking spite her.

Chapter Twenty-Three

Dallas

"We can still make a run for it. I retrieved Madison's ring. The one Romeo threw into the crowd." Frankie paced the makeshift bridal room in von Bismarck's mansion, face wrinkled in concentration, pinching said ring between her fingers. Her saffron cassette silk dress whooshed along the marble floors. "That must be worth something, right?"

My wedding day had arrived. I hadn't seen the groom for close to three weeks. During those weeks, Momma and Frankie had visited me twice, yet I'd never felt more alone in my life.

"Let it go." I glared at the mirror while two makeup artists and a hairstylist fussed over me. "It's a done deal."

My sister would never know how tempted I was to take her advice and run. I'd almost done so the first week after the trick I'd pulled on Romeo. But my friends and extended family began sending RSVPs, reminding me how far down the toilet Romeo had flushed my reputation.

"Is it true that you're pregnant?" Savannah had cried to me on the phone one evening. "People say that your daddy forced him to marry you after he found a pregnancy test in the trash."

Emilie managed to be a little more refined. "Your parents sent me an invitation. Thank you for that. Would you mind very much if I skipped the wedding? I'm not saying that I will. I just need to make sure with my parents that it won't ruin my . . . er . . . reputation. Please, don't be mad at me, Dal. At least you're getting married. And to Romeo Costa, no less. I still haven't received one offer, and I don't want to get a bad rep by being associated with the wrong people."

In the end, the universe provided. Emilie showed up, escorted by her eagle-eyed parents. Sav was here, too, and even brought a date. In fact, I heard that outside, in Oliver von Bismarck's nineteenth-century-era garden, over eight hundred guests mingled, the Licht family among them. My parents had invited them, offering the courtesy of saving face and proving there was no bad blood. No scandal between the two families. Madison was here. The thought made me want to crawl under the vanity and hide. I felt so sorry and guilty for what I'd done. What had caused this chain reaction that spiraled everyone's lives out of control.

"Dal! Oh, Dal, the cake!" Momma burst into the bridal suite, also known as Oliver's twelfth guest room, fanning herself. She sagged against the door, her fingers trembling over her collarbone. "It's an eight-tier cake. All white. The shape of your dress, with edible lifelike roses and custom calligraphy."

Momma was thrilled. Frankie and I had shielded her from the bitter truth about my marriage. I'd spent the past week waxing on about Romeo. What else could I do? Frankie said she'd stopped eating and talking to my father altogether in a bid to bring me back home. No matter how much I loathed Daddy, I still couldn't bear seeing Momma devastated.

"Oh, my." I forced a grin. "Shame I'm probably going to inhale it before anyone takes a picture."

"It's showtime, ladies." The wedding planner kicked the door open, sweating buckets under her designer garment. She wore an earpiece with a microphone hovered in front of her lips. "The groom is already waiting—and looking delicious doing so, I should add. All the guests are seated. It's a go."

Frankie shot me a desperate glance. *It's now or never,* it said. And though I couldn't imagine myself finding happiness with my cruel, beautiful fiancé, I also couldn't return to Chapel Falls a damaged woman and risk Frankie's future. Besides, what kind of future awaited me? No one else would have me. At least with Romeo Costa, I had financial safety, a roof above my head, and a future with children to look forward to.

"Come, my love." Momma shooed away the hair and makeup stylists, pulling me up. Her smile died as soon as our fingers touched. "Your hands are ice cold."

I swallowed. "It's just the nerves."

"Are you sure?" She peered into my face. "You would tell me if you were unhappy, right, Pickle?"

I almost collapsed at the sound of my childhood nickname. There was nothing I wanted more than to return home. Undo my mistake from a month ago.

"Everything is perfect, Momma. I'm the luckiest girl alive."

Chapter Twenty-Four

Dallas

Like all lies, my wedding was too beautiful, well-rehearsed, and above all—soulless.

My dress epitomized regality. Long lace sleeves with a deep-V neckline, clean column satin body, and a round train that covered the von Bismarck mansion's entire grand stairway. Three fashion magazines came to take photos. The profits went to charity—Friedreich's Army. Romeo's idea. Just as with everything else, I didn't have a voice.

The tabloids and local news had reported that the flower arrangement alone cost over 120K. I didn't doubt it. My parents had spared no dime on the lavish event. Momma mentioned earlier that we'd long exceeded the million-dollar budget mark.

The reception—to be held in Oliver's ivy-laced botanic second garden—included signature R&D cocktails after our names, hors d'oeuvres made on the premises by Michelin-starred Italian chefs, and five-figure goodie bags designed to make tongues wag.

I wilted inside the heavy garment, swimming in fabric that burrowed into my ribs. I hadn't eaten anything substantial in weeks. Not since Romeo cleaned the house of anything edible. Hettie snuck me breakfast burritos and bread rolls under her clothes, so the cameras wouldn't catch her defying Romeo's order. Otherwise, all the house had to offer was kale, chicken breasts, oatmeal, and misery.

When I reached the edge of the aisle, I stopped. A screen of hanging white orchids curtained me from view. Soon, I'd walk down the aisle and into the arms of a God of War and become a Costa.

Daddy materialized beside me, knotting his arm with mine. He tried to make eye contact as we stood on the long white carpet swathed across Oliver's five-acre back-yard. I kept my eyes trained ahead on the orchids, my molars smashed together.

"Please, Dallas, can't you see I'm devastated?"

Did he really just make it about himself?

"As you should be."

I clutched my white-rose bouquet. The thorns dug into my flesh. Daddy opened his mouth. Luckily, the music cut him off. With Momma and Monica in charge of most of the planning—I cited headaches and nausea all month—I had no idea what song they'd picked. *Ave Verum Corpus* by Mozart. How apt. I'd always associated it with violent carnage in cinema, à la *The Red Wedding*. Even *that* wedding was better than mine.

I didn't know how I managed to put one foot in front of the other, but I did. At some point, Daddy and I sliced through the orchid curtain and came into full view. Gasps and hushed whispers wove across the aisle. Flashing camera lights licked at my skin.

My bridesmaids, Frankie and Sav, carried my dress train while six flower girls from my local church trailed behind, pelting white rose petals at the guests. I gazed down and avoided eye contact with the guests, who rose to their feet, clapping and cheering.

I wondered if Morgan was here. Somewhere in the crowd. Sipping champagne, entertained by how foolish I looked, marrying a man who still worshiped at her altar. In fact, I wondered if Romeo had seen her in the time between the debutante ball and now. The thought made me nauseous. Not because I liked him, but because I refused to be made an even bigger fool than I already was.

I reached the altar. The man I'd last left chained to my bed, covered in whipped cream, stood before me. Powerful, imposing, and larger than life. The imagery sent sudden, uncontrollable giggles through me. I felt my neck flush. Then I peered up, and the laughter died in my throat.

I'd almost forgotten how glorious Romeo Costa was. *Almost.* He wore a sharp tux. His hair—shorter than I'd remembered, trimmed to perfection—was brushed back. His gray eyes—usually flirting with the color blue—appeared almost metallic silver. His face was neutral and blank as an uninspiring painting in a waiting room. When Daddy stepped aside and I positioned myself in front of him, Romeo surprised me by leaning forward, pressing his lips to my jawline.

Only, he wasn't kissing my cheek. That was just a show for our guests. In reality, Romeo whispered in my ear, "Pull any tricks, and I assure you, your reputation won't be the only thing I destroy."

My brain short-circuited for a comeback. Blinking, I recognized the wedding officiant as a local priest from Chapel Falls.

Father Redd began the ceremony. When my turn came to read from the vow book, I rattled off a wedding speech so cliché and so insincere, I was sure my soon-to-be-husband wanted to vomit from the tackiness. Romeo breezed through his portion.

Behind him, Oliver and Zach stood in designer tuxes. Zach radiated impatience, flicking his eyes to his watch without lifting his wrist. Despite his clean-cut charm and lovely manners, something dark lurked beneath his surface. Something just withdrawn enough to hint that he didn't show his true colors to the world. Meanwhile, Oliver— an open book full of colorful annotations—stared straight past me to my bridesmaids. If he thought Frankie was fair game, I had news for him, which I'd break right along with his balls.

Father Redd flipped a page in his officiant's manual. "Do you, Romeo Niccolò Costa, take this woman to be your wife, to live together in holy matrimony, to love her, to honor her, to comfort her, and to keep her in sickness and in health, forsaking all others, for as long as you both shall live?"

Romeo laced his fingers through mine. They were cold and felt like clay. "I do." A charming smile slashed his face, dazzling the audience. It looked completely photoshopped.

"And do you, Dallas Maryanne Townsend, take this man to be your husband, to live together in holy matrimony, to love him, to honor him, to comfort him, and to keep him in sickness and in health, forsaking all others, for as long as you both shall live?"

Love and comfort him? He was lucky not to leave the premises in an ambulance. My new dream was to contribute to his bodily scars with my own art.

"Hmm."

Father Redd cleared his throat, chuckling. "I'll take that as a yes?"

"I do." I spat out the words.

"You may now kiss the bride."

I didn't know what to expect. Perhaps a dignified peck to seal the deal. But Romeo Costa was just full of surprises. Instead, he stepped forward, wrapped my waist with his strong arm, and jerked me into him. With blood-chilling possessiveness, he cupped the front of my throat, dipped my body, and crashed his mouth over mine, exerting punishing force. The gesture declared one thing—*mine*.

In the background, people went wild, cheering and whistling. Laughter, music, and feminine voices raving about the iconic kiss filled the venue.

". . . as epic as his marriage proposal . . ."

". . . never seen a man so crazy in love . . ."

". . . should be a movie . . ."

I was limp in his arms, even when his tongue darted out and pried my lips open, confidently licking, playing, and exploring the inside of my mouth.

This was a statement kiss.

A kiss designed to inform the world I was now his property.

Trespassers will be shot. Or worse.

I held my breath, ignored the slithering heat rolling down my spine that demanded I kiss him back, and waited for him to pull away. I refused to give in and participate in this debacle.

"Your submission is sweeter than whipped cream, *Mrs. Costa*." He drew back, dragging his nose along the bridge of mine. "How's life away from civilization? Learned how to make fire with rocks yet?"

My response came in the form of sinking my teeth into his lower lip until the taste of copper filled my mouth and I met the resistance of muscle and flesh. He used the back of his hand to wipe away the blood, smirking.

"There she is. I was beginning to worry you lost your teeth."

"You like my teeth?" I pretended to cradle his head, ogling him with mock-adoration. "Good, because you're about to meet my claws."

Then, because I wanted badly to hurt him back, I pulled out Madison's ring, which Frankie had given me earlier, twisting it between my fingers. "Maybe you need better cameras, *hubby*. I got hot and bothered while you were MIA, but the fire didn't come from rocks."

Was I actually alluding to having an affair with Madison? It was reckless, dangerous, yet extremely satisfying. The look on Romeo's face, of a man on the cusp of starting a war, flooded me with adrenaline.

Refusing to show him how miserable I'd been the last few weeks, I smiled. "Enjoy our wedding."

The wedding planner herded the guests to the reception area. Oliver von Bismarck's mansion boasted an entire full-sized ballroom. I swear, his place made the Shangri-La look like a Motel 6 lobby. Round tables cloaked in white lace surrounded the dance area. Antique candelabra centerpieces adorned each. Rustic chandeliers, golden fixtures, and dozens of different flowers—all in white—ornamented the room. I wished this event didn't symbolize my demise, so I could appreciate the place for all its splendor.

As soon as I unglued myself from Romeo, Frankie appeared by my side, clutching my arm and anchoring me to safety. She was so beautiful, my eyeballs prickled. She'd better find a good match. A true love after the sacrifice I'd made for her. "I know we hate him, and in a second, I'll get back to stabbing him with my glares, but I thought maybe you'd be comforted to hear Romeo's kiss dampened every panty on the East Coast."

"Not mine," I lied. "Besides, there's a ton of hot guys in this world."

"Saying your husband is hot is like saying Mount Everest is hilly. Bitch is sizzling. I don't know how you touch him without getting blisters."

I didn't have the heart to tell her Romeo had stolen all of my Henry Plotkin books. I also didn't want her to stab him with one of the decorative icicles that kept the vintage champagne bottles chilled. Momma and Daddy joined us. Together, we visited each table from our side and thanked people for gracing us with their presence. Presumably, Romeo did the same with his family, though I mentally checked out, trying to forget he was in the same room with me. It almost worked.

I'd just started to breathe properly—even the numbness in my fingers had gone away—when Daddy hauled me to the Lichts' table. As his best friend from Georgetown, Mr. Licht showed up despite the bad blood with the Costas. He wouldn't pass on an opportunity to prove he was unaffected by the public fiasco.

"Dallas, congratulations, my dear. You look stunning." Mrs. Licht patted the corners of her mouth with a napkin, though she hadn't touched any of the delicious food in front of her.

I nodded, wooden. My gaze pinned to the floor. I couldn't look Madison in the eyes. Madison, who had let me choose my engagement ring. Who once promised me I could turn a room in his condo into my own library.

"Dallas." His voice was impartial, not a trace of anger in it. I wanted to keel over. Even after his archenemy had sullied me, he still had kindness in him. "Look at me, please. I can't . . ." He tossed his napkin onto his plate, rising to his feet. "I can't bear for you to think that I'm mad at you. We weren't really together. I understand."

I dragged my gaze up from the floor. Madison looked so familiar. With his All-American blond hair and brown eyes rimmed green around the fringes. Though I felt nothing romantic toward him, I'd always assumed the feelings would come. That the comfort would bleed into happiness.

"Dallas." He put his hand on my forearm. "Oh, Dal, please. Come with me." He captured my hand. "Let's wash your face."

I let him lead me out of the ballroom. It was equally sweet and deranged of him to assume I'd let water touch my face after having my makeup done for three consecutive hours.

"I don't want to wash my face."

He stopped and turned to me, his hand still interlaced with mine. "Okay. Know what? Let me get you a plate of desserts. That always lifts your mood. Meet me out back."

I felt comfortable sneaking out of my wedding to the back patio of the ballroom and sitting over the banister. After all, I couldn't give one dang about whether someone discovered me with Madison.

The courtyard overlooked a small lake. Swans and ducks glided over the glacial water. Madison appeared with a plate laden with pink and coral macarons, white-chocolate éclairs, and gold-specked fruit tarts. The desserts looked too beautiful to be eaten. Nonetheless, I shoved a macaron down my throat, barely tasting it.

Madison sat beside me. "Better?"

I nodded, squinting at the never-ending rolling green hills and gardens bracketing von Bismarck's property. "I'm really sorry, Mad—"

"Please, no more of this." He patted my knee, smiling. "You and I both know you didn't really cheat on me. We were always an arrangement. Don't saddle yourself with unwarranted guilt. Was I disappointed? Yes. I liked you. I *still* like you, Dal. But you chose who you chose, and I accept that."

Wanting badly to appease him and also unburden myself from the weight of the truth, I blurted out, "But I didn't choose him at all. It was supposed to be one small kiss before I married you. Everything just snowballed, and now I'm stuck with . . . with . . . this *beast*."

It felt good to be childish and authentic. With Madison, my childhood friend, I felt free to be a version of myself that would be thrown from the halls of polite and mature society.

Madison looked like the sky had fallen directly on his head. "Are you telling me you didn't want to marry Costa?"

"No." I tossed my hands up. "Daddy forced me after he caught us. Romeo planned this entire thing. He set me up."

As I explained the chain of events to Madison, I knew in my heart that I wasn't playing with fire, but rather a full-blown dynamite box. But the temptation proved too much. If the slightest chance of Madison freeing me from this arrangement existed, I wanted to seize it.

It took me three minutes to explain everything. After I did, he gathered my hands in his and faced me. "Are you sure you don't want to stay married to him?"

I didn't even need to think about it. "Confident," I said with conviction. "If there's a way out in which my reputation can survive, I'll take it."

Madison bit his lip. "I can't promise anything, but I think there's a way to take him down." Take him down? It all sounded so *Riverdale*. Desperate times called for desperate measures. I made a mental note to bail on Madison's plan if he formed a red circle.

"When will you let me know? Every minute spent in his house is torture."

Especially since he confiscated the carbs.

Madison sighed, plowing his fingers into his hair. "I'm sorry you got caught up in this mess, Dal. Trust me, I never thought anyone could be as spiteful as to seek you out like this."

"Could you call me when—"

"First thing's first, keep an eye on him for me, will you?" he cut straight to business. "I'm sure he's monitoring your devices, so don't send me anything sensitive in texts. Just call, and we'll meet up. Anything you have for me that smells fishy. Whether business-related or regarding his personal life."

Was he . . . recruiting me to bring Romeo down? I struggled to picture my husband getting caught red-handed doing something bad. He was more sophisticated than that. If anything, he was always stupidly in control. Even when he introduced Scott the Co-pilot's face to the airplane's floor, he seemed calm and collected.

Withdrawing my hands from Madison's, I snatched a fruit tart and nibbled on it. "What if I find nothing? He's not exactly an open book."

Madison pretended to look tormented. He really wasn't a good actor. I'd seen better adult productions at Sav's sleepovers.

"Well . . . I mean, depending on how hard you want to nail the son of a gun, you can always . . . *manufacture* an issue." He chewed on his thumbnail, an old habit I always found off-putting. "You know, bring to light the horrible way he treats you. Anything at all that can tarnish his reputation. This is important, Dal. If you want Romeo Costa out of your life, out of *our* lives—"

"My, my, don't you two look adorable together." Slow, sarcastic claps followed the sharp voice. "The Beauty and the Yeast."

Madison *did* look a little like bread dough.

Out strolled my new husband, twirling whisky in a highball glass, his steps long and confident. He'd shed his blazer sometime during the event. The sleeves of his shirt were rolled all the way to his elbows, exposing tan, muscular forearms.

His hair looked slightly disheveled. Maybe Morgan had ruffled it while they disappeared in one of the twenty-three guest rooms together for a quickie. My heart began pounding out of whack after I remembered that, when we'd last parted ways, I'd shown off Madison's engagement ring.

The latter remained seated beside me. Worse—he draped a hand over my knee, leveling Romeo with an undeterred glare. "I have my eye on you, Costa."

"Your eyes are none of my concern. Your arm, however, is another matter. If you still want it attached to the rest of your body, I suggest you remove it from my wife's lap."

"Your *wife*." Madison snorted. Still, he complied, dumping his hands between his legs. "All she is to you is a way to get back at me for strengthening our ties with the DOD and presenting an impeccable defense package that's too hard to walk away from and twenty percent cheaper than what Costa Industries offers."

"First, I suggest you use punctuation. That was one long-ass sentence." Romeo blinked, as if Madison had spoken in another language. "Second, I wasn't finished."

"That so?"

Romeo spat his gum. It was the first time I'd seen him willingly part with the thing. "Consider this my first, last, and final warning. Each time you come close to my wife, I'll break a different bone of yours. I'm thinking of starting with the femur, though subject to change."

Madison shot up. A blush snaked up his neck. "You have some nerve. After all you've done to me and Dallas—"

Stealing Madison's seat, Romeo flicked lint from the sleeve of his shirt. "Please. This past year, there hasn't been one event we've both attended where you didn't end the night inside a leggy blonde who charges by the hour."

Madison's jaw tightened. He moved it back and forth. "Dallas and I had an agreement." Though no such agreement existed, I didn't flinch.

"Interesting." Romeo swathed an arm over my shoulder, his knuckles caressing the side of my throat, making my flesh warm and tingly. "Tell me, Mrs. Costa, are we going to have the same arrangement? Am I allowed to take on mistresses and parade them around town like prized horses?"

I'd rather die than give him permission to screw anyone else. Only because I didn't want him to have fun. "No." I scowled. "You don't deserve a free pass."

"Guess I'll have to make do with you, then, wifey." He returned his attention to Madison. "I'll give you one thing, Licht. You didn't exaggerate where her looks are concerned. She is ravishing." Romeo twisted his face to me, dragging his hot lips across my jawline. "Who could've guessed she is as delicious as she is spirited? My wife tells me you've had your fill."

I shuddered inside my designer wedding gown, both

from anger and arousal. My eyelids dropped, and I swallowed hard.

"No." Madison's reply reeked of resentment and frustration. "I did not."

"Ah. Now I remember." Romeo snapped his fingers, an evil hollow laugh escaping his throat. "She saved herself for you, didn't she? Lucky me."

Madison watched as Romeo scraped his teeth along my jawline, making my nipples strain against my corset.

"You may leave, Licht." Romeo used his free hand to wave him off. "I've put my point across." He scooped my chin, inhaling my neck as he buried his face in the crook. If only I had the strength to stop him, but it felt too good. "Tell me, Shortbread, will I have to wreck whatever ruins are left of poor Madison Licht's life to ensure he keeps his hands off my bride?"

"I'm fond of him."

He grabbed the back of my neck, angling my body down, so I hovered in the air between the banister and the thorny rose bushes below. The only thing keeping me from falling straight into the mouth of a merciless sea of spikes was his kindness, and we both knew he was hardly familiar with the word, let alone the notion.

Sucking in a breath, my eyes fluttered open. Romeo's face hovered less than an inch away from mine. Madison had retired back to the ballroom sometime after Romeo's threat to put him in a wheelchair.

"Let me be clear on one thing, Dallas *Costa*. You belong to me now. Deed done, contingency lifted, deal fully paid. If I catch Madison laying a finger on you again, that finger will be broken. If he kisses you, I'll cut off his lips. If he fucks you . . ." He didn't have to finish the sentence. The sour taste of bile slammed into the back of my throat. Romeo flashed his teeth. "But I trust you'll behave. Even your stupidity has its limits."

"And you? I suppose you're free to run around, cheating on me with Morgan left and right."

"As long as you fulfill your duties as a wife . . ." His hold on me loosened. I could feel myself almost falling. I wanted badly to clutch his shirt, but I refused to show him my vulnerability. "You won't have to worry about anyone else."

Forcing my muscles to loosen, I sucked in a breath. I hovered an inch away from falling. He inclined me all the way down the banister, so most of my body dangled in the air.

Smiling through the pain, I spat into his face, "Worry? I'd deliver you straight to her door as a Christmas gift, given the chance."

"How foolish can you be?" His face was up in mine, the question delivered with genuine curiosity. "Any girl with half a brain would fall to her knees trying to appease me."

"I have an entire brain, and every single cell in it remembers how badly I hate you."

"Madison doesn't love you." He stroked the edges of my jaw. "The only reason he gave you the time of the day today was because he wants you to conspire against me."

"I know." I smiled at him with a lethal dose of poison. "And I'm *interested*."

I could feel it. The moment his fingers itched to let me fall. It was only by a miracle that he pulled both of us up from the banister, righting us on our feet. I panted hard. Cold dew adorned my forehead and arms. Stumbling as far from him as I could, I made sure he never left my line of sight. I didn't trust him. Romeo's face had returned to its normal princely indifference.

"The good news is that we'll have plenty of time to discuss your plans to ruin me on the plane."

A frown touched my lips. "What plane?"

"Why, Shortbread, did you think I wouldn't take you on a honeymoon?" He feigned surprise. "How else would our union appear believable?"

My face fell. I inched back. "That is wildly unnecessary."

He stepped forward, erasing the distance between us again. "As always, we're in disagreement. One must celebrate their change of status. Especially when all of D.C.'s royalty is watching closely."

I tripped another step back. "We can do something local. Go to New York for a weekend, then split to different hotels."

He advanced, a predator zeroing in on his next meal. "Had I thought we could get away with it, I'd have gladly disposed of you back home and gone my merry way. Nonetheless, you, my dear wife, spent every waking moment from the day we met trying to get rid of me, loudly and publicly. Ergo, we will board my plane to Paris for a long weekend in two hours, so get inside and say your goodbyes."

My jaw nearly dropped. He couldn't be serious. I didn't even get to spend time with Frankie, Momma, and Sav. Never mind that. There was still a twelve-pound cake with my name on it. *Literally.*

Finally, there was no more room left for me to retreat. My back crashed against the glass of the patio door. "But . . . I don't have a suitcase. And . . . and . . . clothes."

"Cara packed you everything you need." He pinned me against the glass, arms bracketing my head, fingers staining the glass. "Whipped cream excluded."

"She doesn't know me."

"Hate to break it to you, but there's more mystery in the contents of a hot dog than the contents of that little head of yours."

"What about my passport?"

"Your mother gave it to me before the ceremony."

Shoot. She probably thought she'd done me a favor.

"I need to rest. The last few weeks have been so stressf—"

"Our mothers did all the work. You've been resting your entire life. This trip is happening whether you want it or not. Now go say your goodbyes."

"I hate you." I tried stomping on his foot, but he was quicker, pulling back.

"How unfortunate." He leaned forward, lips skating over mine. "See, I don't hate you one bit. In fact, you're prime entertainment for me. Like a dozen circus clowns emerging from a tiny car. You're an aerial act, Dallas. When you succeed—I'm impressed. When you fail—I'm amused. But I never, ever care enough to give you hate. That would require you to be my equal."

His mouth was on mine now, touching but not yet kissing. My heart jackhammered through my rib cage, threatening to tear my chest, leap between us, and splatter on his pristine snowy shirt, blood and all. My eyes slammed shut of their own accord. My lips prepared to find his almost-familiar heat.

But instead of being cocooned once again in his addictive hold, a breeze of cool air slapped my face. I opened my eyes and found Romeo two steps away, sneering down at me.

"So naïve." He *tsked.* "You're going to be spectacularly fun to break."

Chapter Twenty-Five

Ollie vB: The bride looked exquisite.

Romeo Costa: Bleach your eyeballs immediately. She wasn't yours to look at.

Ollie vB: So did her sister.

Romeo Costa: Jailbait.

Ollie vB: Come on, Rom. We both know I'm too rich to see a prison cell from the inside.

Zach Sun: Can someone remove the ghost of David Bowie from the chat?

Romeo Costa removed Ollie vB from the chat.

Zach Sun: Why do I always feel like I need a long, scorching shower after talking to Ollie?

Romeo Costa: Because he is sexual harassment packed into a Tom Ford suit?

Zach Sun: Is Denver excited about Paris?

Romeo Costa: I've met cats more excited about their baths.

Zach Sun: Have you considered trying to get along with her?

Romeo Costa: Not once.

Zach Sun: Is there a long version to this answer?

Romeo Costa: I think that ship sailed the day I dragged her by the ear to a state she doesn't know, to live in a house she doesn't like, and marry a man she actively hates.

Ollie vB has entered the chat.

Romeo Costa: How did that just happen?

Ollie vB: I have a software engineer on retainer. @ZachSun hooked me up a few months ago when I had to deal with a dick-pic crisis.

Zach Sun: A crisis aptly titled .Mobi Dick.

Romeo Costa: ON RETAINER?

Ollie vB: @ZachSun, your copywriting talent is heartbreakingly wasted.

Romeo Costa: I repeat: ON RETAINER?

Ollie vB: You'd be surprised how often I get myself into hot water with some of the content I share.

Romeo Costa: Something tells me I would not be surprised at all.

Ollie vB: So, is little Townsend taken?

Romeo Costa: LITTLE TOWNSEND IS STILL IN FUCKING COLLEGE.

Ollie vB: I hate to say this, Costa, but you've always been a prude. Right, Zach?

Zach Sun left the chat.

Romeo Costa left the chat.

Ollie vB: So dramatic. I bet my fifth yacht the girl is eighteen.

Chapter Twenty-Six

Romeo

Dallas Townsend reminded me of a phoenix, rising from the ashes of her poor decisions. An inspiration to the idling masses. In tonight's episode, Shortbread drank herself into a stupor. Ever since I'd broken the tragic news of our impending luxurious honeymoon, she'd guzzled down champagne, slurring her thanks to our guests while zigzagging through the room. Aside from her agreeable looks, I'd met office furniture more lovely to spend time with.

It didn't help that she embarrassed us both by channeling her inner designated drunk aunt at a Christmas dinner, babbling loud enough to be heard from the South Pole. Her family didn't interfere with the spectacle. Shep conducted business, whereas Natasha dedicated all her efforts into finding a suitable match for the other menace she'd spawned. And Franklin . . . Franklin knew exactly how drunk Dallas was. She let it happen, aware that I was allergic to public scandals.

That I managed to shuttle Shortbread into my private jet without losing an eye was nothing short of a miracle. We were Paris-bound, and the excitement level sat somewhere between a three-day-long calculus marathon and a funeral.

"I think I'm going to throw up," Dallas announced, clutching her stomach, still in her bridal gown. Her face was extraordinarily green for someone who wasn't the Grinch.

"Shocking." I flipped the page of my newspaper.

She moaned, tossing her head back on the headrest. "I'm pretty sure I'm about to vomit on this dress."

It appeared as though she suffered from alcohol poisoning. Just when I thought choosing unattractive, sixty-something pilots would ensure an event-free journey.

I dog-eared a page and moved onto the next. "No need to narrate your existence aloud. Truly, no part of me cares."

"Aren't you going to help me?"

"No."

"Well, then. I guess I'll just puke all over your private jet and stink it to eternity."

With a groan, I slid off my seat and hoisted her up in my arms, carrying her to the bathroom honeymoon-style. She was lifeless in my embrace. I wondered if it'd be a good idea to make a U-turn so I could get her straight to the hospital.

Then, in her signature Shortbread whine, she issued demands. "Make sure you pull all my hair up so nothing gets stuck on it . . . oh, and the dress. Take my dress off."

The privilege. The sass. The blind belief that the world owed her something. She was fine.

"Try not to drink like the future of this nation depends on it next time." I plopped her on the floor before we reached the toilet, flipped her on her stomach, and began unfastening her dress. And there was a *lot* of dress to get rid of. She swam in fabric. It took ten minutes to release her from the buttons, zippers, and frills.

Dallas being Dallas, she wiggled, clawing at the thin carpet. "Faster! I can't hold it in anymore."

"Is everything okay?" The stewardess poked her head in from the kitchen, where she prepared fresh fruit and mimosas. It must have looked like I was wrestling a wild boar from that angle.

"Yes."

"Excuse me, sir, but it doesn't look—"

"Am I paying you for your eyesight or to clean my toilets and prepare my snacks? While we're at it, toss the mimosas in the garbage. The last thing my wife needs is more alcohol in her bloodstream." All my employees, top to bottom, signed NDAs. A favorable arrangement, seeing as my manners lacked without a *Bloomberg Finance* mic directed straight to my face.

When Dallas finally escaped her dress, clad only in a strapless beige bra and matching thong, I rolled the elastic off her wrist and tried tying her hair up. "No time!" She *punched me in the face*, frantic. "I need to puke."

I dragged her to the bathroom, flipped open the toilet, and gathered her hair in my hand from behind while balancing her with my other palm. She began projectile vomiting everywhere. As I towered over her, cradling her head so she wouldn't break her spine and introduce me to a world of legal pain, I questioned what kind of idiot married a woman like her. I was normally ruthlessly rational. What on Earth made me think this was a good idea? Even sticking it to Madison Licht wasn't a good enough reason. Shortbread was the human answer to a category-six hurricane. Whatever she touched, she destroyed.

After a few minutes of emptying her gut, she collapsed into a ball on the floor, hugging the toilet. Tears streamed down her cheeks. Her hue shifted from green to dead white. I escaped the bathroom to bring her water and

Advil, purely because I didn't want our next stop to be an emergency one at an Irish hospital.

She accepted my offerings without gratitude. After washing down the pills, she shot me a glare. "Why didn't you bring my toothbrush and toothpaste?"

"For the same reason I haven't drawn you a bath and trimmed your toenails. I'm not your maid." I tossed her empty water bottle in the trash. Not even Oliver had gotten this level of care from me when he'd shown up on my steps shit-faced after a Porcellian Club initiation at Harvard.

She scowled at me through bloodshot eyes, still on the floor. "My mouth reeks."

"The rest of you is not so attractive, either."

"Toothbrush."

"Manners," I instructed in the same grating tone.

"Screw you." Perhaps she considered this a step up, since she didn't scrape my eyes out while she said it.

"Regretfully, I decline. I'll be reading the *Wall Street Journal* outside." I strode away.

"This is all your fault," she cried to my back. "I wouldn't have gotten drunk if it weren't for you." I didn't break my pace. "Oh, fine. *Please*, give me my toothbrush. Happy now?"

I wasn't happy now. I probably wouldn't be happy *ever* after my unfortunate decision to marry this woman. But apparently, I'd found my heartless sociopath limit, because I hauled myself to her suitcase, fished out a pack of toothbrushes along with a tube of Colgate, and brought them to Dallas. I let her shower, brush her teeth, and get back to herself while I skimmed financial news in my seat, sipping lukewarm coffee. She emerged thirty minutes later, hair damp and face scrubbed pink, wearing an MIT hoodie she must've stolen from my suitcase. She seemed grumpy and dazed as she fell onto the couch beside me, digging into the fresh fruit and banh mi.

From the corner of my eye, I watched her polish off two trays of sandwiches and a Diet Coke. Once she finished, she peered around and sighed. "I'm not tired."

I kept my eyes trained on the newspaper. Maybe if I didn't move, she'd think I was dead and stop talking.

"Let's make out."

Since she was still obviously and acutely drunk, and because eau de vomit wasn't a scent I found personally enchanting, I ignored her less-than-stellar offer.

"Come on." Shortbread jumped to her bare feet, padding to me. She flicked the newspaper in my hand away and straddled me. "I'm actually tanked up enough to tolerate you right now. This is a once-in-a-lifetime offer. Maybe getting an orgasm will help me fall asleep." She draped her arms around my neck.

"Give me one reason to help you."

She offered a toothy grin. "Happy wife, happy life?"

Something occurred to me then. "Have you ever had an orgasm?"

"I think I accidentally gave myself one a year ago." Her big, innocent eyes widened. It was in moments like this when I remembered what had lured me into stealing her. Where else in America could I unearth such a blank page for me to doodle, scribble and mold as I pleased?

That piqued my curiosity. "Doing what?"

"Riding a dirt bike."

I flattened my lips so as not to laugh.

"Don't laugh." She furrowed her brows, slapping my chest. "My whole family was there. A moan slipped out, and Momma thought I sprained my ankle. I had to pretend it *did* hurt and even faked a limp for an hour. It was very distressing."

Was I really about to laugh for the first time since age four because of this little headache?

"Get off my lap."

"Or you could get me off *on* your lap." She wiggled her brows. And her ass.

"You're too drunk. Not to mention, I'm not drunk enough."

Her intoxication was the only thing standing in my way of making her come on my fingers. Sadly, the fact that I'd seen that mouth purge out fully digested pieces of macarons, tarts, and custards did not deter me from wanting it wrapped around my cock. I didn't usually lower my standard to *breathing: optional*—that was more Ollie's jam—but I found Shortbread strangely seductive. When Shep had told me his daughter was irresistible, I'd wanted to chuckle. Now I was more worried than amused.

"Can't you see? Me being drunk is the best thing that could happen to us." She slapped her hands over my chest. "Let's have sex. I won't even mind that it's with you. And I've been wanting to lose my V-card for a while." Now wasn't the time to tell her that her V-card would be wasted on my fingers—or my tongue, if I was feeling charitable.

"Evacuate my lap."

Usually, I got off on being in complete and meticulous control. But with Dallas, for a reason unfathomable to yours truly, it felt like a burden to stay in character.

She dragged her pussy—clothed only with a flimsy thong—along my crotch. Of course, I was hard. All she needed was to exist in the same state as me to make my blood migrate to my dick.

She rolled her hips, her slit dragging across the length of my cock again. "Why should I listen to you when you never listen to me?"

My jaw flexed. "Because I'm very close to obtaining an annulment and sending you back to Chapel Falls to be married off to a farm boy."

She smacked my chest again. "Take advantage of me, goddammit."

I wanted to grab the back of her neck, and kiss the shit out of her, and fuck her through our clothes until she orgasmed hard enough to scream. Until she lost her voice. To then guide her down between my thighs and come on that elegant upturned nose, youthful freckles, and big Disney-animal eyes. But I didn't have it in me to do something she might regret later. Though I couldn't be accused of ever being in the same zip code as chivalry, dubious consent was where I drew the line. Especially when it was pitifully obvious that I'd have her on my terms sooner rather than later.

I was about to wrestle her to the sofa when she fell face-first into the crook of my neck. "If you're planning to suck my blood—"

A soft snore broke through my unfinished threat. Then I felt her drool. On my neck.

Jesus Christ.

She'd fallen asleep on me. With my hard-on still nestled between her legs. The smart thing to do would be to put her on the couch and get back to my business. I was going to do it, too. Stand up and rid myself of her.

Only, I didn't.

Perhaps because I couldn't risk her stirring awake and launching into another episode of verbal diarrhea. Or maybe because it wasn't the worst thing in the world to feel her pussy radiating warmth straight into my dick. Whatever the reason, I let her sleep on me. Reading the *Wall Street Journal* and thanking my unlucky stars that, at the very least, Zach and Oliver weren't here to give me shit about how undomesticated my new wife was.

I'd tame her, all right.

After all—I'd already caged her.

Chapter Twenty-Seven

Romeo

Four hours later, the lull of sanity came to an abrupt end. Shortbread was awake and quite sober, judging by the time it took her to tumble to the carpet in a panic, kicking my shins as she realized she'd slept on top of me.

"Get off me," she roared from her place on the floor.

I flipped another page of my newspaper. I'd been reading the same article for approximately three months. It was hard to concentrate with her pressed against my cock. I normally prided myself on being immune to women's charms. Then again, it had been a while since I spent so much time next to a gorgeous one.

"I was never on top of you." And never would be, for that matter.

Shortbread frowned, crossed her ankles, then slapped her forehead. The memories of the last twelve hours must've rushed through her system. I hoped she remembered everything. That we were now legally married. That she'd drunk enough to fill a bathtub. That she'd vomited on everything but the plane's wings, propositioned me with the finesse of a telemarketer, then passed out on top of me.

"I think I'm going to throw up again just from the memory of rubbing myself against you." She covered her mouth, visibly shivering. "I hope I didn't catch an STD from my proximity to you."

"Say all your prayers tonight, and I might just spare you my genital warts." I yawned, though internally, I itched to yell at her that, if she was so worried about sexually transmitted diseases, she should be thankful she didn't end up with Madison A Pack of Condoms A Night Licht. The man had enough notches on his belt to make a pasta sieve.

She eyed me with disbelief. "Be serious. Have you checked lately?"

"No. But I haven't been sexually active recently, either."

She paused, frowning at me. "You haven't?" I shook my head, unsure why I'd chosen to explain myself to this utter hot mess of a human. "Not even Morgan?"

Especially not Morgan. I wouldn't touch Morgan if the world ran out of women and the two of us had to repopulate it. Civilization had a good run, and frankly, it blew it.

"*No one.*"

The wheels began churning in that pretty head of hers, but I didn't care enough to wonder what she was thinking. Whatever it was, suffice to say I'd be in complete disagreement with it.

"Don't tell me you're actually considering being faithful." She pulled a face like it was a bad thing. Was her type cheating scumbags? That would explain why she still pined for Licht.

"A hole is a hole. Might as well be yours."

Tipping her head back, she laughed joylessly. "No wonder your parents named you after the epitome of romantic heroes. They must've known what a dreamboat you'd be."

"My parents named me Romeo after my father, who was named after his father." The buck stopped with me, though. No more Romeo Costas. The world could thank me later.

She bit her lip, still on the floor. "I have been wondering about . . . sex things."

I rested the newspaper on my lap, sending her a leveled look. "Is that an invitation?"

"Will you . . . RSVP?" She bit down a grin. Another laugh fizzed in my throat. When she wasn't a waste of space, she was surprisingly bearable.

I arched a brow. "Is the host still under the influence?"

Her cheeks colored pink. "No."

"Will you try to kill me?" I asked slowly, like a parent chiding a child.

"Not in this instance."

A beat of silence passed between us. I was highly aware of the stewardess busying herself in the kitchen, pretending like she wasn't eavesdropping on our bizarre conversation. I was no voyeur, but I wasn't anxious about the middle-aged woman watching, either.

Tossing the newspaper aside, I patted my knee. "Come sit on my lap."

"Manners," she said, in the same tone I'd used for her toothbrush demand.

It was on the tip of my tongue to tell Dallas to learn about the pleasures of sex through Tumblr and a dildo. Then Zach's words drifted into my memory. *Try to make an effort.* There was no reason to butt horns with this delectable, strong-headed, simple creature before me. Our short time spent together would be more pleasant if I humored her every once in a while.

"Please." The word tasted foreign. I pulled both corners of my lips up, trying my hand at a smile.

"Ugh, stop making that face. It looks like you're planning to eat me." I *was* planning to eat her, though not in the way her innocent head thought. She peeked around, disoriented, completely missing the fact that there was a stewardess behind her. "Oh, whatever. Life's too short, and if anyone ever asks, I'll deny ever getting close to you." She stood and made her way to me. Shortbread draped herself across my lap, blinking up at me expectantly. "What now?"

There were a few options, all of them filthy and depraved, but I figured the safest route to take would be to leave her begging for more. And that meant postponing my own release and prepping her for the future. She would have to adhere to my certain tastes and rules, some of them I had yet to explore myself.

My eyes dropped to the MIT hoodie. "Did I give you permission to wear my sweatshirt?"

"Well, no, but—"

"Take it off. Now."

She opened her mouth, about to argue. I tipped an eyebrow up, daring her to. "Right. Right." She pursed her lips, catching the hem of my sweatshirt and pulling it off, remaining only in her bra. "I guess that's . . . sexy talk, right?"

I couldn't decide if she was adorable or pitiful. More than likely, she was both. But as her magnificent breasts stared back at me, barely contained by her strapless bra and begging for attention, I forgot whom they were attached to altogether. Seizing her by the ass, I pulled her to grind against my cock. She jerked forward, her face an inch from mine.

"This is what you do to me." I lifted her up by the ass, then slammed her back down on my cock. She gasped, her eyes flaring. "I've run beyond the scope of disliking you, Shortbread. In fact, I should invent a new word altogether for what I feel for you. And still, I cannot, for the life of me, resist your temptation."

Instead of quarreling, Shortbread seemed to get the hang of it and shut me up with a dirty, wet kiss. It was all tongue and teeth. An amateur kiss, like a fawn trying its luck on its legs for the first time. Clumsy, yet magical. She didn't even draw back to take a single breath. Her tongue found mine, and she was no longer timid and unsure. She wanted this. Trembling, her hands roamed everywhere. My face, my hair, my shoulders, my pecs, my *scars*. They lingered over the jagged, pronounced skin, and I knew she wanted to know what happened.

My mouth moved south from her lips to her chin, then down to her throat and collarbone, leaving hot, wet kisses everywhere it landed. She tipped her head back and groaned. Her fingers gripped my hair, tugging too hard, too desperately. I yanked her bra down to her waist, popping her tits free.

"We're not alone." She panted, gyrating on my cock. I knew I would regret it when we landed and my balls turned the color of blueberries, but I couldn't stop myself.

"She won't breathe a word. She's under contract." I groaned into her skin, catching her nipple between my teeth and tugging at it until she held her breath.

I felt the airplane lower and knew we must have neared Paris. However, neither the stewardess nor the pilots were dumb enough to approach me while I was busy devouring Dallas's tits like they were my very last meal. I licked and sucked and tugged and scraped at her pale-pink nipples, cupping her tits and giving them a tender slap every now and then. My dick pulsated between her legs. I could tell her clit was pressing over my strained zipper because the friction was driving her crazy.

Her head lolled from side to side. "Oh, Lord. This is so . . . so . . ." But she couldn't find the right word, and I was in no hurry to encourage her to talk.

"Sir . . ." A voice drifted from the background. It was distinctively male, which meant the stewardess didn't want to deal with me herself. She'd sent a pilot. "We're fast approaching Le Bourget. In fact, we're scheduled to land in fifteen minutes and already got the green light from the—"

"No," I said with conviction, my mouth enclosed around Dallas's entire tit. I covered most of her innocence with my arms, but I still didn't like that he hovered next to us like a creep. "Leave."

"Sir, we have to prepare for landi—"

"No, we don't." I lifted my head from between Shortbread's chest, shooting daggers at him with my eyes. "My plane, my rules. We have enough fuel to circle around for another hour."

"An *hour*? That's a waste of—"

"Your entire being is a waste. Can't you see I'm pleasuring my wife? Either you find your way back into the cockpit and circle around Paris until we're done, or I'll kick you out of here myself."

He bolted back into the cockpit, where, I assumed, the stewardess also hid for the remainder of the flight while I showered Dallas's tits with kisses, licks, and sucks.

She giggled as soon as he left and thrust her breasts in my face, basking in the attention. "You're so awful."

"I don't remember you standing up for dear Paddy when I told him to turn the plane around."

I dove right back to doing what appeared to be working best for me and my wife—me driving her to the edge of orgasm without actually taking her to her destination point, and her giggling and pulling at my hair until I went bald.

When the plane landed an hour later, Dallas's chest was red, raw, and full of marks. It was also covered by my MIT hoodie and a coat I threw on her, just in case. Overall, not the best flight I'd had by a long mile. But at least, unlike the one we'd shared from Georgia, I didn't nearly kill anyone.

Which reminded me . . . I hoped, wherever Scott was, he remembered his new life motto.

Never touch what belonged to Romeo Costa Jr.

Chapter Twenty-Eight

Dallas

I didn't have many expectations for my Parisian honeymoon. And *still*, my husband managed to disappoint me. After we landed in Paris, the most romantic city in the world, Romeo and I checked in to the extravagant honeymoon suite at Le Bristol Paris.

What I should've done was tear off his hoodie and rinse away the flush from our earlier encounter on the plane. Instead, I twirled my suitcase by its handle, admiring Montmartre through the open terrace doors. "Do you want to do brunch, then hit some tourist spots?"

Already, Romeo stripped off his tux jacket, laying another crisp suit on our bed. "I have back-to-back meetings with some clients and an old university friend." He was leaving me to fend for myself on our *honeymoon*?

Since trying to appeal to his MIA conscience proved futile, I settled on another approach. The whipped cream tactic. "Sounds good." I shrugged, unzipping my suitcase by the foot of the bed. Cara had packed me enough lingerie to seduce the entire French nation. "I'll see you around when I see you around, I guess."

He stalled in front of the bathroom, scars peeking past his unbuttoned dress shirt, and produced his phone, tossing it into my hands. "Put your number in here. The last thing I need is for you to get lost."

With any luck, I'd be kidnapped for ransom à la *Taken*. Surely, the kidnappers would be better company. I punched in my number, volleying his phone back.

He pressed dial and killed the call when my ringtone pierced the air. *Such trust issues.* "Good girl."

"Bad husband."

"Stop pretending you want to spend time with me any more than I want to spend time with you."

Pathetically, I *did* want to spend time with him. I missed human interaction. I wouldn't exactly define him as human, but he came close . . . ish.

Once he sprung into the shower, I shimmied into a pencil skirt, silk blouse, and sheer black pantyhose with a red line in front. Then I trotted to the nightstand, flipping open his wallet. He'd never offered a substitute to the credit card he'd canceled, so I interpreted his wallet laying out as an open invitation to help myself. And help myself I did. By the time he finished showering, I was long gone, my phone turned off, his Centurion Card in tow.

First, I treated myself to a four-course lunch on Champs-Élysées. When I couldn't stomach more, I spread the wealth, metaphorically and literally, footing the bill for every patron on the premises. After that, a cab escorted me to Rue Saint-Honoré, where I bought myself a few humble wedding presents in the form of three Hermès bags. Since I couldn't possibly embarrass my new beau by purchasing one of the more afford-able (read: less obnoxiously expensive) Birkins, I had no choice but to swing for the respectable limited-edition ones. 120K a pop multiplied by three. An actual bargain. No wonder I returned to purchase one for Momma and two for Frankie.

From Hermès, I moved to Dior, then Chanel, before making my last stop at Balmain. But it would be inhumane to leave without supporting the local designers, so I ended up dropping some serious cash on one-of-a-kind boutique finds, too. The exhausting ordeal lasted ten hours, during which my phone remained off and the Black Card worked out like Tracy Anderson. I'd ironed close to seven-hundred-thousand dollars before hailing a taxi around nine at night.

Paris still buzzed with activity. Dazzling lights glittered like fireflies in the dark. Loved-up couples swarmed the sidewalks. They held hands. Laughed. Fell deeper in love. Did things I'd never do. Things as unattainable as kissing the sun. Jealousy impaled my heart. All the money in the world couldn't buy me what they had. Genuine, content love.

The taxi stopped at the hotel entrance. I tipped five hundred euros and slid out, wrestling dozens of bags. A bellboy rushed to my rescue. He unburdened my arms and transferred my purchases into a golden luggage cart, trailing me. The easy, measured *clicks* of my heels as they slapped the marble lobby didn't fool me. I knew what awaited me in the suite. A furious husband. I envisioned Romeo cracking his knuckles and licking his lips, waiting to punish me. Once I scurried into the elevator, I switched my phone on. Just as I'd suspected, three missed calls flashed across my screen, along with numerous texts.

Romeo Costa: I'm done with my meetings. Where are you?

Romeo Costa: Very typical of you to give me the silent treatment the only time I do not wish for you to shut up.

Romeo Costa: Answer your phone.

Romeo Costa: 200K? Shopping? Have you no concept of what money means?

Romeo Costa: $700,000 IS A WHOLE FUCKING HOUSE.

Oh, boy. He'd used profanity. He *never* used profanity. Somebody wasn't looking at the glass half-full. That card had a 1.5% cash back reward on it. I'd earned him $10,500—and Daddy once complained that I'd flunked algebra.

The elevator pinged open. I stumbled into the hall on wobbly legs. Now that it was time to face the music, I was reminded of how tone-deaf it was to spend enough money to buy an impressive mansion in most states, just to spite my rude husband.

The bellboy wheeled my shopping bags behind me, unaware of the storm brewing. It took four tries to slide my keycard into its slot. As expected, when I flung the door open, Romeo sat in the common area, legs folded at the ankles over a table, chewing gum and enjoying whisky with his suit half undone. His glacial expression didn't change at the sight of me breezing in with half the contents of a Chanel store behind me.

Resting his Macallan on a recent *Bloomberg* issue, he fished change from his front pocket and stood, stuffing a fistful of bills into the bellboy's hand. With a parting thanks, the kid went his merry way, shutting the door with a deadly click. It was just me and Romeo now. Standing in front of one another like two enemies before a duel.

Romeo's languid body language jacked up my vigilance. He cracked one of his rare yet vicious smiles. "Have a good day, sweetheart?"

Would I ever look him in the eye without feeling like I sat on a roller coaster, just about to tip over the edge?

"Fine." I scuttered to the mini bar, collecting an Evian. "Yours?"

"Good. Been anywhere interesting?"

I shrugged, my back to him. Weren't my shopping bags a telltale sign? After draining half, I set the water beside Romeo's whisky when his palm curled around my throat. He applied gentle pressure, sloping my face up so our gazes clashed.

His stony grays penetrated my skull. "I'll ask again, and this time you'll give me a full, satisfying answer. Where have you been, Dallas Costa?"

"Shopping. Where else?"

"Somewhere discreet, where you can spread those nice legs for someone else." His lips hovered a breath away from mine. "Someone like Madison."

Unease slithered down my spine. "Madison?" Romeo's jaw locked. He tore himself from me, stalking to the bedroom. I hated that I trailed him. That my curiosity got the best of me. "What are you talking about?"

"I do hope, for his sake, you fake orgasms better than you do innocence. Don't pretend not to know Madison is occupying the suite two doors down." He faced me. For the first time, a distant cousin of angst swept past his eyes. He was still the same aloof Romeo. But something else lurked beneath the surface, too. A glimpse of boyishness. Uncertainty you'd find on a child's face when dropped off at a new school for the first time.

"I didn't know Madison is in Paris." It was the truth. "How do you know he's here?"

He gave me a *how do you think* look.

I closed my eyes, digging the heels of my palms into my eye sockets. "You're having him followed."

Lord. What had happened between these two?

"Your talent at natural deduction is unparalleled. Are you sure you'd like to keep your major as English Lit when there's so much more you can contribute to the world of mathematics?"

"I told you—I didn't know he was here."

"That would be convincing had you not told me less than twenty-four hours ago you two were conspiring against me. *And* flashed me his engagement ring."

Oh, screw you.

I squeezed past him, scurrying to the bathroom. He followed me, his steps unhurried, his broad shoulders lax.

"Did he steal your ex-girlfriend or something?" I yanked a brush from the vanity and jerked it through my hair. "I know you're not jealous because you give one dang about me, so it must be something else."

"Madison lacks the ability to steal a grain of sand from my backyard, let alone an entire human." His intense stare snared mine through the mirror's reflection. "What is he doing here?"

No clue. But I already knew he wouldn't accept that answer.

"My guess? Playing with your psyche." I sighed, hating to throw Madison under the bus. But I didn't want said bus to run over me a hundred times until it pancaked me to the street. Anyway, Madison was a douchebag. Coming here was provocative and in poor form. He'd placed both of us in danger. It was time I fended for myself—and *only* for myself.

"Perhaps I should beat him to the punch and take your virginity before he does. What do you say?" He advanced toward me. I swiveled, realizing I'd pinned myself against the vanity. My lower back dug into its marble. Romeo was flushed against me in seconds, his hand between my skirt-clad thighs. It was amazing how quickly my body submitted to him, in complete contrast to how my brain fought him every step of the way. I clutched the countertop behind me.

"What do you say?" With a savage sneer, Romeo claimed my lips with his, kissing me hard. He slid his gum into my mouth, and though I'd normally find the gesture distasteful, if not downright gross, I let it rest between my teeth. "Should I show you how it's done?"

I clamped down on the gum, refusing to degrade myself but unwilling to stop him, either.

He dropped to his knees, hiked up my skirt, and tucked it into the waistband of my underwear. I gasped when he tore my designer pantyhose, ripping them at the center, and dragged my panties to the side. He dragged his hot tongue up my slit.

"Ohhh."

Romeo's teeth grazed my pussy. "Or has it been snatched by Madison already?"

He thrust his tongue between my lips, striking my nerves. It felt like he was French kissing me down *there*. Lapping in a sensual rhythm. My knees turned to water, heat spiraled in my core, and my nipples pearled. *Oh, Lord.* It felt better than anything I'd ever experienced. *Definitely* better than the dirt bike.

Romeo removed his tongue from inside me, sucking on my clit now. "Answer me."

All I could do was moan as my first-ever orgasm curled like ivy around my ankles, riding up the rest of my body.

He drove his tongue into me, massaging my clit with his thumb. "Did he take your innocence?"

I knew what he was doing. Tearing me apart. Making sure he destroyed my hymen. And still, every rational thought fled my brain.

I struggled to conjure words. "No, no, I swear. I haven't seen him today."

"Better safe than sorry, I suppose." His tongue sank deep inside me. I arched my back, dropped my head, and moaned so loud I skated on the edge of screaming.

"Ahhhhh."

"I bought the cow. Only fair I get the milk." He explored the terrain—*me*. I felt the tip of his tongue find resistance. Pain accompanied the pressure, but so did pleasure. So much pleasure, I thought I'd die if he stopped. I was so sleek, so wet for him, my lust dripped down my thighs, past my knees.

"Please." My knuckles turned white around the counter. "Please, I'm close."

Another thrust. Then another. Then another.

The climax seized every muscle in my body. Ivy-laced. Head to toe. An odd sensation—of floating in warm water—conquered me. I rocked back and forth against his face, unraveling inch by delicious inch.

A shrill chime clawed through the haze. Just like that, Romeo pulled away, rising to his feet. He pressed his phone to his ear and wiped his mouth with the back of his hand. Pink streaked his tongue and lips. Another trophy of my innocence stained his left cheek, too.

My blood.

Wolfish satisfaction touched his lips. "He's lucky he didn't touch you." His fingers curved around my neck, drawing my ear to his lips. "Or I'd have killed him and made you watch."

Sticky desire glazed my thighs. Probably my blood, too, but I didn't dare drop my eyes to confirm. With Romeo's tongue a safe distance from my sex, my panties had snapped back. Most definitely stained. Most definitely another trophy for my husband.

I was no longer a virgin.

He did it. He claimed me.

Romeo frowned, pressing his phone to his ear. "Did you triple check?"

My pulse charged across my skin. I thought my heart would explode into red confetti in my chest. Why was I so anxious? I had nothing to hide. I'd spent my evening with an army of salesmen. Romeo slid his phone into his pocket, observing me with detached dissatisfaction. As if nothing had happened between us just seconds ago. Like he hadn't taken something so precious from me.

"Wash yourself and put something on. We're leaving."

"You had me followed?" Anger robbed me of my breath. Never in my entire life had I been subjected to such misogynistic behavior. Even in the small, religious town I grew up in.

Romeo turned, headed for his wallet and keycard.

I snatched the hairbrush and pursued him, shoulders quaking with the remainders of my orgasm and fresh, hot rage. "Answer me!"

But he didn't. He just . . . *didn't*. And in that wretched moment, I was so mad, so upset, so lost in this twisted universe he'd tucked me into, I swung the brush back and launched it at him. It crashed into his triangle back with a *thwack!* and tumbled to the floor. He stopped moving. I stopped breathing.

What had I done?

Assaulted your husband.

I'd never hit anyone before. Ever.

It seemed like an eternity passed before he twisted to face me. His eyes turned the color of ash, dead and dusky.

"I . . . I didn't mean to . . ." The rest of the sentence lodged in my throat. I tripped backward as he advanced toward me. There was no anger in his posture. Just measured strides, sensible and proficient. I matched each forward step with one foot back. When my spine thumped against the wall, his arms boxed me in. He fingered my chin, tilting my face up. His hot breath skated down my flesh. He smelled like me. Or rather, like what he'd done to me. A shaky inhale rippled my throat, and I swallowed the gum he'd disposed in my mouth.

"Let's get one thing straight, my beautiful, unhinged wife. Seeing as your ex-fiancé would like my head speared into a dagger on his wrought-iron gate, I will stop at nothing to ensure you and Madison aren't out for my throat. Don't confuse my desire to eat out your cunt with affection. Those two have nothing to do with one another. I will destroy you at the drop of a hat if you show real, potent disloyalty to me."

"I'm not—"

His thumb grazed my collarbone, halting my protest. "As for the shopping . . . This is an open invitation for you to burn my money to the ground, but if you purposefully refuse my calls and shut off your phone, you will be punished. Last but not least, in this marriage, we do not lay a hand on each other without consent. This also applies to inanimate objects, pets, and small babies. Do. Not. Throw. Anything. At. Me. Am I clear?"

I couldn't believe he'd let me off with a warning after I'd narrowly avoided cracking his skull open with the hairbrush. I mean, the momentum was there. The world of shotput had missed out on a natural talent.

Though he'd made himself more than clear, that didn't mean I accepted the terms he laid out for me. But now wasn't the time to argue. Not when he could call the police on me.

Face turned sideways, I answered by freeing myself from his grasp.

"I swear to God, Dallas—"

"You have no God." I tried pushing him away. He captured my wrists in his hands and flattened me against the wall with his weight. His eyes breathed fire. The sharp lines of his jaw were so rigid, I feared his muscles would leap through his skin.

"Whether you like it or not, we are married. That won't change. And the unsavory consequence of my employment includes a real risk to both our lives. Your phone stays on, charged, and ready for use. At all times. As for your questionable lifestyle choices—"

"My worst lifestyle choice is being married to you. Actually . . ." I tried and failed to free myself. "That wasn't a choice."

"Is it really so horrible being married to me?" He seemed puzzled. As if the idea of not being desired was completely foreign to him. I guess it was.

"Yes. *Yes!*" Heavy desperation latched onto my throat. "Are you kidding? Your whole existence gives me whiplash. You force me into marriage, drag me into your house, desert me, threaten me. You eat me out one second and berate me the next. You . . . you—"

"Truce." He pulled away all of a sudden, giving me space.

I nearly collapsed on the tiles without him holding me upright. Slanting my head up, I scowled. "Huh?"

"I'm offering you a cease-fire. A white flag. An opportunity to start over. I'm willing to hear what you have to say and make this arrangement more bearable for you. We both know there is no way out of this marriage for either of us. Might as well make it manageable."

Hard to say no to an offer so charming and romantic. I studied him, unsure. "What's the catch?"

"No catch."

"There's always a catch with you."

"Take my offer or leave it, Shortbread. But if you leave it, don't expect it to be on the table five minutes from now." His jaw flexed. "It's bad business to have bad blood with a person who possesses easy access to your belongings and happens to be tight with a man who wants to take you down." A beat of silence trickled past. "Plus, sampling you wouldn't be the worst thing I could do with my spare time."

"Stop it, I'm getting starry-eyed."

"Sadly, I've yet to reach the height of ardor like Madison Licht, who spent the length of his engagement to you shoving his genitals into every possible hole it could fit into."

"He's really here?" I frowned, remembering how our fight had started.

Romeo nodded. "Did you buy anything interesting?"

I shook my head, relieved he let the subject go. "Just a bunch of designer stuff. Oh, and the entire Henry Plotkin series in French. I collect them in all languages. That was the highlight of my shopping spree."

"Interesting."

"No, it's not. Not for you, anyway." I toyed with the limit-less card inside my pocket. "You know, if I really overspent, you could've canceled the card. I'm surprised you didn't."

"It was the only proof of life I had."

"You mean you're not having me followed?"

"You slipped your security detail after the lunch crowd congregated around your table to thank you for treating them to thirty-thousand euros' worth of overpriced Parisian cuisine."

"If you tried their fricassée de coquillages, you wouldn't find them overpriced."

For once, and despite me doing absolutely nothing different to alter myself, he didn't seem utterly appalled by my existence. He stared at me with reluctant accept-ance. Like I was a chore he needed to get over with. I could tell whatever was happening here was completely new territory for him.

"Let's start over, shall we? I have a reservation at The Eye of Paris. It's on a terrace overlooking the city. You will join me."

I rubbed my ears. "So weird. My hearing must be off, because I can't seem to register the P-word."

"Calling you a parasite seemed unfitting in this instance."

"I meant *please*."

I could tell I was driving him to the brink of throttling me, but I had to score a few small wins after he'd literally snatched my virginity with his tongue, just to make sure Madison wouldn't beat him to it.

He looked like he'd rather rub his genitals against a rusty cheese grater than say the word, but he finally muttered, "Please."

"Let me grab a quick shower and put something on."

Thirty minutes later, an off-the-shoulder olive satin gown with a trumpet silhouette swathed my curves. "You look adequate," Romeo grumbled when we crossed the lobby to the waiting chauffeur service.

"Stop, or I'll swoon."

He opened the door for me. I slid in, unsure how to behave now that we were in a so-called truce.

"Any special requests tonight?" Each word spat out of his mouth like it was nailed into his tongue.

"Drop dead?" I bit out before I could help myself.

"I was thinking more along the lines of a helicopter trip or jewelry."

If my whole body could eye roll, it would.

Uniformed personnel welcomed us at the restaurant entrance and led us to an exclusive table upstairs. After we ordered, I clutched a champagne flute, watching cars zip across the Seine River, waiting for Romeo to break the silence. An array of insults anchored my tongue. I had little to say without their familiar company. The alternative would be to press him about his scars. A question that often occupied my mind. But I knew he wouldn't answer. The sour mood sure to follow would only ruin my parsley-butter escargot.

When our silence began drawing curious looks from neighboring tables, I finally snapped. "When we have kids, I'd like to raise them in Chap—"

"We won't have kids." Romeo snapped his napkin over his lap with a flick of the wrist.

"I don't mean soon." I shot him a murderous glare. It wasn't like I was smitten with the idea of him fathering my children. I could find more emotional intelligence in a key lime pie. More comfort, too.

"We won't have children. Not soon. Not later. Not *ever*."

"And why not?"

Surely, I hadn't heard him correctly.

Forget the poor manners, absence of conscience, and general assholery. *This* was my dealbreaker. In fact, I wanted just one thing in life. Kids. Four of them. I loved children. Loved everything about them. The chubby cheeks, rolling laughter, and pure adoration. Even on that Sunday Romeo had snatched me from my house, I'd spent my time at church playing with the little ones outside. Grandmamma always said a house without a child was like a body without a soul. I didn't disagree.

Romeo piled foie gras on his spoon. "Because I don't want them."

"But *I* do."

"Good luck conceiving them by sucking my cock and having your pussy licked, because that's about the only sexual encounters you'll be having."

A woman behind him choked on her pickled mackerel.

My cheeks flamed. "You mean you don't want to have sex with me?"

"I want to have sex with you. There are few things I want more, Shortbread. Coincidentally, not having children is one of them, so the answer is no. We won't have sex."

I was so speechless, I didn't even care that half the people around us had stopped eating and chosen to watch us like we were a movie premiere.

"Never say never."

"That might be the silliest saying I've ever heard in my life. People say never to many things. Bungee jumping without a rope, hard drugs, pineapple pizza—"

"I like pineapple pizza."

He downed half his drink. "Christ. It keeps getting worse."

I sat back, trying to figure out what I found more unappealing—my husband's personality or the snails on my plate, which tasted like they were 3D-printed.

"Why are you so against children?"

"Other than the fact that I detest them personally? They interrupt your sleep, lower your quality of life, demand every moment of your time, and are generally a crushing disappointment when they reach adulthood."

My glare alone called bull. But since he refused to catch my gaze, I said, "You and I both know that children are a vanity project, not an investment. It is a knee-jerk reaction of civilization to preserve itself. There's something bigger that's keeping you from having children, and it's not discomfort. You're in a financial position to rear offspring without ever having to deal with them."

A flicker of interest zinged through his eyes. "You're not a complete idiot, are you?" I folded my arms, tilting a brow up. "Well, you happen to be right. There is a bigger agenda behind all this. I don't want to have children because I want to cut the Costa dynasty off."

"I thought you and Bruce are fighting over Costa Industries."

"We are."

"Why do you need to inherit this company if you're not going to pass it down to your hypothetical spawn?"

"You do the math, Shortbread."

It took me less than a second to figure it out. *So, he could ruin it. Run it to the ground. Destroy it like he did everything else his cold hands touched.* Such a Romeo thing to crave destruction.

From one family dinner, I'd gathered that Senior cared about one thing and one thing only—Costa Industries. To kill his only love would be a cruel blow before he perished. An act of pure vengeance. The reason behind Romeo's hatred taunted me. I wasn't naïve enough to think he'd actually confide in me. Nonetheless, an idea sprouted in my head.

Romeo didn't want children. I didn't want him in my vicinity. What would he do if I fell pregnant? Would he divorce me or send me back to Chapel Falls with my dignity and wedding ring intact?

The plan wasn't completely ideal. For one thing, it hurt to think my child wouldn't have a father figure in Romeo. But I refused to abandon my dream of becoming a mother. Anyway, this hypothetical kid of mine would have the entire Townsend family at their disposal. Sans Daddy, who was officially stripped from grandfather duties for being a complete wuss.

It was pointless to tell Romeo about my plan for us. So, I sipped my champagne. "Fine."

His eyes narrowed. "Do you take me for a fool? You would never give up so easily."

"Sorry, *hubs*, but your DNA doesn't exactly scream hot commodity."

"You would reproduce with a Trader Joe's organic bag if you truly wanted a kid."

"Would you like me to get down on my knees and beg you?"

"Yes, but not for a baby."

Laughing hollowly, because there was nothing funny about our situation, I pointed out, "You're not wrong. Children are too time-consuming and exhausting for a lazy, messy girl like me. We can have sex without getting pregnant, you know."

"Thank you for the astonishing piece of news." His eyes smoldered as he cut through his dish with the precision of a neurosurgeon. "But it's better to be safe than sorry."

Well, safe was the last thing we'd be. I'd kill his plans by getting pregnant—giving him the heir he never wanted—and free myself from his talons.

His fork hovered before his lips. "Enjoying your dish?"

"Almost as much as the company," I cooed.

For the rest of dinner, we pretended to be a normal couple.

Chapter Twenty-Nine

Dallas

"I've never met a man so eager to lose all of his teeth."

At Romeo's mutter, I peered up from Frankie's text. My heart nose-dived to my gut. Madison sat on the hallway carpet, his back pressed against our door. The bluish light from his phone shimmied across his forehead. As soon as he spotted us, he stood, painting remorse on his disheveled face.

His motive clicked with the force of thunder. Madison and Romeo had begun a calculated game. I was the objective—the *ball*—they kicked back and forth. And suddenly, the plan I'd hatched with Madison seemed like a monumentally stupid idea. One I would no longer proceed with, seeing as my co-conspirator had the survival instincts of a drunk moth.

"Dallas." He'd never been so eager to see me in all the time we'd known each other. "We need to talk. I can't stop thinking about you."

I slowed. For once, Romeo was right. Madison was begging to be killed.

"You lost me at the thinking part. Your measly intelligence merely helps you function." Romeo strode down the hall, yanked Madison by his collar, and hurled him against our door. His voice, as always, exuded calmness. "What do you think you're doing, Licht?"

Madison flailed like an unearthed worm. "Getting back what's mine."

I almost snorted. *What a cliché.*

"Why didn't you say so?" Romeo released him, yielded a blank check from his wallet, and slapped it onto Madison's chest. "Here."

It cartwheeled to Madison's loafers. "What's that?"

"The settlement I'll be paying you after you sue me for breaking your nose."

"You didn't break my—"

Romeo planted his fist square in Madison's face. Blood gushed out of my ex-fiancé's nose. It dripped down his suit, coloring the carpet crimson. He swayed, knocking into the wall.

All the air ripped from my lungs.

"What the fuck?!" Madison moaned, cupping his nostrils between pinched fingers. "I'll call the police."

Romeo feigned genuine interest, guiding his keycard into the reader with ease. "And tell them what? That you came all the way from the States to seduce another man's wife?"

Madison wedged himself between Romeo and the door. "I want to talk to Dallas. I deserve some closure."

I wondered what kind of heinous crimes I'd committed against the human race in a previous life to deserve these two nutjobs as my love interests. Worse—that if I wanted a baby, which I did, it would likely be with Romeo.

I sighed, nudging Madison aside with the tip of my stilettos, careful to avoid a bloodstain. "Could this not wait until we get back home? Sorry, Mad, but this is a bit . . . out of left field. Also, I should probably take you to the hospi—"

"He'll see himself there." Romeo swung the door open and guided me inside, blocking most of Madison from view with his broad shoulders. "It is not the first time a husband has broken Madison's bones, and judging by his antics, it won't be the last."

Madison surged forward. "I didn't even touch Charity."

As I said—heinous crimes.

Romeo lifted a finger to his forehead and pushed, sending a light-headed Madison into the wall. "Next time I see you in my wife's zip code, even God won't be able to help you. Now clean yourself up. You're making Americans appear as gauche as the French think us to be."

He slammed the door shut. The thought of helping Madison crossed my mind for two seconds. Then I remembered he'd come here for a cause, and that cause was likely sabotaging my honeymoon or plotting something against my husband. At all costs. Even me.

Seemed like no one had my interests in mind but me. The more I thought about it, the more compelling I found getting knocked up. It would be the fastest way to get Romeo to send me back to Chapel Falls with my dignity and wedding ring intact. Surely, he'd tuck me where his family couldn't see me. Maybe even grant me a divorce to ensure our child didn't receive any Costa perks.

I rolled back my shoulders. *Forget what just happened. Execute Operation Baby Maker.* Yeah, there were obvious cons to my strategy, but even the slightest chance of having a baby and returning home prevailed.

Showtime.

"Before you whine about Madison's nose . . ." Romeo tore off his blazer, hooking it on a rack. "I draw the line at other men. You are not, under any circumstances while wearing my ring, to conspire or fuck them. That's not too much to ask."

I didn't say a thing. Couldn't find it in me to reassure him. Plus, fighting would hinder my plans for tonight. I backed him into the door, planting a hand on his chest. Above his slow, steady heart. We stood like this for what felt like an eternity.

Finally, he scowled. "Are you casting a Henry Plotkin spell on me?"

Involuntary laughter bubbled in my throat, but I swallowed it. An entire scientific study could be conducted on how a man so cold could possess such penetrating warmth whenever his hands touched me.

I traced a heart over his. "I want you to teach me things."

"Manners, I assume."

"I was thinking more about . . . um, bed stuff."

"Why? Sleeping seems to be your expertise."

"*Romeo.* Be serious."

He licked his lips. It was obvious he found the idea alluring. Our chests strained against one another. I traced his Adam's apple.

He stopped me, clasping my wrist. "Why do I always have the feeling you're playing a game with me, Shortbread?"

Because I am.

Peering at him beneath my lashes, I pouted. "All I want is for us to have a good time together on our honeymoon. I'm tired of feeling miserable."

Then, to show him I meant business, I rolled the zipper down my gown, shrugging off the fabric. It cascaded down my body like a waterfall. Since I didn't wear a bra or panties—the lines would have shown through the garment—I stood buck naked in front of him. His eyes roamed everywhere, caressing every inch of my body. For someone who tried very hard to make me feel bad, he wielded the odd ability to make me feel cherished.

His throat bobbed. I knew that, despite his flawless self-control, he wanted to do dirty, unspeakable things to me. He trailed a finger along my belly, my ribs, the outline of my breasts, lost in thought.

"I want to feel you inside me." My gaze clung to his face. "Will you not consider it? Not even for our first time together?"

"No." The word tore past his lips, croaky and hoarse. His touch sent flames of desire up and down my skin. "But if I start stretching your ass now, I can probably take it by next week after coming back from my Wednesday meeting in New York."

A dozen retorts danced on my tongue. Namely, where he could shove his suggestion. But that would blow my cover. And my cover right now consisted of being an agreeable wife, who wanted nothing more than intercourse with her husband.

"Okay . . ." I cleared my throat. "I'll . . . I'll go buy one of *those* . . ."

Ugh, what did they call them? I wasn't that innocent. I knew what they were. Even spotted one on Amazon.

"Anal plugs," Romeo provided.

"Yes, er . . . those."

"No need. I have an electric toothbrush, an ideal starter kit for anal play. Perfect width and shape, and the vibrations will get you off."

I couldn't believe I was having this conversation with my husband.

I couldn't believe he wanted to stick his toothbrush in my butt.

He studied me, waiting for a reaction. When one failed to arrive, he pointed out, "Give me access to your ass, Shortbread, and I'll make you come for days."

A mountain of curses settled on my tongue, begging for release. What had I gotten myself into? Stupid girl with stupid plans. Being thoughtless always came with a price tag I wasn't willing to pay. Still, I knew he anticipated me backing out of this. No matter how much I dreaded it, I wouldn't hand him this victory.

I looped an arm around his neck. "Okay."

"Okay?"

"You heard me. Getting cold feet, *hubs*?"

He called my bluff, stalking to the bathroom and returning with his toothbrush. I studied it through frantic eyes. It really didn't look too big, but the prospect of shoving it into my most intimate hole induced hysteria. I didn't want this. Not because I thought there was anything wrong with it, but because I still hadn't checked so many other stations on my route to discovering my sexuality. This felt like a leap from two opposite cliffs.

Naked and shivering, I awaited Romeo's instructions.

He flicked on the toothbrush. A symphony of buzzes and hums played between us before he switched it off. "There's no shame in taking your pleasures through paths less traveled." I didn't reply. He toyed with the button again. "Are you sure this is what you want?"

I tried not to quiver. "Yes."

"On the bed, then, Shortbread."

I scooted onto the bed, watching his approach. With each step, my heart sank lower and lower until I could feel it thumping between my thighs.

"Turn around."

I did, scrambling onto my knees. I felt the heat of him from behind. To my surprise, he didn't push it inside. Rather, he snaked his arm around my midriff, drawing me back. His lips traveled up my spine, pressing kisses from the base to my throat. He played with my tits from behind and tongued my jawline, forming a pool of heat between my thighs.

Though I loved his touch, his kisses, his attention, I couldn't stay in the moment. Not with Madison's blood stained on his fingers and the daunting knowledge of what he wanted to do to me. All I could do was stay still and wait for the inevitable, swallowing down my bile.

His fingers reached between my thighs, withdrawing some of my sleek heat. He dragged the wetness from my front to my back, circling the rim at a lazy pace, teasing it. I stiffened all over, shutting my eyes.

He stilled. "Shortbread?"

"Just do it already."

Silence. So much silence. *Too* much silence. That was how I knew I'd messed up. He clutched my waist and rolled me onto my back. I fell onto a cloud of luxurious pillows, not daring to blink for fear I'd pop my tear cherry, too. The stupid toothbrush was still in his hand.

I bit my tongue until I drew blood. "What are you looking at?"

"You're crying."

I wasn't. But I was darn close. The closest I'd ever been, in fact. I pursed my lips, saying nothing. I'd blown my plan. Shattered it to unsalvageable bits and pieces. Stupid Chapel Falls and its stupid rules. Would it have killed the town to give me some experience in seduction?

Romeo volleyed the toothbrush to the nightstand. "You're shivering, too."

I almost gasped when it flew by me, as if it had the power to enter me independently. "I'm just a little cold."

In another twist of events, he gathered me in his arms, plastering me to his chest. I didn't know what surprised me more. The humane response or the steady beat of his heart against my own. All my anger at blowing my plan liquefied into relief. To my horror, I began trembling. I knew he detested weakness. I also knew I'd never felt weaker in my entire life. Lying here, bare and naked, in the arms of a man I hated, leeching his comfort.

He cradled my head as though I were a precious, beautiful thing and stroked my hair, grazing his lips against my temple. I expected his next words to be, *don't cry*. But Romeo refused to fit into the mold.

"You never asked for any of this, Dallas. I'm well aware. Every man in your life has failed you, including me."

An epiphany slammed into me. My mind voyaged to his childhood room, sailing through the photos. The stubs. The *love*. Romeo Costa wasn't born a heartless beast. Once upon a time, he'd loved. *Until Morgan.*

Eventually, Romeo pulled away from our embrace. I peered past the French windows into the inky darkness. It must have been past midnight.

He palmed my cheek. "Forget anal play. There's still plenty we can do."

I nodded. "I know that. I do. I'm just upset because . . ." I reminded myself of my goal while Romeo still straddled the tattered seam between this concerned man and the beast I knew so well. "I'm sad because I'll never know what it feels like to be taken in the traditional sense of the word." I purred, tacking on my most innocent expression. "You've done this before, haven't you? Gone . . . all the way?" Now I was just taking advantage of him.

"You know the answer to that question."

I sniffled. "Yeah, I do."

He paused. "Even if I wanted to show you, I don't have a condom here."

"I understand."

"No, you don't."

"True, I don't. I'll never experience sex, since you'll never give it to me. Of course, I'm sad. I'm allowed to be."

He tore himself off the bed and paced the room. Guilt— so thick and tangible—radiated from him. So, he *did* have a conscience.

My eyes ping-ponged, tracking his movement when he finally stopped in front of the mattress. "Get dressed."

I didn't argue, wading deep in wanting-to-screw-Romeo-up waters. My suitcase fed me white cotton panties and a lavender satin top. I was about to wiggle into matching pants when Romeo interrupted. "That's enough. Go back to the bed."

I scratched my temple. "Didn't you just tell me to—"

"Before I change my fucking mind, Shortbread."

Whoa. "Only because you're asking so nicely." I ambled to the bed, falling onto it.

He stared at me. "Go to sleep."

"What?"

"Go. To. Sleep," he bit out, slower and louder.

"I heard you the first time, but—"

"I'll be back." He collected his wallet and left. Just *left*. Without an explanation. Whatever happened to "before I change my mind"? Maybe he'd changed it after all.

Deciding that today was eventful enough, I did, in fact, descend into the sweet arms of slumber. In my dreams, I drowned in books. Ink-scented hardcovers. With words and universes and creatures far and foreign.

In my dreams, there was no beast disguised as a husband. Most importantly—no heartbreak disguised as marriage.

Chapter Thirty

Ollie vB: Did she break you yet?

Romeo Costa: Consider me unbreakable.

Zach Sun: Consider me appalled by the fact that you sound like a Sia song these days.

Romeo Costa: @ZachSun, since when do you use cultural references that have nothing to do with fine art?

Ollie vB: His parents sent him on a date with an influencer last week.

Romeo Costa: How many of your brain cells survived?

Zach Sun: Nearly all of them. I used concealed noise-canceling earbuds and smiled and nodded at two-minute intervals.

Romeo Costa: Sounds promising. When's the wedding announcement?

Ollie vB: @RomeoCosta, you want to tell me you really didn't taste that sweet, tight pussy yet?

Romeo Costa: I am going to cut your tongue off with a butter knife next time I see you.

Ollie vB: Why a butter knife? It'd only make things unnecessarily long and messy.

Romeo Costa: Exactly.

Ollie vB: @ZachSun, notice how he didn't say yes or no when I asked him about sampling his bride. What do you think?

Zach Sun: Zigzagging over the edge.

Zach Sun: Drunk.

Zach Sun: And legless.

Ollie vB: His fall will be spectacular.

Romeo Costa: Temptation is resistible, believe it or not.

Ollie vB: That might apply to a cake. Not a woman who looks like your wife.

Ollie vB: Is her sister still in high school?

Romeo Costa: It's been ten hours since you've last asked, so yes.

Ollie vB: Time drags when you're waiting.

Zach Sun: Tell that to your prison guard when you get locked up for statutory rape.

Chapter Thirty-One

Romeo

I tramped up and down Rue du Faubourg Saint-Honoré, chewing seven pieces of gum, almost ripping my hair off my scalp. Why the *fuck* had I taunted Shortbread with that toothbrush? The stubborn little nymph almost went along with it, too. It was a dare on my end. One that exploded in my face in spectacular fashion. She'd managed to make me curse. *And* cuddle.

Sure, I could waltz right into a pharmacy and demand a pack of condoms. Double-wrap. Then finish the pack and top it off with another. Then another. And when one of the hundred or so—inevitable the next time Dallas wiggled her ass in the air, welcoming me to park inside her pussy—condoms broke, TLC could add us to the cast of *19 Kids and Counting*. Hard pass.

The pill and IUD had their disadvantages. First off, I couldn't tell her what to do with her body. Second, I'd never trust her to take the pills or keep the IUD in. She obviously wanted children. And finally, the snip. Vasectomies only had a 99.9% success rate. Knowing my luck, I'd be in that point-one percent. After all, I was in that percent in every other aspect—intelligence, looks, tax bracket, and so forth.

An idea formed in my head. I entertained it, stomping up and down the sidewalk. Shortbread begged to feel it *once*.

Just one time with my cock in her cunt. Not too big of an ask. I could get it over with and move on with my life.

Before I had the chance to rethink it, I returned to the hotel. I never actually expected Dallas to fall asleep. Not after the day we'd had. But I'd underestimated my wife's laziness. Not only was she fast asleep, she was also snoring with a half-finished scone plastered to her chest.

I sat on the edge of the mattress, moved the scone to the nightstand, and tucked locks of her wild hair behind her ears. Oliver was right. She was irresistible. Somehow beautiful, innocent, and spirited at once. As exquisite and thorny as a wild rose. I didn't even hesitate before shedding my shoes and pants. In just my briefs, I kneeled between her legs and nudged my nose to her slit through her underwear.

She murmured in her sleep, wiggling her ass a little. A small smile formed on her lips. I pressed my hot tongue to her center. She gasped. The cotton dampened from both my mouth and her body catching up with my intentions. Through the thin fabric, I fingered her and sucked on her clit, teasing her.

Her nipples puckered behind her satin top, and her eyes fluttered open. To my great pleasure, she was still half-asleep, not fully coherent. Perhaps she'd shut up for a change.

With a soft moan, she thrust her pussy in my face. "More."

I sucked harder on her clit, releasing the pressure. Using both my index and middle fingers, I curled them all the way inside her pussy, straining the flimsy panties and finger-fucking her at the same time.

"Mmm. Good."

Good? I hadn't touched a woman in almost half a decade. Good didn't cut it. Shortbread's thighs quaked, bracketing my ears. Her fingers found my hair, tugging viciously. I went harder, rougher, latching on to one of her tits through her top and pinching her nipple. Her eyes finally popped open. She blinked at me behind a curtain of innocent lust.

For a second, I thought I could get used to this. Then I remembered Oliver's words about her. An arrow of possessiveness shot through me, triggering a third finger into the mix. I taunted her clit with the tip of my tongue, circling. She jerked forward, gliding the bud across my nose.

"*Fuck!*" shouted my beautiful, gently bred Southern wife. "No wonder Daddy didn't let us date. If I knew it felt this good, I'd have had sex with every guy in my grade."

I almost choked on her panties. From laughter or outrage, I wasn't sure.

"Yes. Yes. Like that, but maybe . . . maybe even faster."

The childish glee in her voice racketed my pulse. My heart battered my ribs. I couldn't remember the last time I'd felt it working properly. Usually, it did the bare minimum of keeping me alive and not an ounce more.

She writhed and moaned beneath me, clamping her legs around my skull in a death grip, ensuring I didn't go anywhere. It would take three armies and an entire apocalypse to nudge me away. Dallas Costa was fine art. I wanted to frame her in this moment and return to the scene whenever the urge to devour her reared its ugly head. She was so receptive. Brimming with genuine excitement. Nothing about her response to me was premeditated or calculated. She was ruthlessly honest. Honest when she told me how much she hated me with everything she had. And honest when I made her fall apart with my tongue and fingers.

Best of all, she was so different from Morgan Lacoste, who only let go and got off on my tongue when drunk, which was universally more frequent than one should be intoxicated. Ruthless, calculated Morgan cared more about looking good during sex than actually enjoying the act.

"Yes. Yes! I'm coming!" My little undomesticated porn-star pushed me so hard between her legs, my oxygen levels plummeted. She clenched around my fingers through her panties as an orgasm rolled through her in waves. The gush of warmth soaked the cotton. I kissed her through the fabric, again and again, knowing tomorrow everything would return to its proper position—my boundaries, my limits, my hang-ups, my demons.

"Can I return the favor?" Dallas sat half up. "But not through your briefs. Men's briefs always smell like old cheese that's been sitting in a crockpot for days. I know because whenever my housekeeper went on vacation, we all took turns doing the laundry. And, well, I really shouldn't say, but Dadd—"

Not wanting the moment to be ruined with a conversation about her father's underwear, I pulled forward, shutting her smart mouth with a kiss that tasted like her sweet pussy. At first, she pinched her lips and made a face, unsure what she thought about her own taste. But when I dragged the tip of my hard cock along her slit through our clothes, she went wild and kissed me back, shoving her tongue so deep down my throat I thought she would fish out my dinner.

"Yes." She wiggled against me. "Please, sir, may I have some more?"

She'd quoted *Oliver Twist* while getting fucked. Truly, the woman was one of a kind.

Knowing it was idiotic, and dangerous, and deranged, I pushed my tip through her slit. She was tight—tighter, still, through the tattered, stretched cotton of her ruined panties—but wet and sleek, ready for what was coming.

The sensation, how warm and taut she felt, completely undid me. I thrust harder and deeper, entering her through our underwear, fucking her slowly with only flimsy fabric between us. I tore my mouth from hers, eyes glued to my cock each time it sank into her. I could barely fit inside, she was so tight. This was, by far, the best fuck I'd ever had.

She panted. "Is this what people call dry-humping?"

No. Nothing about this was dry. I was basically fucking her through our underwear. Only, explaining to her that this was full-blown sex with a side order of my issues was not in my plans for tonight. Or ever.

"Sure."

Each push brought me closer to a climax. From slow, controlled, teasing thrusts designed to drive her mad with desire, I quickly derailed to jerky, manic, need-to-be-inside-this-woman plunges. Of a man so hungry for human connection, for affection, for carnal needs to be met and satisfied.

My head grew dizzy. I'd taken into consideration the possibility that Dallas couldn't come through penetration. It merely placed her in the same majority as most females on Planet Earth. But she shook, clawed, and reached for me, looking ready to climax. Her tits bounced and jiggled each time I slammed into her. Her mouth opened in awe, probably because this orgasm felt different from the first two. Deeper and more violent.

She clutched the lapels of my shirt, shoving her face in mine. "Lose the underwear." She met my thrust, groaning when my crown peeked past the slot in my boxer briefs. "I want you to come inside me. I want to feel you."

I was about two seconds from fulfilling her demand. Luckily, my logic grabbed the steering wheel, which my cock had seized sometime this evening, and derailed the situation from full-blown calamity.

I managed to wait until she came, just barely, before pulling out, flipping her onto her stomach, and jerking off. I aimed for her bare ass but somehow came on her hair. No matter. She had plenty of time to wash it. Her agenda wasn't exactly full.

Dallas fell back onto the pillows, a lopsided grin on her face. "It's official." She pulled me down with her and peppered my face with wet, sloppy kisses, reminding me, yet again, that the difference between her and a puppy was indeed negligible. "Having sex is my new favorite sport."

"Sex is not a sport."

"It should be. I would do it all day long if that were a thing."

"It is. It's called prostitution."

I fell on top of her with complete disregard to her slight weight, reached for the nightstand, and shoved two mint gums into my mouth. "There won't be another time." I rolled off her, my body sleek with sweat, my muscles calm for the first time in years.

"Sure, honey." She plastered her tits to my arm. Beneath us, the sheets were soaked with everything we'd just done. "Just this once."

But the temptation proved too much. I ended up granting myself a free pass for the duration of our honeymoon. For an entire week, I fucked Dallas through her clothes at every opportunity. And every night, I fucked her through a bedsheet, careful to always come on her face, tongue, and tits. I almost even fucked her bareback in the Louvre. Then I ate her sweet little cunt at La Madeleine. A church of all places, because my troublemaker of a wife simply could not wait until we returned to the hotel. She'd even begged me to finger her on the Dodo Manège. Which meant I also had to suck her tits under a coat I draped over her chest in the taxi back to the hotel.

The pattern was depressingly clear. I married a woman with nymphomaniac tendencies and had zero desire to deprive her of what she wanted. I was pussy-whipped. So pussy-whipped, I forgot to ask, to expect, to train her to return the favor. I was so enamored with her cunt that I forgot it was a Venus flytrap, hungry for my sperm.

One thing was certain. When we returned to U.S. soil, I needed to stay as far away from my wife as I possibly could. Being in close quarters with her would put me at a clear disadvantage in our psychological war. It would take her a month. Two. Perhaps even an entire year. But I knew in my bones that she'd convince me to fuck her bareback. Filthy. Until she filled to the brim with my cum.

Whatever Dallas Costa wanted—Dallas Costa got.

And what she wanted right now was my heir.

Chapter Thirty-Two

Dallas

Romeo's penis could cure depression. Unfortunately, it could not cure hatred. I still had that in spades. I flung my period-stained underwear into the trash, reaching for a tampon. The disappointment that flooded me wasn't because I'd expected to be pregnant so fast. I just didn't want a temporary pit stop in my quest to breaking some sort of Guinness orgasm record.

The jet jostled me like a snow globe. I perched beside the sink, waiting out the turbulence. My sex was already sore, stretched to the max, and ready for retirement after just a week of employment. Each time my nipples brushed against my bra, the numbness axled into pain.

When the plane recovered, I returned to the main cabin in time to watch Romeo flip the page of his newspaper. My butt still tingled every time I caught a glimpse of his strong hands. We'd spent our time in France either arguing or climaxing.

I plopped onto the plush couch, expecting Romeo to ignore me. And he did. In fact, the second we'd stepped onto the jet, he'd shown more interest in his emails than me. *Fine*. Whatever. I FaceTimed Frankie, Momma, and Sav, popping seaweed rice crackers onto my tongue, ignoring the cruel, overbearing ass.

When we returned home, I realized I'd forgotten to ask Hettie or Vernon to water the white rose on my nightstand. *Oops.* I bolted upstairs as soon as I remembered, leaving Romeo in the foyer with our suitcases, confused and—as always—displeased.

"You're welcome for the 1.4-million-dollar honeymoon, Shortbread." I ignored him, taking the stairs two at a time as he muttered to himself, "Anytime."

I barged into my room, panting. Though my thumb veered black instead of green, I hated when flowers died. They symbolized hope and strength. For after each winter, came the spring, bringing blossom with it. A tended flower grew to its full potential. I liked to think about people in the same manner. Could I, too, grow under my current circumstances?

To my amazement, the white rose appeared perfectly in bloom in its makeshift jar. Not one petal out of place. *Phew.* Had Vernon watered it? I fell to my knees before it, noticing the greenish hue of the water it swam in. Nope. It looked like the rose had survived all by itself. *Well, what do you know?* Maybe Vernon was right, and he'd created a rose sub-species that could survive as long as it took to fall in love.

"At least one of us is low-maintenance." I fingered the thorny stem. "Thank you for surviving. You're the real MVP, Rose."

Did I just name my pet rose Rose? *Why, yes. Yes, I did.*

"I see conversing with plants is another quirk I should add to your never-ending list of oddities." Romeo leaned against my doorframe, looking like an ice statue.

I scowled at him. Now that the novelty of Paris's romantic filter wore off and I could no longer shove his face between my legs, I remembered how much I disliked him. Precise quantity: a *ton*.

"Aunt Flow's in town, in case you're here for your . . . er, *snack*."

"Kindly refrain from reminding me you have any relatives. I have intense PTSD from every Townsend I've met so far." He pushed off the doorframe, strolling into my room without an invitation. "As it happens, I'm not here to pleasure you, Shortbread. Believe it or not, my interests run a little deeper than your bed."

"Don't worry. I know your story arc is ruining your father's empire. You're like a badly written Marvel villain, but with a better haircut."

He stared at me, unmoved, towering above me now. "I'm moving out."

My knees remained glued to the hardwood. The scene was gut-wrenchingly degrading, so I shot to my feet, dusting my dress off.

He reached into his metal case, popping two cubes of gums into his mouth. "Work is hectic, with a major agreement with the DOD on the line."

I'd read about it all over the local news. Also filed it under the Don't Care folder in my brain. Just another pissing contest between the Lichts and Costas, to the soprano tune of six-hundred-or-so million dollars.

I rolled my eyes. "Your work's always busy. At least be honest and admit you want to stay away from me."

He observed me with less interest than a traffic report. "You are a distraction, and I do not entertain those."

"I am your *wife*."

"Now you're just repeating what I said." Then, with a sigh, he swept his eyes away from me. "I'll probably visit once over the weekend to check in on the house. You may invite your family members and friends as you wish, two at a time, so long as no men walk through these gates. In men, I also include Madison, though he does not necessarily fit into the category."

"Wait, you can't really leave." I jumped past him, blocking the doorway. I didn't know why I found the concept so hard to digest.

He sidestepped, walking around me. "I am, and you're in my way."

I dove in front of him, bracing an arm on either side of the doorframe. "Guess the only way out is through."

"Very well." He cracked his neck. "Through it is, Mrs. Costa."

Romeo advanced toward me, shoulder-tackled me, and tossed me over his shoulder, strolling through the hallway as if he wasn't carrying an entire person.

I slapped his back, growling. "Let me down, you stuffy . . . coldhearted . . . asinine . . ."

"I'm not asinine." He shifted me onto his other shoulder, and I suspected it had less to do with my weight and more to do with the discomfort it gave me. "The other adjectives fit, though."

My head bobbed, colliding with his back with each stride. He carried me with light breaths and even lighter steps. On the bright side, I obviously had more room to eat, since it seemed I weighed next to nothing. Romeo descended the stairs. I spotted my suitcase alone in the foyer and noticed he'd never wheeled his back into the house. He wasn't lying. He'd never planned on staying.

Romeo rounded the curved stairway and disposed of me in the kitchen, in front of a confused Hettie. "Effective immediately, Mrs. Costa is among your responsibilities, Ms. Holmberg. You are to oversee her behavior, including potential indiscretions and mishaps. You will ensure she stays out of trouble, as the latter seems to have her on speed dial."

Hettie frowned. "What's in it for me?"

"A 150K pay raise and the pleasure of maintaining your job."

"Okie dokie." She whistled, saluting him with two fingers to her forehead. "You got yourself a deal, boss."

I groaned. "Traitor."

"Blue-collar," she corrected.

A few seconds later, Romeo left the house—and my life—as if Paris had never happened.

I turned to Hettie, fuming. "Wow. All it took was 150K for you to turn on me."

Hettie appeared unaffected by my rage. "One-fifty large is a shit ton of money for the average folk, Dal." I knew she was right. But now that Romeo wasn't here, I had to take my anger out on someone. "Plus." Hettie shrugged. "I never claimed to be a *good* governess. My job is to cook his oatmeal. If I suck at my side gig, no one can blame me." She winked.

I grinned. "Thanks."

"Sure. Just don't take advantage of it and throw massive orgies and burn the place down, all right?"

"I'll try my best," I said, inwardly adding that I would do anything and everything short of the list she gave me.

I dragged myself up the stairs and back to my room, where I spent the rest of my day reading and moping. My mind had wandered a thousand miles from the faraway kingdom my book took place in. Before I hopped into bed,

I noticed one petal had fallen off the rose. Just the one.

See, Vernon? The rose is wilting and my hatred toward my husband isn't.

Shaking my head, I crawled into bed.

I'd get back at Romeo Costa. Even if it was the last thing I did.

Chapter Thirty-Three

Ollie vB: @RomeoCosta, your mom just walked out of Bougie Baby with your wife in tow and approximately five hundred bags. Anything you want to tell us?

Romeo Costa: Yes: mind your own business.

Zach Sun: What were you doing in that shop, @OllievB? Anything YOU want to tell US?

Ollie vB: I'll have you know Bougie Baby is right next to my shooting range.

Romeo Costa: Speaking of shooting range . . .

Zach Sun: Don't even go there. That's double homicide. Fifty years in the slammer. Just giving you the facts.

Romeo Costa: She is not pregnant. The only thing she is full of starts with an S and ends with a T.

Ollie vB: Sexiest Alive is actually just the title People Magazine has given me. My real name is Oliver.

Romeo Costa: And your real chronological age is five.

Zach Sun: Strengthening ties with her MIL. Smart move.

Romeo Costa: Unfortunately, she is not as dim as I pegged her to be.

Ollie vB: Admit it, Costa. You miscalculated. You wanted dumb and dumber and got the best and the brightest.

Ollie vB: Alexa, play American Idiot.

Zach Sun: Ollie is right. You thought she'd be your plaything. In reality, you have more control over the weather.

Romeo Costa: Her entire personality is being a toddler. She will tire herself out, eventually.

Zach Sun: Will she? At this point, we're all living in a simulation, and Detroit Townsend has admin access. You cannot convince me otherwise.

Romeo Costa: Detroit COSTA.

Chapter Thirty-Four

Romeo

The way Dallas's brain worked was an absolute crime against humanity. Upon returning to Potomac, the first thing I did was text Hettie, ordering her to hide the baster somewhere my horny wife couldn't find. While I refused to come inside her, I didn't put it past Shortbread to drive to the nearest sperm bank and order two Ventis to-go.

Turned out, abstinence *was* best, because I managed to go four days without liaising with my Wife of Chaos. What I did do, however, was watch her on forty-nine security cameras spread across my estate. Shortbread was bored. And a bored Shortbread, I learned, was a destructive one.

I applauded her talent for doing absolutely nothing, yet achieving so much. The woman spent her days eating, binge-reading books (sometimes finishing an entire series in the span of twenty-four hours), and spending unholy amounts of money. My natural inclination was to suspect she'd racked up my credit card bill solely for the purpose of pissing me off, as opposed to doing so because she genuinely desired the objects she'd purchased. Then I logged onto her Visa statement, noting she'd donated a whole orphanage to Chattanooga, top-of-the-line laptops for an entire school district, and seven-figures to SIDS research. That seemed in line with her inability to keep herself together every time someone in a diaper entered her five-mile radius.

She racked up hundreds of thousands of dollars in bills each day, daring me to step in and put a stop to her spending spree. I'd never been one to blink first. From my air-conditioned corner office, I periodically checked on my lovely wife, day in and day out, watching her welcome her mother, her sister, her friends, and her newly employed private masseuse, pedicurist, hairstylist, and a woman whose sole purpose seemed to be brushing her eyebrows.

I gathered she knew she was being watched. The signs weren't exactly hard to miss. She would sometimes stop in front of a camera and flip me the finger or flash her tits, with little regard to the possibility that my security team might have access to my home feed. That I ended up marrying such a crude woman was a travesty in itself, but I convinced myself that she would grow out of her rebellious phase.

The truth I refused to consider was that this was not a phase. This was her default setting. A feature, not a bug. She was who she was, and nothing and no one could change her.

In the four days we'd spent apart, I shuttled in and out of meetings with Senior, Bruce, and the Costa Industries board, trying to convince anyone with a willing ear that I could secure our grandfathered contract with the DOD before Licht Holdings seized it.

It wasn't exactly a lie. Then again, it wasn't exactly a truth, either. There was valid reason for concern. Senior had decayed Costa Industries to the point where we no longer topped the list of defense companies. And Bruce, being a certified yes-man, let him.

I could've gone an entire week without contact with Dallas if it weren't for the fact that, on the fifth day, something caught my eye on a monitor. I shoved the market report to the corner of my office desk. A commotion had formed at my estate gate. There was never a commotion at my front gate. Or on the property, really, beyond the hundred-fifteen-pound volume of space Shortbread took up.

I'd designed my entire life to fit my solitary tendencies. Which could explain why I felt a baffling rash crawl up my skin the minute I spotted seven luxury cars lined up on my street. The gate pumped open. Slowly, the army of vehicles drove into my driveway. I squinted, trying to see who was inside them.

Cara breezed into my office, carrying a stack of documents. "Mr. Costa, your two-p.m. appointment with Mr. Reynolds from the DOD is here—"

"Not now, Cara."

I recognized the first person to roll in, tucked inside his Rolls Royce. Barry Lusito. A former college buddy and a man I'd personally excommunicated from the industry almost seven years ago when he hit on Morgan while we were still together.

Right behind him, a Bentley cruised up my thousand-foot driveway, driven by one of Costa Industries' engineers—or should I say former engineer. A man I'd fired for sexual harassment shortly before my wedding. What game was Dallas playing now?

After Barry, a few modest cars pulled up with women in them, some of whom I recognized as my wife's new staff. (Why someone with no job, no volunteer work, and no physical ailments needed staff was beyond me.)

And following the herd of women was none other than Oliver von Bismarck, who arrived in his flashy Aston Martin DBX—and had the audacity to wave hello to the camera. Next, Zach emerged in his Lexus LC (he despised overpriced, unreliable cars). Then, finally, Madison Licht. I repeat—Madison Fucking Licht. I couldn't tell for sure, since he'd angled half of himself away from the camera, but his nose appeared to be covered by some kind of nude bandage.

"Sir . . ." Cara adjusted her documents. "You've been trying to get Mr. Reynolds's attention for three weeks now. I'm not sure he'll take well to waiting—"

"My meeting is canceled." I stormed to my feet, plucking my blazer from my headrest and draping it over myself on my way out. "As are the rest of my obligations for today." There was no way I could entertain Thomas Reynolds in our Arlington headquarters while Madison Licht roamed the hallways of my mansion, snooping around.

Cara scurried after me. "Mr. Costa—"

"The answer is no."

"What should I tell Mr. Reynolds?"

"That something urgent came up. Family-related." This wasn't a fabrication. Something *had* come up. My blood pressure. I stormed into the elevator, facing a frantic, frazzled Cara.

"Sir, you have never, in the eleven years I've known you, missed an appointment."

"I have never, in the eleven years you have known me, chained my destiny to that of a beautiful sociopath."

It was the last thing I said before the elevator doors shut in her face.

Chapter Thirty-Five

Romeo

I navigated my driveway, forcing myself to fix my eyes straight. Or risk blowing a fuse that'd end up splattered across every local paper. Not to mention social media, under the ever-growing hashtag I shared with Dallas. I was unable to reconcile the fact that my nineteenth-century estate, which once housed a prominent Union general, had been reduced to the witching grounds of a spoiled Georgian heiress.

People spilled out of my grand entry. Someone body-checked my Bentley, sloshing beer onto the windshield. I didn't recognize a single one of them. My blood, which usually ran as cold as my dormant heart, sizzled hot with anger and the urgent need to inflict pain on someone. A certain lovely someone.

I'd never felt more alive in my life. *Or* as psychotic. Eighteen different cars occupied my sixteen-car garage. It took me eight minutes to locate a parking space on my own property. I stomped my way inside, shouldering past a panicked Vernon, who tried to run back outside.

A flushed Hettie met me at the door, both hands raised. "She said a small gathering of friends. I swear, Rom."

Shortbread's idea of a small gathering, apparently, consisted of an entire country club. Who were these people, anyway? She'd been in Potomac for less than two months. I recognized my friends, the personal shopper at Hermès, two three-Michelin-starred chefs whose restaurants Dallas frequented, and remarkably, what appeared to be the vast majority of people I'd saved on the blackbook spreadsheet in my home office. The do-not-engage-with crowd. People I systematically avoided at all costs. Somehow, she'd found them and invited each and every one of them to my house. Incredible. If I weren't so furious, I'd be deeply impressed.

"Out of my way."

Hettie hung her head, stepping aside. I shoved past the mass of bodies. Most hadn't bothered to dress up, enjoying the majority of the fine liquor from my wine cellar—the bottles I saved for special occasions—in Ferragamo leather slides and Bally tracksuits. A full catering spread stretched across every counter, courtesy of Nibbles, a local boutique service that charged $1800 per head for parties. People laughed, ate, mingled, and helped themselves to tours of my home. Which, by the way, was loud. Unbearably so. My soul, if I indeed possessed one, itched to burst out of my skin like a bullet and run for its life.

I bumped into a shoulder on my quest toward the stairway. The person turned. *Oliver.* The first thing I did was punch him square in the face. Not hard enough to break a nose, but certainly with enough rage to show what I thought of his recent behavior. For reasons pertaining to my shitty upbringing, I possessed an overdeveloped fight instinct. My first instinct in any situation, really. For decades, I'd reigned it in. Already, Shortbread had unleashed it on many unsuspecting victims.

"Aw." Oliver rubbed his cheek. "What was that for?"

"Saying sexist things about my wife, offering her sexual favors to my face, and frankly, because your face is annoying."

He sighed. "Fair enough. For the record—I am no longer interested in joking about bedding your wife. I figured it would hinder any future attempts to get with her sister."

Is anyone in my life over the mental age of thirteen?

"What do you have to say for yourself?"

He took a swig of Belgian beer they didn't even sell in the States. Jesus. How much money had this curse of mine spent during our brief marriage?

Oliver's brows pulled together. "Regarding what?"

I lost patience. "What on earth inspired you to RSVP to her party?"

"*Oh.* There was no RVSP." He twirled his finger. "This little shindig was all spur-of-the-moment. She pulled it together last minute. Incredible, right? She could do this for a living."

The idea of Shortbread possessing a job—or reporting to anyone other than her irresponsible self—was both laughable and inconceivable. This conversation chipped away the remainder of my patience. Oliver lifted the mouth of his beer bottle to his lips.

I held the base in place, forcing him to finish every last drop or risk getting waterboarded by the pilsner. "Oliver. Why are you here?"

When I released the glass, he recovered with a grin, wiping his lips with the back of his hand. "Well, the fact that she throws bomb-ass parties. She said there would be special catering, international alcohol, and fire theater. And so far, Derbyshire hasn't let me down."

Fire theater? In my house?

I fisted his shirt, losing all traces of the control I was so fond of. "Where is she?"

Oliver shrugged—or tried to beneath my fists. "Last I saw her, she was trying on some chick's cocktail dress, and that chick was trying on her dress."

"She was naked in front of other people?" I was going to have a coronary. At thirty-one.

"I can see why you're weathering the storm, bro. She's sex on legs. How's she maintaining that ass? Five hundred squats a day?"

Try two sleeves of Oreos and a McFlurry.

I wrestled my way through dozens of people until I reached Dallas's room. Locked. Of course. I busted the door down with a kick. I wasn't usually fond of damaging my five-thousand-a-pop rustica doors, but desperate times called for desperate measures.

Speaking of desperate, my wife was perched on the edge of her bed, wearing a gaudy, vibrant-green cocktail dress that didn't belong to her. Madison kneeled before her, actively weeping into her lap. The man boasted two black eyes from the DIY nose job I'd given him in Paris. And still, he was idiotic enough to tread into my territory without an entire army by his side.

Dallas looked bored and in character. It was obvious she'd spent a considerable amount of time waiting for me to make my grand entrance. She wanted my atten-tion—and she would now be at the unfortunate receiving end of it.

Madison scrambled to his feet while Dallas took her time rising, a hint of satisfaction on her luscious, plump lips. She'd won this round, and she knew it. I'd cut my day short to be here.

I circled him now, predatorial. My eyes never wavered from his frame. "Tell me, Licht. Were you absent on the day God handed out brain cells?"

"You can't lay a hand on me in public." Madison revealed his cards in our poker game. "And we are, for all intents and purposes, in a public place. There are almost one hundred people here."

He was right. Some of them milled outside the room as we spoke, wondering why the door was currently pancaked to the floor and the three of us looked so tense. It seemed apparent at least one of us would leave in a body bag.

"You're giving me undeserved credit." I cracked my knuckles, feeling dangerously close to dropping my calm and collected façade. "I may very well kill you right here and right now if you don't explain to me what I just walked into."

Shortbread pouted. "We were having a closure conversation."

I read between the lines. She'd chosen to become a player in this mess. And it worked. This marked the moment she ceased to be collateral.

"Or a make-up conversation," Madison countered. "Depends on how you look at it, really."

His attempt at goading me into a mistake was so obvious, he'd be better off taking out a Times Square billboard. And still, for the first time in my life, I traipsed right into his trap. Stopped circling him. Aimed my fist to his throat. I almost cut off his oxygen supply, but someone grabbed my elbow.

"Jesus, Rom. What are you doing?" Zach hissed in my ear from behind, pulling me away from Madison. If it were only Zach, I could probably shake him off. We were similar in size, but I had experience in this field and an extra fifty pounds of rage inside me right now.

Unfortunately, Oliver held my other arm. "I knew he was going to ruin all the fun. Next time, don't invite him, Daly City."

Dallas ignored him.

Madison chuckled. "This is all very middle-school playground, Costa. Can't control your emotions?"

"My emotions are fine. In fact, it *felt* extra nice to fuck your former fiancée with my tongue five minutes after I broke your nose in Paris."

A chorus of gasps ricocheted behind my shoulder. Most people viewed me as an unsympathetic and efficient businessman, who never colored outside the lines or did anything to garner gossip. Positive, negative, or otherwise. That image crumbled to ruins. Because of Shortbread. She'd officially stolen my second scandal, too.

Madison narrowed his eyes, reminding me why shampoo bottles came with instructions. "I should sue you for what you did to me."

"You should. That way, I can sue you for what *you* did to me."

He and I both knew exactly what I'd referred to. His smile disappeared. He edged himself further from Dallas, who had checked out of this conversation minutes ago and was now examining her cuticles. Her downturned lips reeked of dissatisfaction. Good thing she'd invited her nail technician, too.

"All right, buddy. Time to get out of here before I, myself, mess your face up further." With a cheerful grin, Oliver grabbed Madison by the ear like a nineteenth-century principal, dragging him out for all to see. "And

I hate to say this, but from the bottom of my heart, you cannot afford more damage to your already average face."

People spat out nervous laughter. I noticed no phones aimed at us. Shortbread must have confiscated them upon her guests' arrival. *Smart girl.* Dead girl, too, but smart nonetheless.

With Madison kicking, screaming, and threatening legal action while Oliver literally dragged him from the premises, I addressed the real culprit of my life's undoing.

"What do you have to say for yourself?"

"Not much." She pouted. "You seem to be doing all the talking for the both of us. Really, Rom? Telling the world about what happened in the hotel room?"

Not my finest moment, I'd give her that. Not that I was in a mood to admit it. "It was our honeymoon. Not one soul under this roof thought we were playing cards and discussing Dante poems in our suite. Now are you ready to be grounded?"

"Are we role-playing right now? Is this where you spank me, Daddy?"

Much to my horror, my dick stirred. Meanwhile, Zach hovered in the periphery, probably afraid I'd do something he thought I'd regret. Like kick Dallas out of my home and toss her Henry Plotkin books into the Potomac.

"Are you aware that Hettie is responsible for every misstep you make?"

That got to her. Shortbread straightened, meeting me in fast strides. "This isn't her fault. I promised her just a small get-together. But I never expected so many people to show up at your house. I thought they'd all avoid you like the plague."

"And I'm supposed to believe inviting every single person I've ever blacklisted within a hundred-mile radius is a simple innocent mistake?"

She pouted. "I thought it was your friends list. *Surprise*?" At my flat, unamused expression, she rocked on her feet. "How was I supposed to know what that list was? It's not like you tell me anything. I don't know a single thing about you. What city you were born in. The name of your first pet. Your mother's maiden name. Your favorite food as a child."

"You learn things by asking, Dallas. Not by throwing ragers that can be heard from the International Space Station."

"I *do* ask. You never answer me."

"Potomac. No pets. Serra. Anything with calories. See how easy that was?"

"Rom." That came from Zach, who approached my flank. I ignored him. "Anything else you'd like to know?"

"The make and model of your first car?"

"A Porsche Cayenne."

"*Rom.*"

I rounded on Zach. "What?"

"Do these questions ring any bells? From, oh, I don't know . . . The security questions to a bank account, perhaps?"

Dallas launched a fierce glare at him. "So, you can enjoy my party, but you can't help fund it? Are you going to foot the bill if he cuts my credit card? At least stay out of my way while I hustle."

From the hallway, Oliver cackled. "I love her, Rom. I just do."

I hadn't even realized he'd returned.

"Out." I pointed to the door, followed by my two friends. "Both of you. Out. And *you* . . ." I turned to Dallas. "You're coming with me."

"Why should I?" She flipped her hair. It took everything in me not to grab her by the waist and fuck the sass out of her in front of a full audience. The only thing stopping me was the fact that, sadly, it was probably part of her master plan.

"Because I said so."

She gasped theatrically. "Oh, why didn't you say so? In that case, start walking. I'll *surely* follow."

I smiled. "Because Henry Plotkin's entire series is going to look lovely with dancing flames around it when your fire theater starts."

That wiped the satisfied pout from her face. "Lead the way."

The journey to my bedroom passed in utter silence. Between us, at least. The house itself gushed out more noise than a BTS concert. I closed the door, locking it for good measure. Now that we were alone, uncertainty clouded her delicate features. I got in her face, losing the remainder of my composure.

Her back flattened against my window. "Are you having a heart attack?" But the bite had fled her voice, replaced by timidness. "Seeing as you're a neat freak and there's a trillion people partying here."

"Whose dress is this?" I grabbed the fabric of her garment between us, twisting it until it stretched along her smooth skin.

"Morgan's." She stared me down, chin tipped up. "She's here."

I didn't even miss one beat. "Fat chance."

"How do you know?"

"Because after I finished with her, I exiled her to Norway. She hasn't set foot in the States for the past six years. She would take her own life before willingly seeking me out." Cold words. Delivered without an ounce of sympathy. And still, more than what Morgan deserved.

Shortbread looked horrified. "Lord, what did you do to that poor woman?"

"Only what she deserved. Now answer my question. Whose dress is this?"

"Abby Calgman."

Abby Calgman. One of Madison's more prominent hookups. He often paraded her around our circles. In fact, I suspected he genuinely liked her. I'd bet the remains of my estate and the feral wife who'd ruined it that they were still seeing each other.

"I should probably give it back to her . . ." Dallas swallowed. Embarrassment painted her cheeks pink, probably from the fresh memory of showing the entire party her tits and ass. "I should go."

She tried to duck under my arm, but I crowded her more, a vicious smile playing on my face. "Why, Mrs. Costa, I'm afraid I cannot allow you to leave without a proper farewell."

"What do you mea—"

In one smooth movement, I tore the dress from cleavage to bottom, leaving it in a two-piece mess on the hardwood planks. Dallas now wore a black strapless bra and a matching lace thong.

Her mouth hung open. "You're insane."

I began unbuckling my belt. If I had to waste half a work day, something good needed to come out of it. As soon as I released my cock, heavy and engorged, all protests and venom abandoned Dallas. She licked her lips.

"Where do you want it?" I demanded.

Her gaze traveled up, meeting mine. "Inside me."

"*Where?* Specify. You have many holes, and all of them are begging to be fucked right now."

In a rare lucid moment, it occurred to me that Shortbread would see this as a reward not a punishment, and that might come with the unintended side effect of incentivizing her poor behavior. But it *also* occurred to me that, if my intractable wife did not touch my dick in the next few minutes, said dick might actually combust.

Dallas pursed her lips, refusing to play along. The woman harbored too much pride for her own good.

"Here?" I fisted my cock, running it along her slit through her panties.

She shuddered all over. In the back of my head, I remembered her ass against the window. That some of our guests in the garden below were privy to what was happening between us. But I couldn't care less. I'd come to the depressing conclusion that my out-of-control young wife brought out traits in me I'd never known existed.

She tilted her chin up but didn't answer.

"Or maybe . . . here?" I grabbed her by the waist and swiveled her around, shoving her against the glass. I slid my finger into the strap of her thong and moved it aside, letting it slap against her skin. Then I ran the crown of my cock along her ass. A moan escaped her. She arched her back to accommodate half an inch between her ass cheeks.

Still, no words.

My mouth found the shell of her ear. I twisted my hand around her, tugging her nipple. "Perhaps you're finally ready to return the favor for all the times I've eaten you out."

Shortbread gripped the windowsill, bending halfway and pushing into me. My cock slipped through her wet cunt, making me hiss with unabashed pleasure before I pulled out. I wanted to ram into her like my life depended on it, and she knew it.

"Foul play." I pinched her nipple.

She gasped, the inside of her thighs still becoming wetter with her desire. "You started it."

"Ever wonder what I taste like, Shortbread?"

"No."

"Well, you're about to find out."

I turned her around again, slithering my hand between her thighs. She was soaking through her thong, rubbing against me with excitement. Her panting made her tits bounce against my chest. I considered that she'd done all of this on purpose. With this exact reaction in mind. And still, I couldn't bring myself to stop.

"On your knees, Shortbread."

"In your dreams, asshole."

No point in telling her she played a leading role in my nightmares. To my dismay, my cock did not share the sentiment and pulsated between us.

She looked down, licking her lips. "Fine. But I'm doing it for him, not for you."

Dallas dropped to her knees, her hazel eyes avoiding my grays. She wrapped her hand around my cock, and I swear I almost came on her face right there and then. The confidence she displayed, despite her sheer inexperience, did me in. Another woman—basically any other girl of religious breeding and zero flight hours with sex—would ask for directions or apologize in advance for what might be a lackluster performance. Not my wife. No. She existed in her own little universe. A universe in which I, and every other man she captivated, orbited around her.

Shortbread studied my cock inch by inch, not a care in the world that there was an angry, impatient man attached to it, before swirling her hot, wet tongue over the crown. I tipped my head back, suppressing a grunt.

"A bit salty," she commented, then proceeded to, astonishingly, nibble on my cock. Her lips moved along the shaft, half kissing, half licking, as she grabbed it by its root. It was so erotic, so authentic, all I could do was stare in wonder. "You smell good," she observed, seemingly to my cock, not me, pulling back to look at it again.

Then, just when I was about to fall to my knees and beg her to suck me off, she opened her tight mouth, covered my shaft, and gave it a long, greedy suck.

Fuck. Fuck, shit, goddamn, fuck.

All my good manners flew out the door as Dallas serviced me in front of my window. I planted one hand on the glass and laced the other in her lush chestnut hair as she tried to take more and more of me. She made happy noises throughout, driving me over the edge, to the point where I knew, disconcertingly, that my knees would buck and I'd come like a preteen after ten seconds if she didn't stop.

I yanked her back by the hair, refusing to lose face. "On my bed."

On my bed? What in the ever-loving fuck was I asking her? No woman had entered my bed since Morgan—and not by coincidence. Sensing this as a once-in-a-lifetime invitation, Shortbread scrambled to her feet and bolted to my mattress. That train had left the station, and it had no brakes to speak of.

I shoved her down so she flattened against my duvet, head propped up on two of my pillows. Climbing on the bed, I bracketed her with my thighs, grabbed onto the headboard, and positioned my cock in front of her mouth. She stared up at me with pure exhilaration. I was trying to punish her, and she was legitimately going to ask for seconds. Unbelievable.

"I'm going to fuck that smart mouth of yours now, Shortbread."

Any other woman would at least pause to think about it. Eight inches long on a six-inch girth wasn't child's play.

But Shortbread just opened her mouth wide. "Okay!"

I slammed into her, hitting the back of her throat. She made a choking sound. Her eyes watered. I studied her for a second, unmoving, waiting for her to push me away. In a signature Shortbread move, she clutched my ass, drawing me closer to her. Once she grew accustomed to the size in her mouth, she peered up at me beneath a dark curtain of lashes. Excitement leaped from her eyes. My heart beat so fast, I thought it'd rip itself from its arteries and fall into oblivion.

I pulled out, then slammed into her mouth again.

Then again.

And again.

And again.

Soon, I was fucking her mouth without mercy. Without a care for our surroundings. Without a care for the fact that, in doing so, I gave her everything she wanted. The springs of the mattress squeaked. Dallas moaned, peppered by my grunts. Noise cloaked every surface. Yet, I wasn't half as triggered as I normally would be. Each time my cock met the back of her throat, my balls tightened and I was sure I'd bust my load.

Dallas suckled and licked, each movement hungry, taking every inch of me like it was her favorite meal. If this was the way I reacted to her mouth, what would happen if I ever took her cunt?

"I'm going to come in your mouth, and you're going to keep it, open your mouth nice and big, gurgle, taste, and then—and only then—swallow it. Am I understood?"

For all her disobedient ways, when it came to the bedroom, she was surprisingly good at following directions. She nodded enthusiastically. I thrust into her mouth faster, harder, and deeper. Tears ran down her face. It gave me pause that I didn't like seeing her cry, even when I knew it was not from sadness.

My orgasm was a thing of beauty. It had been far too long since I'd climaxed in a woman's mouth—in a woman, *period*. The amount of cum I ejaculated into her was astonishing. Enough to fill a damn Venti. Cum leaked from the corners of her lips down to her lovely throat and full tits.

I pulled back, watching her stare at me expectantly. "Open your mouth."

She did. More cum poured out of it. White and thick. I swiped my index finger along the corner of her lips, taking a few drops and rubbing them against her strained nipple. The rest of the cum I gently tucked back into her mouth.

"Gurgle on it, sweetheart."

She gurgled.

"Do you like it?"

She nodded, her cheeks tear-stained, her skin flushed.

"Let's see if you're telling the truth."

I brought my hand between her legs and slid it past her thong, sinking my finger into her tight pussy. She was so wet, I could shove a hammer into her and she wouldn't even feel it. My dick had already hardened again, and it hadn't even been a minute.

A smirk found my lips. "You'd let me do anything I want to you. Wouldn't you, Shortbread?"

She shrugged, her mouth still full of my cum.

"Can I fuck you in the ass?"

A nod.

"Can I fuck your cunt and finger you at the same time?"

An *eager* nod.

I wasn't going to, but it was nice to know.

I lifted a brow. "Can my friends join us?" This was a trick question, because there was only one answer—hell to the goddamn no. But Dallas nodded, still, a smile spreading across her face, making more of my cum drip down her chin. I fingered the curve of her jaw, closing her mouth. "Wrong answer. Now swallow everything nice and good, and open your mouth when it's clean."

She swallowed a few times. Opened her mouth. Her tongue was pink. Squeaky clean.

As I admired the view, all I could think was that she'd answered yes to fucking Oliver and Zach. I ripped myself off her, tucking my dick back into my briefs and buckling up. "Congratulations. If you wanted my attention, you got it. I'll move back into the house, if only to make sure it remains standing and survives you."

"All I heard was that you missed me," she cooed, spreading her limbs on my bed lazily.

"You need to get your ears checked."

"You need to get your heart healed."

"I like it just the way it is." I opened the door to my bedroom, signaling the end of our conversation. "Covered in ice and beating only for one purpose—my revenge."

I stepped past the threshold. And what did you know? Abby waited outside. In fact, she had eavesdropped, falling to my feet in a heap of limbs. She righted herself in a bout of panic and embarrassment, still wearing Dallas's pink chiffon dress.

"Um, hi, Rom. It's been a while."

"That's because I actively avoid you."

Abby pouted, glaring at me through false eyelashes. "I'm here to collect my dress."

"Did you think it was going to pour into your ear through my bedroom door?"

She blushed, huffed, and parked a hand on her waist. "Am I getting my dress back or not?"

"Not before you give me my wife's dress back."

Said wife remained behind my shoulder, tucked in my bed beneath my covers, cringing at the way I handled the entire situation. Served her right. I refused to touch the fact that I had a woman in my bed for the first time since Morgan with a ten-foot pole. Too much to unpack.

With a growl, Abby began stripping from the pink number. She hadn't worn a bra, thus her tits now dangled dangerously close to my chest. I resisted the urge to vomit on them.

"There." She flung her arms sideways. The dress pooled around her well-heeled ankles. "Happy now?"

"Not in the slightest. Wait here." I turned, retrieved the two pieces of ruined dress from the floor by my window, and hurled them her way. "Send my regards to Licht."

She shrieked. "Wait, the dress is torn."

"So quick-witted."

Abby stomped. "You bastard."

I slammed the door in her face.

Chapter Thirty-Six

Dallas

Romeo moved his things back the same day of my party. Right after he kicked everyone out and called his bi-weekly cleaning service to "bleach the entire house, walls and ceiling included."

I spied from my bedroom window as an army of people on his payroll wheeled his suitcases back inside. I hugged my arms, thinking about what had happened between us just hours ago. When Romeo came in my mouth, I'd saved some of his semen under my tongue. I read somewhere that sperm could still survive in the mouth, provided it remained in its gel-like form. It did.

When I dashed into my room to spit it into a mouth-wash cup, I figured I could try to get pregnant. But leaning against my sink, observing the white thing swim-ming in the small cup, something prevented me from doing it.

My morals, maybe. I still had them, though my husband had lost his somewhere along the way. It was sperm-stealing. It was wrong. And I, unfortunately, had boundaries I refused to cross. Sure, I had no obligation to take the ethical highway. Not after everything Romeo had put me through. He'd deceived me in so many ways, so it was only fair I deceived him back.

Still, my pride wouldn't let me conceive this way. With spat-out semen. In a bathroom. Like a thief.

No. Romeo's downfall would be of his own making. I intended to break him. The cracks were already apparent, imprinted everywhere on his behavior. He wanted me. I knew he did. Even if it was the last thing he needed.

As I watched my beautiful, awful husband weave through the garden, stone-faced, his phone pressed to his ear, undoubtedly discussing something work-related, I wondered what bringing him to full submission would feel like.

I was certainly going to find out.

Chapter Thirty-Seven

Romeo

> **Romeo Costa:** Cara couriered a dress to the house. Be ready at eight p.m. Sharp.

> **Dallas Costa:** Sorry, I have plans.

> **Romeo Costa:** Inhaling pho in front of Dead to Me isn't considered plans.

> **Dallas Costa:** Okay, in that case—sorry. I don't want to.

> **Romeo Costa:** It's for a charity gala.

> **Dallas Costa:** The most charitable thing you can do is send the check and not be there in person to ruin everyone's fun.

> **Romeo Costa:** Be ready at eight.

Shortbread ignored my text. That she'd texted me at all after the incident three days ago was nothing short of a miracle. The read receipt glared at me, ten minutes into my meeting with a Pentagon contact. Unfortunately, Bruce occupied the seat beside me. And also unfortunate was the fact that he was infuriatingly, incomparably phenomenal at his job. In truth, Bruce's only shortcoming was his function as Senior's pet. When it came to business, he deserved his imposing reputation. Walkman, who worked directly under the Deputy Secretary of Defense, latched on to each of his words, promising to sway his boss in our favor.

An hour and a half later, I checked my texts in the elevator to the parking garage. Still no reply. It was obvious Shortbread had no intention of attending the gala. As it was, she had no choice. My father would be there, which meant Costa Industries' entire board would be there. Showing up without my new wife would confirm every tabloid rumor Dallas and I had conjured in the past couple months. It didn't help that Shortbread's party had made the front page of DMV society news.

Bruce unpacked a Treasurer Luxury Black, flipping the cigarette in his fingers. "Trouble in paradise, Junior?"

Sickly sweet peach perfume invaded the tight space. It came straight from Bruce. I was reminded, once again, that Bruce and Senior shared much in common. Like the fact that they both considered adultery their daily cardio.

I pocketed my phone, wishing my penchant for death extended to the tobacco industry. That the cigarette in Bruce's hand would discard of him faster. "Is Shelley aware you've inseminated half of the DMV?"

"Not only is Shelley aware, she is also obedient enough to show up to tonight's gala. What a trooper." He slid the Luxury Black past his canines. "And your undomesticated wildcat? Will she be attending?"

Even if I have to drag her there by the hair, caveman-style.

When I arrived to my home, I found it empty. I checked the kitchen first, then the theater room, and finally her bedroom. No Shortbread. But I did find the signature olive Yumi Katsura box with the gold rose flourishes on her duvet. Unopened. A handwritten *thank you for shopping with us* card still nestled on top.

The entire point of moving back in was to monitor my banshee wife, yet she returned home every night past midnight and woke at three in the afternoon, only to leave the house again. This ended now. I unsheathed my phone from my Kiton pocket.

Romeo Costa: I am at the estate, and you are not.

Dallas Costa: I ate ota'ika and lu sipi for lunch. You ate Brussels sprouts and chicken.

It wasn't a stretch that she knew this. Afterall, I ate the same thing every day. Every meal. Three hundred sixty-five days a year. Even at our wedding.

Romeo Costa: ?

Dallas Costa: Were we not stating things we've done today?

Alas, her capacity for logical reasoning left much to be desired. Exiting the messenger app, I speed-dialed her security team. I found Shortbread in a small indie book-shop on the opposite end of the county. According to her detail, she'd spent the afternoon sampling every bakery on the block before settling on a mom-and-pop Tongan restaurant around the corner. Then she'd made a pit stop at a children's hospital, conjuring a donation so high I considered opening one of my own. And for the past two hours, she'd picked up and put down every book in the Romance and Fantasy sections in this store.

I approached Dallas, dress box in hand. She would have to change in the car and thank her lucky stars that she required no pampering and pruning to be the most beautiful woman in every room she stepped inside.

She startled at my touch when I tapped her shoulder, slumping forward at the sight of me. "Oh. It's you." Her fingers glided over another book, pulling it out. *His Filthy Touch*.

"There's a charity gala tonight. Attendance mandatory."

She slid the book back into its slot and moved on to another aisle. "I know. I read the text. Pass."

That whip-quick tongue of hers ignited a single wick within me. *Impatience*. "It wasn't a question."

"Trust me—so long as I'm an unwilling participant, you don't want me as your plus-one."

Since she had a point, I spoke in the only language she seemed to understand. Food. "The hosts flew in an itamae from Hokkaido."

She finally offered her undivided attention. "Sushi?"

It wasn't lost on me that she'd eaten just two hours ago.

"Yes. An eleven-course menu."

"Hmm . . . prix fixe." She considered it for a moment, pausing between Horror and Fantasy before moving on to Erotica. "I eat everything but roe."

"There is something in the world you will not eat?"

"It's more of a childhood aversion. Emilie and Sav once told me fish eggs hatch in bellies and swim around until they exit . . . *down south*, where they ride the pipes back into the ocean."

"And once a year, a pot-bellied man with a white beard slides down billions of narrow chimneys in a single night."

A wave of amusement crashed into her face. "I was young."

"Youth is not an excuse for stupidity." I forked over the dress box, depositing it on top of the hardcover she held with both hands—*A Lover's Thrust*. "I suggest you keep your mouth shut once we reach the venue."

"Afraid I'll embarrass you?"

"Afraid you'll embarrass yourself. Once you open your mouth, it will become abundantly clear to everyone that I did not marry you for your sharp wit. Whatever they assume after is neither my responsibility nor fault."

"I never agreed to go."

"It was never an option not to."

She peered into the box. "Ohhh . . . this season's Yumi Katsura. They sold out of the gown at Tyson's Galleria. I called the flagship, and they said they were back-ordered."

"Of course, you did."

"I want this dress in every color."

"That's already been arranged." This had nothing to do with affection. The dress was truly magnificent. So was Dallas. They paired well together.

"Okay." She shut the box and shoved it back in my arms, replacing it with another hardcover. This time: *Blindfolded by my Professor*. "I'll consider attending."

"Will you be considering it at the pace you typically process life? The event begins in an hour."

"What did you say the charity was again?"

"I didn't."

"Romeo."

In the interest of time, I caved. "Friedreich's Army."

Shortbread's lips parted. I had no doubt she'd googled the charity after the wedding. That she knew about Friedreich's ataxia. That she'd formed the connection between the disorder and Senior.

245

As expected, it clicked immediately, and she blurted out, "Fine. I'll go."

I chose not to inform her I wasn't attending due to my sick father but rather the swarm of vote-holding board members that trailed him everywhere he went. Let her think that—somewhere deep, deep, *deep* down—I cared about my sperm donor, so long as I did not show up to a public event without my wife.

She sailed past a row of curated sex-addiction self-help books, straight to the sign with five chili pepper emojis beneath a bolded Daddy-Dom-Little-Girl hashtag. "I just need some reading material for when it gets boring." She selected a hardcover that featured two shirtless blue men with horns and tails kneeling before a half-naked woman.

"Absolutely not." I yanked the book from her hands, raising it beyond her grasp.

"Don't be such a buzzkill. I'll cover it with a dust jacket. We can pick one from the classics section."

"We don't have time for this."

She moved onto a row of slip-cased books and slid one from its coffin, fondling the hardcover six different ways. I watched as she held it to her nose and sniffed. Then she opened the pages and checked each and every one. Her fingers traced the case laminate, feeling for grooves. As if she wasn't going to cover it with the dust jacket for *Crime and Punishment* later. And finally, she elevated the book to eye level, angling it at every degree to check for—I didn't know what. Dust? Dents? Her sanity? All of the above?

"Hurry up." I lifted my watch, noting the long arm's dangerous proximity to twelve. "I'll purchase the bookstore. You can return after the charity gala and choose whatever you like. The entire store, if you must."

"You're rich. We get it." She yawned. "The only billion-aires I like are fictional."

"Yet, the only people who can afford your existence are billionaires. And even then, just barely." I made eye contact with the frizzy-haired manager, directing him toward us with a glare. "Is your boss here?"

"Yeah." His hair bobbed with his nod. "Think so."

"Find him, then call him out."

He spoke into his employee radio, shifting from foot to foot. "He's in the stockroom. He'll be out in a sec, sir."

I retrieved my Centurion card from my wallet when my stubborn wife breezed past me toward the exit. Not for the first time, I found myself following her. "You're not purchasing anything?"

She deposited herself in my passenger seat, a frown touching her full lips. "Now that you intend to purchase this place, I can no longer shop here. I don't want to give you any business."

Unbelievable.

Chapter Thirty-Eight

Romeo

"The thing about ice is . . . it's bound to melt." Zach swirled the neat Scotch in his tumbler, studying an Elmer Nelson Bischoff painting in his subterranean garage, which a team of architects had converted into a fifteen-thousand-square-foot gallery.

Zach was sensible when it came to his cars, his clothes, his women, and his career—but he was downright rabid when it came to his art. Since he'd loaned a quarter of his private collection to Sotheby's two months ago, he'd taken the opportunity to fill the space with new findings.

The ice in question was my heart. A specific reference to my showdown with Madison thirteen days ago at Dallas's makeshift party. I was happy to report that, aside from the charity gala she'd spent fleecing a famous Japanese master of his top-secret recipes, I'd passed my rare time at home completely ignoring her, holed up in my office, working nonstop to prove to Senior that I was indeed worthy of the CEO position.

"My heart is not surrounded by ice. It is surrounded by not giving a care in the world about anyone." My voice reverberated over the walls with an echo. I waltzed through the immense space, stopping before a Gerhard Richter abstract painting.

"True." Oliver sloped against an empty sliver of wall, tossing back a shot of something strong. "When I think about someone who doesn't give a fuck, I think about an idiot who almost murdered his archenemy in front of dozens of people in his own fucking home, which is more wired than the goddamn Pentagon. All because the latter mingled with his wife."

"I can't believe I'm saying this, but I agree with Ollie here." Zach raked a hand through his ink-black hair. "She's turning you inside out."

"She's a mess in need of tidying up and straightening out," I countered, moving along to the next piece of hung art.

"Can we at least agree you make a shit-ass cleaner?" Oliver pushed off the wall, advancing toward a genuine Picasso. He reached to touch it.

Zach materialized at the speed of light, slapping his hand away. "What do you think you're doing? It's not a petting zoo."

Oliver yawned, perusing the place, probably searching for the nudity section. "I'll never understand what you see in this."

"In Picasso's *Les femmes d'Alger*?" Zach glared at him as if he'd suggested to replace the piece with a portrait of his own feces.

Oliver strode to the vintage alcohol cart, selecting a decanter of whisky. He circled it in the air by its neck. "Are we all going to pretend not to see that this 'work of art' looks like something a bored Midwestern housewife painted at her local YMCA to express the heartbreak of her broken-down marriage to an insurance broker who left her for his secretary?"

Zach blinked. "That was incredibly detailed and astoundingly ignorant."

I saluted Zach with my beer. "Don't forget condescending and stereotypical."

"Me? Condescending?" Oliver choked on his liquor. "I speak the truth of the average folk. This"—he pointed at Cy Twombly's *Untitled* painting—"looks like the back of my calculus notebook from seventh grade. And this"— he turned to *17A* by Jackson Pollock—"is clearly what happens when a low-quality Christmas sweater and a furball procreate."

Zach crumpled his nose, ambling to the red panic button on one of his walls and pressing it. "Security, I have a man here I need you to escort off my property."

Tilting an eyebrow up, I skimmed over the man in question. "I wouldn't call Oliver a man."

Oliver nodded. "A legend is more like it."

Zach turned to me. "Does she know about Morgan yet?"

"Not exactly."

Shortbread knew bits and pieces but not the parts that had carved the heartless beast out of me.

"What's her game plan?" Oliver set his glass down on the palm of a Grecian goddess. The only statue he—quote, unquote—*understood*. "It's obvious she has one."

The three of us parted, all moving in different directions, orbiting around pieces of art that spoke to us.

I stalled in front of the Jeff Koons balloon dog. "She wants to get pregnant."

Oliver chuckled. "Good luck with that."

I did not confide in him that she was fast approaching her goal, prancing around our home in barely-there nightgowns and constantly trying to seduce me. "At any rate,

Mrs. Costa isn't my concern right now." I finished my beer in one gulp, disposing of the bottle on the alcohol cart. "Licht Holdings went public today."

"I saw." Zach stroked his chin. "Their stock is predicted to skyrocket through the roof."

Which meant it was time to step forward and start meddling with their company.

"I've gone through their audits." I picked up my Burberry coat, sliding it on. "They're not bulletproof. Their revenue hasn't grown exponentially in the past couple years."

"That's because they were working on the technology side of things, not production."

Oliver ran his tongue over his upper teeth, lips tugging up. "And because they still haven't officially stolen your grandfathered agreement with the DOD."

If it weren't for the fact that I, myself, wished to see Costa Industries burned to the ground, I'd find my friend's glee distasteful. Nevertheless, for me to inherit the CEO position, I needed to take care of this matter. No small feat, seeing as Senior had been quite successful in ruining his ancestors' profitable organization.

I tipped an imaginary hat. "If you'll excuse me, gentlemen, I have actual work to do."

Just then, Zach's security team burst into the garage. Igor and Dane automatically moved toward Oliver. It wasn't the first time Zach had kicked him out on the basis of Oliver being a real-life troll.

Oliver followed me out the door. "Don't worry, fellas. I'll see myself out."

We proceeded to our designated cars, which we'd driven despite the fact that the three of us lived on the same street.

Before Oliver slid into his passenger seat, he released an *ask me what's wrong* sigh. I knew humoring him would be a mistake, but not doing so would break a three-decade tradition.

"What's wrong?"

"I don't know how to say this, Rom."

"With as little words as possible and quickly."

"The day your wife threw her little party . . ." He hesitated, scanning me. My guard immediately went up at her mention. "She hit on me."

"Hit on you?" I repeated. "Do you mean to say hit you? That would make more sense." And also fit into her general character.

"She offered herself to me." He rested an elbow on the open door of his Alfa Romeo. "Said she'd do it just to spite you."

That, I could believe. Now that I also remembered Dallas had agreed to be shared with my friends—a dare I'd given to taunt her that had blown up in my face—it started to make more sense. The back of my neck heated. My fingers tingled to strangle him. Feelings that had remained dormant for years crept back, dark and suffocating and full of resentment.

"And how did you react?" I finally spat out.

Oliver flashed his teeth. "I told her to call me after your impending divorce, of course."

That was all it took for me to launch at him. In seconds, I plastered him to the asphalt, fists bunched around the lapels of his collared shirt.

I tugged him until our noses squashed together, shaking with rage. "If you ever as much as fucking look at her ag—"

Before I could finish the sentence, faint clapping came from behind my shoulder. Zach emerged from his garage.

"Fine, von Bismarck. You win 50K. Try not to blow it on prostitutes."

Oliver pushed me off him and stood, brushing his clothes clean. "But prostitutes are my passion."

I straightened, glancing between them, unimpressed. "What was the bet?"

Zach signaled toward Oliver with his chin. "Von Bismarck here said you'd react more drastically than you did after what happened with Morgan." He paused, tilting his head sideways. "Christ, Costa, I've seen more reserved teenyboppers at a One Direction concert. You're a fireball of emotions where she is concerned."

"She didn't really hit on me, buddy." Oliver clapped my shoulder, leaning forward to catch my gaze. "Though you should probably know . . . if she ever does, I'll hit that so hard I'll leave indents the shape of my dick all over her body."

Sometimes, I wished Oliver still had a mother, just so I could fuck her and taunt him about it for eternity. I shook him off, deciding against all odds to end the evening without being arrested. Although I was about to meet Senior, so perhaps I still wasn't in the clear.

"It's different," I ground out. "I'm not jealous. I'm protective of her. Dallas did nothing wrong, other than existing."

"Denver did plenty wrong." A sad smile stretched across Zach's face. "You just keep forgiving her for everything."

253

Chapter Thirty-Nine

Dallas

". . . cost north of six figures to fix . . ."

". . . need more cameras in the East Wing . . ."

"Does anyone know where the damn penis on the Roman statue in the middle of the fountain went?"

The words jumbled together, pinging against each curve of my skull. They came from every direction. From voices I didn't recognize. In elevated pitches that suggested disbelief over the whole ordeal. I popped a single eye open, blinking away blurry white dots. An army of restoration specialists sprawled across the entire living room, where I'd fallen asleep last night during a binge sesh of *Friday Night Tykes*.

They'd come in and out of the mansion over the past few weeks, doing their best to rehabilitate the historic property to its original condition. Apparently, the tiny gettogether I'd hosted had left *major* damage. Silver lining—at least Romeo made acquaintance with people who knew how to party.

Hettie materialized before me, a goblet of green juice stretched between us. I accepted the glass and downed it in two gulps. My brain throbbed from hours of trying to sleep through a symphony of saws, forklifts, and nail guns.

"Romeo left a box on your bed."

I sank back into the couch cushion, uninterested in whatever my husband had to give me unless it required frequent diaper changes and its first word was *Momma*.

"He mentioned something about you not getting to choose the books you wanted before the charity gala."

I flung the throw off me, darting to my bedroom. Sure enough, a giant box of books rested on my mattress. I dove toward it, piling stacks of hardcovers onto my Somerset duvet. There must've been a dozen of them. At least.

A frown touched my lips. *A Radical History of Finance. The Psychology of Money. The Savage Investor.* Each title was worse than the last. We all knew the only books I consumed boasted a liberal dose of the words cock, pussy, and cum. What possessed him to think I'd ever read these? Another form of punishment, no doubt.

Really, I'd done Romeo a favor, seeing as this place hadn't seen a renovation since the 1800s and was in dire need of modernization. In fact, while the restoration team was at it, maybe they could replace the ugly Lincoln-era crystal monstrosity hanging in the foyer with a shiny LED Sputnik chandelier.

I returned all the hardcovers back to their box. In addition to being full of books I'd rather torch my eyeballs than read, I couldn't be certain Romeo hadn't done something to them. Like coat the pages with rat poison. I stared at the box, debating what to do. Whether to donate it or whether he'd tampered with the contents somehow. It would be just my luck to end up behind bars after unintentionally sending poisoned books to the local Salvation Army.

I decided not to chance it, calling for Vernon through the intercom system.

His voice rasped past the speaker a few seconds later. "Vernon speaking."

"I spotted a bonfire pit a few weeks ago. Is that available for me to use?"

"The one on the east side of the property? Overlooking the Potomac?"

"I think so. Can you set up a fire for me?"

"You got it, sweetheart."

Chapter Forty

Romeo

I strode through Costa Industries' lobby, carrying a stack of documents. At almost midnight, I was in no hurry to return to my personal agent of chaos. The building was dead, save for my father, whom, ironically, I *wished* was dead. I barged into his corner office.

"It is common courtesy to knock before walking into someone's place."

I invited myself to the seat in front of him. "It is common courtesy not to fuck your son's live-in fiancée."

Senior's mouth drew in a flat, dissatisfied line. I would never stop reminding him he was in no position to lecture me about conduct. Not after I'd walked into my penthouse to find my father eating my fiancée's pussy for lunch.

She'd sprawled spread-eagle on our dining table, still in the Louboutins I'd gifted her for Christmas. As for Senior, he continued licking his own cum out of her. I kicked Morgan out in her birthday suit, despite the fact that it was mid-December and colder than some chambers of my heart. Enjoyed a whisky from my balcony as she did the walk of shame in nothing more than her heels before a cop car collected her.

Afterward, Senior and I struck a deal. I agreed not to narc to Monica that he cheated on her—*again*. In turn, he made me the youngest CFO in Costa Industries' history. At twenty-four, I handled billions in contracts. I did a fine job, but the master plan was always to reduce everything Senior loved to nothing but cinders.

He wanted heirs. So, I gave him none.

He loved his company more than the oxygen he consumed. So, I vowed to destroy the company, liquidate it, and burn the money, if need be, just to see the pain in his face before he croaked.

Morgan represented my one and only attempt at normalcy.

And my father annihilated this effort.

Senior pushed back in his seat. "Are you going to hold this over my head for eternity?" His hands shook. Lately, they always did.

I yawned. "You didn't dent my car. You fucked my fiancée."

His forehead creased like a crumpled napkin. "You haven't used profanity in years. You're changing."

I was tired of people telling me how much I'd changed since Shortbread waltzed into my life. As it was, even in the midst of conversation, my thoughts wandered to Dallas. Where else? I'd shown little interest in world affairs since my dick found out my wife's pussy was its favorite location.

I boomeranged the documents on his desk. "Let's cut to the chase."

"Licht Holdings went public this morning."

"Thanks for yesterday's newsflash." I rifled through the paper, hunting for a particular one. "I haven't been able to sit down with Thomas Reynolds." Mainly because I was busy breaking up a house party and attending to the important task of fucking Dallas's pretty mouth. "But

258

I spoke to him on the phone last night. He confirmed the DOD is leaning toward not renewing the contract with us."

My father rubbed his cheek as if my words had slapped him. "Did he say why?"

"Our tech is dated compared with Licht's." I found what I was searching for—a list of weapons and artillery Licht Holdings manufactured for a fraction of our retail price—and slid it his way. "Not to mention, they're simply more affordable. They manufacture in the South, while you stayed in New England, where minimum wage is much higher. They also struck some lucrative deals with steel and chip companies."

Senior shoved the document back to me like a toddler refusing new food. "I don't want to see this. I want you to come up with solutions."

"Make me CEO and I will."

"Do it. Then I'll make you CEO."

Senior once enjoyed a youthful, handsome face. When Licht Holdings entered the picture, I'd deliberately failed to stop them. In the years since, he'd sprouted grays, wrinkles, and dark circles. Truth was, he loved Costa Industries enough to bow out and watch me save it. It was his legacy. The only thing his good-for-nothing father (see a theme here?) had left him.

"Look." He tossed his arms up. "It's no secret I'm no longer cut out for this. I've wanted to retire for a year now. The only reason Bruce is even in the running to take my place is because I cannot completely trust you not to do something deranged to get back at me."

He'd hit the nail on the head, then rammed it through a twenty-inch wall. But I'd hardly ever admit it.

"You think too highly of yourself. I want the CEO position because I deserve it. And because no one would take care of this company as well as I would. I am the heir apparent."

"Also, *apparently* a vindictive asshole." He raked his silver hair. "I've seen what you've done to poor Madison Licht for doing much less than I did to you."

"Madison Licht is not poor, and the extent of what he did to me you will never know."

"Even so, relieve us of the Licht problem, and I'll give you the CEO position. One last hoop to jump through. Promise."

I remained silent. So long, in fact, he jerked his leg under the desk.

"I will need this in writing."

He nodded. "I'm happy to sign."

"My lawyers will be in contact with yours." I collected my documents, happy to get as far away from him as possible.

"You should thank me, you know." Because clearly, being an accomplished waste of natural resources simply wasn't cutting it, he had to be delusional about it, too.

"Which part?" I feigned interest. "The crappy upbringing or the bit where you ruined my one and only semi-normal relationship?"

Though it had to be said—Morgan bore responsibility, too. No one forced her to open her legs to my father.

"The part where Morgan clearly wasn't the woman you're destined to marry, just as I warned you. In the few months you've known your wife, you've escaped your shell, lived a little, used your potty mouth again."

"Yes, Dallas deserves a Pulitzer for driving me to sacrilege."

"Point is, you found someone better."

"You've taken a liking to her, haven't you?"

"Of course."

"Last time that happened, you acted on your feelings." I stood. "There won't be a second time, Father. If you get anywhere near Dallas, I'll kill you with my own hands. Make it extra messy, too."

His smile faltered. "Why do you think I'd make the same mistake twice?"

I towered over him. "Because you can't help yourself. From the moment I was born, you wanted everything I had. And me? I've only wanted one thing you own—your title."

Chapter Forty-One

Ollie vB: @ZachSun, want to know what I did with the 50K you gave me?

Zach Sun: Donated it to the tired, the poor, the huddled masses yearning to breathe free?

Ollie vB: Wow. So surprised you never got invited to the illegal raves at Harvard.

Romeo Costa: Go ahead and enlighten us, @OllievB

Ollie vB: I bought a piece of art.

Zach Sun: You did no such thing.

Romeo Costa: @ZachSun I think he's referring to vintage Playboy editions.

Ollie vB: Har har, o ye of little faith.

Zach Sun: Penthouse limited edition?

Ollie vB sent an image to the group.

Romeo Costa: First, assure me that opening this file won't land me on the FBI's watch list.

Ollie vB: The amount of abuse I'm subjected to in this group will land me on a therapist's couch one day.

Zach Sun: You should land there thrice a week regardless. You have more issues than National Geographic.

Ollie vB: Just open the attachment.

Zach Sun: It's a . . . tweet?

Romeo Costa: Of a college girl eating ice cream in a bikini?

Ollie vB: NFT, baby.

Zach Sun: Ollie.

Zach Sun: OLLIE.

Zach Sun: NFTs are the biggest fake news since the Earth is flat.

Ollie vB: Just because all other celestial objects are spherical doesn't mean ours is, too, @ ZachSun. Don't be a blind follower. Think outside the box.

Zach Sun: The oval-shaped box, I assume?

Romeo Costa: You just wasted 50K, my friend.

Ollie vB: But I was specifically told by some guy on Reddit it is going to be worth millions one day.

Zach Sun: He didn't really do it.

Ollie vB: Of course, I didn't. I just wanted to see if you thought I was THAT dumb.

Romeo Costa: Guess you got your answer.

Ollie vB: Yeah. Though it still escapes me how Rom is the one who is married to a Victoria's Secret model and refuses to knock her up and I'M the one with the low IQ.

Zach Sun: You mean QI.

Ollie vB: Fuck you, Sun.

Chapter Forty-Two

Romeo

I slid into a less-than-gallant habit. The habit included watching Dallas throughout my workday via my home security cameras and employing a security detail on retainer to trail her whenever she left the house. Seeing as my contentious industry made me a walking target, I could've given myself excuses about worrying for her safety. But deep down, I knew I had her shadowed because I wanted to be sure she wasn't doing anything I forbade her to do.

Which, in my defense, was one thing and one thing only—other men.

In the weeks since I'd moved back in, my delicate flower of a wife had managed to do quite a bit, including but not limited to officially dropping out of her Emory degree program, single-handedly funding a SIDS awareness month gala, paying off existing medical debt at no less than three regional children's hospitals, and sampling every Michelin-guide restaurant within driving distance.

She spent her days reading books, bullying big corps into donating to SIDS research, and playing board games with Hettie and Vernon. At night, she binge-watched garbage on Netflix and pined over other people's babies on social media. Personally, I didn't see the appeal in children. That she wanted one so bad—let alone multiple—suggested she was in desperate need of a hobby. And no, eating was not a recreational activity, as she attempted to convince me many a times.

She also took it upon herself to rearrange my entire home, pushing furniture into areas they had no business being. Not to piss me off, I didn't think. But rather, because she couldn't restrain her desire to make her environment as chaotic as her.

One morning, I found her in my office, perched on my wheeled wing-backed chair. Hettie sat on the armrest, separating white Oreo filling from its shell.

I strode to my desk and collected my laptop. "What are you doing?"

Shortbread licked the inside of an Oreo. "Hanging up our wedding portrait."

"In my office?"

"Where else would I hang it?" She nodded for Vernon to hike up the left edge, then signaled for him to stop with a raised cookie. "Perfect."

I studied the image, noting one important fact. "I'm not in this."

She beamed. "I know. Isn't it perfect?"

I left the portrait in place, unsure why. But her image haunted me every time I stepped into my office. My stock portfolio, like my net worth, had nose-dived since my marriage, which my friends enjoyed bringing up at every opportunity.

Ollie vB: Looks like you're on your way to becoming a millionaire. Congratulations.

Zach Sun: At this rate, you'll burn through your net worth quicker than Bankman-Fried.

Ollie vB: Whoever thought it'd be a good idea to fork over money to someone whose name, backwards, is Fried Bank Man?

Romeo Costa: Coming from the guy who invested in the Chicago Bulls because, flipped upside down, the logo resembles a robot fucking a crab . . .

Ollie vB: Actually, it's an altar-boy alien reading from the Bible. And you call me a heathen.

Zach Sun: Heathen is too weak a word for what you are. How about pagan? Infidel? The prime symbol for the fall from grace of polite civilization?

For the most part, Dallas and I coexisted in peace by not acknowledging one another's presence. Shortbread ruined the streak when she barreled into my study, days later, drenched in sweat, interrupting my virtual meeting. I exited out, not nearly as irritated as I should be.

Rather than greet me, which would be too mannered for my banshee wife, she planted her knuckles on my desk, sending my mouse flying into my lap. "I need your help."

I inventoried Dallas, taking in the remote clenched in her fist and the angry flush decorating her cheeks. Leave it to her to get so worked up over an episode of *Cheaters*.

I reclined in my chair and laced my fingers together, already debating what I'd bargain for. "If this is about selling tanks to your high school buddy as props for his bachelor party, I already told you, my hands are tied."

"Help me form a political lobbying group for infant product safety." She wiped sweat off her brow. "I know you have connections in D.C."

At this point, her obsession with children made me wary of her kidnapping one to call her own.

I returned my mouse to its rightful place, opening an email from Cara. "While I support the cause, Costa Industries does not engage in politics beyond defense lobbying. It's our corporate policy to maintain bipartisan support."

"Costa Industries won't be doing a darn thing." She jabbed her thumb into her chest. "*I* will work for the lobby.

"*You* are my wife and, therefore, an extension of Costa Industries. Word of advice, lobbying is an impossible job in general, let alone a suitable first occupation. Try walking before you run." I eyed the sweat beaded on her temple. "Just the journey from the couch to my study seems to have taxed you."

"I've had a job."

"Operating the kiss cam for your college basketball team doesn't count. Especially since you were fired."

"*Unjustly.*"

"You turned the kiss cam into a baby cam."

"Your point?" She set the remote down and rounded the desk to my side, standing before me. "The news said there's a bill to repeal the ban on crib bumpers. They increase the risk of SIDS."

What was with her and SIDS? Already, I'd found dozens of charges on her credit card to more SIDS charities than I knew existed.

"I cannot risk any weaknesses for Bruce and Senior to pick apart." I forwarded a document for proofing, moving on to an email from a financial analyst. "This includes breaking a long-standing company policy."

"*Rom.*"

"My answer won't change."

She hesitated a moment, edging back before inching closer. Her eyes fluttered shut. Slowly—so, so slowly—she sank to her knees. For a moment, she didn't breathe. Neither did I.

Finally, her eyes popped open. She rested a white-knuckled fist on each knee, staring so deep into me I wondered if she saw a soul. "I am literally begging you, Romeo."

"And I am literally answering your request in the most pragmatic, logical wa—"

"Fuck your pragmatism!" Her breaths escaped in heavy, erratic jerks, her eyes breathing fire into the room, hiking up the temperature. "Have you ever wondered why I care so much?"

I did. All the time. But I said nothing, waiting for her to continue.

"When I was six, Frankie and I finally got our wish. A sibling. A sister. A beautiful baby girl. Momma let us name her. Victoria." Her throat bobbed. She was looking at me but not really.

I turned rigid in my seat. For the first time in ages, panic wrapped around me, lacing through my bones with startling familiarity. *Shit.*

"She was lovely. So sweet and chubby-cheeked and happy. Healthy. She was healthy, Rom." Still on her knees, Dallas pinched her delicate brows together, as she collected the memory between trembling fingers, weaving together her past. "I remember the day I found her. A Sunday. I woke up extra early to pick matching dresses for church. Victoria—Tory—was only four months old."

She paused, running a hand down her shirt as if she could soothe away the pain. "I found her blue and stiff. She still looked asleep. Angelic and comfy. Just . . . blue."

Her sister died of SIDS. It made sense now. Her fascination with the subject. Her tunnel focus on infants. The first death she'd ever witnessed—a tragedy of magnificent proportions—carved a different person out of her.

And she begged me to help fight this demon.

But I had my own ghosts to slay.

"Romeo." She perched her hands in my lap, gazing at me with defiance, with pain, with rawness—but, I noticed, not with tears. "Please. Help me do this for Victoria. She passed away, but her legacy can still live on."

It killed me to do this to her. To deny her something so profound and important. So uniquely Shortbread.

I fingered her jawline, tilting her chin up, pushing through the lodge in my throat. "You may donate another wing to whatever children's hospital you'd like. Money's no issue. But forming a lobbyist group is out of the question."

Dallas rose slowly, inch by inch. I held my breath.

"You're a coward." She spoke with a voice void of emotions, her expression blank. "Luckily, you're *my* coward. I know your weakness now, Romeo. And I fully intend on using it."

Chapter Forty-Three

Romeo

Days after Dallas detonated a truth bomb in my study, she shimmied into one of her many Chanel gowns, shackled on expensive jewelry, and swiped her favorite red lipstick across her pouty lips.

Shortbread flipped me the bird as she passed a security camera on her way out and slipped into the back of Jared's Maybach, going out for the day.

From my corner office in Costa Industries, I dialed Alan, the trained martial artist I'd hired to tail her. "My wife left the house. See to it that she is safe." I wondered if the lie sounded more convincing to him than to me. "Don't forget to text me where she is and whom she is with at all times."

"Yes, sir."

"Where is Jared taking her now?"

"Looks like she's headed toward your office, sir."

My treacherous, good-for-nothing heart thumped out of whack in its bony cage. I sized up the picture of Shortbread I kept on my desk for appearances' sake. *Did you somehow discover I secretly manipulated the sudden congressional support for your crib bumper ban? Are you on your way to thank me with a sexy number under your dress?*

Dumping my engraved pen over my documents, I reclined against my backrest, laced my fingers together, and tapped them against my lips. I supposed enough time had passed since my last lapse to grant me another taste of her.

The ease in which I snatched the remote to the glass shade and rolled the curtain all the way down in advance should have clued me in to my increasingly poor judgment regarding Dallas. Unfortunately, my brain didn't take the hint.

In lieu of using my brain cells to do something productive like work, I wore down my gum and tidied up my already pristine office space. As though neatness was something she appreciated. When ten minutes became twenty, I began to ponder the eternal question—*what the fuck?* Yet, calling Alan and nagging him about my wife's whereabouts was beneath me. Perhaps they'd hit traffic. Gnarly car accidents were not out of the ordinary in my neck of the woods. Plenty of foreign envoys protected by diplomatic immunity, whose extracurriculars included running over people as if it were a GTA assignment.

When twenty minutes turned into thirty, my fingers itched to call Alan. As it happened, my phone danced on my desk, his name appearing on the screen.

I picked up. "Yes?"

"She reached her destination, sir."

Impossible. Had she truly reached her destination, she would be on her knees under my desk, sucking my cock.

"Is that so?" I smashed my gum between my molars, rightfully wary, given the sovereignty with which Shortbread conducted herself. "Where is she, exactly?"

"She just walked into Le Bleu. Got a street-facing seat on the balcony and a bottle of champagne. Looks like she's waiting for someone."

She sure as all hell wasn't waiting for me. Le Bleu was a two-Michelin-star restaurant right across from my building. In fact, Bruce's office offered a direct line of sight into the place.

Two things became immediately clear to me: 1) This was another power move on Dallas's end, designed to piss me off. 2) This was the last time she would tamper with my life. There'd be no more second chances. No wiggle room for negotiation.

"Check if there's paparazzi nearby." My jaw locked around my gum. I'd bet my entire personal wealth and right testicle there was.

Alan cleared his throat, taking a moment, presumably, to search. "Yes, sir. There is. Across the street." Another company's headquarters all but kissed the Costa Industries building. Licht Holdings. "Sir, someone is approaching her. I'm going to hang up and initiate a video call, so you can—"

"No need." I stood, shouldering into my coat. "Let me guess—tall-ish man, blond hair, and busted-up nose, sporting a tailored suit and zero charisma?"

"Wha—how did you know?"

"I'll be there soon."

I hung up, proceeding to the conference room across the hall. Somehow, Shortbread had spotted her tail, didn't like it, and retaliated by meeting with Madison somewhere public.

Message received.

Now it was time to deliver mine.

Madison's objective in this arrangement could be spotted blindfolded from the top of the Washington Monument. Being seen with my wife—documented by the local tabloids, no less—humiliated me. But I played the long game. Besides, every passing minute I didn't burst into the restaurant and cause a scene would increase their discomfort.

My index finger sank onto the intercom button. "Cara."

My assistant materialized, scurrying behind me on high heels, an iPad clutched between her manicured fingers. "Yes, Mr. Costa?"

"I'll send you a list of people I need to be put through with for an urgent call."

"Urgent when?"

"Urgent now."

For fifty-five minutes, Dallas and Madison simmered in their own awkwardness as I finished a conference call, followed by a full plate of Brussel sprouts and chicken breast prepared by the company chef. Alan's texts buzzed through in periodic increments.

> **Alan Reece: Very odd, sir. They're just staring at each other without talking.**

> **Alan Reece: Looks like they're waiting for something?**

That something was me.

> **Alan Reece: They're both eating bluefin tuna. The man is checking his watch every two seconds.**

If Madison hoped for me to beat the living lights out of him in public, he was in for crushing disappointment. I'd give my young wife one thing. For a man who prided himself in having a flatlined range of emotions, she somehow made me feel. Anger, frustration, annoyance, and disgust—but feel nonetheless.

Finally, an hour after Dallas and her ex-fiancé paraded into Le Bleu, I made my way there. I met Bruce in the elevator downstairs.

"Seems like there's more drama with your little Southern belle." He pressed the lobby button, watching the numbers atop the sliding doors roll down. He must've seen Madison and Dallas from his office. Hard to miss the sea of paparazzi out front. "Can't be good for your reputation."

I smoothed a hand over my suit. "Neither would a *Page Six* item about a certain CEO candidate's affair with a golf-course attendant."

His smile disappeared faster than a complimentary bread-stick basket in front of Dallas at the Olive Garden. "That is a blatantly malicious rumor."

"Tell it to little Ginny, who promised me she'd write a tell-all about you if I cover her student debt."

As soon as I marched through the revolving entrance door of Costa Industries, the paparazzi circled me like hungry piranhas, snapping hundreds of pictures. Sixty minutes of smug anticipation melted together as I crossed the street. Shortbread was slouched on the edge of a Wassily chair atop Le Bleu's balcony. At the sight of me, her back went ramrod straight. She pored over every inch of me, hawkish eyes desperate to read my blank face.

Following her line of vision, Madison glared at me, too. With a rare sunny smile—and using every drop of serenity in my bloodstream—I breezed up three flights of stairs to the restaurant. At the double doors, a hostess and two waiters offered deep bows as they opened both sides.

So. Word had gotten out to management. Already, I enjoyed the fruit of my labor.

I proceeded to Shortbread, seized a chair from an occupied table without permission, and invited myself to join my wife and her ex-fiancé. "How's the tuna, my dear?"

I swiped her fork and carved myself a nice, juicy piece, popping it into my mouth. Dallas scratched her temple, brows squishing together. Camera flashes glittered in my periphery.

"Darling, please close your mouth." I used the tip of my finger to shut it for her, then speared a chunk of dead fish, hovering it between us. "It is so unbecoming to look like what you eat."

Madison cleared his throat. "We were in the middle of something." Sweat bled from his pores, as he sought a meltdown that would never come. "No one invited you to join us."

I faced him. "You're absolutely right. But I'm here with a proposition."

He arched a single eyebrow. "Whatever it is, it won't allure me."

"Humor me."

"Romeo . . ." Shortbread captured her glass. Water sloshed to the rim, courtesy of her shaky hand.

Whatever happened to the fountain of defiant attitude she drowned me in every waking moment of the day? Surprisingly, I did not find this timid version of her as appealing as the fiery one I'd grown accustomed to. That I thought of her enough to develop preferences should have concerned me.

Madison's jaw flexed. His failed attempt to stare me down elicited rare, genuine laughter from me.

I plucked Dallas's linen napkin and patted the corners of my lips. "Since you two obviously find it difficult to stay away from one another, I have come to the inevitable conclusion that I can no longer stand in the way of what is clearly a once-in-a-lifetime love story."

The silence at the table was so thick and loud, you'd think this was a morgue.

Madison spoke first. "You married her."

"That, I did. See, there is a certain invention called divorce. It is incredibly effective and quick, especially for people with iron-clad prenuptial agreements such as ours." I squeezed Dallas's rigid hand. "Isn't this true, sweetheart?"

She was pale as freshly fallen snow—and just as frozen. As always, her feelings were clearly written on her face.

Yes, your plan backfired. Yes, I know you want Madison Licht a little less than you want to have your limbs amputated by a shark. And yes, we both know that Madison is, in fact, more rotten than yours truly.

Madison tossed his napkin over his plate. "You took her virginity."

"Don't be such a prude, Licht. Your own virginity was lost so long ago and so scrupulously, I'd be surprised if it's even in the same cosmos as us. Besides . . ." I spun my head back to Dallas. "Isn't that what you've always wanted? A way out of this marriage?"

"Yes." The word shoved past her lips. "But not so I could enter another toxic relationship."

Tsking, I fingered my jawline. "Should have specified."

Madison's eyes darted to Shortbread. "I'm not marrying her."

She pushed back in her chair, unaffected by his rejection. "Same."

"How devastating." I yawned. "And here I thought an angel would earn its wings through my matchmaking skills."

When I stood, they mirrored my movements, glued to me with an intoxicating mixture of horror and trepidation. "Mr. Licht . . ." I angled my entire body toward him. "Kindly evacuate the premises."

Madison pulled his shoulders back, straightening to his full height, ready for the showdown he'd anticipated. "You can't tell me what to do. This is not your restaurant."

"Actually, it is." I collected my phone and slanted the screen in his direction. "The deed was signed earlier this hour. Admittedly, waking Jean-Pierre from his slumber in France to convince him to sell me this fine establishment was a challenge, but as you're well aware, I never shy away from those."

Madison gaped at the contract. "You *bought* this restaurant just so you could kick me out of it?"

"And every other restaurant and food cart on this street," I confirmed, aware of the cameramen still surrounding us, too far away to eavesdrop. "Which means lunch breaks have become particularly challenging for you."

"You can't do that."

"What is the point in telling me I cannot do things I clearly just did?"

"You've officially lost it. I heard rumors, but now I see it's true."

"Doubt I ever really had *it*." I sighed. "Any parting words before I call security?"

Sadly, if there were such, I did not get the opportunity to hear them, because Madison all but stomped out of the place without as much as a farewell to the woman he'd shared brunch with.

I swiveled to Shortbread. This was the second workday in a single month she had completely ruined for me. Though one couldn't blame me for not being fond of Senior's company, I needed to at least pretend to care about it.

"Feel free to enjoy any of our wonderful desserts. My apologies for your lack of company." With that, I strode away.

She followed me, as I knew she would. I slid into the back seat of my Maybach, not sparing her a glance when she scooted in from the other side, uninvited.

"You have two options." I lounged in the brown leather seat while Jared weaved his way out of Le Bleu's parking lot. Dallas leaned closer, drinking every word, knowing her entire life depended on them. "Since I know how badly you want to both have children and return to your family, I shall grant you neither, instead tucking you away in my Hamptons mansion, where you will remain far enough from everything and everyone you love while stripped of your ability to inflict serious damage on my life. Or . . ."

I stroked my chin, giving it some thought. As a general rule, I did not reward bad behavior. But in Shortbread's case, I often found myself making exceptions, including but not limited to the box of books I'd gifted her for attending the charity gala despite her unruly behavior during the third dinner course. (She'd tried to take an uni shot off a pop star's tits. When I'd pried her away and lectured her on behaving in public, she shrugged me off and informed me that with great power comes great responsibility.)

And this time, the same forgiving part of me I'd never unearthed before she'd swaggered into my life wanted to give her a second chance. Or rather, a trillionth chance. I chucked it to my ruining her life. That must have been the reason I still possessed an iota of patience for the creature in front of me.

Shortbread's eyebrows flew up, almost kissing her hairline. "Or?"

"I will give you what you want. I'll grant you a divorce. You will return to Chapel Falls and become a living, breathing scandal. Ruined for all intents and purposes. You will probably marry a widower or a divorced man with kids. But you will have the freedom you crave so much."

It angered me to no end that my breath recoiled in my lungs as we stared each other down, waiting to see which option she would choose. I purposefully left out anything remotely appealing for her to fall back on. Dallas needed to comprehend the graveness of the situation.

Finally—*finally*—she ruptured the silence. "Can I think about it on our way to the house?" Somehow, it was the worst thing she could have said. The waiting would be pure torture.

I shrugged, diverting my attention to my texts. Once Jared dropped us off, a waiting Hettie and Vernon stood on the driveway.

"Well?" Hettie said before Shortbread's door even opened all the way. "Did you piss him off?"

Vernon ambled forward after her. "Will we finally have a little munchkin in the house?"

I entered my home first, which meant my disloyal staff—turned against me by my own wife—fell back, furious blushes glued to their cheeks, eyes pinned to the floor. "Both of you, get the hell out."

Vernon, the gentle giant, blinked. "But where should we go?"

"Anywhere out of my eyesight if you want to keep your jobs," I advised, ridding myself of my coat and advancing to the stairs. I did not spare Shortbread a look. "You have another thirty minutes to consider your answer while I make some calls. I'll come to your room when I'm ready."

Through the tall glass window sprawled along my stairway, I witnessed Shortbread collapsing on the bottom stair in her beautiful dress, her head tucked between her arms, her hair cascading all the way down her back.

She wasn't going to get a baby.

She wasn't going to get a divorce, either.

All she would get was a reality check.

As for me? I always, *always* got what I wanted.

Chapter Forty-Four

Romeo

Forty-five minutes after I left her to sob on the stairs, I skulked to Shortbread's room. It did not surprise me to find it empty. The silly rose she kept in the Q-tip jar had shed petals all over the place. That the cleaners hadn't wiped the nightstand surface beneath it must have been my unkempt wife's doing. It was not lost on me that she had fused herself into my home so thoroughly, it would become an entirely different place should she choose to leave.

I stalked the hallways in search of Dallas. Rain pelted the roof, knocking on the windows. The temperature had plummeted since our return from Paris. The cold never bothered me—I was used to it inside and out. But it occurred to me that my wife might not be enchanted with the bitter frost that arrived once fall drifted away, making room for winter.

Not in the mood for playing hide and seek, I produced my phone and checked her whereabouts through the security cameras. Rewinding the videos, I found footage of her dragging an oversized Louis Vuitton suitcase to the subterranean garage, two balled fists clutching the handle as if it sheltered a dead body.

A suitcase.

I bolted in that direction. A potent potion of anger and alarm bubbled in my stomach. What did she think she was doing?

Choosing one of the options you gave her. Leaving, you moron.

It no longer surprised me that I had a reaction to Dallas—a fact at this point. But it twisted my gut and every inner organ, pretzeling them in a ball of apprehension, to admit just how deeply she dug into my skin. So deep, she seeped through flesh, blood, and bone. Through stem cells, cerebral scars, and dense layers of ice. She hit right where it was raw and tender. Where the pain was inescapable. Not because I liked her—for I truly did not like Dallas Costa.

But because I *wanted* her.

Craved her.

Because touching her was the only goddamn thing I could think about.

By the time I burst through the doors of the underground garage, I had enough rage in me to light up Vegas. Nonetheless, my composure remained impeccable. Dallas perched atop a mountain of suitcases beside the Maybach, snacking on a small box of strawberry-covered Pocky sticks. Her legs dangled in the air, like a child's. It sickened me to see someone so unsophisticated hold so much power over me.

I circled her with my hands knotted behind my back. "Going somewhere nice?"

"Any place away from you is lovely."

Inside, something—*someone*—screamed at me to force her to stay. Not because I could tolerate her, but because losing her meant losing to Madison.

Instead, I feigned indifference. "Chapel Falls or the Hamptons?"

"Chapel Falls." She sucked the strawberry coating clean before dropping the bare stick back into the box. "I don't mind marrying someone with kids. More children to surround myself with."

What was with this woman and small humans?

"I'll call Jared." I brought my phone to my ear, unbelieving that, for the first time in my thirty-one years, someone had called my bluff—and that that someone enjoyed Henry Plotkin books and *Cheaters*.

"No need." A satisfied hum buzzed up her throat at the taste of another Pocky stick. "I already called him. He's on his way."

You gave her an ultimatum. She chose. Now walk away with your dignity intact, and find another way to taunt Licht.

I pocketed my phone. "My lawyers will send you some papers to finalize the divorce. Shouldn't take too long because of the prenup."

A sweet, toothy smile grew around her snack. "Great!"

"Although . . ." I advanced a single step. "With the amount of time we've been married, perhaps an annulment is a better option." An annulment would make her a sinner to Chapel Falls. The town would never let her live it down.

Dallas flipped her hair onto one shoulder, unmoved. "Listen here, Costa. I don't care if you send me back with a pack of Chippendales at my side covered in used condoms. Anything is better than living in a prison, where I am constantly monitored, simultaneously ignored, and refused the only thing I want from you—a baby."

"Is this truly the height of your aspirations?" I scowled. "To become a vessel to carry someone else, then their servant for the next eighteen years?"

"Yes. And before you tell me I need to smash the walls of patriarchy, wanting to fulfill myself as a mother and recognizing this is my passion is a choice just as noble as becoming a neurosurgeon."

I was in complete disagreement with her, as usual, but it was pointless to debate the matter. A few seconds passed in silence.

"Why're you still here?" She yawned. "Go away. Jared will be here any moment, and I'll be nothing but an unfortunate memory."

I should go. Pivot and leave. To my relief, I started doing just that. The echo of my footsteps bounced on the bare walls. I did not look back. Knew that if I caught a glimpse of her again, I'd make a mistake. This was for the best. It was time to cut my losses, admit my one mistake in my thirty-one years of life, and move on. My life would return to normal. Peaceful. Tidy. Noiseless. *Unexpensive.*

My hand curled around the doorknob, about to push it open.

"Hey, asshole."

I stopped but didn't turn around. I refused to answer to the word.

"What do you say—one last time for the road?"

I glanced behind my shoulder, knowing I shouldn't, and found my soon-to-be ex-wife propped on the hood of my Maybach, her dress hiked up her waist, revealing she'd worn no panties. Her bare pussy glistened, ready for me. A dare. I never shied away from those.

Throwing caution to the wind (and the remaining few brain cells she hadn't fried with her mindless conversation), I marched to her.

When I reached the car, she lifted her hand to stop me, slapping her palm against my chest. "Not so fast."

It is going to be fast and a half, seeing as I'm about to come just from watching you like this.

I arched an eyebrow. "Cold feet?"

"Nah, low temperature is your thing. Don't wanna steal your thunder. Either we go all the way, or we go nowhere at all. It's all or nothing."

It infuriated me that each time I gave her a choice, she fabricated another. If I gave her an option, she swapped it with one of her creation. And now, on the heels of my ultimatum, she'd dished out her own.

And like a doomed fool, I chose *everything.*

I chose my downfall.

We exploded together in a filthy, frustrated kiss full of tongue and teeth. She latched on to my neck, half-choking me, half-hugging me. I fumbled with the zipper of my suit pants, freeing my cock, which by this point gleamed with precum, so heavy and so hard it was uncomfortable to stand.

My teeth grazed down her chin, trailing her throat before I did what I hadn't done in five fucking years and pushed into her, all at once. *Bare.* My cock disappeared inside her, hitting a hot spot, squeezed to death by her muscles.

Oh, fuck.

My forehead fell against hers. A thin coat of sweat glued us together. Never in my life had anything felt quite so good. I wanted to evaporate into mist, seep into her, and never come back. I wanted to live, breathe, and exist inside my beautiful, maddening, conniving, infuriating curse of a wife.

She was the one thing I never wanted and the only thing I craved. Worst, still, was the fact that I knew I couldn't deny her a single thing she desired, be it a frock or piece of jewelry. Or, unfortunately, my heart on a platter, speared straight through with a skewer for her to devour. Still beating and as vibrant red as candied apples.

I retreated, then slammed into her harder. Pulled and rushed back in. My fingers gripped her by the waist, pinning her down, wild with lust and desire. I drove into her in jerky, frenzied movements of a man starved for sex, fucking the ever-living shit out of her.

Now that I'd officially filed a restraining order against my logic, I grabbed the front of her throat, sinking my teeth onto her lower lip. My spearmint breath skated over her face. The hood of the car warmed her thighs, still hot from the engine, jacking up the temperature between us even further. Small, desperate yelps fled her mouth.

The only sounds in the cavernous space came from my grunts, our skin slapping together, and her tiny gasps of pleasure. The car rocked back and forth to the rhythm of my thrusts. Dallas latched on to the forearm of my hand curled around her throat and plastered her back against the hood of the car as I continued fucking her hard.

The door behind us opened, and Jared walked in. "Oh, sorry. I didn't mean to—"

"Get the fuck out," I roared. My demand shook the walls so hard I was surprised they hadn't cracked. The door promptly closed.

Perhaps because it was, by far, the most pleasurable experience I'd ever had, the orgasm wasn't instant. It skulked forward, gripping each of my limbs with its claws, taking over me like a drug. I knew I'd regret what was about to happen. Yet, I could not even entertain the idea of stopping.

Dallas quaked beneath me. The muscles of her thighs

strained. Sliding into her hot tightness a few more times, I finally erupted inside her. It was glorious. And at the same time, felt as if someone had sucked my chest empty. I came, and I came, and I came into Dallas's cunt.

When I finally pulled out, everything between us was sticky. I peered down between her legs. My thick white cum dripped from her swollen red slit to the hood of my car. Pink flakes of blood scattered inside the cloudy, milky liquid. Panting and out of breath, I realized this marked the first time that I'd lost myself to a moment. That I'd forgotten everything. Including the fact that *she* was present.

My gaze rode up her bruised pussy to her torso. Sometime during sex, I'd torn the top of her dress without even noticing. Red marks covered her exposed breasts. Full of scratches and bites. Her neck still bore the imprints of my fingers—how hard had I grabbed her? And though I dreaded seeing the aftermath on her face, I couldn't stop myself.

I looked up and nearly keeled over to vomit. Flushed pink cloaked her face. A single silent tear traveled down her cheek. A glossy sheen coated her hazel eyes, almost golden in their tone and empty as my chest. The corner of her lips had produced a thin line of blood. Her doing. Not mine. She'd bitten them to tamp down her pained cries. Shortbread wanted me to fuck her bareback so badly, she'd suffered through the entire ordeal.

Incomparable guilt slammed into me. Bitterness hit the back of my throat. I'd taken her without considering her pleasure. Against my better judgment. And in the process, I'd ruined her first genuine experience of sex.

"Sorry." I jerked away from Dallas, shoved my dripping half-mast cock back into my pants, and zipped up. "Jesus.

Fuck. I'm so—" The rest of the sentence vanished in my throat. I shook my head, still in disbelief that I'd fucked her to the point of blood and tears. Without even sparing her a glance.

She sat up. That lone tear still shimmered from her cheek, somehow even worse than a loud sob. "Do you have any gum?" The perfect, even composure braided into her voice rattled me. In fact, everything about Dallas rattled me.

On autopilot, I produced two pieces of gum from my tin container, forking them over to her. She tucked both into her pretty pink mouth that I would never kiss and fuck again.

"Shortbread . . ." I stopped. An apology wouldn't even begin to cover it.

"No. It's my time to speak." She made no move to flee. To slap me. To call the police, her parents, her sister. My cum still dripped fat white drops through her exposed pussy. A single streak of blood smeared across the hood of my car.

I stood far enough from her that I wasn't a threat and listened.

"I want you to stop having me followed." The words came out as if they were spoken within the cold, clinical walls of a boardroom. Before an army of shareholders, not a husband. "No more cars tailing Jared. No more security detail. And no more monitoring me through cameras. I feel like I'm a *Big Brother* contestant. Only, I can never win." She threw her hands up. "I want this to be my home, not my prison."

The surprise from hearing she wanted to stay nearly brought me to my knees. I remained standing, though, my face impassive. If there was one thing I'd learned from my father, it was to stand tall and proud, even when you had nothing to be proud of.

She sank her teeth into the gum, a blank expression on her face, reminding me of myself for one startling moment. "Tell me you understand and it will be done, or I am moving out and giving you the divorce you want so much."

It was on the tip of my tongue to tell her I was calling her an Uber that would take her back to Bibleville. However, my rationality wouldn't allow my pride to override my senses.

"That's acceptable."

She drew in a ragged breath. "I want to have a baby."

And what *I* wanted was for her to take Plan B. But such a request would be cowardly. It wasn't her fault I'd lost control. We both played to win. The home team—me—had suffered an unexpected loss today. No need to cheat her out of her victory. No matter how big it might turn out to be. She could get pregnant. These past twenty minutes could determine the rest of my life.

I retrieved my tin container, popping a piece of gum past my lips. "Well, I don't."

"Why are you so against procreating?"

"Trauma."

"Are you ever going to tell me?"

"No."

She didn't seem surprised by my answer. Or upset. In fact, as I advanced toward her, I noticed tiny bubbles peppering the tear, which *still* hadn't evaporated. No. Not a tear. Was that . . . *spit?* I realized, for the first time, that I'd never actually seen Dallas cry. Ever.

Something shifted in me just then. I no longer saw Dallas Costa as a nuisance. After all, she held the upper hand in almost all of our mental games. And this time, she'd brought me to the brink, then tipped me over the edge. Made me fuck her bareback, and feel guilty about the whole thing, *and* bargain with her, too.

Dallas Costa was no plaything. She was my equal, and it would be wise to treat her as such.

Shortbread frowned, most likely debating what she wanted to bargain for in our negotiation. If I gave her the opportunity to speak first, the request would probably be every inch of my soul.

"I'll give you freedom if you give me time." The words rolled off my tongue of their own accord.

"Time for what?"

Time to discard of you on my terms after completing my task of ruining Madison Licht.

"To think about babies," I lied. She considered this. Before she could answer, I added, "But I have a condition, too."

She licked her lips, nodding. "I'll never meet Madison again."

"Promise."

"I promise."

She hopped off the hood of the Maybach, her dress still askew and tucked around her waist. My cum dripped down her thigh, traveling to her knees and ankles. Dry, matted blood the shape of clouds stamped to her inner thighs. We both watched them in silence.

"Want me to lick it better?" I heard myself grunt out.

"Yes, thank you."

Chapter Forty-Five

Dallas

It could be claimed, with some justification, that I often overestimated my acting abilities. But not today. I did something a little bad. Okay, a *lot* bad. I faked a tear. What can I say? After Romeo chose a company he hated over SIDS prevention, it was a cathartic experience watching him fall all over himself because he thought I was distraught.

I wasn't distraught. Not at all. In fact, I loved it when he grabbed my throat, adored it when he bit my nipples, and got off on it when he thrust into me so hard, I felt him reach my belly. And when he lowered to his knees, licked his own semen from my legs, and trailed his tongue further north until it disappeared inside me—licking, suckling, kissing my clit, and scraping his teeth on it until I came on his face—I was just about ready to donate both my kidneys *and* my liver to get a repeat.

Could goading Romeo with Madison for the millionth time be classified as immoral? Sure. Was guilt-tripping my husband into considering babies a new low? Perhaps. But did I feel bad about it? Not in the slightest.

Hours later, I pranced around the house in Disney pajamas I'd bought on the Internet. No way would Romeo approve of them—an extra bonus that led me to purchase the set in all colors.

After dinner, which he'd taken in the dining room while I ravaged mine straight from the oven, Romeo tucked himself into his study, probably doing boring, grown-up things. I gossiped with Frankie on the phone, munching on a sugar cane. Each time I remembered my agreement with him, a smile lifted my cheeks.

Sure, my first full-blown sexual experience was . . . *weird*. I never orgasmed. Well, not until he ate me out after. And the too-tight fit pained me. But there was something thrilling about seeing my husband truly lose control for the first time since we'd gotten married.

"Is he still giving you a hard time?" Frankie cooed on the other line. "The hot, irritating bastard."

I couldn't very well tell her he'd given me a few other hard things. She wouldn't understand. In fact, *I* didn't understand what was happening between me and Romeo, either. I knew a fat red line existed between love and lust, but what happened when you straddled it? I didn't want to find out.

"He's horrible!" I said cheerfully, crushing the cane between my molars. "The absolute worst. I constantly do things to make him mad. Just today, I went on a lunch date with Madison. And invited the paparazzi."

"Ugh. Madison." Frankie gagged. "He was in Chapel Falls last week. Did I tell you? Went around moping about how much he misses you. The lying scumbag. Took both Deidre Sweeting and Jean Caldwell into his bed with his crocodile tears. Everyone's talking about it."

"Frankie. Mean gossip is beneath us."

"Aw, Dal." I could picture her exaggerated frown. "But nice gossip is so boring."

We both giggled.

"How's school?" I changed the subject, from fear that if we spoke about Romeo for too long, I'd break down and confess that no matter how much I hated him outside of bed, inside of it, I was his number one fan. "Anything interesting happen?"

"I failed most of my midterms, which I guess is fascinating. At least to Momma, Daddy, and our nosy neighbors."

I sighed. "You need to make an effort, Frankie."

"Oh, but I am. I'm making an effort not to lose my V-card before marriage. And that's plenty difficult."

"Frankie. You know what happens if you give the milk before he buys the cow."

"Maybe I don't want to be bought. Maybe I want to partake in the goddamn twenty-first century."

If only things were that simple. We both knew we were products of our upbringing. That we played by the rules of the place we came from. Human nature, for all the progress it had made, was still tribal by nature. Moving to Potomac had freed me, though I'd exchanged one cage for another.

"Is there anyone in particular that tickles your fancy?" I glided down the banister from the second floor to the first, just to see if Romeo would bark at me for doing so. To test whether he'd stopped watching me through the security camera. The house remained eerily quiet. So far, he was fulfilling his part of the bargain.

My sister's grin traveled through the line. "There are lots of somebodies." Her voice became somber at once. "Are you sad, Dal? That you might never have sex because you are married to a man you hate?"

I couldn't do it. Couldn't tell her I'd already done the deed. That it was primal and exhilarating and celestial. That all I wanted to do was have sex with my husband—and the things that came with it. I especially didn't want to tell her how fun sex was when she toyed with the temptation of having it herself—and out of wedlock. I was no prude, but I also knew what troubles awaited her if Chapel Falls deemed her compromised. Unfortunately, I knew it firsthand.

I froze by the kitchen's entrance, barefoot. "I'm sure it'll happen for me one day."

"Yes. You'll break him at some point, and he'll give you a divorce. I'm sure of it."

But that would mean no more life-altering, earth-shattering sex with my ridiculously hot husband. No more orgasms beneath his talented tongue. No babies with his gray eyes. No. I didn't want a divorce. Not at all.

After I hung up and finished my third dinner for the day (Hettie's bistek tagalog and fried lumpia), I retreated to my room to read my Henry Plotkin books, which Romeo had returned from exile. Time for a reread ahead of the fourteenth and final book in the series.

"Shortbread." Romeo's arrogant voice snarled from the jaws of his study. "Come inside."

You mean . . . just like you did today?

Giggling to myself, I followed his instructions. He sat behind a mahogany desk, working on his laptop, a library of literally every unreadable book I'd ever come across behind him.

"Yes?" I bent down to tug my funny socks up over my Minnie Mouse sweatpants.

"Is it Halloween?"

"No."

"Then why are you dressed as a toddler?"

I swaggered deeper into the office and flashed him a sunny smile, knowing those, in particular, soured his mood. "Comfort first, right?"

"Wrong." His fingers skated over the keyboard. "Comfort is what mediocre people strive for once they realize the currency of success is hard work."

Naturally, I gravitated to his library and noticed the bottom row of fifteen or so books. Linen hardcovers, absent of dust jackets and any indication of the contents within.

I fingered one, teasing it out of its slot before poking it back in. "Are these for decoration?"

He didn't even turn to see what I'd referred to. "No."

"How can you tell which book is which?"

"By opening them."

"Is this some weird aesthetic thing rich people do to keep paupers guessing what they read?"

"*You* are a rich person."

"Yeah, but I'm an abnormal rich person."

"You're an abnormal person. Period. And no, this is not *some weird aesthetic thing rich people do to keep paupers guessing what they read*."

"Then . . . the bookseller sold them like this? That should be criminal."

"They came with dust jackets."

My lips parted, appalled at the idea of trashing them. "What happened to them?"

"They're now on the books I gave you."

"What books?"

Surely, he didn't mean *those* books.

"*His Filthy Touch. A Lover's Thrust. Blindfolded by my Professor. Dominated by Two Alien Alphas.* Must I continue? I lose a brain cell for every second we discuss them."

I tried to remember if I'd taken the time to peek past the dust jackets and see what the books beneath actually were. I hadn't. *Oops.*

"Oh. Those books."

Romeo's eyes narrowed. "Yes. Those books. Have you finished them?"

Oh, they're finished, all right . . .

"You could say that . . ."

"What happened?"

I yawned, covering my hand over my mouth to obscure my next words. "I might have burned them."

"You *burned* them." His jaw ticked. The slightest movement. If I weren't paying attention to every painstaking detail of my husband, I wouldn't have noticed it.

I toyed with the edge of my shirt, staring down at Minnie Mouse. Figured it was too late to apologize. Bygones and all. "Yeah." I waved a hand. "Happened ages ago. No need to revisit the past."

"While we're at it, we may as well ban history courses. K-through-12 education, too."

"Mm-hmm. We should." I nodded fast, beaming at Romeo. "Worked super well for women in the past."

And nope. Still couldn't bring myself to apologize. Why was I like this? Better question—why was *he* like this?

I boiled in his potent silence, fanning my cheeks with an unidentifiable linen hardcover. Romeo continued to type on his laptop. He paused for a moment, unsheathed his old tin can, and fetched a white rectangle from within, popping it into his mouth. His gum.

I wanted to inch closer. Dive into his past. Sneak a peek of the container, which I noticed for the first time *did* possess a single flaw. A tiny dent in the corner that marred the otherwise smooth matte surface.

Instead, I made a show of continuing my perusal of his shelves. My fingers brushed each naked spine. The books, I had no problem apologizing to. In fact, I would've held a candlelight vigil, too, if I didn't think it'd be poor taste, considering how their jackets had met their untimely demises. I pressed my palms together and offered a silent prayer to each and every one whose skin I'd burnt to a crisp in the bonfire.

Please, Lord, wash me of my sins and find these books a better home in the afterlife. Preferably with someone with taste. The Vast History of Financial Statements? *Really?*

On the bright side, I'd finally discovered Romeo's addictions, other than gum and my misery—money. His entire bookshelf consisted of rows upon rows of finance books. It struck me as odd. I could've sworn, based on my stellar snooping skills, that he'd studied engineering during undergrad and focused on Entrepreneurial Management for his MBA.

I slanted my head, realizing something. "You memorized the books I picked up at that indie shop?"

He finally broke his silence and faced me, answering my question between bouts of drilling a hole into my head with his frosty grays. "Nothing more than a byproduct of my superior memory. *No need to revisit the past.*" He pried the book from my fingers and wedged it into my mouth, right between my teeth. "Are you done?"

He didn't wait for me to reply, returning to his laptop.

Spitting the book into my hand, I advanced toward him. "You should get into finance. I bet if you do something you enjoy, you would abandon your *Mission Impossible: Getting Back at Daddy for Being a Meanie* plan."

"Great plan. Just neglect my entire career at Costa Indus—"

"It's not a career. It's a revenge quest. And it's childish. It sucks the joy and soul out of you." I waved the disrobed hardcover nestled in my palm, which was probably titled *Generational Wealth: The Imperial History of Mediocre Nepo Babies* or something equally snooze-worthy. "You *love* working with money. Life is too short to not do what you love."

"Life is long enough that I might get to do both."

The sudden urge to hug him seized me. "Oh, Romeo. You never know if your next breath is going to be your last. How foolish of you to not seize the moment."

On the television mounted on the wall beside him, a news segment flashed across the screen: **Hacker Attacks Licht Holdings, LLC**. The rolling headline reported that an anonymous hacker had stolen and duly leaked key blueprints of a new technological weapon online, rendering the entire production worthless. This had my husband's fingerprints all over it. The man wouldn't rest until he' had Madison by his throat.

Pouting, I squinted at the segment. "Wow. I didn't know Zach meddles with hacking."

Where was he when Sav taped me stuffing my bra with Choco pies at Emilie's sleepover and leveraged the footage for my limited-edition Jimmy Choos?

Romeo didn't lift his eyes from his screen, still typing. "He doesn't."

I didn't really expect him to confide in me.

"So, why am I here?"

"I have a surprise for you."

My heart immediately did jumping jacks, expanding and contracting at record speeds. Pressure built between my legs. "Can we do it on your desk? Oh! Can I go upstairs and dress like a sexy secretary?" *Finally*. An opportunity to use all those pencil skirts Cara had gotten me. And to think I'd almost taken them as Romeo's subliminal message to get a job.

Those arctic-grays swung up from his screen, surprise and . . . was it delight? coloring them. "I wasn't talking about sex."

"Oh."

"But good to know I didn't scar you for life after this afternoon."

The look he gave me told me he knew I'd faked those tears, did not find it amusing, and would punish me later for it. Hopefully, in the bedroom. Over his knees. As I wore the school girl uniform that I'd purchased in anticipation of this exact scenario.

I brushed his judgment off. Returning the hardcover, I parked my butt on the edge of his desk. "Okay. What do you have for me?"

He leaned back in his chair, gripped my outer thigh through my sweatpants, and ran his rough palm up my hip until he clutched my waist. "Since I was foolish enough to buy your tears today, I donated two buildings in our family name. One to Georgetown and the other to Johns Hopkins."

I blinked, not yet comprehending. "Are you going to turn them into libraries for me? Seems a bit extreme to rob so many students of their degree—"

"You can now take your pick at which university you'd like to complete your college degree." His upturned chin told me he thought he'd done me a favor.

I, on the other hand, wanted to slap him silly. What a horrid thing to do. Didn't he know me at all? Maybe

I'd gone overboard on giving him hell for plucking me midway through my degree.

Misinterpreting the surprise on my face for awe and gratitude, a wolfish smirk tugged at his delicious mouth. "I will take my thank you in the form of dick sucking, although I am partial to eating you out on the kitchen counter, too."

I flung my hands in the air, groaning. "How could you do that to me?"

That wiped the smile off his face.

"You dropped out of Emory," he pointed out, as if the detail had escaped me.

"Yes." I stubbed an accusing finger into his chest. "And that was literally the only thing I looked forward to when you took me as a wife."

"You don't want a college degree?" The mask of indifference returned to his eyes.

"Of course not." I shook my head. "Do you know anyone worth their salt who has one?" He stared at me in a way that suggested I'd spoken in an entirely different language. I sighed, listing the greatest minds of our generation, all degree-free. "Steve Jobs, Mark Zuckerberg, Bill Gates, Jack Dorsey—"

"Shortbread." He frowned. "I don't think you're at risk of depriving the world of a budding tech genius. In fact, when your phone freezes, you smash it against a hard surface instead of restarting it. I've seen you do it. Multiple times. You know nothing of technology and social media. Plus, virtually all of those people dropped out of Ivy League schools, which they did not require entire building donations to get accepted into."

"Are you saying I'm stupid?" I added an insulted lilt to my voice, mainly to veer him off the topic of my unfinished college degree.

"No. You've proven to be incredibly smart."

"Then, what's the problem?"

"I won't be married to an uneducated woman."

"You should've thought about that before kidnapping one." I began moving things around—pens, stapler, paperweight—just to leave my mark on this usually untouched room. Now that I thought about it, it could use some artwork. A splash of color, perhaps?

"You will finish your degree." He clasped my wrist, gently drawing me from further messing up his workspace. "And that's that."

"Or else what?" I slid from his desk, straddling him in his chair now. I wrapped my arms around his shoulders, peering into his face. "You're going to kick me out to the Hamptons? To Chapel Falls?"

We both knew I wasn't going anywhere. I didn't know why or how, exactly, this had become a silent agreement between us, but I think in some messed-up, completely unhealthy way, whatever was brewing inside this mansion was better than the reality we both had lived before.

He grabbed my ass, grinding me against his erection. His jaw muscles jumped, eyes hooding. "Fuck it. I'll buy you a degree."

"I'll burn it," I countered. "I want people to know I'm self-taught."

"At what? Sitting on the couch and licking Oreo cream?" His hard length parted my slit through our clothes, colliding with my clit. "At least become the chairwoman of a non-profit."

I shook my head. "I'll continue giving to charity behind the scenes."

He examined me, perplexed. "Why?"

"Because I don't need to impress anyone, and neither do you." I leaned down to kiss him. He caught my lips in his, drawing me into a deep, tongue-filled kiss. "Now, should I get naked?"

"Certainly." He pushed me off him, returning his attention to his work. "But only because what you're wearing is an eyesore. I'm busy."

Even though he low-key threw me out of his study, I was actually quite happy when I swaggered my way outside. This was our first non-toxic interaction. How pathetic that it made me elated. But alas, it did.

I went back to the kitchen to get a water bottle—I always got extra thirsty after our encounters—strolling past his office again on my way upstairs.

I halted, noticing he no longer had his eyes trained on the screen. His elbows now rested on his desk, and he cupped his head, staring downward.

He looked exasperated.

Dissatisfied.

And no longer in hate with me.

Chapter Forty-Six

Dallas

Romeo and I slid into a routine. A routine where I did whatever I wanted whenever I wanted, and he stopped bothering me about it. This mostly consisted of lunch dates with Hettie, trips to local libraries, and Henry Plotkin binges in anticipation of the fourteenth and final one. Not exactly life on the edge.

This evening crawled by like any other. While I hovered over the stove, forking down adobo pork belly before Hettie could even plate it, Romeo ate his boring chicken in his boring office. God forbid he get caught being civilized with his wife in front of his staff.

"You're not a mop, Dal." Hettie jerked the pot away from me. "You don't need to lick the cookware clean."

"It's called efficiency. I'm saving water for the drought."

"The one across the country?"

"It's called patriotism, Hettie."

"We both know you finish dinner in point-two seconds every night to kick me out early so you and Lucifer can get freaky."

Since she'd spoken nothing but truth, I did exactly that, ushering her and Vernon out the door. By the time Romeo slipped into my room, I awaited him on my duvet, naked, Henry Plotkin in one hand and a highlighter in the other.

In truth, I counted the days, the hours, the minutes until my period. I wanted so badly to wake up in the morning (okay, afternoon) and discover I was late. Nothing would make me happier than being pregnant. I was sure of it. Even if my blessing would be Romeo's curse.

Romeo strode to me and attempted to pry my fingers off the hardcover.

"Wait." I pouted, tugging it back. "Madison is about to—"

He stood deathly still. "Madison?"

"The *character*. Henry's sister."

Madison the Scumbag, on the other hand? I hadn't heard from him since the showdown at Le Bleu. I'd be lying if I said I felt good about the way we'd left things. Not from guilt. Madison used me as a tool against my husband, who then used me as a tool against Madison. If I were a judge, they'd *both* be convicted of crimes. It just sucked to know the three of us were stuck in this power, ego, and money limbo.

I released the book, allowing Romeo to set it on the nightstand. Then he proceeded to show me heaven in a place that should have been my personal hell.

We did everything but sex. Spent hours exploring each other's bodies. Each muscle. Each curve. All licked, kissed, scraped, and sucked. He knew my body inside out. The beauty mark below my right hip bone. Each individual freckle on my shoulder. And I'd studied him acutely, learning exactly where he was ticklish (between his six-pack and hip bone), what made him suck in a breath (when I covered the crown of his cock with my mouth, then blew air on the tip), and what he merely tolerated because he knew I enjoyed it (when I licked the shell of his ear. It gave him goose bumps).

At two past midnight, he slid his pants over his legs. I lay in bed, lips puffed, hair a mess, body deliciously aching.

Romeo glanced at the poor flower and muttered something that sounded suspiciously like, ". . . incapacity to care for a houseplant, let alone an entire child."

Vernon's rose had prevailed the impossible—me. My sun-deprived room, the dirty water it marinated in, and my general inattentiveness. From time to time, Romeo would tend to it, swapping out fresh water. Once, he'd even taken the tiny scissors I used to trim my eyebrows, clipping the tip of the rose. Maybe that was why only one petal had fallen from it since we'd started regularly hooking up. I didn't know what impressed me more—Vernon's ability to create a sub-species of rose or my husband's hidden trait of caring for things with the gentleness of a doting father.

The next morning, I danced around the kitchen island with Hettie, immersed in a chocolate challenge. Every single brand under the sun sprawled before us. Godiva, Cadbury, Dove, Ghirardelli, Lindt, and La Maison du Chocolat. Vernon, our judge, sat on a barstool, atop four thick finance textbooks I'd stolen from Romeo's office for added height. Not that Hettie or I could see him through our blindfolds.

I munched on a raspberry ganache pearl. "Godiva."

Vernon cleared his throat, interrupting my 4-3 lead. "Mrs. Costa, you have a guest."

As always, he insisted on calling me Mrs. Costa. And as always, I visibly shuddered.

I ripped the blindfold off my eyes, gasping. "Frankie!"

But it wasn't her. Not Momma, either. My lungs emptied, a gust of air whooshing past my lips.

Shepherd Townsend stood before me.

He hovered by the doorway, hat in hand, shifting his weight from one foot to the other. He wore that suit I liked the most. Black with yellow stripes. A hilarious combo that earned him the nickname Bubba Bee. Those days seemed eons ago.

I wasn't laughing now.

"Dallas. You haven't been taking my calls."

I pushed the chocolate aside. "Yes, I am aware."

"I was hoping we could talk." He lifted a shoulder, unsure of himself for once. It tugged at my heartstrings, if not completely knotted them together in a tangled heap. Despite his actions, I couldn't hate him all the way.

I gestured to the dessert-laden table in front of me. "Clearly, I'm busy."

Thorny anger climbed up my throat. It went beyond the act of promising me to Romeo without my consent. Daddy had done that before with Madison, too. What charred me inside-out was the eye-opening moment my now-husband hauled me from my childhood home, barefoot and in my sleeping gown. In that instant, with the clarity of a newly polished mirror, I knew my father would not save me. Fathers were supposed to protect their children. Not their family's reputation.

Shepherd Townsend operated in a man's world. Where women were a novelty. Simple, ditzy creatures to be quieted by the drop of a credit card. He believed I'd find happiness with Madison, just as he'd wagered I'd grow accustomed to Romeo. After all, they were both easy on the eyes and filthy rich. What more could a woman want? *What, indeed?* Perhaps a voice. Agency. Respect.

My father was a chauvinist. Just like the rest of Chapel Falls. Now that I no longer lived under his roof, I could show him exactly what I thought about his worldview.

A wave of surprise drenched Daddy's face. "Surely, you could spare me a few minutes."

While Hettie and Vernon scurried away, giving us undesired privacy, I gallivanted around the island, gathering the ingredients for homemade whipped cream. "What makes you so sure? Because I don't have any children to raise? Any floors to sweep? Luncheons to organize? Because I'm a woman, Daddy?"

At this rate, he would need a forklift to return his jaw to its upright position. On the bright side, perhaps he could apologize to society for his chauvinism by donating his eyes to science. I didn't even know those puppies could grow that big. Or be that empty. Like two deserted planets.

"Where is this coming from? You used to be so sweet." Daddy's hat slipped from his fingers, feathering to the floor. "What happened to you?"

"What happens to every girl who escapes Chapel Falls." A sad smile hovered at my mouth. "I grew up and realized there is life beyond the ivy-laced walls of Chapel Falls. That in this life, women are allowed to make mistakes, to be human, to experience life as fully and as wholly as men, without paying a horrible price."

"You knew what would happen if you got caught with a man before marriage. I didn't make the rules. Society did."

"Two thousand years ago. Most of American society doesn't live like us anymore."

"You've been mad at me since before you moved to Maryland."

Somehow, he looked smaller. Older. Far less powerful than I remembered. Time apart had extinguished that supreme glow that once radiated from him. The one every girl saw from her daddy before reality scrubbed it raw.

"Yes." I rinsed my hands, wiping them on a rag, along with every illusion regarding my father's concern for me. "I realized, after you gave me to Romeo, that I'd never chosen Madison, either. At the time, I agreed to avoid upsetting you. You've never given me a voice. How ironic that I found mine, anyway, and in the gilded cage you sent me to, no less."

Daddy observed our surroundings. The beauty. The lavishness. The wealth. "I thought he'd be good to you. Costa's reputation is unimpeachable. Is it really so bad here?"

No. Not at all.

But it wasn't my *choice,* either.

Just as I readied to give him a piece of my mind, swift footsteps echoed down the corridor. The pace. The quiet confidence. It could only be my husband. Two things happened at once. First, my heart somersaulted, eager to see him again, though only three hours had passed since he'd feasted on me for breakfast. Second, my nerves—already strained so taut I feared they'd snap my skin like rubber bands—jumped to attention.

Romeo strode in, larger and more forbidding than my father. Than the kitchen. Than his *mansion.* How had I not noticed it before? That my husband—dressed to the nines with his too-sharp jaw and ashen eyes—was a weapon of war himself.

He shouldered past my father, caught my expression, and swung his glare on Shep Townsend. A chill zigzagged between us.

"Have you an invitation to be here?"

Ego puffed up Daddy's chest. Earlier, wrinkles had pleated his forehead, betraying his frustration with me. At

Romeo's words, they ironed out. Shepherd Townsend refused to be schooled by a man half his age. "I don't need an invitation. My daughter—"

"Is my wife, my responsibility, and therefore my business. She currently does not want to speak to you. Unless I'm mistaken?" Romeo swiveled to me, raising a brow. I didn't need to shake my head. He read my eyes. He read *me*. He turned back to my father. "Leave."

"Dallas . . ." My father—no longer Daddy to me, I realized—wrung his suit in his hands, attempting eye contact. "Are you really going to treat your own dad this way?"

Guilt burrowed through my chest, past my ribs, and into my heart. I ignored it, folding my arms.

He tossed his hands up as Vernon materialized behind him, guiding him away by the elbow. "You told Momma you were happy."

"I told Momma a lot of things so her heart wouldn't break." I swallowed. "Your heart, however, deserves to crumble to dust."

"Allow me to make it easier for you, Shep." Romeo planted a hand on my father's shoulder. I was surprised the latter didn't sink all the way through the floor and disappear between its cracks. "If I catch you here one more time, uninvited and unwelcome, I will cut your legs off to ensure your mistakes do not become a habit. Do not underestimate my mean streak. After all, I *did* ruin your firstborn's reputation, engagement, and life, all within the span of one evening. I am terribly proficient where cruelty is concerned. It's an inherited talent. Making me an enemy is not for the faint of heart."

The steel calmness that settled into my shoulders at the sight of my father's forced removal should have rattled me. I didn't recognize myself. Yet, I knew I would never return to the old me. No matter what happened.

Georgia would always own my soul, but I suspected my heart lived here. In Potomac. Dangerous hope bubbled inside me. Maybe my pregnancy wouldn't tarnish Romeo's immaculate existence. What if I could convince him that giving someone else life was worth more than ruining his father's?

My eyes clung to Romeo, who braced the back of an upholstered stool, glaring at me with a mixture of tenderness and aversion. In the rare times he showed me kindness, he despised himself for it.

He scowled, misreading my longing stare as an accusing one. "I thought you wanted to get rid of him."

"I did."

"Why are you looking at me, then?"

"Don't I normally look at you?"

"Only when you want to be eaten out or you've lost your credit card and need a new one."

Lord, was that true? I'd been so busy comparing him to Shakespeare's love-struck character that I'd failed to notice I hadn't earned any Wife of the Year awards, either.

"Well, I'm looking at you now," I snapped. "And I like what I'm seeing."

He jerked his head back. "Are you drunk?"

"Can't I pay you a compliment?"

"I'm the one who does the payments in this relationship. Whatever you're doing, stop it immediately."

Somehow, our gazes had tangled so thoroughly, I didn't know how to pull mine away.

He retreated first with a shake of his head. "I'm going to the gym."

I would've followed him. Truly. But exercise equipment resembled distant cousins of the guillotine. Not my fault I'd entered this world with sky-high self-preservation instincts.

I pouted. "You're always going to the gym."

"That's right." Romeo threw the fridge open, snatched a water bottle, and downed the entire thing in one go. "I want to see a greater age than thirty-three, and your sole mission in life seems to be wearing me down." He crushed the plastic in his fist, tossing it into the recycling bin.

"Will you come to my room afterward?" I immediately regretted the question. It sounded clingy. I never waited for Romeo to arrive. He simply did. And on the rare occasion he didn't, I pretended not to notice.

Romeo turned to me fully, taking me in. "*Why?*"

Okay. I could've done without the incredulity.

"Maybe I've missed you," I muttered.

"I should hope not. We may not be enemies anymore, Shortbread, but we will never be lovers." He brushed his shoulder against mine as he exited the kitchen. "Make sure Hettie cleans all the melted chocolate from the counter. Heads will roll if I find an ant inside my mansion."

Chapter Forty-Seven

Dallas

After Romeo clubbed me with the truth stick, I drew a bath to scrub his words off my skin. I wanted us to be a couple. A *real* one. Not sure when that had happened, but now that I did, any other outcome would end with devastation.

The second blow of the day came in the form of a pink spot splattered on my underwear. Big, bold, and unmistakable. *And* a day early. I held the cotton to the light as if any doubt existed as to what it was. The sight sliced me open. Misery poured in through the gaping wound. The stain felt like betrayal. Like grief and self-loathing.

I introduced the fabric to my sharpest scissors, shoved the tattered remains into the trash, and yanked the bathtub plug, refusing to fester in my own blood. If I didn't smell like a brothel from this morning, I would've forgone a shower entirely. Instead, I made it quick, shrugging into my most comfortable, childish pajamas and crawling beneath my comforter.

The third blow came when I willed myself to cry, failing to conjure the tears that had eluded me all my life. I needed relief. In any form it would come. Yet, once again, my body failed me. In tears. In fertility.

Fine. It wasn't my eggs' fault that they suffered a sperm drought. I just preferred not to acknowledge the simple truth. Romeo refused to have sex with me. No matter my advances. No matter every delicious, toe-curling, orgasm-inducing, *almost-sex* activity we engaged in.

The beginnings of a storm teased my ankles, curling around them. My father's unannounced visit. My husband's rejection. My period. My general sex-free existence. They swirled together, gaining force, brewing into something sinister and dangerous.

So, hours later, when the door wailed open, I knew the visit would not end well. Romeo never knocked, and I never cared. Only, tonight, I did. His shadow glided across the sleek darkness. He stopped just above me, the scent of him—of spearmint, cologne, and potent man—sailing into my nostrils.

He came.

Because I'd asked him to? Because he missed me? Or because his needs required fulfilling? I never could tell.

Romeo trailed his knuckles along his favorite constellation of freckles on my cheek. "What's on the menu tonight, Mrs. Costa?" The husky, low tone seeped straight through me. "Another sixty-nine, or can I finally fuck your tight little asshole?"

At his words, the storm transformed into a hurricane, festering somewhere deep below and rising to the surface. Unlike the natural calamity, its speed and ire didn't weaken upon hitting the ground. It increased. Tenfold.

I slapped his touch away. "Get out of my room and never come back."

I hate you. I hate you with everything I have in me and more.

Lord, had it always hurt this much to breathe? It was true, what they say. There's no law of conservation for love. You don't get what you give.

"Is this about our conversation earlier?" His light, unbothered tone might as well have been a dagger. "Dichotomy is a simpleton's best friend. You should aim higher than that, Shortbread. Love isn't in the cards for us, but that doesn't mean we can't enjoy each other's company. If I truly couldn't suffer through our brief encounters, I would have granted you the divorce you desire so much."

I don't want a divorce, you stupid, selfish fool.

I wanted dinners in front of candlelight, movie dates, and inside jokes that no one else understood. I wanted kisses, comforting words, to be his shining light when gloom seized him.

I flung the duvet over my head. "Just get out."

"What's the matter with you?" The temperature in the room dropped, indicating his shift in mood. "You've been acting strange all day."

"You know," I murmured into my pillow. "I don't think Leonardo DiCaprio truly made it big in *Romeo and Juliet*. I think what put him on the map was *Titanic*. And I think everybody felt sorry for him. That dang door clearly could've fit both him and Rose."

The silence that followed sent a wave of panic into my gut. Surely, he didn't actually leave.

Alas, he did not. "I'm sure there is logic behind your words, though for the life of me, I cannot find it."

"I want to have sex with someone who'd grant me a place on the door!" I tossed the comforter away, glaring at him in the dark.

He appraised me as if we were meeting for the first time. Sizing me up, taking notes, deciding how he wanted to approach the matter. "We don't have to go on cruises. Personally, I have a strong dislike of yachts—"

"Arghh, Romeo." I bolted out of bed, pushing his chest. Desperation practically oozed out of me. For what, I didn't even know. "I'm not talking about yachts right now."

He flicked the light on. Neither of us said anything. He waited for me to make sense. I decided to put him out of his misery.

"Congrats." I stomped to the door and opened it, waiting for him to leave. "I got my period."

Romeo just stood there. Silent. I didn't get the sense that he was happy. I didn't get the sense that he was sad, either.

"I'm sorry." The words dripped obligation.

"No, you're not." I swung the door wider. "Now leave."

"Will I be invited back in the near future?"

"Only if you want to have sex like a married couple."

"Boring, fast, and every other week?" I could tell he didn't want to argue, didn't want to return to being foes, but also didn't want to meet me halfway, however that might look.

"Without a condom."

Before, I'd considered the emptiness inside me bottomless. But as he left, as stone-faced as he'd come, it grew and grew, until I was certain if someone screamed into my mouth, a terrible echo would follow.

I knew he wouldn't return. Not tomorrow. Not next week. Not even next month. He'd dodged a bullet, and he wouldn't dare mess with a loaded gun again.

I had one chance.

And my body blew it.

Chapter Forty-Eight

Dallas

I found the will to lure my husband into unprotected sex on the fifth day of our cold war. With the end of my period, I woke up re-energized, eons before my two p.m. alarm, and spent an obnoxious amount of time prettying up, even shaving everything south of my chin.

Since our fight, Romeo had avoided me at all costs. That ended now.

I arrived at the dining room with flourish, at six in the morning on the dot, knowing Romeo would be there after his five-mile run and ice-cold shower. Truly, *I* should be the one wary of breeding with him. Weren't psychopath genes hereditary?

When I tornadoed in, Romeo flipped his newspaper, a steaming cup of coffee to his lips. I helped myself to a croissant, Vermont butter, and two Danishes from the pastry tray Hettie baked each morning. Then I slipped into the seat across from him.

Romeo didn't look up from his paper. "Good morning, Shortbread. Am I hallucinating, or are you out of bed before three?"

"You're definitely hallucinating."

"Seeing as you swathed four fingers of butter on a single croissant, I don't think I am. This is too you to

317

be a mirage." He closed the paper and folded it in crisp squares by his side. "Are you feeling better?"

"Yes, no thanks to you."

He set his coffee down. "Believe it or not, I intended to check on you this weekend if you hadn't shown your face by then."

I rested a hand over my heart. "And they say romance is dead."

"Romance *is* dead. Dating apps killed it years ago. You're the only one who still believes in it. I'm half worried you spend unholy amounts of time watching *Ghostbusters* in the event that you encounter a ghost."

I wolfed down my croissant in two bites. "I want you to entertain me today."

For a reason unbeknownst to me, I knew he'd humor me. He always gave me some kind of version of what I wanted without fail.

He finished his coffee. "I can visit your room at the end of the day, should my schedule permit—provided you loosen your intercourse rule."

"I meant during the daytime."

"And what of the pesky thing that is my work?"

"So, take me to work."

"No, thank you."

"I wasn't asking."

"I wasn't offering." There was a pause. He used it to exhale, so as not to strangle me. "Not today. There's an arms demo, and I'm required to be there. It's dangerous."

"I like danger."

"And I like you in one piece." As an afterthought, he added, "As one of my most expensive possessions, of course. You cost hundreds of thousands of dollars to maintain. Per month."

"I'm coming to work with you today."

"No."

I pouted, rolling a lock of hair around my finger. "You know what happens when I'm bored." I was, of course, being deliberately petulant, knowing it ground his gear.

My reflection shined through his dead shark eyes. In it, the past several months played out. The amount of crap we'd put each other through. Ultimately, though, Romeo never feared my bad behavior. And this time, his intentions flashed across his forehead. *A concession for a concession.* What a foolish thought. Naturally, I hoped he continued thinking it.

We stalled at an impasse. Finally, he stood, checking his Rolex. "I'll send Jared to pick you up at noon. The demo takes place on a tarmac outdoors. Expect wind, chill, mud, and a healthy dose of discomfort. Don't wear anything to attract attention, including and especially high heels. While there, you will not leave my side, you will not wander around, and you will not do anything that is not in the instruction manual I'll email you after I leave."

"Okay, Zaddy," I purred.

"If you behave, which I greatly doubt, we could go for a late lunch afterward. Do not make me regret this, Shortbread."

I shot up, punching the air. "I won't!"

He shook his head, draped his blazer over his forearm, and strode out. Could've sworn I heard him mutter, "I already am."

Maybe Romeo needed to better define what *an outfit that doesn't attract attention* meant. Because when I sashayed from the Maybach through the endless tarmac, he did not look impressed. And by not impressed, what I meant was, he'd gladly shove me off a cliff should one zip within his line of sight.

It marked the first time I'd seen fire in his eyes, and that fire wished to burn me to death. If you asked me, there was nothing wrong with my strappy black mini dress. The tiny patches of sheer nylon that covered my modesty could only be described as high fashion. I wore five-inch Louboutin boots to complete the look—and so Romeo wouldn't tower over me completely. The patent leather stretched up my legs, cutting off midway at my thighs.

Nestled in the outskirts of Alexandria, dozens of uniformed men milled around the asphalt, where a house-sized Humvee had parked. And all of them were looking at me, mouths ajar, eyes glazed over. I swung my hips as I cat-walked to my husband, his father, and his nemesis. They stood beside a helicopter with noise-canceling earmuffs, eyes pinned to me.

I supposed I'd achieved my goal of reminding Romeo how desired his wife was, considering every man I passed undressed me with his eyes. The sunny smile on my face only hardened Romeo's glare. He tore his muffs off, shoving them into Cara's hands.

Senior studied my cleavage like he'd lost his car keys inside it. Beside him, Bruce looked ready to volunteer as tribute and dig for them.

The helicopter's blades whisked air around us. Still, I heard Senior crystal-clear through the roar. "What is she doing?"

"Making sure I lock her in a cell until she hits menopause." Romeo had already started for me, even outpacing the wind dancing between us. We met halfway on the runway. My skin blossomed with awareness, knowing we held every eye in a one-mile radius.

"Hey, hubs." I laced my arms around his neck, rising in my heels to give him a kiss. His mouth was cold and unresponsive as it covered my lips. I darted my tongue across the seam then sucked the lower one into my mouth.

He refused to budge. "You look like a slut."

The word cut off my air supply, rendering me dizzy. I lost my balance, almost tripping if it weren't for his hand on my back. He'd never called me that before. Not even when I'd thrust my genitals in his face, demanding to be satisfied, which occurred daily. The Romeo I knew did not view sexually liberated women as sinful. Something had triggered him.

Or maybe you are trying to excuse his toxic masculinity.

His expression remained as hard and unrelenting as his shoulders. "That was your intention, was it not?"

I hated that my argument died before it could gestate, grow limbs, and strangle him to death. To be fair, I'd seen pornstars screwed in lingerie with more fabric than my dress. If the wind blew the wrong way, every man in the vicinity would enjoy an open view of my breasts. And there was *a lot* of men in the vicinity. Plenty of wind, too.

"Fine. If you want me to treat you like one, congratulations. I'll let you be my little slut."

I tore away from him, wounded and feverish. Even at the height of our hatred, he'd never dared speak to me like that. There'd always been an undercurrent of respect. There wasn't now.

He advanced, searing his hand on my waist until I thought my bones would char to dust. His lips dragged across my cheek, settling on the shell of my ear. "Get on your knees, take out my cock, and jerk me off until I come all over your 'outfit.' Go ahead. Do it."

My left knee buckled on instinct, but I forced myself to remain upright. Brutal wind lashed at us. The curls I'd worked so hard on earlier whipped around us like blades of a blender. I was distinctly aware that the only thing keeping my nipples from the eyes of every man here was the nervous sweat that glued the tiny scrap covering them to my skin.

If only I had the guts, I'd call his bluff. Lower to my knees. Take him into my mouth in front of all his employees. But I didn't. Instead, I rooted to the ground, afraid I'd topple if I moved, yet knowing Romeo would never let me fall.

"That's what I thought, Shortbread." His fingers coasted just beneath my dress, digging into my thigh. "I'm going to burn this outfit to the fucking ground, along with everything else I find unsuitable, as soon as I arrive home tonight. Guess you'll be free of me after all."

"Free?" My mouth dried. I didn't want that at all. Quite the opposite. "Where are you going?"

"Jail."

"What?"

"Where else would I land after I rip out the eyes of every man who used them to undress you?"

Searching his face for sarcasm, all I found was crisp blankness and a warning of what was to come. Across the tarmac, the car beckoned me, inviting me to flee. But I refused to lose face in front of his father and colleagues. I'd never give Romeo the satisfaction.

"Aww." I brushed invisible lint from his suit. "Scared I'll run off with a real man? Maybe one without daddy issues the size of Viet Nam?" I ignored his hard glare. "Did I say Viet Nam? Too small. I meant China."

"Watch your mouth." He plowed his fingers into my hair in what might've looked like a tender caress from afar, but there was no mistaking the warning in his tug. "Or tonight, I'll fuck it so hard you won't be able to eat for a week."

His words shouldn't have dampened my panties.

They did, nonetheless.

More than anything, I was pathetically glad he still wasn't done with me.

I pasted on a smile. "Try and put your dick in my mouth, baby. I'll bite it off and fulfill your wish to never have kids in this lifetime."

"Dallas, honey." Senior waved a hand for me to join him. "Come on. We're about to start the drill. You don't want to miss this thing of beauty."

I hurried to him, mainly so I could escape Romeo before I lost it. When I reached Senior, he kissed my cheek, handing me plastic glasses. "I hope my son isn't giving you too much trouble."

Bruce forked over noise-canceling earmuffs. "Junior can be a bit immature."

I turned away, trying to focus on the Humvee. Khaki-colored, with wheels big enough to flatten a strip mall, and probably paid for by my tax dollars. Well, Romeo's tax dollars. Perks of unemployment.

Senior gestured to the vehicle. "We're the sole contractors for the U.S. Army's eight prototype Humvees. This is our latest creation." He planted a hand on Bruce's forearm for balance. "We produce over twenty thousand Humvees a year, but none are half as sophisticated as this baby right here. The HMWWV3."

I could think of a catchier name, but it probably wasn't my place to suggest a marketing overhaul. Plus, weapons tended to sell themselves without the help of jingles and radio ads. I nodded and glared at the machine-gun mount, channeling all my efforts into ignoring the prior showdown. I'd never been as humiliated as today. Just when we'd approached some kind of a ceasefire, too.

I forced myself to focus, refusing to search for Romeo. "What's so special about it?"

"Glad you asked." Senior laced his arm with mine and approached the Kevlar door, his steps uneven and weak. "The battlefield glass is resistant enough to survive a direct hit. It's also lightweight. Our fastest Humvee to date. It can carry triple the military equipment of our competitors and includes shock absorbers capable of withstanding most ballistic missiles."

"Oh."

Lovely contribution, Dal. What next? A dissertation?

What I really wanted to know was where Romeo went. It struck me as bizarre that he'd miss out on any opportunity to trample Bruce in front of his father.

We stopped before a row of men, adorned in a uniform of black fatigues, protective glasses, and helmets. All four blinked back at me like I'd just paid them a visit straight from space. Maybe I did go a little overboard with the outfit. Still, Romeo's outburst was completely uncalled for.

Senior gestured to the man closest to the Humvee. "This is Matthew Krasinski, one of our top engineers. Matt, this is my daughter-in-law, Dallas."

Matt reached for my hand. "Pleasure."

I shook it, eyes darting everywhere in search of Romeo again. I couldn't find him anywhere. Panic overtook me.

Was this the straw that broke the camel's back? After all we'd been through? A stupid La Perla mini-dress was going to send us to the lawyer's office to sign divorce papers?

Then it hit me. The thing I'd known in the back of my head for weeks now but refused to articulate in my mind—I didn't want a divorce. I wanted the opposite of divorce. And the old tricks in my hat—of pressing his buttons with my messy, lazy, unapologetically shocking behavior—didn't work. I wasn't drawing him closer. I was pushing him away.

Matt motioned to the monstrous tank. "Are you ready to see this baby in action?"

Not even a little.

"Sure."

But the Humvee didn't move. Neither did the men around it.

Finally, Senior shook his head, chuckling. "Okay, I see everyone's a little distracted. Let's give them some space, Dallas, shall we?" He set his hand on my back, leading me toward the helicopter while Bruce trailed us.

I swept my eyes across the tarmac. "Where did Romeo go?"

Bruce settled on my other side. "Probably to sulk. Junior does that often. He can't stand when people are nice to his father. Such an unbecoming trait in someone expected to inherit a leadership position."

Senior nodded his agreement. "He's not making you miserable, is he?"

"No, not at all," I shot out. An odd sense of ownership seized my throat. Only *I* could take jabs at Romeo.

"You can always come to me for anything. I should've mentioned it earlier. I'm here if you need me."

"Er . . . thanks."

325

I continued searching, mildly aware something was amiss—and not just my husband. Senior's hand slipped, hitting the curve of my butt. I startled, shoulders sagging when he hiked his hand up my back again.

Red-hot mortification dusted his cheeks. "My apologies. My hands aren't what they used to be, unfortunately. Not as steady."

I gave him the benefit of the doubt, because the alternative struck me as too outlandish.

Bruce rushed to Senior's side, offering an arm. "Where is Junior when his father needs him? He really is unreliable."

As soon as the drill began, I understood why Romeo didn't want me here. The experiment consisted of the Humvee, driven by a trained professional, sailing across the tarmac as everything from nature to man-made catastrophes attempted to wipe its existence off Earth. The vehicle galloped into an array of dangerous obstacles: mud, ice, water, and fallen trees. Meanwhile, dozens of armed men shot bullets into the rear. Just when the noise died down, an explosion quaked beneath my heels. I wobbled, one teeter away from face-planting on the harsh cement. Senior seemed worse off, barely able to maintain balance, which he already struggled to do on a regular basis. Bruce flew to the rescue, offering his forearm again.

The tank lulled to a stop, engine cutting. A man holding an orange light stick directed the vehicle to move past us for the second obstacle course. My mini dress rode up, exposing the edge of my butt. I forced myself to watch, quivering in my stupid outfit, cursing myself for ignoring Romeo's weather forecast.

Senior brushed Bruce aside, retrieved his phone, and aimed it at a rocket launcher, recording the display. "This is my favorite part. You'll see how the vehicle gets out of all of it unscathed."

But apparently, this almighty Humvee could not withstand a simple ten-foot drive, because as soon as it roared to life again, it drove directly into a ditch.

"What in the absolute cluster?!" Senior staggered toward the tank, which protruded perpendicular to the road, stuck hood-down in a six-foot-deep trench. "What happened?"

The driver crawled out, ripping his helmet off.

Matt sprinted over to help him, sparing me a glare. "Your daughter-in-law happened, sir. Steven couldn't stop staring at her and got distracted."

Steven lurched to his feet, a rooster-red blush pecking his cheeks. "I'm so sorry, sir. This isn't . . . I mean . . . look, sir, you could see her entire, hmm, *you know*, in that outfit."

"Check yourself, boy." Senior swayed with the force of his shout. "You shouldn't be commenting about my daughter-in-law's outfit, let alone what's beneath it. Where's my son?" He scanned the growing crowd while Matt yanked Steven away.

"Should be here any minute." Cara materialized, tucked into a sensible coat. Such a lovely, fully functional coat, too. My teeth chattered, fingers invading frostbite territory. "He went to grab something from the helicopter."

"For fifteen minutes?"

Cara propped her chin up. "He had an important call to take."

There was no call. I knew that as perfectly well as I knew Romeo had disappeared so he wouldn't kill me in front of an audience.

"He missed the drill?" Senior gaped. "What the hell is wrong with him?"

"Such a poor example for our employees," Bruce added. Why was this cretin even here?

Okay, fine, I had no real reason to be here, too. In fact, I regretted ever showing up.

Cara pursed her lips. "I don't mean to overstep, Mr. Costa, but Romeo warned you that Steven is too inexperienced for the job."

Senior spun to me. "Let me take you to lunch, Dallas, since my rude son is too incompetent to keep his own wife entertained."

"I'm not hungry."

Not only was it the (surprising) truth, but Senior also never really un-plastered his hand from my lower back, even though we'd reached the helicopter. If I had to guess, he kept it there for the sake of being seen like this, which I didn't appreciate at all.

"Sir." Matt jogged to us, stopping a few feet further than necessary when he spotted Senior's arm around my waist. The only reason I hadn't slapped it away was because I wasn't sure if I'd overthought it. "We'll need about forty people to drag the Humvee out of the ditch. We don't have enough manpower. I've called for help."

Senior jabbed a finger at the ditch. "That it cannot see its way out of a hole without assistance is a travesty in itself. A four-by-four can outperform this piece of junk." He flashed me his teeth. "You really are a little troublemaker, aren't you?" Before I could tell him to get his hands off me—was it really important if I was overthinking? I didn't feel safe, and that was enough—he pinched my hip bone. "My, my, have you got meat on you. Much more than Morgan. I can see why he is so territorial of you."

A terrible realization ambushed me. What a nasty, lecherous, horrible excuse of a man. Not a shocker that Romeo loathed his father so much. All the puzzle pieces fused together.

Senior and Morgan.

Morgan and Senior.

No wonder my husband almost blew my head off when I showed up looking like fair game. He didn't want his father thinking I *was* fair game. Pain, desire, and truth were the DNA of love. He'd checked two of the boxes, and I'd desperately craved the third. Now that I had it in my grasp, I dreaded the consequences.

"Get your hands off my wife before I break them both in front of your entire staff." Romeo's icy voice chilled the air.

"Junior," Bruce purred. "And here we thought you'd left to get your diaper changed by Cara and wouldn't be gracing us with your presence."

I whipped my head around, watching Romeo round the helicopter. He shouldered off his cashmere Burberry coat. Senior retreated from me as he draped it over my shoulders. Bruce, too, knew better than to stand in his way. I didn't know whether he'd covered me up so I wouldn't show my goods to his staff or because it was cold, but gratitude swam laps inside me, nonetheless. Not just gratitude but elation. Lord, was I screwed. The sight of his face restarted my heart, and the idea of not seeing it again . . .

He buttoned the coat around me like I was a small child, ensuring I was snug inside it. I swore he smelled of alcohol and blood. Anger slashed a deep line between his brows, the hard set of his jaw rendering him unapproachable. Still, I needed to try.

"Romeo, I'm so sor—"

"I'm not interested in your standard 'sorry' that usually follows despicable behavior, for which you never shoulder the consequences." He turned to Cara. "Take my wife back to our house, and see to it that she doesn't leave until I get there."

Cara white-knuckled her keys. "Of course."

It seemed obvious now that I'd figured it out. Cara knew what had transpired between Morgan and Senior. After all, she'd referenced it the day she brought my new wardrobe. Another obvious thing—how much Cara loathed me for the trick I'd pulled today. I couldn't even blame her. I'd begun to dislike myself for all the punishment I'd inflicted upon her boss.

Cara led me to Jared's car. I craned my neck, desperate to catch Romeo's gaze, but he refused my attention. He kept his eyes trained on his father. The father he couldn't punch the daylights out of right now, even though it'd be completely warranted, since he was vying for the CEO position.

In the background, bulky men unloaded from Jeeps, jogging toward the ditch. What a disaster. And it was all my doing.

I wanted to call Romeo's name, but my voice perished in my throat.

Darkness seeped into me, cutting clean through my flesh and bones, straight into my soul. The realization something terrible had happened to my husband—and that it was inflicted by his family—gripped me like a rust-clawed demon.

How could I be so blind? I should've remembered what I learned from books.

Beasts were never born—they were made.

Chapter Forty-Nine

Ollie vB: Holy shit. I cannot believe Rom just WENT THERE.

Zach Sun: Maybe he wasn't the one to do it? Maybe mainstream media got something right for a change?

Romeo Costa: It didn't.

Zach Sun: This is why optimism should be outlawed. It is basically free false advertising.

Ollie vB: Is the story true?

Romeo Costa: It is.

Ollie vB: This is great.

Zach Sun: Great for whom? Not for nature and certainly not for humanity.

Ollie vB: FOR ROM. Thanks, Zach, for shitting on your best friend's parade. You do know there is CON in the word conscience, right?

Zach Sun: There is also cute in execute. Does that mean murder is adorable?

Romeo Costa: @ZachSun, stop. You'll make his head explode.

Zach Sun: Speaking of exploding matters, word around town is the drill today didn't go fantastically.

Romeo Costa: You can credit my wife for the disaster. That cost us 800K, excluding the extra manpower.

Ollie vB: Her talent of burning money is astounding. Have you considered enrolling her in America's Got Talent?

Zach Sun: How is Des Moines, anyway?

Romeo Costa: Not speaking to me.

Ollie vB: Marriage is great.

Ollie vB: @ZachSun, coming soon to the reality near you.

Zach Sun: I'll never marry a (clearly imbalanced) complete stranger.

Romeo Costa: Never say never.

Romeo

I resisted the urge to check on Shortbread through the cameras. Unlike Senior, I honored promises and contracts I committed to. I kept opening my desk drawer. Each time I did, I cooled off a little more.

A Glock 19 nestled inside. Unloaded. A comfort blanket of sorts. Every time Senior drove me to the brink of madness, I'd stare at it and remind myself he'd soon be dead. Nothing but a distant memory and rotting bones. His impending death put me in a decent mood, but eventually, my mind circled back to the sight of him touching Dallas. If I'd been there, it wouldn't have happened. As it was, I'd locked myself in the helicopter as a preventative measure. What, precisely, was I preventing? Making good on my threat to pluck out the eyeballs of everyone who'd gaped at her.

In the helicopter, I nursed a tumbler of whisky, crushing it from the blunt force of my fist. The glass sliced through my skin. Cara had to stitch me up once she returned from escorting Dallas home. As for Senior, I should've known he couldn't help himself. Shouldn't have assumed he had no interest in her, just because he'd only taken Morgan as a lesson for me.

But Dallas wasn't Morgan. She was indisputably, *irrevocably* mine. An utterly nonnegotiable constant in my life. One I'd go to frightening lengths to broadcast.

Including, apparently, calling her a slut. Few words revolted me. This one did. There existed no creature more spineless than a chauvinist, which I'd exhibited in spectacular fashion. Today marked my first time using it. And my last time. Wielding it to goad her was an act of juvenile rebellion. An apology was in order. Since I'd never apologized to anyone in my life, I was ninety-nine percent sure I'd fuck it up. Also—that seemed to be the general theme of our marriage.

Cara breezed into the office with the documents I'd requested. "I forgot to tell you something. I found it so endearing." She always found charming things about Dallas, though whenever they shared a room, she hardly doled out positive attention.

I slammed my drawer shut, accepting the speech she'd printed. "I doubt I'll share the sentiment, but carry on."

"She changed into her pajamas as soon as she set foot inside."

"Are you sure the word you were looking for is endearing and not lazy?"

"But what she did after that, when she thought I wasn't looking, was so sweet. She dragged your coat around the house like it was a little fluffy toy, sniffing it when she thought no one was looking."

Shortbread had begun to show signs of domestication. You'd think I'd take pleasure in that. After all, I wanted to keep her. Sadly, it brought me no pleasure to see my naïve wife confusing lust with something deeper. I wasn't a lovable creature. I wouldn't pretend to be one.

I skimmed the speech, lips pursed, making quick changes before the urgent press conference I'd scheduled an hour from now. "Thank you, Cara."

"And if it makes any difference at all . . ." Cara loitered, sighing. "She looked really shaken about what happened. I think she regrets it. I do, Rom."

I hated that Cara knew Morgan cheated on me with Senior. Hated that she'd broken the news, requesting my urgent presence at the penthouse all those years ago, because she'd known I needed to find them myself to believe it.

"I'm utterly disinterested in my wife's mental state." I stood, handing her the speech changes while snapping my gum, surprised my jaw was still intact with how excessively I'd chewed today. "Have this edited, proofread, and returned to me in the next twenty minutes. And get me my gold tie. The one best suited for cameras."

She pulled a face, accepting the papers. "You're projecting, Rom. Dallas isn't Morgan. She's just a kid. A wild kid but a good one. She shouldn't pay for Morgan's sins."

Shortbread wasn't Morgan, all right. She would never be in a position to hurt me.

My walls were too tall, too thick, too cold for her to slip through.

Chapter Fifty

Romeo

If only I could see Madison's face as I delivered this speech, I'd frame it in Zach's gallery. As it was, I did, in fact, hire Alan to capture it, which was why I'd tacked on an extra hour before this press conference. The man needed time to find the perfect angle.

I settled behind the Costa Industries podium in our head-quarters press room. I'd practiced this face in the mirror a few minutes ago, since it wasn't one I had experience in using. Remorseful, dedicated, and somber. No hard feat, seeing as I'd spent the majority of the afternoon pep-talking myself into not murdering my father.

A bevy of reporters, journalists, and photographers from national and international media outlets sat before me. I deliberately took my time, careful not to unleash my satisfaction on my face. Well, the little gratification I possessed. Shortbread had ensured the thorough ruin of my day. *And* life.

"Ladies and gentlemen. Today, at approximately 10:30 a.m. Eastern Time, news broke that Licht Holdings Corporation, whom we considered colleagues, peers, and co-pilots in the effort to strengthen the U.S. Army, disposed of dozens of toxic PFAS chemicals in the water stream in Newsham, Georgia, a small blue-collar town in which Licht Holdings manufactures weapons."

I paused, frowned, pretended to give half a damn. Enough to convince people I genuinely cared—and so they wouldn't suspect me of tipping off reporters about the story. "Upon a detailed investigation, we've confirmed this has caused high rates of cancer, depression, suicide, learning disabilities, and asthma within this already struggling community."

Another pause. "We are still in the process of discovering all the suffering and pain this thoughtless, reckless move by Licht Holdings has inflicted. However, I would like to assure you, right here and now, that Costa Industries condemns these actions. We are, and always will be, committed to serving the communities we are part of and not vice versa."

A few journalists raised their hands. Photographers snapped pictures, buzzing with energy. You couldn't tell a story like this without pictures, so I'd paid a hefty sum to the families affected by the toxic chemicals to share photos of their dying relatives, ruined lungs, infested limbs, and chemotherapy journeys. I didn't feel half guilty about it. Not the part where I paid distressed people to share their tragic stories. And not about bringing this to light, preventing other companies from exhibiting this behavior in the future.

"While I share little about my personal life in public, I'd be remiss not to mention my wife is Georgian, born and bred. Thus, I am especially fond of the state."

A ripple of giggles rolled through the crowd. At least complete strangers considered me a heartthrob. Too bad Shortbread's parting words were a promise to bite off my cock if I got close to her again.

"I've met Madison Licht, the son of Licht Holdings CEO Theodore Licht, many times and considered him a peer in the industry. The Lichts both share deep ties to Georgia, so I am staggered, if not completely floored, to discover they would do this to their own people, their own state, their own beloved natural resources."

I laid it on so thick, I was surprised my own eyes didn't roll out of their sockets. Time to wrap it up before I sailed into overkill territory.

"As we face this new era of uncertainty, trauma, and dramatic loss of precious lives in this great nation, I would like to make a vow, on behalf of Costa Industries, to never fail the people of this country. Of the states that host us as manufacturers."

More hands shot up, waving now. *Journalists*. So impatient.

"Furthermore, I would like to announce that, in light of the recent findings regarding the PFAS damage, Costa Industries has donated fifty-five million dollars to workers and residents of Newsham, who are currently suffering the consequences of catastrophic policy, irresponsible management, and a poor example of a defense company."

Claps erupted across the room. Some people stood, particularly the ones I'd planted in the crowd to egg on support.

"Thank you for trusting Costa Industries. We promise not to betray your faith."

I soaked in the applause, allowing photographers to capture every angle before I strode offstage.

Our public relations officer sauntered onstage, smiling big in her crisp dress suit. "Mr. Costa will not be taking questions. Understandably, he'd like to be with his loved ones today and make sure he shows support to his wife's family."

The Townsends lived nowhere near Newsham. And Shep Townsend was about as blue-collar as I was a Hooters waitress, but calling on my bluff didn't fit the media's narrative.

As I marched backstage, Cara and Dylan, my financial analyst, followed, jogging to match my long steps.

"Give me good news." I jerked my tie loose, strolling to the elevator. I'd done a lot of legwork to ensure this story found itself in the hands of every major media outlet in the United States.

"Their stock is tanking." Dylan's eyes remained glued to his iPad. He pushed his glasses up his bridge. "This is catastrophic for them. We're talking a fifty-percent slash in value. At least. Honestly, unheard of. Not even after Parkersburg. And Licht's stock was rocky in the first place, since it just went public."

He didn't tell me anything I didn't know. This should've been my moment to relish in the damage and misery I'd leveled at the Lichts, yet all I could feel was the nagging, persistent stab of guilt that poked at me like a humming-bird. *Dallas*. She always wormed her way into my psyche.

"Sir? Did you hear what I said?" Dylan waved his iPad. "Their stock is crashing. Why aren't you happy?"

An excellent question. I wanted the answer just as much as he did.

Cara answered her phone. "Yes. I'll tell him. Thank you." She didn't have to tell me who it was nor what he wanted, but she did. "Your father requests your presence in his office. He sounds very pleased."

Almost pleased enough to give me the CEO position. I could feel it. I'd won him over. He'd made me jump through fire hoops—and so far, the flames hadn't licked me.

"I'll see him right away."

Victory was within reach, so potent and sweet, I could almost taste it.

Chapter Fifty-One

Dallas

"And what's he doing now?"

I flipped on my back, setting my book on my mattress, feet dangling in the air. Hettie leaned beside my doorframe. I wasn't sure at what point, exactly, I'd lured her into my camp, but I no longer worried about whose side she was on.

Sometimes, it felt like we were roommates in a dorm. Or maybe teenagers stuck in a long summer camp abroad. We shared the kinship of two young women forced to face an arduous man, who somehow stood their ground.

Hettie squinted into the sliver of space between the hinges. "He's still pacing from side to side, mumbling to himself that he knows you're here."

Snorting, I shook my head and reopened my book. After a few pages, I asked, "And now?"

Hettie leaned forward and squinted, brows furrowed, hands pressed against the wooden panel. "I think he's trying to call you again."

I didn't bother checking my phone, which vibrated on my nightstand. Last time I did, it had racked up sixteen unanswered calls. That was two hours ago. The clock flashed ten at night, and Romeo still showed no signs of determent by my reluctance to see him.

"I can see you, Hettie." His words seeped through the door. "If you don't open up, I will fire you."

Hettie cupped her mouth, suppressing a giggle.

"You'll do no such thing," I yelled, flipping a page. "And if you try, I'll rehire her and pay her to be my friend full-time."

"With whose money, pray tell?"

"Mine. Oh, I forgot to mention. I sold a couple of your designer watches to ensure I'm not low on cash. You don't mind, do you?"

The silence on the other side of the door told me he was using every available drop of patience to make up for his cutting words to me earlier. "Open the door, Shortbread."

"Give me one good reason," I challenged, enjoying the exchange between us.

"So you can explain to me how you managed to defy the laws of gravity—and in my eleven-million-dollar house, no less. My bathroom ceiling is splattered in green."

This was what he cared about right now? My little skin-care-routine accident? I sure hoped liquid chlorophyll was as effective for my face as the magazines claimed, because it was absolutely effective on Romeo's precious crown molding.

"You should thank me. Your house needed some color. Everything is cream and beige here."

"Open the door." Boy, he sounded like a broken record.

"Apologize first," I cooed.

"For what? Tarnishing my house with a vile green color or ruining a drill with a prototype that cost over eight hundred thousand dollars?"

"My Lord, so expensive, and it doesn't even have a sunroof."

Though I wanted to drag out our beef into the next century (and maybe the one following it), I knew things weren't black and white. His father *did* hit on me today. Blatantly and in front of people, disrespecting his honest, loyal, and hardworking son. If my suspicion was true, Romeo had been subjected to a terrible betrayal by Morgan and Senior. I was rabidly curious.

"Okay if I go?" Hettie faced me. "I mean, clearly, he'll sleep in front of your door if you don't open up."

I nodded, closing my book, rising to my feet. "Just make sure he doesn't come in when you slip outside."

"You got it."

I hugged Hettie goodbye. As soon as she darted out, I shut the door and locked it for good measure. Romeo pounded on the wood from the other end. *Someone* was fast approaching the end of his patience.

"You have exactly five seconds to open this door before I tear it down. Fair warning: I will not be reinstalling it, and your privacy will go up in flames, right along with your sexy clothes."

It didn't surprise me in the least that he'd follow through with burning my revealing frocks. Just because he'd said something he shouldn't didn't mean he thought he was wrong.

Leaning my forehead against the wood, I closed my eyes, drawing in a breath. "I have conditions."

"Your only condition is insufferable." But the bite had fled his voice, replaced with something different, almost coaxing.

I ignored his words. "You need to apologize for calling me a slut today. And promise me to never, ever say that again. Not about me. Not about anyone. It's a degrading word, designed to make women feel shameful for having the same needs and urges as men."

Utter quiet wedged between us. For a few seconds, I thought he might've taken off somewhere else. Maybe to find an agreeable wife.

"Fine. I shouldn't have said that. I'm sorry I did. I don't think you're a slut, and I share the notion women shouldn't be shamed for their sexual urges."

Though it never occurred to me to consider it before, his words incited a wave of relief. After all, we *did* get together after I snuck behind Madison's back with him.

"It'll never happen again," he promised, somber. "Even if you decide to walk around naked. Which, regrettably, I am unable to rule out at this point, knowing you."

A smile touched my lips. I spun, eyes landing on the white rose. The rose that still survived. Kind of like our unlikely relationship.

"What's the other condition?" A soft thud told me he'd leaned on the other side.

I pressed my palm against the wood, where I imagined he rested. "You need to tell me about Morgan and your father." I swallowed. "Everything."

The words soared past my lips before I could chicken out. Part of me wanted to take them back. To turn back the wheel and spare him the heartache. But what about *my* anguish? As long as he punished me for someone else's sin, I'd never find true happiness.

Silence seeped through the crack, lacing around my ankles, rooting me in place. This time, I knew he was still there. Heard his labored breaths. Could almost feel his heartbeat thumping through the wood.

Finally, he broke it. "Why?"

"So, I can help you heal. Because you want to destroy whatever little is left of your father's life more than you want to enjoy your own. And since my destiny will forever be chained to yours, I deserve to know where it all went wrong. When you decided that hate was more worthy than love."

"Hate *is* a more powerful drive than love."

"Nonsense." My fingertips ran over the wood like it was his face, like I could caress him. Touch him. Take away his pain. "Love always wins. After every war, there's a baby boom. After every storm, spring sweeps in and everything blooms. It's always darkest before the dawn. Love is an effortlessly potent fuel. It is easier to maintain than hate. It doesn't consume—it *fuels*. You're running on the wrong energy, dear husband."

Another pause. Another breath. Then his footsteps carried him away from my room. My heart sank. He left. I squeezed my eyes shut, thumping my forehead against the door.

Stupid. Stupid. Stupid.

What did you do that for? Why did you force him to open up when he clearly wasn't ready?

The steady thud of his footsteps reemerged after a few minutes, nearing my bedroom. "Open the door."

I swiveled, turning the key ever so slowly, knowing what awaited on the other side wouldn't be pretty. He stood before me, eyes bloodshot, hair tangled in an unkempt, devastatingly sensual mess. His tie hung past the lapels of his work suit, the buttons of his dress shirt half undone. The sharp contours of his pecs peeked past. He held two tumblers of whisky.

We stared at each other, and I knew nothing would be the same between us after this talk.

He offered me a glass. "What I'm going to tell you won't leave these walls."

I stepped aside, head bowed. "I'm not Morgan, Romeo. I'll never let you down."

344

Chapter Fifty-Two

Dallas

"I met Morgan at Monica's summer party in our Hamptons house."

Romeo reclined on the other end of my rug, rotating the simple wedding band on his finger. He never took it off. Not once since we'd exchanged vows. I always assumed he sought the perks of his good-boy reputation. Not what was right in front of me—Romeo Costa was loyal to a fault.

"She was the au pair for a couple across the street. A charming Midwestern ballerina. Blonde, beautiful, bewitching. She attended Juilliard on a full ride and had a dimpled smile and impeccable manners. And she was great with kids. Very endearing."

He picked up his tumbler, twirling the tawny liquid. Specks of gold shimmered inside it. He studied them with a deep frown.

"I was twenty-one. She was nineteen. I was rich. She was . . . not. It didn't matter to me then. It doesn't matter to me now. But as soon as Senior caught me looking her way, he informed me blue blood doesn't mix well with that of mere mortals. '*Treat her like the ocean, Son. A few dips won't hurt—but don't go in too deep.*' I ignored him. And what started as giving her rides after she clocked out for the day quickly escalated to sex in my back seat, skinny-dipping in the ocean, and talking from night till morning until our mouths dried."

Jealousy clasped my gut in its tight fist, twisting it painfully. This unattainable, larger-than-life creature who'd strode into a ballroom months ago, able to have his pick of every available girl at the event, had boyishly courted an ordinary girl. One whose daddy didn't own a key American company and whose last name didn't open doors.

He sipped his drink, still staring at the wall. "By the time summer ended, it was clear Morgan and I weren't a seasonal fling. She quit Juilliard to move in with me while I finished my degree. A move Senior had anticipated. He claimed women of her pedigree could never stand toe to toe with men like us. That Morgan was too blinded by my fortune to be my equal. I refused to take love tips from a man who notoriously cheated on my mother my entire life." The flex of his jaw told me he regretted not listening to the advice. "At any rate, Morgan moved in with me, and Senior fumed."

I knew where this was going. I tucked my legs under my butt, gulping down whisky to calm my nerves.

"Morgan slipped effortlessly into a life of luxury. While I attended classes, she shopped, got her hair done, worked out, and stepped into the role of a trophy wife. Only we weren't married yet. Not even engaged. And that was a problem for her."

A wry smirk touched his lips as though he remembered something particularly unpleasant.

"She waited until I graduated before she told me she expected me to propose."

"You were so young."

He shot me a glance. "Still older than you are today."

346

I knew in that moment he regretted taking me against my will. Which, sadly, only made my stomach churn further. I couldn't imagine losing him, even if he was never truly mine.

"I was born to be a wife and a mother." I crawled to him, skimming his knuckles. Although he didn't pull away, he also didn't lace his fingers through mine as I wished. "I know it sounds old-fashioned and small-world. But we cannot help the things we desire. Please, carry on."

He worked his jaw, palming it in his free hand. "I was ready to propose. I knew I loved her, flaws be damned. God knows I had my own. When I notified him of my intentions, Senior blew a gasket. He informed me he wanted me to marry. But on his terms. Someone he could flaunt. A woman with an influential last name who would bring her own fortune to the table and make us even richer."

A woman like me.

I knew I was never my husband's choice. That I was convenient because I once belonged to Madison and wielded acceptable lineage, but the reminder sliced through me with a blade so sharp, I could feel the burn on my skin.

"Senior told me it was time to face reality. He even suggested I pick up with her again after marrying a suitable girl. I believe his words were—*everyone does it, Sonny. Monogamy is an upper-class creation to oppress the middle class. We needn't adhere to it.* Monica, herself, came from a very wealthy family. Her parents footed the bill whenever Costa Industries needed outside capital. To Senior, a marriage that didn't include a business contract was utterly pointless."

I withdrew from his knuckles. "But you didn't listen to him."

"I bought Morgan a ring. I was twenty-two; she was twenty. I didn't want to buy the engagement ring off my parents' credit card. It seemed wrong, considering they both opposed the union. Monica less adamantly—she always saw Morgan as a gold digger but let me live my life. So, I bought the ring with whatever money I had saved up from my TA gig."

That couldn't had been much. A hunch Romeo confirmed by tipping back his tumbler, polishing off the rest of his drink.

"I presented Morgan with a ten-thousand-dollar ring. She was livid."

A gasp bunkered in my throat. "Did she say no?"

Romeo chuckled. "Oh, no. She said yes. But she also said other things—how I didn't truly love her because the engagement ring was an embarrassment compared to those of her new rich friends. That she couldn't be seen with it at her country club. She complained I wasn't serious enough. That she quit Juilliard for me. Put her entire life on hold."

"Did you ask her to do all that?"

"Not once. Then again, I was young and thoughtless. I happily accepted her sacrifices without considering she'd demand a reward for each."

I dug my nails into my palms, nodding for him to continue.

"Around that time, Licht Holdings entered the game as a serious competitor. Morgan and I patched things up. I took her on vacation to the Bahamas. When we returned, I started working for Costa Industries while applying for my Masters.

"My first year at Costa Industries seemed to balm the strain in our relationship. I earned real money and aged into my trust, which meant she spent a lot more. I'd take her to weekly dinners with my parents, hoping she'd win their hearts. Monica thawed, but Senior remained unwavering. At the same time, he always flirted with her at the dinner table. I hadn't thought much of it. Almost three decades separated them. Not to mention, she was my fiancée."

I winced, bracing for the worst.

"Things unraveled when I started my Masters while employed full-time at Costa Industries. I spent little time with Morgan, which she resented. She began hanging out with Madison's crew. The rich Georgians who flooded Potomac seemingly overnight. She liked them. They found the place boring and made frequent trips to New York. She joined them often. I didn't mind, since I couldn't give her the time she required. Back then, Madison and I were friendly."

Did Morgan cheat on him with Senior *and* Madison?

Romeo stole my whisky, bringing it to his mouth. "By the time I finished my Masters, Morgan and I were little more than roommates who occasionally had sex. My love for her turned into obligation. I could tell she begrudged me for being obsessively laser-focused on my career. But I had a goal."

"To take down Costa Industries?"

If Morgan's affair hadn't triggered his revenge quest, what did?

"Yes." He didn't elaborate. "I can't deny being an inattentive fiancé, but I was also reliable, faithful, and gave her every penny I had. So, when we drifted apart, I doubted whether the marriage could work. Still, Morgan always lured me back into her web. I felt guilty enough for ripping her from her previous existence to see it through.

"The day of my first promotion, Senior called me into his office and informed me he'd selected prospective brides for me. That if I didn't break things off with Morgan, he'd do it for me. We had a nasty argument, but I thought nothing of it. Days passed, then weeks. One day, Cara, who routinely bought groceries for us, called. I was on my way to Zach's. I'd been hanging out with him and Oliver more often, since home felt like anything but. Cara urged me to head to my penthouse. Said there was something there I should see. And there was."

The storm brewing in his gray eyes swept me into emotional turmoil.

"I found my father eating out my fiancée, who wore nothing but a pair of heels for him. He didn't even stop when I walked in. Just stared me right in the eye and told me that was what happened when you chose a working-class girl instead of a classy, workable girl. She'd always choose money over you." He paused while I fought the urge to throw up. "And he was right. All it took for her to spread her legs for him, to do this to me—to my *mother*, who fed her every Sunday at her house—was a black card and an empty promise he'd divorce for her."

"Oh, Romeo." I cupped my mouth.

I understood his mocking approach to marriage now. He'd hardly seen a good example. His parents were miserable together, and his one and only girlfriend cheated on him in the most despicable way.

He returned my drink. "Spare your tears for someone who deserves them. Power is a great substitute for love. And I have plenty of it. Life is much easier once you accept the fact that everyone will hurt you."

I held the whisky to my chest, my heart hammering against the glass. He was right, but he'd also missed the most important part. Everyone will hurt you. The key to happiness is finding someone worth enduring the pain.

"After I threw Morgan out to roam the streets naked, I watched Senior tuck himself in and realized he was right all along. The working-class fiancée. The ability to get away with absolutely anything if you possessed enough influence. I could've beaten him to a pulp. I have experience in that field, after all."

He leaned against the bed base. "But revenge is a dish served cold. And I'd already enacted plans to ruin the thing he loved most—his business. That would be my moment of reckoning. This, and killing the Costa dynasty with my last breath. After all, Senior always planned on having more children to ensure a line of succession. Didn't work out so great."

A bitter smile found its way to Romeo's lips. "So, I've played the long game. Garnered control and clout to use against him. I agreed Morgan was a mistake. Sat down with him for a drink. And vowed to give him what he wanted in due time—a filthy rich bride of high ranking."

Siring an heir for Romeo meant giving in to his father's wishes.

I hugged the glass so tight, its edge left a mark on my skin. "You had a drink with your father immediately after you discovered him sleeping with your fiancée?"

"Indeed, I did."

"This is sick."

Romeo shrugged. "Love doesn't exist. Marriage is a means to an end. My only regret is dragging someone else down this grim path of mine. Before I met you, it was easy to write you off as an upper-class version of Morgan. A ditzy woman who didn't mind whom she married, so long as her quality of life remained unsullied. I didn't think you'd care if I stole you from Madison. In that aspect, I'm no better than your father."

I regarded him with fresh misery.

He turned away, not wanting to see what was smeared on my face.

"Why do you hate Madison so much? What was his role in this?"

Romeo worked his jaw again. I noticed he wasn't chewing gum and realized he felt uncomfortable without it.

"After she realized my father had tricked her, Morgan tried crawling back into my good graces. Didn't happen, obviously. She'd leave me hourly voice messages. Long ones. Begging me to take her back. She knew my tidiness didn't allow me to overlook the red alert on my phone. In one of her ramblings, she mentioned something about how she 'didn't even tell Madison anything that could come back to hurt *me*.' The moron essentially outed herself. I found out Madison paid her the last six months of our relationship to collect intel against Costa Industries through me. And that was why I finally exiled her somewhere she couldn't hurt me."

That sounded like the Madison I'd grown to know and dislike in Potomac. It also sounded like my ex-fiancé was the first to initiate this war between them. The hatred burned with a never-ending flame.

"What did he find out?" I swallowed hard, dreading the answer.

Romeo's eyes met mine, dead and cold. "Not much he could work with but plenty to embarrass me. Morgan never cared about my business. Never wanted to know much about it. So, in order to cut a nice check for herself, she resorted to telling him my secrets. My fears. My . . . *complex* childhood." His nostrils flared. A faraway look curtained his face. "She did something far uglier than giving him trade secrets. She told him my weaknesses and how to use them."

"Where is she now?" Part of me didn't want to know. I was liable to make the trip and strangle her myself.

"Norway." His lazy tenor told me not to ask any more questions regarding the why and the how. "Working a retail job and keeping her nose out of my business. She is not doing brilliantly. Still single. She spent the money Madison gave her within weeks of our breakup, so no sound investments were made, either."

"Do you think you'll ever see her again?"

He shook his head. "She is dead to me, and she knows it."

"Then, there's no reason for her to remain there. You need to let her come back to America."

"No."

"*Yes.* You can hate someone for all the right reasons and still wrong them. Revenge is the act of stooping as low as the person who hurt you."

He stared at me miserably. "Loathing you was so much easier when I thought you were silly."

Silence blanketed the room. Surprisingly, I didn't have many questions to ask. Only one, really. Everything else was crystal clear. His motivations. His desires.

"This all happened years ago," I pointed out. "Why did you take me as a wife just now?"

"A few reasons." He tucked a lock of hair behind my ear absentmindedly. "First, I'm now the CFO of Costa

Industries, within reach of CEO. Senior is seriously ill and will step down any day now. And you and Madison only recently made the engagement official to the general public. I was unaware of your existence until the week we met. Plus, for the longest time, I couldn't tolerate the idea of having a woman by my side, even as decoration. Time dulled the anger, but it did not cloud the memory."

I pulled away from him. "That all women are the same?"

He shook his head. "No, my precious Shortbread. That once broken, a heart can never mend. Function—yes. But you cannot repair something that is already in pieces."

I didn't agree with him. Then again, my heart had never been broken. Although, currently, it felt like it treaded dangerously close to this territory.

"So, now you know." He collected our glasses, standing. "Why I hated seeing you parade yourself in front of Senior. Why he touched you to make a point to me—that you were fair game, too. Why I'll never have children."

He left no room for negotiation. No room for thought. I studied him from my spot on the rug, realizing he'd given me exactly what I wanted—the truth—and that it didn't get me any closer to defrosting his heart. If anything, the mission seemed more impossible than ever.

"I will never love you, Dallas Costa. For that, I am truly sorry. Because you are certainly worthy of love."

Chapter Fifty-Three

Zach Sun: Is it just me, or have we not seen Rom in weeks now?

Ollie vB: It's not just you. He's been busy with his sweetheart.

Zach Sun: Detroit?

Romeo Costa: @ZachSun, you are aware that this joke was not funny the first time around, let alone the fiftieth, right?

Ollie vB: There you are, sunshine. Where'd you disappear?

Romeo Costa: Life is hectic.

Ollie vB: Too hectic to join our annual pre-Christmas snowboarding vacation?

Romeo Costa: I'm afraid so.

Ollie vB: Lies. You're not afraid of anything. Other than catching feels.

Zach Sun: @OllievB, can you hear the meows?

Ollie vB: Of @RomeoCosta, being pussy-whipped? Yup.

Zach Sun: @OllievB, remember when Rom had his balls?

Ollie vB: @ZachSun, yeah. They were beautiful. When he ran, they'd clank against one another. It sounded like wedding bells.

Romeo Costa: Speaking of weddings, when is yours, @ZachSun?

Zach Sun: Never.

Romeo Costa: I'm giving it three months.

Ollie vB: I'm going to be generous and give him six months.

Romeo Costa: 100K?

Ollie vB: Deal. Whoever's closest wins.

Zach Sun: I hate you both.

Ollie vB: I hear wedding bells again.

Romeo Costa: False alarm. It's just Zach's balls shaking.

Chapter Fifty-Four

Romeo

A week after Shortbread had pranced around in little more than a Post-It note covering her privates, I wined and dined Tom Reynolds at Le Bleu. This meeting was long overdue. Last time, I'd canceled after Dallas channeled her inner Great Gatsby, throwing the mother of all house parties.

Today's agenda included convincing Tom to reverse the DOD's decision to grant Licht Holdings our forgone renewal. Cautious optimism settled into my shoulders. Licht Holdings sat amid a PR disaster. With far too many fires to extinguish to fulfill the monstrous contract.

Jared slammed the brakes, narrowly avoiding a Tesla that cut him off.

"*Ooof.*" Shortbread careened into my side, sloshing sparkling apple cider onto my Bruno Cucinellis.

I jerked the bottle from her grip, sending it into the trash. "We're minutes from the restaurant. Is this necessary?"

"I'm pregaming."

"You're *spilling*."

And that brought me to the only downside of Tom inviting his wife—Shortbread had to tag along, too. There was nothing wrong with my wife whatsoever. Stunning, entertaining, and sweet as sin, she provided a welcome distraction for Casey, who I doubted wanted to hear about drones, tanks, and semi-automatic weapons. There was only one issue with Dallas—I could hardly think of anything other than burying myself inside her whenever she entered my vicinity.

Shortbread pouted, yanked tissues from the tight corset of her gown, and dabbed my loafers, presenting an unimpeded view of her generous cleavage.

"*Dallas.*"

"Hmm?"

But what could I say? Put your tits away before I spring a rifle-sized hard-on that'll make Tom wish he never asked to see my weapons?

I extended a handkerchief. "Clean yourself up."

Instead of using it to wipe the sticky cider off her hands, Dallas brought the square to her nose, inhaling my cologne. "You know, just because I agreed to come tonight, doesn't mean I approve of your job."

I swiped the fabric from her, collected her heeled foot, and dabbed the alcohol off her myself, ignoring her words.

"I mean, I don't trust humans to take care of the planet, and all they need is literally not to suck. Why would I trust them with heavy artillery?"

"You're not supposed to trust anyone with heavy artillery. That's its entire purpose. The quickest war to end is the one that never started."

"So profound." She batted her lashes. "The Nobel Peace Prize is on the way. Make sure your suit is ironed."

It infuriated me to no end that this was the woman I'd entrusted my truth to. I knew she'd keep my secrets safe. That offered me absolutely zero comfort, seeing as I wanted to pinpoint, dissect, and devour each flaw of hers. Anything to make her less appealing to me.

She had plenty of faults, too. I remembered how easily I'd spotted them when she'd first moved in. But everything I'd detested about her—her rolling, loud laughter, her messiness, her uncanny ability to befriend anything and anyone, potted plants included—no longer irked me.

True, she wasn't academically accomplished, but she'd read half the local library in under four months and whipped quips at a frightening pace. She flaunted a knack for numbers, too, crushing Vernon in chess and Zeus on the Loose.

Her food obsession bordered on unhealthy, but her knowledge in all things culinary fascinated me. Mostly, it disappointed me that my wife wasn't truly lazy. She was just waiting to become a mother so she could channel all her energy into her spawns.

Presently, though, I discovered a good reason to be unhappy with her as we strode from the Maybach to my newly acquired restaurant. She was panting like she'd just finished a marathon.

"Must you breathe so loudly? Aliens can hear you from neighboring planets."

"You believe in them, too?" She perked up before side-eyeing me, noting my flat expression. "Wait, you're annoyed with my *breathing* now?"

I opened the door for her. "You're young and, for an unfathomable reason unrelated to your lifestyle, seem to be in excellent shape. Why are you breathing so hard?"

"I'm breathing regularly, Rom. Maybe you're just super attuned to me, so you can hear me even when I'm quiet."

Rom. My nickname spoken from her rosebud lips sounded like the most beautiful word in the English language. When Oliver and Zach called me that, I wanted to punch them.

"Keep dreaming, Shortbread." I settled a hand on her back, leading her to our table. "And while you do that, don't forget to be courteous, friendly, and well-mannered. I need Reynolds's business."

"Ugh. I planned on eating directly from their plates, but now that you asked . . ."

Tom and Casey already awaited us at the table. They weren't alone. They brought—I shit you not—their toddler. Thus, a flurry of cooing and kissing ensued. Casey immediately gushed about Dallas's hair, dress, eyes, and general existence. Meanwhile, my wife physically snatched the toddler and cradled it to her chest. "Who do we have here?"

"Freida. Her nanny bailed on us last minute." Casey sighed. "You don't mind, do you?"

"Mind?" From the extent of Dallas's outrage, you'd think Casey just suggested a couples swap. "Children are my passion, and this one is just extra delicious, aren't you, sweetie?"

Despite that last sentence potentially landing her in the FBI's watchlist, a twinge of pride pricked my chest. I studied Dallas, seeing her from a stranger's eyes. Her beauty remained unrivaled. Yet, more than her looks, I admired her endurance, sweetness, brash honesty, and devotion to children.

I wasn't so arrogant as to think she was content with what we shared. She wanted more. Feelings. Romance. Dates. *Heirs*. She deserved all those things, too. But the only way I could grant them was to let her go, and I refused to do that.

The mindless chatter began as soon as we settled into our seats. Little Freida—curly haired with a yellow plaid dress—sat in Dallas's lap and ate squished food from between her fingers. I asked after Tom's parents, golf tournament, and drone-flying hobby, all of which I cared about a little less than Kanye West's opinion about marginalized minorities. Through bits and pieces, I overheard Dallas and Casey discuss the grave matter of surgical brow lifts.

Idiotically, and for no reason other than my inability to let the matter be, I tuned out Tom Reynolds, whom I'd courted for weeks, listening to Shortbread's conversation. Her steady breaths lingered in my ears, accompanied by her boisterous laughter, the crunch of her complimentary bread, and the little gulps her throat produced as she sipped a pink martini. The way she blew raspberries into Freida's neck and stroked the child's shoulder every time she fussed. Was she right? Was I simply hyperaware of her? The very thought made me shudder.

It took me a while to slide in to business mode, but once I did, I forgot Dallas's existence. She seemed to amuse the Reynolds females. I made a mental note to reward her cooperation in the form of fucking her. I'd be smart about it. Now that I knew her period cycle, I'd fuck her when there was little chance of getting her pregnant.

"I'm going to be honest. Things aren't looking well for Licht Holdings." Tom blew out air, shaking his head once we finally cut to the chase. "I doubt they'll be able to honor our contract even if we were willing to overlook the public outcry to boycott them. Which, I have to say, the Secretary of Defense isn't eager to do. Cameron Lyons is Georgian, if you might recall."

I poured Tom another glass of wine. His words were silence to my music-allergic ears. "Have their productions reduced significantly?"

"I'm not in a position to discuss their business with you. You know that as well as I do, Costa." Reynolds scanned the heavily jeweled diners, voice lowering. "But with their Newsham manufacturing base shut down and another one in Alabama under heavy investigation, I just don't see how they can pull it off without missing the deadline by months. We're talking a backlog that could cost the Pentagon billions."

"We'll be able to take their load and hit the deadline. Perhaps even hand over some equipment early. As you may be aware, we just recruited five hundred workers at our Smethport factory. Call it the Prophecy of Dry Bones. The resurrection and restoration as you return to your promised land—Costa Industries."

If things went my way—which they historically had—the DOD and Reynolds would have no part of their contract fulfilled. Costa Industries would be long gone by then. Duly crushed, liquidated, and dormant. I didn't care one bit. As Dallas loved to point out, I was in the business of death and intimidation.

Reynolds nodded, stroking his chin. His daughter gurgled in the background. "I'll talk to Lyons. He initially wanted to try Licht Holdings for their attractive prices, but that's out the window, so I'll see what we can do—"

A loud bang exploded in my ears. The double entry doors collapsed on the floor. People shrieked. Utensils and champagne flutes shattered to the hardwood in a symphony of broken glass. Waiters dove, seeking safety under tables. Four men dressed in cargo pants, black Henleys, and balaclavas tromped through the restaurant. I immediately recognized them as the ring of high-end robbers responsible for terrorizing Potomac. Still uncaught, after all this time.

Next to me, Dallas shoved Freida behind her back with no regard for her own safety.

A robber pointed to the ground with the tip of a Savage 64F. "Phones on the fucking floor or everyone's dead." Dozens of iPhones boomeranged toward his feet.

Everyone dead? By an outdated hunting rifle? Wouldn't bet on it. And while interrupting my meeting, no less. Irritated, I draped an arm around Shortbread, who tucked Freida against the wall, sliding both our phones on the Bocote planks. I'd read the news. Knew what these morons were about. They robbed fashionable, rich diners, took cash from registers—not much, this was the twenty-first century, everyone paid by card—and left victims scandalized but unharmed. Unlike the previous places they'd raided, the minute I bought Le Bleu, I'd installed a Costa-owned security system so advanced and sophisticated, the cops must've left before the robbers even entered the premises. External security personnel monitored our cameras twenty-four seven.

Shortbread's skin chilled. I squeezed my grip around her, pushing her head under my chin. Not because I cared, but because it looked great in front of Tom and Casey. Who, by the way, appeared stricken with horror. Casey shot Shortbread grateful stares for hiding Freida. The toddler shook, but my wife made funny faces to stop her tears.

"Hands in the air, everyone." Another robber with a Glock raised his arm, shooting at the ceiling. The clown hit the chandelier, which crashed at his feet, causing everyone to scream and cry.

"Now I'm going to go to each table with my friends here, and you're going to hand over everything you have that's worth shit. Jewelry, watches, cash, fucking coupons.

And you'll wait with your hands where I can goddamn see them until I get to you, or I put a bullet through your head."

I turned to Dallas. "Do as he says. Nothing bad will happen to you."

Her throat bobbed with a swallow, though she didn't sob like Casey, who crumbled to hysterics that rivaled the other diners'. I'd long suspected my wife was what Gen Z ridiculously referred to as a bad-ass bitch. As always, I was right.

The robbers worked quickly, grabbing everything of value and pouring it into backpacks. The one with the Glock reached our table, while the three others milled around, emptying pockets and bags.

Casey yanked off her rings, as well as her earrings, necklace, and Chanel clutch, sliding it to him. Tom and I offered our wedding bands, watches, and the little cash we carried. Dallas handed over her engagement and wedding rings, a bracelet, and a Birkin. Freida was still hidden behind her back, away from view. She glowered at the masked man like a disapproving teacher. Laughter fizzed in my throat. She was giving him sass at gunpoint. Classic Shortbread.

"The earrings, too." The man behind the balaclava pointed at them with his gun.

Shortbread fingered the simple pearl stud, shaking her head. "No. I can't do that. They belonged to Grandmomma. And she died—"

"I don't give a flying fuck about how your mee maw kicked the bucket. Hand the earrings over, bitch."

What was she doing?

Being sentimental and sweet. The things you mock her for so often.

364

She splayed her fingers flat on the tablecloth. "I'm not giving you my earrings."

Freida began to cry. The shrill shriek echoed off the walls like a bullet.

"Sweetheart." I didn't call her by her name, since it'd be dumb to tell them who we were.

"No." She tucked the child under the table and glared right into that asshole's eyes, issuing an unspoken challenge. "Shoot me if you'd like. But you're not getting my grandmomma's earrings."

His face twisted in rage, visible even through the black fabric. "I'm going to fuck you up."

He raised his pistol to hit her. Dallas slammed her eyes shut, bracing herself for the pain that never came. I'd blocked the barrel an inch from her face.

I held it in a death grip. "I'm going to make a pen holder out of your fucking skull if you so much as glance in my wife's direction."

He jerked the gun back, sweat staining his balaclava. "Who the fuck do you think you are?"

"I said what I said. Put the gun down and walk away."

Freida wailed harder. Frankly, I couldn't fathom Dallas's fascination with children. They were incredibly loud for their size.

"I'll shoot the bitch if she doesn't give me the earrings."

"Come on, T. We gotta go." Urgent calls from the rest of the robbers made "T" swing left and right, panicked. His esteemed colleagues already hovered by the door, backpacks slung over their shoulders. An arsenal of police sirens wailed, assaulting my ears and signaling the end of this nonsense.

"Not before she gives me the fucking earrings. I will shoot her fucking kid."

He thought Freida was ours. That made Dallas really lose it. She rushed to unfasten her earrings.

"No." I put my free hand on her arm. "Your earrings stay."

"T, the fuck are you doing?" a robber cried out. He sounded young.

"She's not going to disrespect me." T pointed his Glock at Shortbread.

Something strange happened in my chest in that moment. An eddy of frenzy. An intolerable appetite for blood and violence. I shot up, blocking his view of Dallas. He stumbled back when I got in his face, pushing him off. His friends ran away, leaving him behind—*cowards*—while he struggled to regain his balance. I snatched the gun by its barrel.

"Stop!" T tried jerking back his weapon. "Fucking let go."

"I told you not to threaten my wife, did I not?" I pushed the gun downward and snatched T by the throat with my free hand, squeezing so hard his eyes bulged out of their sockets, pink and round and petrified. "Play stupid games, win stupid prizes. *Nobody* threatens my wife and lives to tell the tale."

He gurgled. Foam bubbled out of his mouth. In the background, I registered the sirens nearing, people gasping, and Dallas begging me to stop. But I couldn't, even if I tried. All I could think about was how he'd aimed his fucking gun at her, all because she wanted to keep her grandmother's heirloom. A grandmother I'd never meet. There were so many things about her I didn't know, and this idiot almost ensured I'd never discover them. If he did something to her . . . if he hurt her . . .

I clasped his throat so tight, I felt the bones inside it strain, on the verge of breaking.

"Oh, Lord," Dallas shouted, just as the robber collapsed to the floor beneath me from lack of oxygen. I didn't think he was dead. Brain damaged, maybe. No great loss, considering his less-than-intelligent actions so far. "Romeo." Dallas sprang on me, clutching my shoulders. She handed Frieda to Casey when she saw my face. "Are you okay?" She cupped my cheeks. Her hands shook. Those beautiful hazel eyes glittered with tears. "Please, please, tell me you're okay. Tom called 9-1-1. The ambulance is on its way."

"I don't give a rat's ass about this punk. For all I care, he can die right here on my floor."

"Not for him. For you!"

For me?

I inventoried Dallas first. Arms. Legs. Neck. Everything seemed intact. A sudden burst of pain struck my left arm. The same left arm that now felt like deadweight. Like it no longer belonged to my body. I looked down and realized I stood in a pool of my blood. My gaze rolled up to my arm. I'd been shot. Grazed, to be more accurate.

Well, this was inconvenient.

As the adrenaline subsided, pain began trickling in.

Dallas waved a hand in front of my eyes, trying to capture my attention again. "Hello?" She tapped the center of my forehead. "Anyone in there?"

I tore off some of the tattered fabric. "Fortunately, there's a great deal of distance between the bicep and the brain."

"A bullet hit your arm." She fawned over the gnashed skin, jumping from side to side as if it would vanish at a different angle. "How can you be so calm about this?"

"Would running around hysterically with tears streaming down my face close the open wound?"

"Do you test your own products or something?"

No, but I've survived worse fights.

Dozens of cops burst inside and collected the knocked-out man beneath us, cuffing him. A commotion of people swirled around me, with Reynolds and two cops trying to push them away to give me space. I detested attention, especially the positive kind.

One of the police officers pulled Dallas aside. She kicked, yelling at him not to touch her, refusing to leave me. A fact that surprised and delighted me.

With my uninjured arm, I drew her to my chest. "My wife stays."

The ambulance arrived soon after. A paramedic ushered me inside, cutting through my clothes to reach my wound. We both examined it through sober eyes. Shortbread stood beside the open doors of the compartment, growling like a guard dog at any reporter who neared.

"Looks like a shallow wound. I could use some stitches, but it seems like a scrape." I nudged the paramedic's hand away. "I can do it myself. I don't have time to play around at the hospital for hours."

He dabbed the wound with antiseptic. "Protocol says you have to accompany us to the hospital."

"Fuck your protocol."

"You can't—"

"Are you going to take me against my will?"

"No, but—"

"Then, I can."

Dallas's head whipped toward us. "You should get this stitched." The sheer worry clinging to her voice thrilled me, which was how I knew I was completely and utterly screwed.

"I will. I know what I'm doing." I hopped out of the ambulance, making my way to our Maybach, where Jared awaited. "Come, Shortbread."

She looked torn between trying to convince me to go to the hospital and doing as I said. In the end, she seemed to remember her husband answered to no one, not even her, and joined me.

When we slipped inside and I bled all over my leather seat, shirtless, Jared didn't ask any questions. He knew his place.

Shut up and drive.

Chapter Fifty-Five

Romeo

It seemed Shortbread had a bone to pick. Or in her case—break. I ignored her, striding into my room, still bleeding. She followed the scarlet drops of blood, like Hansel and Gretel chasing a candy trail. In my bathroom, I yanked out a first-aid kit and sanitized the wound again. I'd suffered scrapes worse than this, but it looked nasty.

Dallas hopped on the counter by the sink, cradled her knees, and rested her chin on them, studying. "Need help?"

I dabbed the area dry and pulled out a needle and thread, frowning down at the bicep I needed to sew. "Do you know how to stitch gunshot wounds?"

"No."

"Then, how do you suggest you help me? Cheering from the sidelines, holding a sign of my name?" She blinked at my harsh words, obviously hurt. Sliding the thread through the needle's eye, I added, "You may leave now. You did well today. I think we saved the contract."

"Is that all you care about?"

I ran the tip of the needle along my skin, searching for where it had broken. What a lousy angle to stitch myself from. "Of course not. I also care about the damage they inflicted on Le Bleu. Cara will need to talk to the insurance company and authorities. Bureaucracy is a real bitch."

"You saved my life."

"That clown wasn't going to inflict any serious damage. He was just a kid."

She hopped off the counter, ducked her head under me to catch my gaze, and palmed my face. "No, he was angry and provoked. You took a bullet for me, Romeo."

I scowled. "Don't be dramatic."

"Thank you."

Since I'd made no progress finding the starting point to stitch myself, I cleared my throat, stepping back. "You're welcome. Now leave."

"I want you." Her hand ran the length of my chest up to my shoulder.

I want you, too, which is why I need you to get the hell away from here. I no longer recognize myself or my actions where you're concerned. You've become a liability I cannot afford.

Rather than kick her out, I set the needle and thread down. "You can ride my thigh."

"I want to ride your *cock*." She teased up the short hem of her olive satin dress. "When you forced me to tag along to Le Bleu, didn't you say you'll fuck me if I behave? I behaved."

"I said I'll fuck you when you're on your period."

"I interpreted that differently."

"It's not a Benedict de Spinoza book. It was not open to different interpretations."

"Whatever. That last time wasn't so great anyway." Contrary to her words, her dress inched up, flirting with the border of her lace panties. "It happened so long ago that I don't even remember much. Was I even there? Were *you*?"

Egging me on wouldn't work. Sadly for her, I was more sophisticated than that.

She continued, undeterred. "Oliver told me you're a born-again virgin. You know your pee pee has other functions, right?"

"Leave, Dallas."

But she didn't leave. Instead, she dropped to her knees and began undoing my belt. I leaned on the edge of the sink, powerless to stop her. My fingers curled around the counter.

"I'm going to bleed all over my floor." A last-ditch effort to stop her.

She pulled out my heavy, engorged cock. Her fingers circled it all the way without touching. I loved how tiny she was compared to me. How unlikely a pair we were. How people must've wondered how I fit into her. The delicious answer, by the way, was *barely*.

"It'll compliment all the green I splashed on your ceiling." She wrapped her lips around my cock, taking it inch by inch. Her warmth engulfed it. I shuddered when she flattened her tongue against my shaft.

I dropped my head back and groaned. Dallas was a great dick-sucker. She had the stamina, since her jaw worked out all day from eating. *And* she was enthusiastic. I could tell she loved going down on me. I'd had my dick sucked by enough women who only did it to warm my bed. They'd blink up at me, examining me through their lashes with what they thought were seductive grins, suckling gently, stroking my dick up and down like it was a cello.

Not Shortbread. Shortbread loved it all—the sucking, the spitting, the kissing, the way my cock hit the back of her throat when I grabbed her hair and fucked her face. She loved gagging on it and often tried to take me all the way to the root. In fact, this seemed to be the only aspect in Dallas's life in which she was *not* lazy.

Tilting my chin down, I watched as she sucked me off. Crimson drops ran down her glossy hair, trailing along her forehead. Seeing her tainted with my blood did something to me. Gave me a sense of ownership I normally did not allow myself to contemplate.

Perhaps it was the blood loss, but I didn't want to finish like this. Coming in her mouth wouldn't cut it. Lacing her long brown hair in my fist, I tugged her away from my cock. She pulled back, blinking at me expectantly.

"You want me to fuck you?" I leaned down, bringing her face to mine so our noses crushed together. I grabbed the front of her dress, twisting, tightening it against her skin until the fabric began pulling apart and tearing. "You want me to knock you up?"

"Yes," she breathed out. "*Yes.*"

I dropped to the marble, resting my back against the vanity. "Ask nicely."

"Please."

"Nicer."

She crawled toward me on all fours, straddled my lap, and grabbed my hand, bringing it between her legs. Her fingers guided mine into her slick pussy, two of hers joining mine inside her warmth. My lips found her nipple, biting down through her dress. Together, we fucked her cunt down to our knuckles, curling until her walls pulsed. I watched our fingers disappear inside her. She arched her back, trying to accommodate as much of us as she could.

Her lips drifted to the shell of my ear. "Please, please, *please.*"

I tore my fingers out of her, ripped her dress down the middle, and captured both sides of her waist, sinking her onto my cock, down to the hilt. Her head fell forward. She bit my shoulder, drawing blood, her hips bucking. She was so tight it felt like I was fucking her ass. Her walls squeezed around me, milking my dick for cum. I let her ride my length until my impatience won over, and I pulled her off me, flipped her over, and lowered her on all fours.

The marble was cold and hard against her knees. I love seeing that spoiled little brat take all of my cock, feeling the discomfort of it. My silver-spooned nymph.

I entered her from behind. She drove back, meeting each of my thrusts. My fingers curled around her neck and steered her upward until her back plastered against my front. She craned her head around and captured my lips, slipping her tongue past my teeth.

Her back arched, fingers dipping between her legs, searching for her clit. I smacked them away, then landed a palm on her ass.

"Rom," she whined. "I need to come."

"What you need is to be fucking grateful." My blood brought my point home, covering every inch of her back, arms, and tits, matting her hair in clumps.

I released her throat and pet the crown of her head, whispering praises into her ear. "Such a good girl." Words I never thought I'd say. Especially to this particular girl, who was anything *but* good two hundred percent of the time. "If only you took directions so well when you're not filled with my cock."

I reached around her and found her clit, rewarding her with a single flick. She cried out and fell forward, on her hands and knees again, pushing onto my cock. More crimson drops splattered onto her back. I'd reopened my wound, and fresh red painted her spine. I dipped a finger into it, then spelled my name across her back dimples.

"Who owns your ass?" I growled.

"You."

"Louder."

"You."

"Now crawl forward and show me your cunt from behind. I want to see if it's worth my cum."

With a reluctant moan, she inched away from my cock, writhing about two feet away. She started to turn when I hissed, "I don't want to see your face, Mrs. Costa. Just the cunt I stole from my enemy."

She spread her thighs apart, exposing her pussy. It dripped on my floor, her juices mixing with my blood, creating a pink puddle at her feet. I stroked my cock, coated with her wetness, scented by the wife I couldn't get enough of.

I grinned, the release tickling my shaft. "Embarrassed?"

"No. Empty."

Fuck me sideways. How this woman would ever end up with a wuss like Madison, I had no idea. She would make meatballs out of him before the reception.

"Keep looking straight ahead. I'll fuck you when I see fit."

I lasted less than two minutes before hammering into her from behind. Her elbows bucked and she let out a surprised gasp.

My balls clenched. I growled and drove every inch of me into her.

I came inside her. In thick, never-ending ropes, the head of my cock pressed as deep as it would go. When she realized what I'd done, her entire body tensed. Her pussy erupted around my cock, slicking it with her release. I slid out, watching as our cum cascaded past her lips and onto the marble. She collapsed on the tiles, resting on her back, a lazy grin adorning her face.

I reached two fingers out, gathered my cum spilling out of her pussy, and tucked it back inside her cunt, remembering her words from earlier. "Is this what I do with my pee pee?"

Arms sprawled out like a snow angel, she released a delighted giggle.

In the pleasure meter, making her laugh came close second to making her come.

"You came in me," she whispered, almost bewildered.

"I did."

And unfortunately, I wanted to do it again.

And again.

However many times she'd let me.

She stretched, propping one of her feet over my thigh. "That glass heart of yours, Romeo . . . One day, I'm going to break it."

"If anyone can, Shortbread, it's you."

I could give her a child without giving her my heart.

And that was damn well what I planned to do.

Chapter Fifty-Six

Dallas

Romeo and I had sex. *Real* sex. In fact, he seemed to almost accept the idea of expanding our family. Not to mention, he saved my life last week at Le Bleu. The man took a literal bullet for me. Without even hesitating. On paper, I should've been elated. So, why wasn't I happy?

For starters, two more petals fell from Vernon's rose. *My* rose. The more it shed, the sadder the fragile stem appeared. It swam in a pool of withered white, since I refused to discard a single corolla. And somehow, that made it barer. A lonely soldier in a forgone war.

And second, despite all Romeo's concessions, gestures, and devotion—he still kept me at arm's length. Still hadn't taken me on one proper date. I knew genuine adoration when I saw it. Shep Townsend might be a terrible father, but he loved my mother with everything he had. Meanwhile, Romeo spared me no real attention. To him, I'd become a fixture. A piece of furniture. A distraction. The realization gutted me. After all, there was no greater pain than unrequited love.

Unfortunately, I felt foolish explaining this to Hettie. So, instead, we played Connect Four, the television murmuring in the background.

"Wait." I latched onto her forearm. "Turn up the volume."

"Dal, you can't change the rules every time you lose."

"No. The news."

"Holy crap." She snatched the remote, blasting the mini flatscreen in the kitchen.

A cheery reporter folded her hands on a curved anchor desk. "An anonymous source reports that Costa Industries' demo artillery exploded mid-field test, leaving three staffers hospitalized. Investors are questioning whether the company can successfully fulfill their Pentagon contract, given this massive engineering setback." An infographic flashed across the screen. "As you can see, shares have nosedived since initial reports of the fiasco."

This "leak" had my dear ex-fiancé's paw prints all over it. I'd almost forgotten about Madison. Hadn't even heard from him since our brunch at Le Bleu, and I preferred to keep it that way.

A cut-out of my husband's smiling face at a charity event popped up beside the reporter. What I didn't expect, as she read out his official comment, was for said husband to burst into the kitchen. The clock read two past noon. Romeo never made it home before six.

Hettie turned to me, slurping on the Vietnamese egg coffee we'd ordered on DoorDash. "I think your husband just walked into the kitchen."

Shaking my head, I tried hard not to blush. "Nah. Must be the edibles we took earlier. No way would he miss out on all the office fun."

We never took edibles, but I always liked to keep Romeo on edge, forever guessing. It made him pay me a sliver of attention, and I, the beggar that I was, scrambled for whatever crumbs he threw my way.

"Dallas." He ignored Hettie's existence. "We have something to discuss. Follow me."

My smile evaporated. Was I in trouble? If so, how come? I hadn't spoken to Madison in ages. Plus, what happened today had nothing to do with me. In the background, news about Costa Industries' mounting troubles continued rolling.

I feigned a yawn, but my heart galloped. "Whatever you have to say can be said here."

He leaned a shoulder against the doorframe, folding his arms over his chest. His muscles bulged beneath his dress shirt. I knew he was wrapped up, in stitches and in pain under his sleeve. That made me yearn to kiss every inch of him better.

"This is a private matter."

Hettie shifted in her seat, clearly wanting to be anywhere else but the position I'd put her in. Beneath the counter, she pinched me.

I pinched her back. "This is private enough. Hettie is family."

"No, she is not. Even if she were, the latter shan't be privy to all things passed between a husband and his wife."

Again, he spoke like a nineteenth-century duke. I couldn't deny it made me rethink my stance on historical romance. Still, I refused to be subjected to him while he suffered from a foul mood, which he clearly did.

"I beg to differ." I straightened my spine. "Whatever you need from me, here and now is good enough."

He skimmed Hettie, not really paying her any heed, and shrugged. "Very well."

In two swift steps, Romeo hoisted me up, perched my butt on the kitchen island, and began unbuckling his pants between my legs.

Gasping, I turned to stare at Hettie behind me. "What in the Lord's name do you think you're doing?"

He flattened me on the counter. My hair tickled Hettie's elbow as he flipped my shirt up, exposing my midriff. His tongue trailed upward, toward my breast. Violent shivers of pleasure circuited my body. In an instant, I dampened between my thighs.

"You said whatever I need from you can happen here. In front of Hettie. I'm having a bad day and need a pick-me-up. Came here to cream pie in my wife's tight cunt and slap her tits a little. Hettie is welcome to leave at any point." His head disappeared inside my shirt, his teeth already nipping at my nipple through my bra.

"And Hettie is leaving right now before she can never look either of you in the eye ever again . . ." Her chair scraped. In a blonde blur, Hettie dashed out of the kitchen.

Vernon, who was on his way in, did a U-turn, too, muttering, "Goodness gracious."

"This is unsanitary," I pointed out as Romeo discarded my shirt and bra. His mouth devoured the side of my neck. "People are supposed to eat here."

"I *do* intend to eat here. Your pussy."

"I thought you were mad at me." I propped myself on my elbows, watching him, fascinated.

He tugged down my jeans and panties, burying his face between my legs, eating me out with the urgency of a man starved. His hot, wet tongue stroked my insides, his nose massaging my clit.

"Why would I be mad at you?" The words were murmured into my core.

"Because of the stock . . . Madis—"

"Do not speak his name when my tongue is deep enough in your cunt to reach your uterus."

The familiar burn of a blush crept up my neck. "I worried you thought I had something to do with it."

With much reluctance, he tugged his eyes up, understanding words needed to be exchanged between us. He sighed, kissed the inside of my thigh, and straightened, staring me in the eye. "I know you're not seeing him anymore."

"How do you know?" Somehow, I was sure as the morning sun that he'd stopped having me followed. Romeo kept his word. He always did.

"Because you and I both know that I would exile you from Potomac and file for divorce if you betray me after everything that's been said between us." Fire ignited his glacial gray eyes. Despite the malice inside them, his gaze showered me like sunshine, warming me down to my fingertips.

He now cared enough to get hurt. It wasn't much—but it was enough to make my head spin with joy.

"Now." He dipped two fingers into me, curling them as the sound of my juices clinging to him filled the air. "May I kindly eat out my wife, then fuck her, then eat her out again? I canceled all of my meetings for today, just so I can do that."

He withdrew his fingers and sucked them clean of my desire for him.

I grinned. "You may."

I was so satisfied and exhausted, every muscle in my body ached. Romeo stood at the stove, heating milk for my hot cocoa. White drinking chocolate from L.A. Burdick, which he'd specifically instructed Hettie to order for me ahead of winter. It marked his first time doing anything semi-romantic for me.

It means nothing, Dal.

Still, I couldn't heed my own warning.

Romeo sifted two scoops of shaved Burdick blend into the pot. "I used to take a cup to class every time the temperature dropped. Even while at MIT where the closest locations are all the way in Harvard Square or across the bridge."

I pretended to gasp. "You mean, there exists something beyond Brussel sprouts and chicken breasts that you eat?" My eyes glued to his sinewy forearm as he whisked the mixture. Good Lord.

"You'll understand when you try it."

To be honest, it could taste like liquid manure and I'd still demand seconds if only for the first-row seat to his forearm porn as he assembled it. I feasted on the sight of him. Shirtless, gloriously powerful, and *almost* mine. His taut muscles flexed every time he made the lightest move. A thin coat of sweat still clung to his tan body. I watched him with pleasure from my spot on the chair Hettie had occupied only an hour ago.

"I ordered replicas of your engagement and wedding rings." Romeo poured the drinking chocolate into my cauldron-shaped mug, littered with Henry Plotkin spells. "They should arrive late next week."

My stupid heart fluttered in my chest. It was so hard to keep my feelings at bay when all I wanted to do was let them loose. Watch them grow, develop, and evolve.

I feigned boredom. "And what about your ring?"

He sucked his thumb of milk residue, setting the mug in front of me. Fresh whipped cream and peppermint shavings. Just as I liked it. Had he been paying attention?

Romeo sat across from me. "My wedding band should arrive around the same time."

I was hearing everything I wanted to hear. Why wasn't I satisfied? Was it the rose that was slowly dying before Romeo had time to fall in love with me? Was I just being moody? Hormonal? Homesick?

I spun the teaspoon in my hot chocolate, channeling all my concentration into it.

"Shortbread?"

My eyes snapped up. "Yes?"

He frowned. "Why do you look so glum?"

Because you still feel nothing toward me. You simply accept me as yours. As one accepts a new colleague or neighbor. Someone random who entered your life and was here to stay.

I tried to swallow my frustration, but I couldn't. The idea of slipping into bed with him tonight—of sharing my body with him without sharing a single thought—haunted me.

I motioned between us. "Because this isn't real."

"Elaborate."

"This. *Us.*" I sighed, pushing the cocoa away from me. Things were serious when I wasn't in the mood for something sweet. "We share so much together, yet nothing at all. You don't know me. Not really. You haven't even attempted to learn more about me. You've opened up to me, and for that, I am grateful. But you know nothing about me. No enticing bits and pieces that would make me more endearing in your eyes. You don't know what my favorite color is. My favorite food. What my dreams are—"

"Your favorite color is blue." Lord, could he sound any more disinterested?

But he was right. And I was shocked.

He reclined against the backrest, shrugging it off. "You always wear blue. It complements your tan. And you gravitate toward blue things. From your Henry Plotkin

383

phone case to your favorite Chanel bag—all blue. As for your favorite food, that would be lomo saltado. Extra aji verde." Even the tiniest smirk from him directed rays of lust straight to my bloodstream. "You order it in three times a week. The delivery guy practically has our gate code. You always switch things up for variety when you order from any other restaurant. Other than Peruvian ones."

Spot on. Again. Maybe I was more transparent than I'd thought. I suppressed a smile, knowing if I unleashed it, he'd see how stupidly in love with him I was. *Oh, no.* I was, wasn't I? In love with Romeo Costa. The coldest, least sympathetic man on Planet Earth. The God of War.

All moisture fled my mouth. The adrenaline in my body awakened me from my orgasm-induced sleepiness. "But you don't know about my dream. My real dream. Not the ones I joke about."

He arched an eyebrow. "Children?"

I shook my head. "That's a goal, not a dream."

"Then, no. I do not. What's your dream, Dallas Costa?"

To be Dallas Costa because it's your choice and not a part of your plan.

I had a much older dream, though. "I want a house that is also a library."

"A library in your house?" he corrected, frowning.

"I said what I said. I want a house gutted from within and turned into a library. Every inch of it. Every room would have shelves, wall-to-wall, floor-to-ceiling. No matter where you walk. Kitchen. Dining room. Bathroom. Everywhere."

He studied me like I was an intriguing piece of art he'd just stumbled upon at the museum. Completely new to his eyes. Slowly, he nodded, unfastened his tin of gum, and placed a square on his tongue. "Now I know."

Well, that was anticlimactic.

I swallowed hard, feeling stupid and childish. I changed the subject. "So, you felt bad today and came to see me. Careful. I might suspect you're developing feelings for me." The joke came out all awkward and wrong. More accusing than flirtatious.

"I needed a quick fuck to get rid of the excess pent-up rage." He reached for his water bottle, taking a sip. "Do yourself a favor and don't read into it. I'd hate to hurt your feelings, Shortbread. They're so very precious. So are you, by the way."

It was the most patronizing, backhanded, terrible compliment I'd ever been paid. And I couldn't even tell him that, because then he'd know how much he'd hurt me.

"Hey, Romeo?"

"Hmm?"

"Have you noticed you haven't been chewing on gum excessively in the last few days?"

I had. I noticed everything about him.

Romeo tilted his head. "That's right. It's been a few days."

"One of these days, you're going to have to tell me why you like gum and silence so much," I teased, my foot finding his under the table.

"Why are you so fascinated with it?"

"Because our habits tell us who we are. Your quirks are a piece of you." I paused. "And I want to piece you together, Romeo Costa. That is, if you'd let me."

He shot up, taking his bottled water with him. "I'll be in my office, working. Thanks for the fuck, Shortbread."

Chapter Fifty-Seven

Romeo

Thanks for the fuck, Shortbread?

I deserved to be slapped by every woman on Earth. Still, I meant what I'd said. Though her feelings *did* matter, it would be wrong for Dallas to mistake our cordial relationship for a romantic one. To be honest, Morgan had nothing to do with it. My heart had long decayed by the time she'd entered the picture.

No. What alarmed me wasn't my dead heart. It was the danger of what my wife might do to it. Blow off the dust with her sweet breath. Soap off its tombstone with her capable hands. Breathe life into it with her unbearable, undeniable sweetness.

From her portrait in my study, Shortbread loomed over me. Her eyes clung to my profile as my loafers flattened the rug. Back and forth. Sure, we had something good going on. I trusted her. Enjoyed her company, even. Her cunt was by far the sweetest thing I'd ever tasted—perhaps as a result of the industrial amount of sugar she consumed. But there would never be more than that. And how could I keep my wife while offering her a fraction of what we both knew she deserved?

I didn't enter her room that night. Or the next night. Instead, I drove to Oliver's mansion with Zach. They'd just returned from our annual pre-Christmas snowboarding vacation in Colorado, which I'd skipped out on for the first time. Ever.

The guys played pool while I nursed a bottle, perched on the vintage Pac-Man machine. A Commanders game danced on the television in front of them. All in all, a pleasant night. I should have missed these gatherings with them, now that I spent most of my scarce free time with Shortbread. Yet, somehow, I didn't.

"So, when do you think you'll grant her a divorce?" Oliver lit a cigar and plucked a thong from the crease of his cedar leather couch, tossing it into the trash. Christ. I'd forgotten his place was an STD lab designed to create new diseases.

I strode to the bar, studying his impressive selection. "Who said we're going to divorce?"

Zach chuckled from the pool table. "*You.*"

"Several times, in fact," Oliver added.

"Six." On top of being a genius, Zach also appeared to possess the memory of an elephant herd. "I can recite them if you so wish, including dates and contexts."

Oliver scratched his temple. "I think your exact words were, 'Art rarely hangs on the same wall forever.'"

I opened the liquor fridge. "Dallas and I have reached a mutual understanding."

"Nice try." Oliver tucked a red-lace thong into his pocket, a swirl of smoke escaping his mouth. "You and your wife barely even speak the same fucking language."

I tried another tactic. "If we get a divorce, it will be some time from now. I'm in no hurry. Neither is she. I have more pressing issues to tend to."

Zach and Oliver knew my plans for Costa Industries. And why. I hid nothing from them, other than my complex feelings toward Dallas. But these were a recent development, and there wasn't much to tell.

"Not that far off." Oliver orbited his media room, unearthing pieces of lingerie in different sizes, styles, and colors, throwing them into his trash can. "She'll want kids at some point."

"I'll give her that," I snapped, annoyed.

Zach missed the cue ball, striking the side rail. Half a dozen bras tumbled out of Oliver's hands. Both their brows kissed their hairlines.

Zach digested the news first. "Will you, now?"

I grabbed a beer bottle by its neck without even reading the label, unscrewing it. "I need an heir. She needs a hobby."

"Since when do you need an heir?" Oliver tipped his head back and cackled. "Last we spoke about the subject, you developed a crust of hymen over your cock to avoid children."

"Someone needs to inherit my fortune."

Zach re-racked the pool table. "Pull a Gates and MacKenzie Scott. Donate most of it."

"Do you know me?" I scowled. "If Philanthropy met me in a dark alley, it would play dead, and I would *still* kill it just for the blood sport."

He clucked his tongue, chalking the tip of his pool cue.

"So, what I'm taking from this is that you're absolutely, certainly, without a doubt fucking your wife." Oliver finished fumigating his man cave of his hookups' lingerie and graduated to collecting empty condom wrappers from the floor. Why on Earth did I think this brothel was worthy of my wedding? "And that she gives *great* head."

"Lernaean Hydra." Zach nodded. "One head isn't enough to chip the ice. I'm thinking five, minimum."

"Stop talking about my sex life," I barked.

Oliver grinned. "Is her sister eighteen yet?"

I hurled my half-full beer in his direction.

Jackass.

I didn't visit Dallas's room that night. Mainly to prove to myself that I still had control over the matter. Our time together was not compulsory. I wasn't obsessed. In fact, I did not miss her warmth and cunt and kisses at all. Not as I laid in my frigid, too-vast bed. And not as I stared at the ceiling, wondering what fresh hell I would prepare for Madison Licht tomorrow.

Chapter Fifty-Eight

Romeo

From the start, Dallas scheduled Christmas with her family while I spent it with mine. An arrangement we had made in the rare times we'd spoken before shedding our clothes. One we thought would work well. Problem was, I'd wondered how I would tolerate five entire days without Dallas beside me.

The haunting prospect urged me to try an experiment. I planned to avoid Shortbread for a few days to prove to myself that I could, indeed, live my life without sinking my cock and tongue inside her, just as I had the thirty-one years prior to meeting her.

On the first day, I came home late enough that she'd already fallen asleep.

On the second, I arrived with a guest. Oliver. That would surely keep her at bay.

To my surprise, Shortbread wasn't in the kitchen when we entered, her natural habitat. She wasn't in the living room or my study, either. (In the latter, she enjoyed reading and leaving snack crumbs, just to remind me I'd never have a tidy house again.)

Oliver helped himself to whatever Hettie had prepared earlier, while I pretended not to be puzzled by Dallas's behavior.

"Hettie," I barked, interrupting her struggle into a puffer jacket. "Is Shor—Dallas here?"

She turned, frowning. "Isn't it the official first sale of the fourteenth Henry Plotkin book? She's probably lined up in front of the Potomac Yards Barnes & Noble, trying to snatch a signed first edition."

Of course. She loved those silly books.

I peered outside, scowling. Snow piled in giant white boulders. "Was she bundled up when she left?"

Oliver's head shot up from the bowl of pepper pot soup. He gaped at me, a spoon tumbling out of his lips.

"Oh, I didn't actually see her leave. I've been present shopping." Hettie triple-wrapped a scarf around her neck, shoving her hands into mittens. It was so cold, she wore layers for her short walk across the lawn to her residence.

My nostrils flared. "She probably wore a baby doll and sandals there."

Hettie laughed. "Knowing her, probably." She waved to me and Oliver before leaving.

I remained rigid for a few more beats while Oliver ogled me. He ladled his spoon inside the dish, gulping down a bite. "You can just call her, you know."

I could. But she wouldn't answer. I suspected she didn't like that I'd disappeared the last few days. "I'm going to grab a coat and scarf for Jared to drive to her." I shook my head, feigning exasperation, though I was more worried than infuriated. "I'll be right back."

On my journey up the stairs, I reminded myself I owed Dallas nothing. We'd always been an arrangement, and she knew it. So what if we hadn't seen each other for days? She hardly sought me out, either.

When I reached Dallas's room, I was surprised to find her still inside it. Even more so that she laid in bed. Shortbread didn't contemplate sleep before one in the morning. Yet, a neon-red seven glared at me from the alarm on her night-stand. The rose beside it had wilted, with only two more petals clinging on for dear life. I couldn't understand why she hadn't gotten rid of the stupid thing by now.

"Let me guess." I tromped into her room. "You hired someone to stand in line for you, so you wouldn't have to move your precious ass—" The rest of my sentence died in my throat as I finally caught a full glimpse of her.

Probably for the first time in her life, Dallas Costa looked terrible. A cherry flush stained her cheeks, but all color had drained elsewhere, leaving her as pale as her dying rose. White flakes peppered her lips, depleted of moisture, while a dull glaze coated her eyes. I rested my hand on her forehead. Furnace-hot.

"Jesus." I pulled back. "You're burning up."

She was too narcoleptic to speak. Or move. How long had this been going on? Was she like this yesterday? Had I missed her illness in my quest to prove to my brain that my dick wasn't the one behind this train wreck's wheel?

I touched her forehead again. It sizzled. "Sweetheart."

"Please get out." The words clawed past her throat.

"Someone needs to take care of you."

"That someone definitely isn't you. You made that clear these past couple days."

I said nothing. She was right. I hadn't bothered to check on her. Perhaps I'd wished *she'd* check on *me*. In truth, she'd already gone beyond any expectations in trying to make whatever it was between us work. Meanwhile, I'd shut her down. Repeatedly.

"Shortbread, let me get you some medicine and tea."

"I don't want you to nurse me to health. Do you hear me?" She must have hated that I'd seen her like this. Weak and ill. "Call Momma and Frankie. It's them I want by my side."

I swallowed but didn't argue. I understood she didn't want to feel humiliated. To be taken care of by the man who ensured she understood her insignificance to him. How did her bullshit meter not fry? How could she think I really felt nothing toward her?

"First, I'll get you medicine, tea, and water. Then I'll call for Hettie to stay with you. *Then* I'll notify your mother." I tugged her comforter up to her chin. "No arguments."

She tried to wave me out, groaning at the slightest movement. "Whatever. Just go. I don't want to see your face."

I gave her what she wanted, though as always, not in the way she expected. The sequence of actions didn't proceed as promised. First, I contacted Cara to dispatch the private jet to Georgia. Then I called my mother-in-law and Franklin—separately—demanding their presence. Only then did I enter the kitchen to grab water, tea, and ibuprofen for Shortbread's fever.

Naturally, like the chronic idler he often proved to be, Oliver still sat at the island, now enjoying an extra-large slice of red velvet cake I was pretty sure was meant to be consumed by Dallas.

"What are you still doing here?" I demanded, collecting the things I needed for her.

He scratched his temple with the handle of his fork, brows pulled together. "You invited me here. You wanted to watch a soccer game, remember?"

I did not remember. I didn't even remember my own address right now. "Get out."

"What about the—"

I snatched the plate from his fingers, admitting to myself that I'd treaded into feral grounds. "This cake wasn't for you to eat."

"You've gone insane in the ten minutes you were gone." Oliver gawked at me, wide-eyed. "What happened to you? Did Durban not get her hands on the latest Henry Plotkin book and take her anger out on you?"

Shit.

The Henry Plotkin book.

I shoved Oliver out with a fork still clutched in his grimy fist, dialing Hettie with my free hand.

She half-yawned, half-spoke. "Yes?"

"Dallas is ill. You need to come here and take care of her until my in-laws arrive in about two hours."

"Oh, yeah?" Her energy returned tenfold. "And what the hell are you gonna do during this time?"

"Freeze my balls off."

I could have sent Cara to do this. It wouldn't have been the most gallant thing I'd ever done—Cara straddled the thin border between fifties and sixties, suffered a busted back, and deserved her time off on Christmas—but not unheard of either. Hell, I could've sent any of my six lower-grade assistants. But I didn't.

Something compelled me to join the three-hundred-strong line outside my local Barnes & Noble for a chance to get my hands on the brand-new fourteenth and final book in the Henry Plotkin series—*Henry Plotkin and the Cadaverous Phantoms.*

And by "chance," I meant I would definitely get it for Shortbread. Even if I had to pry it off the hands of a terminally ill, orphaned kindergartener. I had no qualms about setting the entire place on fire if it meant returning with the treasured book. It was what she wanted—what she had planned to do with her time tonight—and by God, she was going to get it.

A scowl stamped on my face as a few reporters interviewed people in the freezing cold about how long they'd been standing in line (four to seven hours), how they planned to pass the time until the store opened in the morning (with hot drinks and sleeping bags), and what they thought would happen in the book (I tuned out that part).

I pondered how I'd reached this new low in life. I'd never done anything remotely as uncomfortable for anyone. Even for my ex-fiancée, whom I thought I'd tolerated. Morgan could only dream I'd stand in line an entire night for her. I used to get furious whenever she sent me on a tampon run if it was past nine at night.

Maybe guilt could be blamed for making me suffer in twenty-five-degree weather, but I didn't think so. For one thing, I had no conscience. For another, even if I had one, I'd put it to work forcing her to marry me—not failing to check on her for forty-eight hours.

Every now and then—re: seven-minute intervals, on the dot—I texted Hettie, demanding an update regarding Dallas's health.

Romeo Costa: How is she feeling?

Hettie Cook: Not well, but you already know that. She took Tylenol and drank some water. I'm making her avgolemono soup right now.

Romeo Costa: Is her fever down?

Hettie Cook: Between five minutes ago, when you last asked me, and now? No.

Hettie Cook: Fevers always spike in the evening, so don't worry about it.

Romeo Costa: I called the doctor. He is going to pay her a visit in the next forty minutes.

Hettie Cook: Forty minutes?

Hettie Cook: I hope she's going to make it till then.

Romeo Costa: ???

Hettie Cook: I'M KIDDING. SHE IS JUST A LITTLE SICK. JESUS. CHILL.

I was so chill, I couldn't feel my nose, let alone my balls.

Romeo Costa: You're fired.

The night crawled, minute by minute, refusing to disperse into morning. The doctor arrived and determined Dallas's fever needed to break, winning the Most Useless Doctor Award in my head. He prescribed her rest, fluids, and cold compresses. For what it was worth, Hettie agreed with my analysis.

Hettie Cook: Did you have to hire the Director of EMERGENCY Medicine at Johns Hopkins? The poor dude looked so confused when he realized Dal isn't on her deathbed.

Romeo Costa: You thought he was useless, too?

Hettie left when Franklin and Natasha arrived, which forced me to tone down my texts. I attempted to be reserved with my sister-in-law, seeing as Dallas particularly enjoyed talking shit about me with her.

Romeo Costa: Is she feeling better?

Franklin Townsend: Like you care.

Romeo Costa: It's a yes or no question.

Franklin Townsend: No improvement.

Romeo Costa: Keep me posted.

Franklin Townsend: You're not the boss of me.

Romeo Costa: God, you're a brat. I wish very much for Oliver to end up with you when you finally come of age.

Franklin Townsend: What?

A decade after the night had begun, the sun finally cracked through the silver sky, pale and reluctant. The store opened. People rushed in. It took me fifteen excruciating minutes to make it to the register.

The prepubescent cashier opened the book, leafing through it while he rang me up. "Can't wait to see how Henry handles The Duke of Hollowfield, huh?"

I yanked my card from my wallet. "Mind the spine before I break yours."

He gaped at me, almost fumbling the hardback in his rush to close it. "Bag?"

"Give it to me. I don't trust you not to wrinkle the book any further." I tucked it inside the bag and wrapped it tight.

As Jared wove through tree-lined streets, passing mammoth mansions, manicured lawns, and lavish holiday decorations, I couldn't help but feel a little unsteady about my newly acquired Christmas gift for Dallas. Originally, I'd purchased a spa weekend in Tennessee for her to enjoy with Franklin, but this seemed so much more significant. I would not call the unsettling rush coursing through me giddiness, but I was definitely not unhappy in this moment.

When I reached the house, it was still early enough that Vernon hadn't arrived. A sleepy-eyed Hettie stumbled into the kitchen, retrieving the pastry dough she prepared each night for Dallas's breakfasts.

I stopped by the island, clutching the book in a death grip as though it was in danger of being stolen by the furniture. "Is Dallas in her room?"

"She was asleep when I came in, but Frankie said her fever went down."

"How's she feeling?"

Hettie yawned, collecting her pink-tipped hair into a high ponytail. "Good enough to reject every brand of cough syrup we've given her."

"Why?"

"Says they taste bad."

"It's medicine. It's not supposed to taste good."

"It's pretty bad. The label says it's grape, but it smells like pickles and spam." Her nose scrunched. "Between Vernon, her family, and several of the staff, we checked every pharmacy in the DMV for pills. Sold out. The pharmacist says there's a nasty bug going around."

"I'll take care of it." I snatched the offending bottle from the counter. "Are her sister and mother with her?"

398

"Frankie, yeah. Natasha went to sleep in a guest room. Guess she felt like she could take a break because Dal's feeling better."

I took the stairs two at a time. With each step I climbed, my spirits lifted. The lilt of Shortbread's sweet, bell-like voice filled the corridor. Quiet, but unmistakably her. Why did it take me until today to realize I enjoyed her voice? Her sound? Her general existence? Maybe because it marked the one thing that wasn't complete silence that my ears cherished.

When I reached her door, I raised my fist, intending to knock. I couldn't wait to show her the book. Childish pride filled me. I supposed this was what kids felt when they did something they knew would grant them their parents' approval. I wouldn't know. My parents rarely paid attention to my existence.

". . . can't believe you didn't tell me you two were having S-E-X." Franklin abbreviated the last word, whisper-shouting in excitement.

A chuckle lodged in my throat. I wasn't one to eaves-drop, but staying back for a few moments to hear Dallas's response wouldn't enter the list of top ten-thousand worst things I'd done in my life.

"How's the sex?" Franklin demanded.

"It's okay, I guess." Dallas coughed, still weak. "I'm not suffering."

Understatement of the generation, sweetheart.

"Does that mean that you like him?" Frankie gasped, holding her breath. For an odd reason, I did the same.

There was no pause, no hesitation, in Dallas's response. "My Lord, Frankie. Of course not. I told you, he is the human answer to a potassium-chloride injection. That didn't change one bit."

It hit like a punch straight into my stomach. So much so that I staggered back a step.

What did you expect? For her to fall in love with you after you forced her hand in marriage and spent months berating her?

"Then, why are you having S-E-X with him?"

Why, indeed?

"Because he's never going to release me from his arrangement. I might as well get some fun out of it, right?" Shortbread sniffed. "Plus, I really want a baby. You know I've always wanted a big family, Frankie. Just because I don't like my husband doesn't mean I cannot raise a family I love. In fact, the sooner I get pregnant, the sooner I can return to Chapel Falls. He won't want me around him when I'm pregnant, anyway. He hates children."

I didn't hate children. Okay, I did. Only recently— the last few days, to be precise—had I begun to think it wouldn't be so terrible if Dallas and I had a child. Particularly if that child inherited her exploring hazel eyes and endearing laughter. Except now I'd come to discover the only reason my wife had been riding me like I was her favorite roller coaster was because she wanted to flee to Chapel Falls.

"That's the plan." Dallas's voice drifted into the hallway. "Keep coming here to get knocked up and run back to Georgia until I have three or four children. I'm sure he won't miss me, either."

My fingers shook, tightening around her book. Tense, labored breaths billowed in my throat. I'd offered her a divorce—why didn't she take it and leave? But the reason flashed before me in neon lights. She'd be a ruined woman, just as I'd pointed out. She would need to start from scratch, settle for the scraps Chapel Falls offered, and endure a terrible reputation for the rest of her life. If she got pregnant with my child, she could come and go as she pleased. She would still be the wife of one of the wealthiest people in America. No one would dare utter a negative word about her. Her family's respect, dignity, and good reputation would remain intact.

"I hope you get knocked up soon." Frankie giggled. "I miss you so much. I can't wait for you to come home."

"Me, too, Frankie. Trust me."

It shouldn't have felt half as bad as it did to find Morgan sprawled on my dining table, being eaten out by my father. Yet, it felt a thousand fucking times worse. It felt as if Dallas had taken a knife, carved out my guts, then fed it to the wolves. The level of betrayal was incomprehensible.

How ironic that I thought her disloyalty would come in the shape of Madison Licht, when all along, Dallas did not crave someone else.

She simply didn't want *me*.

Turning, I zipped through the hallway and down the stairs, dumping the stupid book in a random trash can on my way out the door.

If she wanted nothing to do with me, she did not have to say it twice.

I'd give her all the space she needed.

And then some.

Chapter Fifty-Nine

Romeo

Perhaps recognizing this as a genuine moment of crisis, Zach offered to let me crash at his place through the holiday. Christmas Eve, I dragged my miserable self to my parents', mainly because I knew my father itched to retire. The CEO position had never seemed more within reach. Despite feeling like I'd been run over a million times by our failed Humvee, I decided to dutifully finish what I'd started and kill Costa Industries.

The anticlimactic event that was Christmas dinner consisted of Monica moaning over Dallas's illness—apparently, she'd paid her a visit earlier in the day, reporting a tenacious fever—and Senior studying his food without an appetite.

Zach and his parents vacationed in Plitvice, which gave me the opportunity to stay at his place all by myself and dwell on the information my mother-in-law had texted when I returned from the mediocre meal.

> **Natasha Townsend: Hello, Romeo. I wanted to keep you posted, since your staff is away on vacation. Dallas's fever is persistent.**
> **According to her doctor, she also developed pneumonia. He prescribed her antibiotics.**

> **Franklin and I will stay in your guest rooms. Have you plans to pay your wife a visit anytime soon?**

The passive aggressiveness didn't escape me. I couldn't blame her. I was MIA when her daughter—my wife—suffered from pneumonia during the holidays. The epitome of a crappy husband. Yet, I doubted she would appreciate the reply I kept on draft for her.

> **Romeo Costa: Hello, Mrs. Townsend. My apologies for being away. I am currently occupied with the grave task of alternating between drinking myself to death and picking bar fights to release my rage, as your daughter made it perfectly clear that what I thought was a true relationship was actually her desperate account to escape me. I shall be there as soon as I get over the fact that I am nothing more than a bag of money and dildo full of sperm to her.**

As I sprawled on the minimalist leather couch in Zach's living room, cradling expensive whisky, I knew one thing was for certain—I was in love with Dallas Costa. In love with her, with the ground she walked upon, with her laugh, with her freckles, with her obsession with books, her messiness, her joy, her unapologetic personality. Every bit and piece of her, I adored.

I had no idea at what point, exactly, Shortbread had bewitched me. I only knew that I was helplessly and inappropriately in love with her when I didn't want to be. In fact, one of her few appeals when I'd initially taken her as a wife was what I'd thought was the absolute certainty that I would never develop feelings for her. Everything I'd once found awkward and unrefined about her ended up being my kryptonite.

The drink in my hand turned into three, which turned into five and then some. With Jared on vacation, I ended up in an Uber, a Burberry scarf wrapped around my face three times to conceal my identity. For a reason unbeknownst to me, I'd chosen Costa Industries as my destination. Not a soul occupied the building beyond a graveyard security team, so I sprawled across the lobby marble, chugging down whisky straight from the bottle.

I released a humorless laugh.

You took a bullet for her.

You broke your no-heirs rule for her—or at least, you intended to.

I had spinelessly accepted her demands, her flaws, her passions, and her ways. And still, she did not want me. There was little point in trying to convince her otherwise. The worst part was, although I loathed Dallas for acquiring my love, I still worried about her. Even after everything she'd said about me to Franklin, I wanted to be by her side. Hold her hand. Tend to her.

I was wrong. I'd never loved Morgan. What I'd felt toward her was ownership and entitlement. *This.* This was what love felt like. Like an organ of mine was in someone else's hand, and I couldn't retrieve it if I tried.

I hated every moment of being in love with Shortbread.

But that didn't make it any less true.

I stumbled through Costa Industries' rotating doors, bumping into the sober, stone-faced oaf. Unfortunately, I wasn't drunk enough to fucking hallucinate. Yes, it was

Madison Licht, standing before me in all of his five-foot-seven glory. Or rather, modesty.

"Well, well. What do we have here?" The frigid air lashed at both of us, but since he shared the same pallor as a melted snowman, his cheeks were the only ones to turn clown-red. "Getting into the Christmas spirit by solo drinking?"

"Not everyone can bask in the pleasure of seeing their company crumble to rubble. How's Licht Holdings doing, by the way?" I palmed my phone, calling an Uber. Five goddamn minutes.

"We'll bounce back." Madison ground his molars. "We always do."

"Word around town is, in addition to your mounting legal troubles, you've also failed more audits than the Pentagon. If only you knew a financial expert with nearly a decade of experience in Defense."

"I'd rather die than accept help from you."

"I was hoping for that option." I flicked the empty whisky bottle into a nearby trash can. "Let's proceed with your untimely death."

"So smug." His nostrils flared as he sneered at me through a mist of red fury. "You think you're so untouchable, don't you?"

I knew he'd leaked my failed demo to the press. That he thought he'd done something other than handed me one giant wrapped gift ahead of Christmas.

I barked out a laugh. "Oh, I'm touchable. Your ex-fiancée touches me all the time. *Everywhere*. She's delectable. Thanks for that, by the way."

Madison advanced, fisting my collar, something he'd never do—or get away with—had I been sober. His rotten carp breath rained down on my nostrils. "Don't forget that I know your little secret. That Morgan revealed all your deepest, darkest fears to me before she fucked off."

"My secrets can't kill me," I said, realizing for the first time that it was true. The past was just that—the past. As unbearable and painful as it was.

He released me, brought his thumb to his neck, and sliced it across, holding eye contact the entire time.

"But *I* can."

I woke up on Christmas Day with a raging hangover and a text from Frankie, unsure which of the two was worse.

Franklin Townsend: Momma and I are leaving tomorrow. You better come here and take care of your wife, or I swear to God, you will have nothing to return to. I am going to wreck your entire house, Costa.

Rage certainly ran in the Townsend blood.

I continued day drinking, ignoring the Townsend women while they tried to reach me on my phone, through Zach, and his landline. Obviously, I'd arranged for Hettie and Vernon to arrive a few hours before Natasha and Franklin were due to board a plane back to Georgia. They'd take care of Dallas while I wallowed on Zach's couch.

At some point, I grew bored of drinking and staring at the walls and ventured out of his place. The bitter cold nipped at my face as I trudged through unplowed snow. A ghost town of closed bars and restaurants met me at every turn. I roamed through the streets until frostbite formed on my cheeks, then returned to Zach's place and caved, bending to my heart's will.

Romeo Costa: How is she doing?

Franklin Townsend: Come and see for yourself, jerk.

Romeo Costa: I'm busy.

Franklin Townsend: So am I. Don't text me anymore.

Damn her.

A sleepless night followed the miserable day. Once the sun skulked up the sky and I glanced at my watch, realizing Frankie and Natasha had already taken off to Georgia, I called Hettie.

"Are you there?" I paced the living room, wearing out the rug beneath my socks (the Sun household enforced a strict no-shoes policy). "Is she okay?"

"Good morning to you, too." I heard the crunch of melted snow and ice crushing under her boots. Her labored breaths heaved across the line. "Actually, I'm stuck in New York because of this shitty-ass weather. Buses and trains are down. They're only now salting the roads, so—"

"And you're telling me now?" I roared, darting to my shoes and shoving them on, policy be damned. I laced them in record time, already slipping into my coat. "Vernon won't be there until afternoon. Dallas is all by herself."

The thought made my skin crawl. She was sick. She might have loathed me, detested me, and wanted me nowhere near her—but she was still sick. I zipped out of Zach's door, advancing toward his Tesla. Surely, he wouldn't mind. And even more surely—I did not care.

"Well, to be honest, Romeo, you're literally in town, so . . ." Hettie trailed off. She thought I'd stayed with my parents.

"Just get your ass there as soon as possible."

I hung up and floored it so fast back to my house, I beat Waze by fifteen minutes.

Utter silence and an empty house greeted me when I arrived. I cursed myself a thousand times over as I darted up the stairs to Shortbread's room. I opened the door without knocking. Niceties were a luxury I couldn't afford.

A duvet draped over her succulent curves. It was only when I got closer that I noticed her closed eyes. Blotchy red spots peppered her cheeks. Her fever must have persisted. Strewn across her nightstand were tissues, an assortment of liquid medicine, and bottled water.

The gravity of her illness slammed into me. Yet again, I found myself sick to my stomach with self-loathing. How had I chosen my precious ego over my beautiful wife?

"Sweetheart." I rushed to her bedside, setting a hand on her forehead. Oven-hot. "When was the last time you had a shower?"

"Leave me alone," she croaked, her eyes still closed. "You seem to be good at that lately."

"I'm sorry. I'm so sorry." I kneeled next to her bed, taking her hand in mine. It felt lifeless between my fingers. I pressed my lips to it. "I'm drawing you a bath."

"I don't want you to do anything for me. Hettie will be here soon enough."

She would rather wait for someone else to help her. Dallas twisted her face to the other side, so I couldn't see it. Each time I thought the knife in my heart couldn't twist deeper, she proved me wrong.

I filed into her en suite, drawing her a bath. While I was at it, I swapped the water for her rose, since I knew how much she liked the ugly, bare thing then made her tea and peanut butter toast.

I settled on her mattress and fed her, bringing the bagel to her lips and uttering coaxes. "Just one more bite, sweetheart. You can do this. I know you can. I'll buy you all the Peruvian food in the world if you finish this bread."

She didn't answer. Certainly didn't thank me. Just swallowed small bites of the toast without tasting it. I couldn't blame her. Regardless of how she felt for me, I knew for a fact she would nurse me to health had I been in her position. I was a coward. A childish fool for punishing her for not loving me.

Once the tub filled up, I stripped her clothes off and guided her inside, dragging a chair over from her vanity. Judging by her soft groans, I gathered I didn't do a terrible job massaging shampoo into her scalp. After rinsing, I lathered every inch of her body with a soft sponge and soap. Simply breathing seemed to pain her.

Great job, you bastard. How could you be so selfish?

At some point, the water turned cold. I carried her to bed, set her on a sprawled towel, and patted her dry, hiking panties up her legs. Then I removed the towel and swung the comforter over her shoulders.

"You forgot the rest of my clothes." She moaned, too weak to properly scold me.

"I didn't forget. We're going to break your fever."

Hopefully before you break me.

She watched through sluggish eyes as I stripped down to my briefs, lifted the comforter, and slid in next to her. I wrapped my arms around her from behind so she couldn't see me.

With my nose nuzzled in her hair, I decided in that moment that if she was crazy enough to give me another chance, I would give her everything she wanted, no questions asked, and demand nothing in return. If it meant I got to keep her, I would endure an entire lifetime of her stringing me along, getting pregnant, fleeing to Chapel Falls, and returning here only when it suited her.

Shortbread quaked in my arms. I squeezed her close to my chest, my throat tightening with all the words she deserved that I never got to tell her.

"Are you shivering, sweetheart?"

Her shoulders shook. After a long pause, she said, "No, I'm sad, you idiot."

I didn't know why it made me chuckle. "Why?"

"Because you deserted me."

"I didn't desert you." I kissed her jaw from behind. "I didn't think you wanted to see me."

Close enough to the truth, I supposed.

"You're my husband. Who else would I want to see?"

Your mother and sister, to whom you declared you cannot stand me.

"I'm here now, and I'm not going anywhere." I stroked her hair. I couldn't stop kissing her jaw. My body sucked the fever out of hers, our skin plastered together, our flesh melting into one unit.

"I hate you."

"I know. I hate me, too."

Leaning forward, I kissed her cheeks, absent of tears. I noticed she never cried, even when I most expected her to. Yet another thing I'd never asked about. I hoped she'd give me the chance to.

Dallas shivered inside my arms until her breathing evened out and I knew she'd fallen asleep. Another thing that fell asleep was my arm beneath her body, but I didn't dare move an inch. Not even when an hour turned into two, then three, then four, and I was certain I would have to amputate the whole limb after she woke up.

In fact, I didn't give much attention to my arm at all, because finally—*fucking goddamn finally*—Dallas sweat out her fever. I knew her fever broke when the sheets beneath us pooled with scentless perspiration. She squirmed and groaned as the sickness escaped her body. I couldn't do much but stroke her damp hair, kiss the back of her neck, and watch as she crawled back to health.

The entire time I held her, I was in awe of how I felt. How I was capable of giving someone love without expecting them to return an ounce. In awe of how I senselessly slipped back into her bed. The place where my heart would surely be broken.

Chapter Sixty

Dallas

I stirred to life in the darkened room, stretching in my damp sheets. White stars danced across my vision as reality seeped in. Romeo lay beside me, his muscular body draped over mine. *He's still here.* I wiggled my fingers and toes, trying to keep calm.

I decided not to tell him he shouldered the blame for my body's reluctance to heal. But in my heart, I knew the truth. From the moment he stormed out of the kitchen and ignored me, venomous unease slithered into my limbs, latching onto each organ until I struggled to stand, breathe, *exist.*

While my tear ducts never seemed to get the memo, the rest of my body remained in perfect sync with my soul. Both craved Romeo. And both stubborn entities went on strike until they got him. Yet again, my romance books proved right. Love is an accident. Something that occurs completely out of your control with no regard for your safety.

At first, the desire to reach out enticed me. Then my fever spiked, my bones descending into unending ache. The more time passed, the worse I felt. The worse I felt, the angrier I got that he hadn't even checked on me once.

He was here now. I didn't know if it was out of obligation, reluctance, or genuine worry. It didn't matter.

Stupid gratitude fueled each breath. I felt all better now. Brand new, in fact. And eager to find my way back into my husband's good graces. How convenient, then, that we were both naked in my bed. I wiggled my butt against his cock, springing it to life within seconds. For someone so against breeding, he wielded a reliably virile response.

Plastering my back to his chest, I propped my head on his shoulder and reached for his cock.

He clasped my wrist before I slipped my fingers into his briefs. "No, thank you."

My breath hitched. Blood roared between my ears. I met his eyes. Cold and lifeless, they belonged to the man at the debutante ball. Not the one who made me hot chocolate and agreed to give me the baby I longed for, to sacrifice his own plans and dreams for my own.

"You don't want me anymore?" I tried to sound casual.

"I want you more than I want my next meal. My next sleep. My next breath. But I cannot afford you, Shortbread. Giving in to you just might kill me."

Feeling my eyes flare, I jerked my face back. "What are you talking about?"

He slid aside, swung his legs over the edge of the mattress, and slipped his pants on with his back to me. "Are you well?"

"I . . . uh . . . yes." I sat up, dizzy. I told myself it was from the sudden movement and not the direction of conversation. "I don't think I have a fever anymore."

"You don't." So, he'd checked. "Hettie is here. Vernon, too. I spoke to Dr. Reuben. He'll arrive later tonight to check on you. He recommended an extra dose of medicine to ward off the remnants of illness."

I scrunched my nose. "It's gross."

413

"It's medicine." He reached for the tiny plastic cup, filled it to the line with purple cough syrup, and pressed it against my lips. "Drink it."

I shook my head, my lips zipped shut.

"Shortbread."

Another head shake. I knew if I opened my mouth, he'd tip it in. Not only did it taste expired, it also came with an hours-long aftertaste.

With the cup still kissing my lips, Romeo lowered his nose, tracing it up my neck, along my jaw, and to my ear. I released a moan, just in time for him to tip the medicine into my throat and whisper, "Swallow it." *Fair play* didn't even exist in his dictionary, did it?

Frowning, I gulped every drop. "It's disgusting."

"Good. Remember the taste, and never get sick again."

"It wasn't my fault."

"Did you or did you not go ice skating without wearing a coat? And don't deny it. You left time-stamped receipts to the rink in Rockville Town Center on your vanity. Plus, I confirmed with Hettie."

"Fine. I should've layered up."

He collected his wallet and phone, shoving them into his pocket.

"Are you leaving?" I squeaked, watching him button his shirt. My eyes missed him so much, they didn't dare blink.

He shoved his feet into his shoes. "Yes."

My bottom lip quivered. "But . . . why?"

"Because all you want is for me to knock you up so you can waltz back to Chapel Falls. And all I want is to bury myself inside you and never leave your bed. You're a weakness. An addiction. A distraction."

I flung out of bed. The abrupt movement sent nausea spiraling down my gut. My knees failed me. Romeo was there in less than a second, righting me in his arms. And still, his gaze remained flat and unforgivingly dispassionate. I could liquify into a puddle of regret right then and there, at the feet of his Bruno Cucinellis.

"What you're saying is nonsense!" I pounded his chest, furious. "No part of me wants to go to Chapel Fa—"

"Stop lying!" It was the first time he'd raised his voice at me. Ever. He ripped himself from me, plowing a hand into his messy, ink-black hair. "Stop lying to me, Dallas. I overheard you telling your sister how much you hate me. How you want me to knock you up so you can go back home."

Oh, no. No, no, no, no, no.

I couldn't believe he'd overheard that. What a disaster.

"Lord." I tipped my head back, forcing out a laugh. "I lied to her, Romeo."

"Why?"

"She found out we were having sex. My sheets reeked with the scent of us. I had to make an excuse for allowing you into my bed. I hadn't confided in her. I've never kept a secret from Frankie. She felt deceived and pushed back. She was hurt." I never stopped to think he might get hurt, too, if he heard my words. But I should have. Not one of them had rung true.

He arched a brow. "And telling her we were getting along wasn't a suitable answer?"

"No."

"Why?"

I sighed. "Because she wouldn't understand."

"Wouldn't understand what?"

That I am in love with you. With my captor. My enemy. My beast.

"Because we're complicated, and she doesn't understand relationships. Trust me, Rom. I don't want to go away. I don't want to return to Chapel Falls. I lied to my sister, and I'll make this wrong a right. I promise you that. But you have to believe me."

I clutched the lapels of his shirt. If he walked out right now, I knew my life would be over. Or at least, the life I wanted for myself.

He peered down at me. I could tell he didn't want to believe me. That his overdeveloped self-preservation instincts begged him to guard against another heartbreak. I couldn't believe I made him taste betrayal again. The thought sickened me.

"I have no reason to trust you," he finally said. Deathly quiet.

"I know." I clung to him. We were so close, I could smell him. I wanted to drown in him and never resurface.

"Then, why should I?"

"Because I'm asking you to." I licked my lips. "And because that should be enough."

His nostrils flared. I knew he didn't want to give me a chance. I also knew this was exactly why he'd ghosted me. He wanted to step back from the intensity of our relationship. Well, I wasn't having it. I wanted him. All of him.

Palming his cheeks, I lowered his face down to mine. Our foreheads met. The tips of our noses touched.

I breathed hard, my lips moving over his. "You are not the only one here with a dark corner to your soul. I will go to extreme lengths to make sure you are mine. I want you. And I won't give you up just because you decided you want to try out life without me again."

That was all it took for his lips to fuse with mine. Before I knew what was happening, he grabbed the backs of my thighs, hoisted me up as my legs wrapped around his waist, and carried me across the room. He thrust his tongue past my lips, kissing me deeply and furiously.

I moaned into his mouth, giving the kiss all I had before coming up for air and realizing we were in the hallway now. "Where are we going?" I nipped at his chin, already working on unbuttoning his shirt. I couldn't believe we'd gone over an entire week without sex.

"My room." He sucked the side of my throat, moving my panties aside and fingering me with the hand that wasn't holding me wrapped against his body. "*Our* room."

"Our room?" I pulled back, staring at him, wide-eyed.

"I am fucking done asking permission to see you every night. You're moving in. Starting now."

The next morning, Romeo was already in his study when I woke up. He obviously didn't bridge Christmas and New Year where work was concerned. I splashed in his massive bed—*our* massive bed—grinning to myself. Somehow, yesterday had resulted in shattering a mental wall of his. I now budged closer to becoming his wife not only in name but in purpose.

My stomach growled, royally announcing it was back in business, demanding to be filled with decadent holiday pastries. But the rest of me had more pressing issues to tend to. Like moving all my things to the master bedroom before Romeo changed his mind.

I hurried down the corridor before remembering that I needed to pee. Slipping into a bathroom, I crouched on the toilet and giggled to myself. From the corner of my eye,

I glimpsed something in the trash can by the sink. After wiping and flushing, I fished it out. *A Barnes & Noble bag?*

Heart stammering, I tugged out the item inside, though I already knew what it would be. The new Henry Plotkin book. The thing I wanted more than anything else.

Shallow breaths sweltered in my throat. I closed my eyes, pressing the backs of my hands to my hot and tender cheeks.

He went there. Romeo. Waited outside the store all night to get me the book I wanted, knowing I couldn't go myself.

Then he returned in the morning, only to hear me trash him to Frankie . . .

No wonder he was so angry. So miserable. After opening up to me. After sharing his body and future. After everything.

And still.

He cared about me. He worried for me. He nursed me back to health, tended to me, and bathed me when he thought I felt the worst about him.

I wasn't falling in love with my husband. I was crashing straight into the arms of unhealthy, frenzied obsession.

If he left me now, I would never get over him.

He would forever be my perfect, dark Romeo.

Chapter Sixty-One

Dallas

Neither Romeo's aloof demeanor nor his thirst for revenge rattled me. It was his ability to distance himself from every living being that proved to be fatal. Especially when that comprehensive list included me.

Every night, we shared a bed, but as soon as the sun crossed the horizon, we went our separate ways. Clearly, his survival tactics included convincing himself that his affection for me could be managed.

Though I longed to seek his attention, I refrained. Somehow and somewhere along the way, I'd put his needs before my own. Which was how I learned how deeply I'd fallen. Grandmomma was right. Love is an illness, and the first symptom is prioritizing their happiness over yours.

At least we had unprotected sex. At least I'd soon shelter a piece of him—something uniquely Romeo Costa—inside of me.

In my spare time, I accepted invitations to galas, charity events, and even a New Year's party. Meanwhile, paparazzi captured my husband swirling an attractive lady on the dancefloor at some billionaire's private party.

"Your husband is hot." Hettie enlarged the clip on the gossip site. "So is Zach's mom."

I watched through a green fog of envy as Romeo's eyes crinkled with laughter. When he dipped her, Mrs. Sun beamed with all the adoration and love of a mother. Genuine affection I'd never seen Monica offer him.

In the middle of January, I decided to visit Chapel Falls.

"It is time." I shoved frocks and heels into the open mouth of my suitcase. "I was supposed to go there for Christmas, anyway. This is long overdue."

Not a lie, per se, but not the whole truth, either. I needed to escape. Recently, I'd noticed the fact that I watched the clock every evening, anticipating my husband's arrival.

Romeo's long limbs enveloped the recliner in the corner of our room. "That is fine. An entire week, however, is a stretch." He snapped his gum, discarding the *Financial Times* on his lap. The only man under sixty who still had a subscription to a magazine that didn't include topless women. "What on earth will you be doing there for so long? There are no theaters, no Michelin-star restaurants, no culture."

"There's plenty of culture." I flapped my suitcase shut, struggling to clasp it. To no one's surprise, I wasn't the type to travel light. "Besides, it's my home. I don't go there for the entertainment. I go there for the people."

Romeo stood, zipping it with ease. "You feel more fondness for a Cheetos bag than you do for your father."

"To be fair, a Cheetos bag will never do me wrong." I tucked a few hair bands into the front pocket. "It would never hand me over to a complete stranger for marriage. The worst it can do is stain my fingertips orange."

"I swear, next time I see him, I'm going to punch the daylights out of him for handing you over to me so quick."

I shook my head, dragging the luggage off the bed and onto the rug. "Do you not see the flaw in your own statement?"

"Three days," he bargained, blocking my way out the door. "It's plenty of time to unwrap presents and pretend your sister is a tolerable human. If you still want to return, you can do so after Easter."

"Why are you so adamant I return quickly? It's not like we do anything together."

His forehead creased. "We do plenty. Three times a day, minimum. Five, if you include oral."

"I'm not just talking about sex." *For a change.* Sex was all I seemed to think about whenever he neared. "I'm talking about date nights, watching the same shows, eating dinner together . . . you know, couple stuff."

By the way his eyebrows shot up, I almost suspected he wasn't aware of the concept.

"You've had a fiancée before," I pointed out, slanting my head.

"Yes, but she mainly spent my money and left me to my own devices. I worked most of the time and took her on vacation once a year."

Oh, my. His idea of love was giving shelter, food, and a credit card to the woman by his side.

"And were you both happy like that?"

He shot me a *what do you think* glare. *Oops.* I already knew the ending to that movie.

Placing a hand over his chest, I hopped on my tippy toes to kiss the base of his throat. "Would you like to do more things together when I return?"

He squinted. "Like what?"

For the first time, I wasn't the inexperienced and awkward one in the relationship.

Happiness bubbled in my chest. "You can take me out on a date. Dinner, then a movie. *Then* I can read with my head propped on your shoulder while you go through your money paper."

"Finance news." He brought my hand from his chest to his lips, kissing it distractedly. "Fine, if you wish. But I still think you should return after three days."

I skimmed his jawline, my smile tickling his stubble. "Why? Will you miss me?"

He pursed his lips. "Longing is a Jane Austen invention premeditated to sell books."

Tipping my head back, I laughed so hard, my stomach hurt. "You'll survive seven days without me, hubs. You'll see."

Chapter Sixty-Two

Romeo

I did not, in fact, survive even *two* days without her.

The first day, I sulked, firing incoherent orders at Cara, Dylan, and everyone else in my vicinity. The second day, I picked mundane arguments with Senior, Zach, Oliver, and a Starbucks barista who offered me a straw ("Do you like shitting all over your planet? Do you have another one stashed somewhere I should know about, for when the time comes and this entire place is underwater?").

By the third one, I was climbing the walls. *Literally*.

Zach barely lifted his head from his laptop, in the middle of a virtual shareholders meeting. "Move away from my wall, Costa. It's a high-ceiling house. It'll be a bitch to repaint."

"Your wall is two different shades. I just noticed." Beige and swan white.

"And you're fifty shades of pussy-whipped." On the other end of the study, Oliver engaged in his favorite hobby, sifting through his laptop for high-quality porn. "You look like someone killed your pet hamster."

I paced the room. "I'm bored."

"I would offer to entertain you the way your wife does, but my New Year's resolution includes only fucking people I find attractive."

423

The rug flattened beneath my bare feet. Back and forth. Again and again.

Zach groaned. "You're giving me a headache, Costa."

"Maybe it's your two-shade wall." I stopped, frowning out the window. My parents lived across the street from Zach. Sometimes, when I was here, I looked outside hoping to catch an ambulance rolling up the hill to my parents' place, plucking my lifeless father from his bed. For a dying man, he seemed to be hanging in there. When was he going to appoint me as CEO?

"What's the weather in Georgia this time of year?" I wondered aloud.

Zach snapped his laptop shut. "I don't know, but if you don't leave to find out, I'll personally drag you there by the ear. Just admit defeat. You fell in love. With a minor."

"Can we please normalize sexual relationships with women who are of age by law?" Oliver grumbled.

"No," Zach and I answered in unison.

"She's with her family." The words shot out. Like I'd given it some thought. *Had* I given it some thought?

"You're a part of her family now." Oliver settled on a video of a housewife being pounded by both her husband and his brother. They were sharing the same hole. Even from my angle, all the way across the room, I could tell the idea might be hot, but the execution would likely send at least two out of three participants to the ER.

"What if she doesn't want to see me?" Since when did I *care*?

"Then, at least you know where you stand." Zach rose to his feet, advancing to the door. He flung it open, waiting by its side. "And whatever that place might be, it is far away from my fucking house. Goodbye, Costa."

★

Returning to Chapel Falls sat somewhere on my to-do list above moving in with Oliver von Bismarck and below undergoing a pubic-hair transplant. Yet, here I was, on the doorstep of Dallas's childhood home. It seemed fitting that I now did what I should have done before—held a bouquet hoping to receive the affection of the woman I'd chosen for myself.

At the sight of me, Shep shuffled two steps back, shoulders solidifying. "Dallas said you knew she was here." He reared his head as if preparing for a slap. To be fair, the thought *had* occurred to me once or twice, but as his daughter pointed out, I shared the blame for what had happened.

"Clearly. Thus, here I am."

He gathered the pathetic remains of his spine and inclined his head, deciding to put up a fight. "She's having fun. Don't ruin it for her."

I shouldered past him, just as I had all those months ago. "I have no desire to ruin her fun."

He followed me, still on edge. "Then, what brings you here?"

"I miss her."

I couldn't fault Shep for his shock. After all, even I couldn't believe that I'd shown up. Turns out, there is no reason when it comes to love. It exists to destroy. Even logic.

I followed the church-bells laughter. The one I used to loathe and now, evidently, could not survive forty-eight hours without hearing. It came from the kitchen. Naturally. Shortbread's favorite room in any house she entered, excluding libraries. Dread accompanied the anticipation swirling in my stomach. She was having fun without me, while I was incapable of doing the same without her.

I strode the length of the hall, then leaned against the kitchen doorframe, observing as Dallas, Franklin, and Natasha made an apple pie. Shortbread rolled out the stripes. Flour dusted her freckled nose and cheeks. Her eyes glittered with happiness as she swirled in her spot, noticing my presence for the first time.

Her lips parted. "Romeo? What are you doing here? Is everything okay back home? Is it Senior?"

Home. Is that really what my mansion is for you?

"Everything is fine. My father is still depressingly alive." I trained my eyes on her, refusing to see Franklin and be reminded of the harsh words Dallas used to describe me. I had no idea if Shortbread made good apple pies, but she made darn perfect humble pies.

"What's going on?" She rested the dough on the counter, approaching me. I placed the white roses in her hands. Her fist wrapped around them, a million questions dancing in her eyes.

"Nothing." I slipped a hand around her narrow waist, drawing her to me, not giving a single lonely damn that her entire family watched. "I just thought I'd take you up on that offer for the date."

"The date was supposed to take place when I returned from Georgia."

"That timeline doesn't work for me."

She scrunched her nose. "Why not?"

"Because I cannot stay away from you for longer than forty-eight hours."

At last, she seemed pleased by my words. By my presence. She set a hand on my cheek, grinning up at me.

I shot a quick glance at Franklin. She looked as though I'd just declared my intention to eat my own arm on live television. Again, I found myself uncaring of what a literal teenager thought of my affairs. All I knew was, it felt ridiculously good to hold my wife again.

Dallas peered up at me. I couldn't help myself. I kissed away the sprinkling of flour on her nose. "We can have it now if that works for you? The date."

"Now's perfect timing," I confirmed. "My schedule is wide open."

"Let me just change."

I kissed her forehead. "I'll wait."

Forever and beyond, if need be.

She squinted at me. "Last time, you timed me."

"Last time, I was an asshole."

She giggled, stars in her eyes. Stars I'd put there. "And what are you now?"

Now, I'm in love.

Chapter Sixty-Three

Romeo

I understood now why men would go to drastic lengths to claim a woman. Why the Achaeans invaded Troy for Helen. Or, in my case, why I paraded through a provincial, coma-inducing small town for Dallas of Chapel Falls. Shortbread beamed, bouncing with each step as she commandeered our date. Our first destination: the public library.

"This is where I had my first date with Mr. Darcy." She swooned over a chipped wooden bench by the cafeteria. "And this is where I had my first kiss—with Lars Sheffield, my high school's quarterback."

"Pity you mentioned him by name." I laced my fingers through hers. "Now I have to kill him."

She giggled. "Want to play a game?"

Naturally, my first instinct was to say no. "Sure."

"I used to play it with Frankie all the time when we were kids. We write general topics—mammals, seasons, flowers, *whatever*—on slips of papers, fold each, toss them into a hat, and shake, drawing one subject at random. The first one to find five books in the theme wins."

"Wins what?"

She wiggled her brows. *Ah.* There was certainly a leap of logic in the reward system, since the loser and winner would both benefit from paying the price, but I saw little point in bringing it to her attention.

Shortbread jotted down a few subjects, landed a ball cap from a random stranger, and selected a subject. *Fruit.* She squealed. "This one's good. I've never had it before."

We ventured in search of fruit-themed covers and titles. I had to admit the game wasn't completely stupid. I picked *Apples Don't Fall, The Grapes of Wrath,* and *Fried Green Tomatoes at the Whistle Stop Café.* Tomatoes were a fruit like any other. And yes, that was my hill to die on. Speaking of fruit, I became increasingly hungry. I hadn't eaten prior to the plane ride here, too preoccupied to notice my hunger.

"Got it," Shortbread announced in the middle of the library with no regard for her volume, the stack of books cradled in her arms concealing her face. An old librarian shushed her. Dallas didn't even notice as she hurried to me, showing off her finds.

"*The Curious Charms of Arthur Pepper?*" I glared at her. "That's a vegetable."

"But it's as sweet as a fruit."

"That is a very loose interpretation of fruit. By that logic, vodka is a type of bread, since both contain grains." My stomach rumbled. We needed to stop talking about food.

"Well, maybe it *is* a type of bread." Dallas wrapped her arms around my shoulders, joy plastered all over her pretty face. "Anyway, I win."

"Great. Let's go grab a bite and check into a hotel where we can pretend I'm a stranger you picked up at a bar." I needed to make up for the fact that she would never be with another man, because there was no way I was letting her go.

"Oh, do we have to?" Dallas's face fell. "I wanted you to see my favorite lake. I wrote a poem about it, and it was published in the local newspaper."

I hadn't eaten in ten hours.

Not a big deal, I reminded myself. *You're a grown man. You can go without.*

"Let's do that, then." I pressed a hot kiss to her jaw. "And then, I'd like you to read the poem for me."

She lit up. "Really?"

"*Naked.*"

She swatted my shoulder. "Pig."

Great. Now all I could think about was bacon.

Off we went to her favorite lake, where we rested against her favorite oak tree, and Shortbread did her most favorite thing in the world—talked about food she wanted to try and where she would try it. Japan, Thailand, India, and Italy topped her list. An hour passed, then another. My stomach began to physically hurt.

"We need to get going, sweetheart." I stood, offering Dallas my hand. If I didn't eat soon, I might commit capital murder.

She rose to her feet, her face clouded. "Do you regret coming here for our date?"

"No." I frowned. "Why would you think that?"

"Because you've wanted to go ever since we started it."

I felt like a childish idiot. "I'm just a little hungry, that's all."

She laced her arm through mine. "Okay, let's go eat, then."

Unfortunately, Chapel Falls's residents were as incompetent as they were judgmental. The first three restaurants we tried downtown did not have any availability. The fourth had temporarily shut down due to remodeling. By the time we nestled into a sticky booth at a small, unremarkable diner, I shook with hunger.

I ordered a burger and Diet Coke. Shortbread requested pancakes. She tried to engage me in conversation, while I pretended to pay genuine attention. Twenty minutes after we ordered, the waitress swept by our booth, tacky pink uniform and inflated blonde hair intact, and announced that they'd run out of burgers.

"How does a burger joint run out of burgers?" I seethed, lips pressed tight to avoid roaring.

She shrugged. "Ask the owner. I'm just here taking orders."

"Then, take this one—get your ass to the kitchen and bring me the manager. Now."

Shortbread gasped, spinning to me. "Romeo, is everything all right?"

"No, nothing is all right." I slipped out of the booth, striding to the kitchen myself. Surely, they'd have something to eat. At this point, I was open to gnawing on someone's leg if it meant feeling satisfied.

Throwing the saloon doors open, I waltzed into the sizzling kitchen, bypassing the cooks and the dishwashers, marching straight to a man in a cheap suit. Dallas and the waitress pursued at my heels.

"Hey!" He swung in my direction, holding a clipboard. "You can't come in here."

I cornered him to the wall. Clanging pans and rushed shouts filled my ears. I hated noise. The only noise I could ever tolerate was of Dallas's making.

"You ran out of burgers." I fisted his shirt and lifted him in the air, slamming him against the industrial freezer.

431

"Romeo!" Within seconds, Dallas heaved herself over my arm. "Let the man go. Jesus Christ, what's happening to you?"

"W–w–we still have steaks." The McManager's eyes nearly bulged out of their sockets. "S–sorry about the burgers. We had an office party earlier. A lot of people ordered it—"

"I don't want a steak. I want a fucking burger."

"I'll see that someone goes to the grocery store to buy more—" A red rash unfurled across his cheeks, sweat hailing down his temples in buckets. "In the meantime, we'll send complimentary onion rings and fries to your table."

Shortbread finally managed to push me away. "Romeo, let him go."

Reluctantly, I disconnected from him. She wedged herself between us, her face singed pink. Her expression pulled me back to earth. What the hell just happened? Edging a few steps away, I raised my hands in the air, signaling that I'd finished manhandling the staff.

Dallas flashed an apologetic smile. "Thanks for the offer . . . and the onion rings, but we'll go someplace else."

She shoved me out of the kitchen then the restaurant. Dazed, I let her drag me into the passenger seat of Natasha's car. Cold sweat itched at my neck. Dallas slid into a drive-thru and purchased two massive burgers with all the frills, fries, and sodas.

She thrust the food into my hands before she even slipped her card back into her wallet. "Eat."

"I'll wait for you."

"Eat right now, or I'll shovel it down your throat, Rom. I swear to God."

Well, she *did* insist.

I devoured everything within minutes. All gone by the time we rounded two blocks to a park tucked behind a residential neighborhood.

Shortbread killed the engine and turned to me. "You had a panic attack."

Shame trickled into my system. In fact, it had never really left. I stared right ahead, at the slides and swings. I never allowed myself to go over four hours without food. Not for decades. That was the whole reason I ate low-calorie, nutritious meals. I needed to constantly consume food to keep the anxiety at bay.

"I was just hungry."

"Bull-crap. You're the most meticulous creature I've ever met. You've never lost your temper before. You were triggered by something. What was it?"

Haven't you had enough of my secrets? Of my flaws? My glaring imperfections? Must you know every single dreadful thing about me?

The questions must've been written on my face, because she nodded. "I'm your wife. Your safe haven. I need to know everything. As I said before—I will never betray you."

Fine. If she wanted a private view into my soul, she'd get it. Though nobody should be unfortunate enough to witness that mess. At the same time, I was helpless to deny her anything. My secrets. My thoughts. My heart. All there, on a silver platter for her to gobble. The woman had me in such a chokehold, I'd follow her to the pits of hell if she wished to enjoy its warm weather.

Gathering the burger and fry wrappers, I crinkled them in my fist, avoiding eye contact. "As I once mentioned, Morgan wasn't my father's first rodeo in Cheatville. Even before her, Senior had the irritating habit of dicking down anything with a hole and the faintest interest in him."

Her eyes clung to the side of my face, heating my skin.

"He cheated on Monica on and off. Theirs was an arranged marriage by the book. She was born into wealth; he wanted his hands on it. Their families were both Italian. Both Catholic. Both ambitious. It made sense. Unfortunately, Senior took it for what it was—an arrangement with benefits—while Monica fell madly in love with him, demanding his loyalty."

Love was a terrible thing. It brought the ugly out of people. Though I'd begun to see it brought the beauty out, too.

Shortbread rested her hand on my thigh, squeezing it.

"My parents would go through vicious cycles. Romeo cheated. Monica kicked him out. Then, eventually, he crawled back to her for a second chance. Always wanting to impregnate her again. Rinse and repeat. Except the baby never came. Monica was completely barren, save for lucky old me."

A bitter smile found my lips. I'd lost count of the times I'd wished I wasn't born at all.

"When I was six, Monica discovered Romeo cheating. Not just cheating. An actual affair. The woman moved into his downtown penthouse. Brought her shit in. Kid included."

The same penthouse I'd occupied on and off while Shortbread turned my world upside down. The same penthouse I'd shared with Morgan. Come to think of it, I couldn't find a more suitable destiny for said penthouse than to be burned to the ground.

"As a little boy, I grew accustomed to caring for myself while my parents entered crisis mode. I prepared my own showers, clothes, lunch, homework. Monica paid little to no attention to me, dedicating her time to failed seduction plots and impregnation attempts. Never mind that she couldn't care for her existing child. So, at first, when she kicked Senior out, I managed."

Releasing a breath, I cupped Shortbread's hand, still on my thigh.

"Then I started first grade. Soon enough, it became apparent that I had no grown-ups in my life. I arrived to school late—if at all—since Monica's driver often ran errands for her, leaving no time to take me. I was unkempt. Smelled. Fell behind on homework. By the end of the first semester, CPS knocked on our door."

Shortbread's fingers tightened over my leg. I studied the sunroof, refusing to see the pity in her face.

"The natural solution would be to hire nannies, but my parents had been burned before. Past nannies constantly broke their NDAs, blabbing to the press. Zach's mother offered to take me for a few weeks, months—however long it took."

By then, Zach and I had become inseparable brothers.

"Ultimately, Senior couldn't bear the shame it would bring to his doorstep if people knew he handed his only child over to strangers. He was bitter and angry at Monica for failing her only job—to be a mother. So, he found a solution. He sent me to his younger sister in Milan."

Sabrina Costa was the definition of hot mess. The love child of privilege and stupidity. The woman spent her time jumping from one toxic relationship to another without taking a breath. She filled her days with parties, shopping, and scoring cocaine without her family's knowledge. Her drug habit had taken her across the ocean, to somewhere her parents couldn't monitor her every move.

Dallas brought my hands to her lap, wiping them of burger grease. "They uprooted you in the middle of a school year?"

I nodded. "Since I didn't speak Italian, my parents decided I should be homeschooled by Sabrina, who I doubt possesses more knowledge than a Little Einstein music box." Perhaps I was being harsh. Surely, the music box knew more colors and animal sounds than my aunt.

"The minute I arrived in Milan, I realized where things were headed. Sabrina didn't spare me a single minute. She constantly went out, partying and staying with her rotating boyfriends. I was alone in her apartment. Just me and the textbooks Senior dropped me off with. Once a week, she would return with a bag or two of groceries, but those hardly covered two days of meals."

Shortbread's jaw tensed as if bracing for a physical hit.

"I managed, okay?" A hollow chuckle escaped me. "I always found tins of food lying around. Sometimes, I'd only eat a few spoons of tomato paste a day. Dry pasta—I didn't know how to make it. Tuna cans were a real treat. Whenever she brought some over, I had a blast. Eventually, even those deliveries stopped. One of her boyfriends took over."

Dallas stiffened beside me, the wet nap clenched in her fist. Darkness blanketed the park. Somehow, we'd missed the sunset.

"The first day I met him, he took me out. I was so happy. It marked my first time leaving the apartment since I arrived almost a month before. I thought Sabrina finally found someone who wasn't a total piece of shit. Gabe told me he'd take me to eat, and he did, only it wasn't at a restaurant. We arrived at a fighting arena in the outskirts of Modena."

Shortbread's eyes saucered at the word *arena*. And still, she said nothing.

"He led me to a cage, locked me inside, and told me if I wanted to eat, I needed to win. I didn't. Not for the first four rounds. In fact, I didn't even fight the first two matches, I was so stunned. They opened the cage and nudged me to the center of the arena with a cattle prod, where an orphan a few years older beat the shit out of me."

The wet napkin slipped out of her hand, sailing toward the pedals.

"I later learned to fight harder against the heavier orphans. They were hardened, more vicious, filled out from countless victories, each of which was rewarded with a meal. A small meal, but food was food. I hadn't eaten in days. After the fifth fight, I snapped. I kicked, punched, clawed. Anything to win. And I did. They had to pull me off the kid. He was probably a year older, seven, but I'd beaten him so bad, they had to carry him away.

"They gave me my meal. What Gabe never told me was how good it'd be. I hadn't had a cooked meal in a month. So, when they offered me half a plate of risotto, I would've fallen to the ground if I weren't already on the dirt in my cage. Gabe took me home and told me he broke even on his bets that day. That with a little practice, he saw great things in my future. He even stopped at a market to get me junk food. That got me through a few days, and I was happy to please him if it meant I could eat that risotto again.

"We went to the arena every weekend. When I won, the hosts offered me a home-cooked meal. Gabe would drive me home, dish out fighting tips the whole way, and buy me groceries. But I never wanted to leave the arena.

I wanted to fight. I wanted to *eat*. Eggplant parmigiana. Linguini alle vongole. Ricotta gnudi. They gave me barely enough to survive the days between my fights. I was so jealous of the orphans, who got to stay and fight every day. The others—kids like me and poor kids with families—only came weekends."

I swallowed hard, finally daring to meet her eyes. They were dry, accompanied by a tight jaw. She refused to see me as the charity case I was, and for that, I was grateful.

"Eventually, I learned to carry a container with me. A little tin I'd dump my reward into to stave me over while I waited for the next fight." I flipped it in my hand. The gum inside rattled against the metal.

"It was only six months. Four of which I spent with Gabe. He was Sabrina's longest relationship. Still is, probably. He kept her supplied, so she kept *him*. But eventually, it ended, and I never saw Gabe again. The day he left, he told me good luck. That he wouldn't visit. I got so angry, I tossed this"—I lifted the case, pointing to the tiny dent in it—"at his head. Then I bawled like a fucking baby. With him gone, I was back to relying on Sabrina for food."

I didn't tell her that some days I had nothing to eat. That my weight deteriorated until I looked like a four-year-old. That my bones stuck out of my skin so badly, it hurt to lie in bed and sleep. I didn't tell her two of my teeth fell off. That my hair became brittle and thin, hanging like a gloomy cloud atop of my head.

"My aunt had little food in her apartment, but she had plenty of gum. Her jaw used to lock from all the cocaine she snorted, so she stocked a good amount. It helped dull the hunger. I would chew it throughout the day."

I'd only made the unfortunate mistake of swallowing gum to fill my stomach once. It resulted in a pain so bad, I crawled my way from spot to spot for two whole days. It reminded me I couldn't go to the hospital should I need to. That I had to take care of my body and never put myself in a situation like that again.

"That's why you're obsessed with gum." Shortbread fingered the case still in my grip, almost reverently. "It's your safety blanket. It helped you through your worst nightmare."

"It helps me stay calm," I admitted.

"And the noise? Why do you hate noise so much?"

"It reminds me of the arena. Of the audience. They had their favorites—me, mostly. I fought the hardest. Won them the most money. Eventually, they cheered every time my cage shot open. Each time I landed a punch, broke another kid's ribs, whatever—they roared out their satisfaction. It felt like the noise would drill into my skull."

"The scars." She nodded to herself, as if putting together all my screwed-up pieces. "So, what happened? Who took you back?"

"Senior." I opened the door to toss the wrappers in the trash then returned. It took no more than thirty seconds, but it provided me with the fresh air I needed. "He came at the end of the school year to check on me. Didn't like what he saw, to say the least. Flew me back to Potomac, hired two nannies, and warned Monica that if she didn't pull herself together, he'd divorce her and gain full custody of me."

Wow—she shaped her mouth around the word, rather than said it. "Seems like he had a glimpse of realization he should do better by his son."

"More like he realized Monica wouldn't provide him with any more heirs and wanted to keep the one he had alive." I snarled. "So, this is why I keep myself well-fed every four hours. Why I chew gum. Why I hate noise. Why I'm quick to fight like it's an instinct—because it *is* an instinct. I strive for control. Anything short of complete power is unsatisfactory to me."

An emotion I couldn't pinpoint erupted across her features. Something between anger and pride. She leaned over the central console, taking my face between her palms. "You prevailed. Look at you. Gorgeous. Successful. Accomplished."

"*Fucked up,*" I completed, my lips chasing hers, demanding to be kissed.

She kissed me slow and steady but kept the passion out of it. When she pulled back, she patted my stomach. "I hereby promise to make sure your tummy is always full. It will be no hardship, trust me. I'm a huge fan of food myself."

She was trying to make light of it. While I appreciated it, there was no need.

"I'm better now." I brushed my thumb over her maddening freckles. "Well, mostly."

"I will be a good momma to our children. I promise. I'll put them first, always. And to heck with their daddy."

I believed her. It was one of the things I enjoyed most about Dallas. She had the instincts of a mother. Her child would never go unclothed, hungry, or dirty.

Dallas clutched my shoulders, pressing her forehead to mine, breathing me in. "I know you've been hurt beyond words. The people who were supposed to be your protectors—Monica, Senior, Morgan—all failed you. But if one day your heart opens up . . . I hope I'll be the one with the key to it."

I am already indecently in love with you. Only, you can never know.

Her power over me would be so complete, so destructive, if she ever knew the strength of my feelings for her.

Dallas Costa frightened me. She wasn't Morgan. She didn't need a key to my heart.

She'd already kicked down the fucking door.

Chapter Sixty-Four

Dallas

The idea of parting with Romeo once we returned to Potomac horrified me. But he had a job. Responsibilities. A life beyond me. And me? I felt like gravity had abandoned me. As if I floated above Earth, struggling to ground myself in my new reality. A reality of childhood arena fights, complicated relationships with food, and justified revenge.

I wanted to hug him. To heal him. But most of all, I wanted to curse myself for judging him. There were no beasts. Only people whose pain was carved on the outside.

Each night, Romeo crawled into our bed and supported *my* dream. We had sex. Lots of it. Bareback. In the kitchen. The theater room. The sauna. Even at the gym when he'd dragged me there for a spin class with Casey Reynolds—the point of which still evaded me. Why would someone hop on a bike to ride nowhere?

A week after returning from Chapel Falls, I lounged on the living room couch, sifting through wedding pictures with Hettie. This time, I intended to print one with my husband in it. "What about this one?"

"Dude, for the fiftieth time, you both look unreasonably hot in every picture. I think I actually hate you for it."

"Fine, fine. We can stop. For now."

"Oh, thank God." She palmed the television remote and exited the photo casting app. "Let's put on *Friday Night Tykes* again. Nothing beats watching grown men get irrationally angry over ten-year-olds chasing a ball."

Something flashed across the screen before she flipped the channel.

"Wait." I latched onto Hettie's arm. "Go back."

She pressed a button, revealing a breaking news report. A headline rolled across the screen: **Licht Holdings stock crashes again.**

The reporter spoke into her microphone. "Our cameras are on the ground in front of Licht Holdings as CEO Theodore Licht and his son Madison are being hauled away in handcuffs by DOJ Special Agents from the Fraud section. Our sources in the Department of Justice indicate that the Licht duo have been arrested on corporate fraud charges. With Licht Holdings's chances of ever working with a governmental body gone, who will take their place? More details coming to you tonight."

Hettie muted the television, turning to me. "*Oh. My. God.*"

I sucked in a breath. I knew what this meant. And contrary to what she might have thought, it wasn't good. Over the course of my stay in Potomac, I'd realized the sheer level of pettiness Madison exuded. He needed to have the last word. No way would this be the end.

A cornered Madison was a dangerous one. In fact, on our flight from Chapel Falls, Romeo mentioned his Christmas encounter with him.

My hands darted to my phone. With unstable fingers, I speed-dialed Romeo.

He answered on the first ring. "Shortbread?"

Hettie cleared the room, giving me space.

"I saw the news."

"You don't sound happy."

"I'm not. I'm worried." I began pacing, gnawing on the tips of my hair. "It's a corporate fraud charge. He'll be out on bail in no time. We have to deal with him roaming the streets until the trial concludes. That could take years, Romeo."

"I hired a full security detail. Starting tomorrow, when you leave the house, a trained martial artist will follow you. Promise me you'll let him."

"I'm not worried about me. I'm worried about *you*."

"Don't be. Costa Industries is the safest building in Arlington County."

"The Pentagon is in Arlington County," I pointed out.

"I said what I said." I could hear the smile in his voice, but I couldn't find it in me to match his amusement.

I stopped pacing. My lips parted. Three words weighed down the tip of my tongue. I wanted to release them. To launch them into the universe. To hear him say them back. I didn't. It felt foolish to confess it now—over the phone, on the heels of Madison's arrest.

I swallowed the words.

Unaware of how much I'd come to regret it.

Chapter Sixty-Five

Romeo

For the first time in more than a decade, I existed beside my father without wanting to punch him in the face. After all, I needed his mouth functioning for the announcement he planned on making in—I checked my Rolex—the next eighteen minutes.

We sat before the entire board and major stockholders during Costa Industries' annual shareholders meeting. It couldn't have come at a better time. We'd collectively spent the first thirty minutes gloating over Licht Holdings's downfall, this morning's leaked mugshot of Madison and his father blown up on the projector screen behind me.

Things had fallen into place. And soon, after the short recess, Senior would officially announce his retirement and nominate me to take his position. In the corner, Bruce sulked, clenching a complimentary breadstick in his fist.

It was a pity I derived no triumph, no pleasure, from knowing I would soon be announced as the CEO of Costa Industries. I didn't actually want the position. Only for as long as it took to destroy the company. As for Bruce, he'd never sparked genuine conflict in me. I knew as soon as I pushed him out of my path, he'd be unmemorable and insignificant, despite his lingering sour presence. Kind of like a fart. But one on a fat payroll.

I checked my group chat when a message buzzed in from von Bismarck.

Ollie vB: How much do you guys wanna bet the local prison population also finds Madison Licht's face punchable?

Romeo Costa: I would honestly rather they find it fuckable.

Zach Sun: Never mind that. What's happening with the CEO position, Rom?

Romeo Costa: It's mine. Any minute now. Licht Holdings is out of the game. Bruce is eating his emotions. While I was pulling extra hours, he was pulling the new receptionist. Barely twenty-two years of age. Senior didn't like it. Neither did her husband, who is threatening to pen a tell-all.

Zach Sun: I'm proud of you.

Zach Sun: (Pretend I care enough to mean what I just said.)

Ollie vB: Don't mind him. I'M proud of you. Your dedication to ruining others can only be paralleled with that of Stefano DiMera.

Zach Sun: I am unfamiliar with this name. Politician? Historical figure?

Ollie vB: Days of Our Lives character. Super villain. Makes Billy the Kid look like a kitten.

Romeo Costa: One question, @OllievB—why?

Ollie vB: You forget my life consists of breathing and getting paid for it. Daytime TV was all I had going for me before streaming networks got into the game.

I frowned at the text box on my phone, losing both the thread of conversation and my patience.

Ollie vB: Don't slam it before you try it. That time when Marlena was possessed by the devil was wild. The exorcism scene is some of the best TV I've ever seen.

Zach Sun: That's because amateur porn comprises most of your screen time.

Ollie vB: Amateur porn just hits you different. You can suspend your disbelief that these people are actually stepsiblings, you know? You can never do that with established porn.

Zach Sun: Suspend your disbelief? You just recited a plotline from a soap opera in which a woman levitates around the room with no eyeballs.

Zach Sun: You know Santa doesn't exist, right?

Ollie vB: Of course, he does. I saw him at the mall just this Christmas.

Zach Sun: You desperately need a hobby.

Ollie vB: I know. But Rom won't give me his SIL's number. :(

Romeo Costa: She is too young fo

I was about to inform Oliver of how close he was to being canceled by his childhood friends when I noticed something astray. Whispers ping-ponged across the room, volleying from one shareholder to the next.

Cara dashed to me from the refreshments table, pocketing her phone along the way. She leaned into my ear, voice low. "Madison and his father are out on bail."

Shit.

"Already? It usually takes forty-eight hours for a bail hearing."

"Their lawyers expedited the hearing, and well, the Lichts still have many friends in D.C."

Madison's threat echoed in my skull. The cretin had the spine of a gumdrop, but when it came to Dallas, I refused to chance it. I palmed my phone, shooting a text to Alan, who I'd rehired this morning. He wasn't set to resume his protection duties until tomorrow.

Romeo Costa: Can you start early?

Alan Reece: Early when?

Romeo Costa: Early now.

Alan Reece: I'm on a flight to Potomac from New York. I'll land at BWI in an hour.

Thank fuck.

Cara left while I issued an alert to my estate security team, demanding them to raise the threat level to yellow and follow proper protocol. Beside me, Senior rose, taking his place before the microphone on the podium.

"Welcome back, gentlemen."

In the audience, Marla Whitmore's lips pinched together. As our only female board member, my father relished in pretending she didn't exist. It made the fact that she refused to kiss his ass far more enjoyable.

"As we resume this meeting, I'd like to make an announcement. It's one I'm sure you all have expected for quite some time."

At the edge of the room, Cara waved her phone, capturing my attention again. Mine buzzed with a text seconds later.

Cara Evans: Emergency.

Romeo Costa: Can it wait? He'll make the announcement any minute now.

And sure enough, Senior did. "Effective immediately, I am retiring as the CEO of Costa Industries. My last act as CEO will be to announce my nominee as successor . . ."

Cara Evans: I just got word that Madison Licht is on the way to your home.

Dallas is home.

I shot out of my seat, sending it flying behind me. It slammed against the wall, leg snapping.

My father chuckled into the mic. "Easy there. I haven't even announced your name yet, Romeo. Kids these days . . ." He shook his head. "So vigorous."

Scattered laughter bounced off the walls. I strode straight toward the exit behind Senior, eliciting a frown between his sunken cheeks.

"Where are you going, Son?" His words traveled through the mic to every speaker in the room.

I didn't answer him. He gestured for security to block my way. Four suits surrounded me, fanned out in a semi-circle. I could take them. I had ample experience fighting and panicked urgency fueling my cells.

But in the interest of time, I turned to Senior. "Madison Licht is out on bail and headed toward my home. Toward my *wife*."

"Alert your security."

"I did."

Around us, whispers from the shareholders gained volume. Bruce poked his head from the pastry tray he'd taken his emotions out on, seeing the sun peek past the clouds for the first time since my father informed him of his decision.

Senior cleared his throat, unused to having his authority questioned in such a public manner. "There's nothing more you can do. The annual shareholders meeting only comes once a year. Sit down."

I pivoted to his lackeys, ignoring my father. "One million dollars to each of you if you step aside."

They glanced at each other, trying to gauge whether I'd follow through on the promise.

"The offer reduces by a hundred K with each passing second. One—"

They scattered out the door.

From the podium, Senior still hadn't gotten the hint that destroying Costa Industries meant jack shit compared to Dallas. "Sit down, Romeo Costa Jr., or so help me, you will never step foot in this room again, let alone as CEO of Costa Industries."

I bolted out the door and never looked back.

Chapter Sixty-Six

Romeo

The Maybach stalled at the curb by the time I escaped the building. Cara must've alerted Jared. I hustled into the back seat, producing my phone from my pocket.

"Where to, Boss?" Jared examined me from the rearview mirror, tipping his hat down. Dallas once pestered me about relieving him of his uniform. Claimed he must have felt like a circus monkey in it.

Dallas. Next time she made a suggestion, even if it was donating both my kidneys to science, I would fulfill it without delay. *If* there was a next time.

"Home." I managed not to shout. "As fast as you can."

Jared offered me a curt nod and fished a bottled water from the mini fridge next to him, handing it over to me, as he always did. I didn't have any goddamn time for his routine.

Tucking it under my arm, I shot a text to Zach and Oliver.

> **Romeo Costa: @ZachSun How fast can you track Madison Licht's location?**
>
> **Ollie vB: County jail? FBI holding facility? Or, if there is a god, a CIA black site?**

451

I sipped the water, trying my hardest not to lose my composure as I waited for a real response. I'd get there in time. I had to.

Romeo Costa: He's out on bail.

Ollie vB: Shit.

Zach Sun: If he has his phone on him, a minute. Hold.

Romeo Costa: @ZachSun, you done? It's been a fucking minu

A chill bolted through my skin, hiking up every hair on my body. As if I'd been electrocuted. *Must be static friction.* But I couldn't finish typing out my sentence. A roll of nausea crashed into my gut like a fist. A guttural growl escaped my lips. I raised the water bottle, intending to sip again, and noticed my hands shaking.

My hands *never* shook.

I inventoried my symptoms. Trembling hands. Sluggish breaths. Hazy vision.

My entire body twisted inside out like snakes slithered within it. Jared's eyes met mine across the rearview mirror before scurrying back to the road ahead. I knew guilt when I saw it. And I could taste betrayal from a thousand miles away.

I'd been poisoned.

Madison or Bruce? I didn't even have to think twice. Madison, of course. Bruce was conniving but too conventional to murder. The man was as edgy as a softball.

Madison must have paid my driver to kill me. Problem was, I had no idea what he'd laced into the water. No way of knowing how grim my situation was or what the antidote might be. I doubted Jared knew, either. One thing was certain—mentioning it to him now, while I was too weak to breathe properly, would be a mistake.

Returning my attention to my phone, I wrote one word.

Poisoned.

Within half a second, Zach's name flashed on my screen. I accepted the call, too ill to speak. Just as well, as Zach didn't want my conversation. He needed my location through his GPS app.

"I can't wait to get home," I croaked out, so he could hear where I was headed. Judging by the scenery, I'd make it there in four minutes.

Texts darted down my screen.

> **Ollie vB: I sent an ambulance over to your house. Heading there now.**

> **Ollie vB: Side note—I love how you insisted on putting a period after the word poison, even on your deathbed. Your passion for good grammar is commendable.**

> **Ollie vB: Oh, and keep whatever you drank or ate with you, so we can run a check and see what's in there.**

I was grateful my friends, despite exhibiting the mental age of thirteen normally, were resourceful in crunch time. Relief swept through me when I realized Madison would probably leave Shortbread alone. No point harming her without me alive to witness it.

Jared's shoulders rattled with nerves. He tossed glances at me through the mirror, clutching the steering wheel in a death grip, leaving indents of sweat on the plush leather cover. He either expected me to drop dead and was wondering why I was still seated, looking calm and collected, or was having second thoughts.

There is minus-zero chance I'll let you walk away from this. If *I get out of this alive.*

I'd never been a big fan of life. Growing up, I'd spent countless days wishing I'd never been born. So, the foreign panic that seized my chest surprised me. And with it, came an unsettling realization—I didn't want to die.

I wanted more time with Dallas "Shortbread" Costa. With my wife.

I wanted to hear her laughter. To try new food with her. To dance together in ballrooms—this time because she wanted to give me those dances, not because of societal pressure.

I wanted to seduce her and be seduced by her. I wanted a do-over of our Parisian honeymoon.

Hell, a part of me wanted to see our child. Would it be a boy or a girl? Hazel or gray-eyed? With her temper? Or my dry sense of humor? And her laugh? Was she already pregnant?

Fuck, what if she was?

I wasn't ready to say goodbye.

The car pulled in front of my mansion. The thought crossed my mind that it could very well be the last time I greeted Dallas in our home. If she was still there.

Pushing the door open, I stumbled out, zigzagging my way to the door.

Jared flew out the driver's side, hot on my tail. "Boss, you don't look well. Should I—"

I burst through my entryway, collapsing to my knees. My body was shutting down. One organ at a time. Crawling toward the stairway, I passed Hettie on her way from the kitchen, a bag of oranges cradled in her arms.

"Keep Jared out of the house," I mumbled.

She didn't ask what was wrong. She did as I said and blocked the driver with her slender body.

The journey up the spiral staircase was excruciating. Each step seemed to cost me a year of my life. Sweat rolled down every inch of skin. White dotted my eyesight. Finally, I reached Dallas's bedroom. Though she slept in ours these days, she still loved the room she first occupied when she moved here.

It was full of her books. Of her scent. Of her sweet existence. She spent most afternoons reading on the windowsill.

The relief I felt at seeing her curled in front of her window, a paperback in her lap, was immediate. At the very least, I could tell her what I wanted to say.

She looked like a painting so unique, so special, even Zach wouldn't be able to get his hands on it. In a pale turquoise dress. Her backdrop a winter realm of pearl-hued snow. Tendrils of her hair escaped her messy bun. I cursed myself for all the times I wanted to tuck them behind her ears but didn't. Life was too short not to be crazy fucking in love with the girl who wore you down.

Shortbread's gaze hurdled from the pages of the book to me. Her jaw slackened.

The sky was falling through the reflection of her eyes. Even if I never heard her return the words I was about to say, I knew that was enough.

"Rom!" She tossed the book aside. It ricocheted on the floor. It gave me great satisfaction that she mishandled her book for me. Her books were her entire world.

She rushed to me, collecting me in her arms. Crouching down, she lifted my head, cradling it. I gathered I looked about as ghastly as I felt because her fingers shook so much, she dropped me on her lap with an unceremonious *thump*.

"What's going on?" Her pupils danced hysterically in their sockets. "Why do you look so pale?"

"Poison." I didn't even have the energy to tack on the "-ed" on the end.

She sucked in a breath and pulled her phone out, calling 9-1-1. I somehow lifted a hand, knocking it back. I couldn't feel her touch. Her warmth. It felt like I was cocooned in a temperature-less cotton.

"Ambulance on the way."

"I'm going to kill him." She buried her nose in my shoulder. I couldn't smell her rose-scented hair. "Madison. He did this to you."

My eyelids fluttered shut. I harvested every ounce of my remaining strength. I would only get one chance to say this. It needed to be firm. Clear.

Our eyes locked.

"I have something to say."

Oddly enough, I was busier telling her what I came here to say than being furious at Madison. Turned out, Dallas had been right, after all. Love trumped hate. Good conquered evil. When you drew your last breath, you didn't think about the people you loathed. You thought about those you loved.

"This is very important, Shortbread. Are you listening?"

Though I couldn't feel her body, I could feel her pain. She looked like heartbreak. The way she had on the night I'd met her at the debutante ball. Oh, fuck. Even back then, I was powerless against her, wasn't I? From the moment I saw her in that ballroom, in her own little universe, surrounded by sweets and a head full of faraway fictional lands, I wanted her.

"Yes." She trembled, clutching my cheeks harder. Our faces fused together. "I'm listening, Rom."

"I'm in love with you, Dallas Costa. I love every piece of you. Every cell. Every breath. Every laugh. You've bewitched me, and I don't want to leave this world thinking you don't know how much you've changed me."

"No, Rom. No."

Dallas rested my head on the floor. The realization that I'd lost complete control over my body boomeranged into me. She unbuttoned my shirt in a desperate attempt to save me. Her eyes roamed my skin, searching for a telltale sign. A bite mark. Anything she could work with.

For the first time since I met her—and knowing her, maybe this decade—a single tear beaded in the corner of her eye. It crawled down her cheek, trudging past her chin. Just one tear, yet that tear brought me the most joy I'd ever felt in my life. Turned out, my defiant, stouthearted wife *could* cry. And it only took me dying to happen.

Suddenly, tears washed her cheeks, splashing from her chin to mine. Her brows furrowed at the sight of liquid trickling down my jaw. She catalogued my eyes before realizing it hadn't come from me. With an unsteady hand, she brought a fingertip to her cheek, collecting a tear.

Dallas studied it, almost bewildered. "I'm crying."

I love you, too, Shortbread.

Ambulance sirens filled the room with their hysterical shrieks. I shut my eyes, wondering why I couldn't even die in fucking peace in the arms of the woman I was reluctantly in love with.

"They're coming to save you. Please, wait." Dallas kissed my cheek. My forehead. The tip of my nose. My eyelids. When had I closed my eyes? I couldn't remember, but it happened, because I couldn't see her anymore.

I needed to see her.

Just one more time.

"Please, Rom, stay awake. *Please*. For me?"

"I'll do anything for you," I heard myself say, before the world turned black and the ambulances ceased to whine. "You're my favorite plot twist."

Chapter Sixty-Seven

Dallas

So, this was what it felt like to cry. As if death strangled me in his cruel hands, and I struggled in his grip despite yearning to join him. Heavy tears tumbled down my cheeks. Guilt consumed me like a bloodthirsty monster, feasting on my organs.

You did this to him. It's your fault.

As Romeo lay motionless in my arms, I couldn't help but wonder where the thing that poisoned him was and how I could get my hands on it to join him in eternal slumber.

The wish I'd made refused to stop ringing in my ears.

My one and only wish is for you to die in my arms, Romeo Costa. I want to see you when you draw your last breath. To feel your skin turn cold and lifeless beneath my fingers. My wish is to witness your nostrils struggle to move as you consume oxygen for the last time. I want to watch you suffer for all the suffering you did to me. And there is nothing and no one I want more in this life.

My fantasy turned into my reality, and my reality turned into my nightmare.

I rocked back and forth, trembling with sobs that tore at me like sharp knives.

"You can't leave me. Not now. Not when you finally love me. You can't die. You've survived too much."

I cupped his cheek, so pale and frozen beneath my fingertips. "My dark Romeo. My misunderstood beast. You're stronger than poison, than mortality, than *death*. I never got to say I love you. Wake up, and I promise to say it back."

He didn't budge. Didn't blink. Didn't *breathe*. Time is regret's weapon of choice. And this time, it struck me so hard, I knew I would never recover.

I pressed our foreheads together, begging to take his cold and exchange it for my warmth. "Please, come back to me. I love you more than I love everything in this life combined—my family, my friends, my books, myself."

I tilted my head up and caught a rose petal as it floated down, landing on the nightstand.

The last petal dropped.

Just when Romeo told me he loved me. Long after I'd fallen for him. And I'd keep falling. Plummeting down the endless depths of my love for him.

But ours wouldn't be a fairy tale with a happy ending. Instead, what I got was a cautionary tale.

My arms wrapped tighter around him, even when I felt a hand rest on my back.

"Come on, Dallas." It was Zach, with his velvety voice. The man could announce the apocalypse on national television and still sound like he was coaxing you into bed with him. "The paramedics are here."

It took his gentle force to loosen my arms from my husband, as paramedics circled Romeo, hoisting him up onto a gurney. I was limp and boneless in Zach's arms. He tried righting me up to a standing position, but I collapsed into a fetus-shaped blob on the floor.

Parking his hands on his waist, he glared at me from

above. "Yours is the sappiest marriage of convenience I've ever witnessed."

"I love him." I moaned into my chest, a pool of tears gathering on my neck. "I love him so much. I can't live without him."

Zach stepped back, as though feelings were a contagious disease. Oliver powered into the room as they ushered Romeo out. I knew I should have chased the paramedics down the hallway. Joined them on the ride to the hospital. Asked questions. *Anything* other than stay here. But I felt too empty to move.

Oliver cocked his head. "*Uh-huh*. What do we have here?"

"A distressed Juliet. She says she can't live without him." Zach's tone matched that of a pharmaceutical commercial. The voice that rattled off the nasty side effects of the advertised drug. He produced hand sanitizer from his pocket and squished a good portion onto his palm.

"And her way of showing this is taking a nap on the floor?"

"I'm not taking a nap on the floor, you asshole." I shot to my feet. Fresh anger sizzled through my bloodstream. "I'm going to fight for him. I have to show him what he means to me."

I didn't know why I'd told them this. Maybe I needed to verbalize it to myself.

Oliver swung his keys around his finger. "I'll drive her to the hospital."

Zach nodded. "And I'll hunt down Jared, bring him to the police, and catch them up to speed on Madison's bullshit."

Maybe they were doing it for my sake, but their utter calmness almost made me forget the last time I'd held

Romeo. He was as cold as the marble floor in the ballroom where we first met.

"He'll be okay, won't he?" I clutched Zach's lapels. I had a feeling Oliver's tongue could not be trusted, be it with his words or the pleasure he brought on women.

Zach looked away, ushering me out of the room by the small of my back. "Let's go."

I turned, staring at the spot I'd last held Romeo. I'd never realized it before. That marriage is a mirror, showing you exactly where your empty parts are before it fills them up. And if Romeo left me, I'd be forever empty.

Chapter Sixty-Eight

Dallas

I didn't leave his hospital bedside.

Not to eat. Not to drink. Not to shower.

Frankie, Momma, and Monica rushed to my side as soon as the news broke. They took turns bringing me food and clean clothes but could only ever persuade me to take bathroom breaks. Even then, I went about my business quickly.

Days ate at each other. Time was not my friend, slipping between my fingers like quicksand. One minute, I was ecstatic that Romeo was not dead, that his heart still beat, that he'd soldiered through, fighting for each breath. The other, I crumbled in complete despair. He wasn't getting better. He existed as a glorious statue. Still but beautiful.

The revolving door never ended. Zach. Oliver. Mrs. Sun. Cara. Monica. Senior. Momma. Frankie. Hundreds of flower arrangements and food offerings arrived every day from colleagues and friends. I donated them all. They made it feel like Romeo was no longer alive. The very thought made me want to hurl myself out the window.

On the fourth day of Romeo's medically induced coma, his lawyer waltzed in, along with Senior. Jasper Hayward. I recognized him from the day I'd signed a prenup.

463

My spine snapped straight. I wiped away the tears and cobwebs from my eyes. "What are you doing here?" I shot to my feet, looking between the men. "There is no reason for you to pay him a visit. There is no change in his condition, and the doctors haven't discussed taking him off life support, so there's absolutely no way—"

"Dallas." Senior put a hand on my shoulder. I jerked away, stepping back. "Don't worry so much. Mr. Hayward is here to go over some documents. That's all."

Documents, my butt. I trusted Jasper Hayward like I trusted the pull-out method as contraception. And I trusted Senior even less. I'd seen the leaked video from the shareholders meeting. As soon as Romeo left the room to save me, his father had followed through on his threat and announced Bruce as his replacement.

My guarded gaze traveled between their faces. "Make it fast. I'm going to be here all the while."

Senior blinked at me. "You truly love him, don't you, child?"

I leveled his glare with my own. "I would *kill* for him, sir."

After the awkward silence that followed my overdramatic yet truthful declaration, Jasper shuffled to Romeo's bed, drinking in an eyeful. My fingers twitched. I resisted the urge to block his view of my husband in such a vulnerable position. I couldn't remember him ever looking anything short of an untouchable emperor. The sight never ceased to jar me, even four days later.

Jasper flapped open his case, rifling through some documents. "Obviously, we're all hoping and praying for Romeo Jr.'s quick recovery. In the meantime, though, I would like to inform you that, should Mr. Costa take a turn for the worse, he made it clear what he wished for his wealth and estates. And though there is no prenup, there's a will."

Blinking slowly through eyes so swollen I hardly saw anything through them, I shook my head. "No. You're wrong. There is a prenup. I signed it myself. Right in front of you."

That seemed decades ago, but I knew my memory didn't fail me.

Jasper Hayward frowned. "Mrs. Costa, I thought your husband told you."

"Told me what?"

"Told you he stopped by my office a few weeks ago, tore the prenup to shreds, and dictated a will, instead. He left you everything he has. Every single thing."

I staggered back, almost fainting. It was only by a miracle that I stayed on my feet. "Are you serious right now?"

"I get paid way too much to joke about such things."

Romeo left me everything. His money. His mansion. His cars. All of it. I knew the why. He'd told me, seconds before he'd skidded out of consciousness. The question was—when did he write his will? At what point did he decide he loved me?

"When was that?" I demanded, clutching onto this new information like it had weight. Like it could bring him back to me. "When did he come to you? What day? What date?"

Jasper opened his mouth to answer, just as my favorite sound in the entire world filled the room.

"*Shortbread?*"

★

He's in a medically induced coma. There is no way you heard his voice.

Still, it sounded so real. So heartbreakingly perfect. I turned around slowly, worried I was now hallucinating on top of suffering a mental breakdown. I *did* only sleep about an hour every day. But when I looked at Romeo's bed, he was inside it, staring at me with his pale eyes that never seemed to dim, even under the harsh hospital light.

"Oh, Lord." I dropped to my knees, grabbing his hand in mine. "Please, tell me this is not a figment of my imagination and you really are awake. I'm too much of a snowflake for crushing disappointment."

A gruff chuckle rumbled his chest. He attempted to curl his fingers in mine. "It's not your overactive imagination."

Behind me, Senior strode toward the bed. "Son."

Romeo didn't even look up from my face when he said, "Senior? Jasper? Get the fuck out. Now."

They fled within seconds. I cupped his cheek, brows squished together, delicious sparks electrifying my fingertips. Should I not be at least a *little* concerned about my husband defying the laws of science?

"I thought . . . I thought they put you in a medically induced coma?" I rested my chin on the edge of his mattress, priding myself in my self-control. I had yet to jump on him with kisses. "I mean, they had. For the past four days. Your systems were in total shutdown. Barely functioning at some point."

"Some bedside manner my wife has." He gave me a slow onceover. I couldn't help but laugh, shoulders shaking. "Don't cry."

"I never cry."

But that wasn't true. Not anymore.

A lopsided smile touched his lips. "You cried for me. While I appreciate the sentiment, if you do it again, my systems will suffer another massive breakdown."

"You signed a form to pull him out of the medically induced coma yesterday." Oliver breezed in without knocking, as though he owned the place. "You must've forgotten, seeing as you've been running on coffee, angry outbursts, and the thoroughly stabbed voodoo doll of Madison Licht that Frankie stitched for you."

I glanced at the couch I'd occupied these past four days and the pincushion of a voodoo doll Frankie crocheted for me. It resembled a rag doll with a yellow receding hairline and Sharpie'd goofy smile.

Romeo laced his fingers with mine. "Oliver."

He batted his eyelashes. "Yes, dear?"

"*Leave.*"

"Not before you give me Frankie's number."

"I'll give you a punch in the face first," I warned. I couldn't think of a more ill-suited candidate for my sister.

Once Oliver left, I returned my attention back to my husband. Romeo raised his hand, tucking a lock of hair that escaped my ponytail behind my ear with a devious smile.

"Rom?"

"Yes?"

"When did you rewrite your will? Canceled your prenup?" I wanted to know when he first realized he loved me.

"The day after you threw a party in my mansion and forced me to move back in."

I frowned. "You hated me back then."

"Baby." He cupped my cheek. "I never hated you. I went from indifference, to being petrified of what you might do to my heart, to so disgustingly in love, I half wished you'd dump me just so I could tell myself *I told you so*."

"The night after the party." I squeezed his hand, humming. "Wow. Do I really suck cock that good?"

He laughed, even though I could tell he was in pain, drawing me to a kiss. "It's difficult to say. Perhaps you'd be as kind as to give me a reminder?"

Epilogue

Dallas

Six months later

"For the last time, I promise that Franklin Tabitha Townsend has never been possessed in her life. How many times do I have to say this?"

I stop myself just short of tossing my hands up, not wanting to distract Romeo from the road. With Jared (and Madison) in prison, awaiting trial, he hasn't found a replacement. Romeo insists he's *happy* he got poisoned, since attempted murder charges mean Madison will rot in maximum security, not some cushy facility with tennis courts, Swedish massages, and Wagyu Sundays.

Romeo flicks the left signal. "Dropped on the head?"

"Not that I know of."

"Did she ever peel lead paint off the walls and eat it as a baby?"

"Nop—" I stop. I don't lie to Romeo, and since that sounds like something a baby Frankie would have done . . . "How would I know? I was a toddler then."

"She's not living with us, Shortbread. She can take the penthouse in D.C., but no way will I have that gremlin marching down the halls of the place I expect to sleep safely at night."

"Fine. Deal."

I recline in the passenger seat, satisfied that he offered the solution Frankie rooted for in the first place. Romeo *did* say he wanted to destroy the place. I can't think of a better harbinger of destruction than Franklin Townsend.

"It's only for a few months." I pull a snack out of the glove compartment. "Until Daddy cools down and her college un-suspends her." Shep is back to being Daddy. For now.

"How could she flood an entire dorm building?" Romeo turns right, exiting to the freeway from the private airport. "How is that even possible?"

Since I once spilled chlorophyll on our ceiling, I'm in no place to judge. In fact, the green specks are still there. Scattered between the lighting like a Rorschach painting. As for Daddy, he blew a gasket when the school sent a twenty-three-million-dollar bill for the damages. Took it right out of Frankie's inheritance to teach her a lesson, which will most definitely go unlearned.

"Does it matter?" I kick my legs up on the dash, munching on Pocky sticks. "I share some blame in this."

"You're not the one who flooded an entire college dorm building in the middle of finals week."

"Sure, but I *am* the reason Daddy gives Frankie so much freedom."

Daddy's version of an apology to me. Sometime this year, he gifted Frankie all the freedom he never gave me to prove he changed. While I'm happy for her, I'm also dreading the consequences. Already, there was the Home Depot debacle, the Swiss ski-trip fiasco, and the near international incident in Dubai.

Romeo stops at the light, turning to face me. "Or your father can man up and apologize to you with words. Then we can all move on to the next chapter of our lives. One where Frankie is not kicked out of her home to learn responsibility the hard way."

I wave his words away. "Speaking of moving on, when are you gonna hire a driver?"

Six months since Jared's arrest, he *still* hasn't finished running thorough background checks on new applicants. To be fair, his old driver *did* try to kill him. Can't blame a poisoned man for being thorough.

"Cara emailed me the background checks this morning."

Ah. Cara. The only remnant of Costa Industries in Romeo's life. When he left (okay, was fired), she left, too. He rewarded her loyalty with a massive raise. Turns out, my husband is better at selling stocks than, well, *stocks*.

Romeo rolls through our iron gates, up the quarter-mile driveway, and past a forklift.

"Why is there a forklift on our property?" I swivel my head to stare at the obnoxious thing as we whizz past. "Is there construction going on at the house? I didn't break anything before we left. Not this time."

He frowns. "They were supposed to be gone by last night. I paid them an extra mil to get it done by the time we arrived."

"How much work are we talking here? It's only been three months since we left on our food tour."

Three months of bliss. Hopping from country to country, eating everything we could, from street food to high-brow Michelin-starred restaurants. Not only did he remember every country on my To Eat list from our Chapel Falls date, he also set up a food itinerary for each. It helps that Romeo is currently unemployed. Okay, fine. Trading stocks. (He swears it's a job. I'll take his word on it.)

"I hired a team to redo the home."

My jaw practically unhinges. "The entire thing?" *Without consulting me?*

Romeo kills the engine in front of the door, handing the keys to a waiting Vernon.

Hettie swings my door open, giggling when I launch into her arms. "I can't wait for you to see it. It's amazing."

I send an accusing glare to Romeo. "Did everyone know about the renovations but me?"

Hettie loops an arm through mine, leading me to the entrance. "You're gonna melt into a puddle of chocolate. It's everything you ever wan—" At Romeo's expression, her words die.

"Out." He pries her arm from mine and nods in the direction of the staff's quarters behind the main house. "Before you ruin the surprise."

"Fine, fine."

It's too late. I'm already racing toward the double doors, thrusting them open. I know what lies inside, because I know my husband. The man is hell-bent on making me happy.

Just as I expected, he turned our home into a library. Every inch of wall space is covered in floor-to-ceiling shelves. The living room. The halls. The theater room. Even his study. My legs carry me from room to room at the speed of light. Though I hurry about it, my eyes don't miss a thing. How he catalogued everything by genre, by spines, exactly the way I envisioned it. Horror and mystery in the study. Travel and cooking in the kitchen. Romance and erotica in the bedroom.

I spin to Romeo, who has finally caught up to me, and fling myself onto him, showering kisses all over his face. "Thank you, thank you, thank you."

"I'm already regretting it," he informs me as he carries me up the stairs and into our bedroom. "The books in the shower will probably mold."

"I'll waterproof them."

"The ones in the kitchen may catch on fire."

"I'll fireproof them."

He presses a kiss to the tip of my nose. "Is it exactly how you wanted it?"

"Even better."

Romeo

A year later.

> Romeo Costa: Rain check for tonight. For some reason, my wife has locked herself in her reading room with three pints of Morgenstern's egg custard ice cream.

> Zach Sun: Maybe she is homesick?

> Romeo Costa: Maybe your brain is homesick. THIS IS HER HOME.

> Ollie vB: Take Daytona to eat KFC. She'll cheer right up.

> Romeo Costa: She's from Georgia, not Kentucky, you uncultured buffoon.

> Zach Sun: Is there really a difference?

> Ollie vB: KFC = KOREAN Fried Chicken.

> Ollie vB: You uncultured buffoon.

I pocket my phone, taking large strides to Dallas's former bedroom. Loud wails seep into the hallway from the crack beneath the double doors. My wife, who has only cried *when I almost died*, is bawling.

"Dallas?" My palms meet the wood, slamming down. "Open up."

No answer.

"Dallas."

Still nothing.

My fists pound harder, but they're drowned out by her cries.

"Dallas Maryanne Costa."

Wretched panic sails down my throat, sinking to my gut like an oversized anchor.

"Are you okay? What happened?"

And *still*. No answer.

"Damn it, Dallas. I will blow down this door if you do not open it right now."

She doesn't.

True to my word, I lift my leg and kick it at the seam, splintering the wood into pieces.

Splayed across the floor, surrounded by a séance circle of ice cream tubs, Dallas clutches a clear glass display box. The one with the fourteenth Henry Plotkin book inside. She usually keeps it on the opposite side of the room, hanging beside the pressed petal painting Vernon made from the remnants of her white rose.

Sheets of tears shoot past her cheeks and ricochet on the pearl marble, where they plunge into an ocean of their peers. Okay, not really. But my legs don't get the memo as they lurch forward at the sight of three tiny tears chasing one another down her cheek.

I take the box from her, set it aside, and lift her onto my lap, her legs on either side of my thighs. "What happened, baby?"

"Yes."

Huh?

I tuck a tendril of hair behind her ear. "Yes, what?"

"Exactly."

"Dallas, you're not making any sense."

As if she just realized I'm here, she squeals, launching her arms around my neck, almost strangling me to death. "A *baby*. We're having a baby."

"A what?"

"I'm pregnant, Romeo. *Pregnant*."

"But we just started trying three weeks ago." *Re*-started, more like. After I was poisoned, Shortbread and I decided we weren't quite ready to expand our family and wanted to enjoy one another a little more before we devoted ourselves to someone else.

"I know. Isn't it wonderful?" She leans down and pats my dick, speaking directly to it. "Thank you for your wonderful contribution to this family." Her head tips back, addressing the ceiling this time. "I can't believe they worked."

Dread churns in my gut. "Who are *they*?"

But it's too late. My personal agent of chaos is already sprinting down the halls toward our bedroom. I run a hand down my face, a little concerned about how hectic this house/library/whatever will be in nine months if my child takes after their mother.

I'm still dumbstruck. It must have happened during our sixth honeymoon—the redo of our Parisian one. The shock soon molds into excitement. *Shortbread is going to be a mother. I'm going to be a father.*

Within minutes, I'm on FaceTime with Oliver and Zach, who started the call.

I frown at Zach. "How did you know already?"

"Decatur called to thank Mom." Zach is in Korea on business, brushing his teeth in his lavish hotel room.

"For?"

"Mom took Davenport to a temple to get Guan Yin talismans." At my blank expression, he adds, "Fertility talismans."

Of course, she did.

Helpful as always, Oliver chimes in, "If it's a boy, you should name him Romeo Costa the Third."

"Kindly go fuck yourself."

"Good idea. I haven't man handled the ham candle in sixteen hours now."

Is he even speaking in English?

Zach sinks into a couch, the camera shaking with the movement. "At least we found out within a reasonable timeframe this time."

"Three seconds is actually unreasonable," I point out.

They ignore me, still bitter about what happened a few months ago.

In fact, Zach cuts right to it. "Is there a reason we found out your father died on the six o'clock news?"

"It wasn't newsworthy enough for the nine o'clock cycle?"

Oliver scratches his temple. "Zach, don't you ever worry that Romeo's a sociopath?"

"I'm not a sociopath." Why am I speaking to these people instead of being with my pregnant wife right now? Oh. That's right. Because I can hear her and Hettie gushing downstairs and know it will be at least ten minutes before I can safely approach her.

"Debatable." Zach sets his phone down, slam-dunking his electric toothbrush into a glass cup. "Do you remember what you said when we came to offer our condolences?"

"I barely remember your hair color."

"*Welp. You win some, you lose some.*" He mimics me down to the timbre of my voice. "*And I just won some. Where's my congratulations?*"

"I mean, an 'I'm happy for you' would have been nice."

If anything, I went easy on Senior during his life, for the sake of Dallas. I abandoned my revenge plans. That was generous enough. Even Morgan got a free pass to return to America. Last I heard, she's living in a commune in the Appalachians.

Oliver tilts his head. "When I croak, will you deliver my eulogy speech? I need someone who's emotionless enough to form words in the wake of my death. Everyone else will be too busy bawling."

"You mean bowling." Zach shuts the lights in his hotel room. Behind him, a sweeping view of Namsan Tower looms. "There will one hundred percent be a party."

That's my cue to hang up. I press the end button, figuring Dallas has had enough time to do whatever she needed to do with Hettie. By the time I enter our bedroom, she's sitting in a sea of bright yellow paper, her arm shoved under our mattress, yanking more and more out. They keep coming like a clown's handkerchief with no end in sight.

She holds one up to the light like it's money she needs to check for authenticity. "These babies must've worked as soon as I got them. Maybe too well. What if we have twins? A triplet?"

I lean against the door, watching my wife exist.
Loudly. Messily. Unapologetically.
Just the way a woman loved is meant to bloom.
Like a rose in spring.